Cowboy Seeks Husband

By
Leta Blake &
Indra Vaughn

An Original Publication from Leta Blake Books

Cowboy Seeks Husband
Written and published by Leta Blake & Indra Vaughn
Cover by Dar Albert
Formatted by BB eBooks

First Print Edition, 2019
ISBN: 979-8-88841-011-0

Other Books by Leta Blake

Any Given Lifetime
The River Leith
Smoky Mountain Dreams
The Difference Between
Heat for Sale
Stay Lucky
Stay Sexy
Omega Mine: Search for a Soulmate
Bring on Forever
Angel Undone

The Home for the Holidays Series
Mr. Frosty Pants
Mr. Naughty List

The Training Season Series
Training Season
Training Complex

Heat of Love Series
Slow Heat
Alpha Heat
Slow Birth
Bitter Heat

'90s Coming of Age Series
Pictures of You
You Are Not Me

Co-Authored with Indra Vaughn
Vespertine
Cowboy Seeks Husband

Co-Authored with Alice Griffiths
The Wake Up Married serial
Will & Patrick's Endless Honeymoon

Gay Fairy Tales
Co-Authored with Keira Andrews
Flight
Levity
Rise

Audiobooks
Leta Blake at Audible
Indra Vaughn at Audible

Free Read
Stalking Dreams

Discover more about the author online:
Leta Blake
letablake.com

Other Books by Indra Vaughn

The House on Hancock Hill
Patchwork Paradise

Christmas Books
Dust of Snow
The Winter Spirit

Shadow Mountain Series
Fated
Fragmented

Co-Authored with Leta Blake
Vespertine
Cowboy Seeks Husband

Gay Romance Newsletter

Leta's newsletter will keep you up to date on her latest releases and news from the world of M/M romance. Join the mailing list today.

Leta Blake on Patreon

Become part of Leta Blake's Patreon community in order to access exclusive content, deleted scenes, extras, bonus stories, rewards, prizes, interviews, and more.
www.patreon.com/letablake

Acknowledgements

Leta would like to thank the following:

Mom and Dad, without whom I couldn't be following my dream of being a writer. Brian and Cecily, my lights to travel home to. All the wonderful members of my Patreon who inspire, support, and advise me. Delphine Dryden for early draft editing. DJ Jamison for final draft editing.

Most of all, thank you to our readers for making all the blood, sweat, and tears worthwhile.

Indra would like to thank the following:

Belgium for welcoming me home, nursing for giving me independence and steadiness, and my son for bringing me joy. Our editors, Delphine Dryden and DJ Jamison. And, of course, thank you to the patient readers of the world who have been so generous and understanding as I have transitioned in my life to a new and different horizon.

Dedicated to Marsha – so long and farewell.
You're loved and missed.

CHAPTER 1

WALKER REED DUSTED off his gloves against his old Wranglers, pushed his hat off his forehead, and wiped at the sweat dripping from his hair. He gave the shimmering horizon a pained look and only then did he give in to the insistent buzzing in his right pocket.

"Great," he mumbled, tugging one glove off. Each call always seemed to be from a different number but the same area code, so he knew what to expect at a glance. He removed the piece of hay he'd been chewing on from his mouth and pressed his phone to his ear. "Walker Reed."

"Hey, Walker, it's Molly."

"Afternoon, Molly."

A heifer nudged his hand and he scratched it absentmindedly between the eyes.

"It's so charming that you actually say things like that," she said with a laugh.

Walker rolled his eyes. The producer, Molly—not to mention the director, Andy, and the rest of the film production crew with the reality show Walker had foolishly signed on for—made it out like his manners and his Louisiana twang were either the cutest things ever or evidence of his lack of brainpower. He didn't see any sense in reminding her that he was from the South and southern boys greeted ladies politely when they called, even if they were nuisances who interrupted his workday.

"Anyway, babe," she went on, forcing another roll of his eyes.

That was another thing. These Hollywood dodos all called him babe whenever they were getting ready to strong-arm him into something new and definitely not in the contract. It was a tell not unlike his Aunt Jenny's tendency to call him 'sug' whenever she wanted him to donate use of a field for her son's motocross hobby.

Molly was still talking. "Andy wanted me to reach out to you for confirmation of a full day sometime early next week for us to shoot the intro."

"Next week? I've got a heck of a lot on my plate between now and then, Molly. Besides, it was my understanding—"

"Andy said you might be busy," she interrupted, sounding intensely empathetic. But then she went on like those words were meaningless and all that mattered was the answer she wanted to get. "But we have to get on with this. So when's a good day for you?"

"I thought filming didn't start for another two weeks." Bad enough he had the *Queer Seeks Spouse* production crew running under his feet all day long, trying to turn one of his unused barns into something worthy of reality TV. All the effort, though, didn't mean they were actually doing quality work on the place. They were fixing things up just enough to make the barn-cum-house look all fancy-pants through the lenses of dozens of remote-operated cameras wired in all over the place, and, hopefully, the starstruck eyes of the home viewing audience.

The hot Louisiana sun beat down on Walker, and he wiped at his forehead again while Molly muffled the phone with her hand and barked out orders to other unknown minions at her end of the line. Molly's position as a producer came with a lot of power and an attitude to match.

"Andy says it won't take long. And the contract states—"

"I know what the contract *states*." Walker kicked apart the hay bale he'd just dumped down and walked back to his tractor. "I have inspections on Monday. Tuesday's out too. That's the day I'm expecting the trucks to pick up our calves. That might run out to Wednesday, but if it does, Marlon can take over. On Thursday, I'm riding out to check the cattle, so it's either Wednesday or Friday."

"Well…" Molly hummed, then her voice went muffled again. Walker resisted the urge to turn on his tractor and make it impossible for the conversation to continue. He could just imagine Andy Towes, Showrunner and Director, standing right next to Molly while she did the dirty work. "Okay, so we want some outside shots, and Friday's weather looks awful, so Wednesday it is. We'll start bright and early."

Walker snorted, said a brisk goodbye, and hung up.

Bright and early, his ass.

To limit grazing on ryegrass Walker put out hay for the cattle regularly, and he needed to get on with it, not sit and stew in annoyance. But before he let the tractor roar to life, he sent a quick text to Tessa, asking her to check the weather. The humidity in Louisiana was never ideal for making hay, but a run of dry, hot days like predicted for the beginning of next week wasn't something to miss. Especially if it was going to rain on Friday.

It was dark by the time he walked through the back door, and the house smelled of garlic and gravy. Kicking off his boots in the mudroom, he wondered what he needed more, a shower or food. The Dutch door into the pantry was half open, and a pie cooled on the wide ledge there. He lifted it gingerly and took a deep sniff before putting it back down.

His stomach won out over the shower, and he scrubbed his hands in the old farmer's sink in the kitchen that had definitely seen better days.

"Walker, is that you? Finally." Tessa, his step-mom, stuck her head around the door and smiled at him. "Hey, baby. Your dad and I ate already."

"That's fine. I got another call from a producer, and it put me off my schedule." It felt better to blame his lateness on Molly, even though the call had barely taken two minutes of his day, than to admit he'd let himself be distracted by it. He'd stewed over her call—questioning every choice that had led up to it, and back again—so many times that there was no doubt he was the one really to blame for his screwed up schedule.

She raised an eyebrow but said nothing, knowing full well he'd come out with it in good time.

"What's for dinner?" he asked, kissing her on the cheek as he followed his nose into the kitchen.

She swatted his ass with a towel. "It's in the oven, see for yourself."

Walker got his plate, not bothering with oven mitts, and hurried to the old worn table tucked against the kitchen wall. Tessa rolled her eyes when he blew at his fingertips and sat down. "Thank you, Tess."

She'd become Walker's assistant during the day when he'd officially taken over the ranch from his father, but at night she was the closest thing to a mom Walker had ever known.

"What time did Dad come in?"

Tessa glanced at the door leading to the hallway and into the living room, then said, "At three."

Walker almost swore under his breath but managed to keep his face fairly blank. "Did you check the weather?"

"Yep. It looks good. I called Marlon and Dennis. They can start haying on Monday."

It wasn't ideal since that was when the inspectors would be roaming the property, and Tuesday the cattle trucks would begin arriving, but they needed to get on with it if they wanted to have enough dry hay stored up for the wetter months. "Thanks," he said.

When she turned to the sink to deal with the last of the dishes, he quickly fished his phone out of his pocket and texted Marlon.

Fences?

The reply came almost immediately. *Checked and mended, boo.*

With a sigh of relief, Walker pushed his phone aside and dug into Tessa's buttery garlic mashed potatoes. At least those fences were one thing he could scratch off this week's to-do list. He needed to figure out if he could give Marlon and Dennis a pay raise if they had to double check his dad's work all the time. Maybe after the show.

"How's he doing?" he asked when Tessa sat down, her hands red from the hot dishwater.

She gave him a strained little smile. It pulled at the corners of her eyes, creating deep lines. Her gray hair was gathered back in a ponytail, and she'd captured the flyaways in a red, paisley scarf. Since she'd recently stopped dyeing it, she tried to keep the roots hidden, but Walker loved seeing the white mixing with the dark brown.

"Tired. He slept from the minute he came home until dinner, and I wouldn't be surprised if he just fell asleep again in front of the news."

Walker pushed his empty plate away. "He should get himself checked out. This can't be right."

Tessa jerked her chin toward the door. "Go on then," she said. "You convince him of that."

Holding up his hands in defeat, Walker leaned back in his chair. "Okay, I hear you. Still, I'm going to reduce his exposure to the hard labor. I can't risk anything happening when he's out there checking the fences."

Tessa sat forward and reached for him. He slipped his hand underneath hers and felt a rush of affection for the strong, caring woman who'd raised him pretty much by herself while running half the ranch. "Diabetes or not, he's also just plain old, Walker."

"I know."

He'd been born to older parents, which was, some said, the reason his mother hadn't made it through his birth. Though Tessa always poo-pooed that, claiming that it was "just one of those terrible things" and there wasn't a bit of blame to assign to anything or anyone.

She'd married his father when Walker was six, his father almost sixty, and she'd been in her forties herself. Tessa had loved them both heart and soul, dedicated her life to them and the ranch, and kept them in line from their marriage day forward. God only knew why Walker had never called her Mama; sometimes, he wished he'd tried. She deserved the title.

Tessa squeezed his hand. "Sooner or later, something's going to happen to him. It's inevitable, baby. And I know for a fact your daddy wants to go out doing what he loves best. And that ain't sitting on a couch wasting away."

Walker gritted his teeth but let the subject slide. "That Molly girl called earlier."

"The producer. You mentioned it." Tessa waited for him to go on.

He sighed and ran a hand through his hair. Despite the hat he'd worn all day, a small cloud of dust drifted down. Damn, he needed a shower. "They're coming on Wednesday to shoot…something or other. The intro, I think." He looked into Tessa's light brown eyes. "I'm regretting this already, Tess."

She casually shrugged, squeezed his hand, and let go. Rising to her feet to take his plate to the sink she said, "It's only six weeks. It'll all be said and done by the time we've gathered the bulls for their checkups in July. Just keep your mind focused on what you're gonna get out of it."

"It's not like they're even doing a decent job on remodeling the barn."

"It's better than it was. And three hundred thousand dollars prize money ain't nothing to sneeze at, Walker Reed. Even *you* can smile for the camera to get your hands on that much dough."

"I smile," he mumbled. Tessa laughed and tweaked his jutted-out lip.

"At your cattle, maybe."

He remained quiet even though he wanted to keep complaining. She was right. Six weeks of inconvenience was nothing compared to that amount of money. They needed the cash infusion badly if they had any hope of keeping the ranch going, and this stupid television show Marlon had signed him up for got the job done. Walker wasn't fooling himself that he might actually find love, too.

Everyone knew reality shows were rigged at best and entirely faked at worst. Heck, the showrunner, Andy, had chosen *him* for the new program's very first bachelor, hadn't he? Out of how many applicants?

Walker had no idea, but it had to be in the thousands, at least. Tons of queer men with interesting careers had thrown in their lot hoping for a chance to earn a heap of cash while "courting" a bunch of handsome guys. Being on one of the first *Bachelor*-esque reality shows to feature LGBT contestants would be a feather in many a man's cap. So, Walker knew he should count himself lucky, even if none of this had been his idea.

Somehow, out of all those men, Andy Towes and Company had chosen Walker. Despite knowing he was nearly broke and despite his own reluctance. Why? Well, Walker figured it was because they could use him all the same. After all, they planned to portray him as a wealthy cowboy for the viewing audience.

"There's nothing more swoony-worthy and All-American than a cowboy," Andy had said that first day over the phone. "And with your face and body? Baby, there was never even a contest about who we'd choose to star. You're the one for this show. Hell, kid, you could be living in a swamp and we'd still want you. We can gild any pig with the glow of television romance, sweetheart. It doesn't matter how broke you are. Trust us."

In fact, Walker suspected the way Andy saw it, the broker he was, the better. He knew the contract he'd signed would chafe anyone with its terms and privacy violations, but he'd been desperate enough to sign it anyway, with only a brief check from a local attorney who specialized in farm contracts, not entertainment deals.

Walker assumed they would be more honest with the contestants regarding his prospects and his true motivations, but so what if they weren't? All the contestants were in it for the per-episode money anyway, not to mention the potential of half the grand prize split by the bachelor and winning suitor. So why should it matter if Walker was in it for money, too? The idea that any of these men would be on the show because they wanted to find true love was laughable.

So, yes.

He'd do the shoot like they wanted. Of course he would. In the end, the money would be worth it. Even if his colleagues and neighbors made fun of him for the rest of his life. Who cared what they thought?

He'd save Reed Ranch and that would be enough to satisfy him.

"PERFECT. PERFECT," ANDY murmured as he eyed the four-camera setup. He was an older, effeminate man wearing a pair of what looked like women's shorts and a light T-shirt. At least he wasn't complaining about the heat. Yet.

One camera was angled to be on Walker at all times, the other on the host, a man named Luke Montgomery, who was handsome in a hyper-but-sexy way. Tall, dark, and yet vibrating with barely restrained energy, he made Walker think that he'd be the result if Ryan Seacrest and Tom Selleck somehow had a baby together. The third camera was positioned back farther in the field and held a steady, panoramic view on them both. A man braced a fourth camera on his shoulders, moving back and forth to test different positions.

Walker started to sweat. Nothing seemed to be expected from him right that second, so he tuned out all the endless "getting ready to begin to start" activities and turned his gaze onto Marlon and Dennis in the far distance. They were mowing the hay fields, and Walker wished he was there with them. He loved the fresh scent of newly cut hay and the satisfaction of laying it out to cure. It was a tight squeeze, though, for this final pasture. The cut grass would only have two days in the sun before they'd need to have the balers out there on Friday morning, pounding it all into bales before the storms hit.

Because of the noise of the mowers, they'd had to move the filming site to one of the outer pastures, not used for growing hay, where they'd set up two barstools of all things. Walker was sitting on one of them with a fence at his back. It was a nice spot, really. The cattle weren't grazing this field at the moment, so the growth was long and green, and the air smelled fresh and sweet.

He should probably tell Andy and the others to check their ankles for ticks later.

Nah.

Andy came to stand beside Walker and did that ridiculous camera square thing with his hands in front of Walker's face. "Yes. Perfect. That profile is divine. You're stunning, babe." He winked.

Walker fought a blush.

"Don't worry, he's just stroking your ego," Luke said after Andy darted off to consult with one of what seemed an endless stream of assistant producers about something important on their clipboard. At least, Walker assumed it was important, given the way Andy was frowning at it.

"His husband wouldn't be happy if he wasn't. Joking, I mean," Luke went on, fidgeting on his barstool. He adjusted his collar, and instantly a woman with makeup appeared and started dabbing at the skin showing where his top button opened.

"I wasn't worried."

Walker had already figured Andy out. The show *Queer Seeks Spouse* was Andy's baby, and he loved it too much to taint it with any sort of scandal. Half of the reason Walker had signed the contract, despite feeling like a disingenuous fraud, was because of Andy's excited claim that he was all about offering queer reality show content that wasn't just about titillation, but about true romance.

If "true romance" was entirely made-up bullshit. But whatever.

Walker liked that Andy seemed determined to present queerness as normal, unremarkable, and yet worthy of the same attention as any straight but entirely bullshit reality TV romance. Luckily, a progressive streaming media company had agreed, and the budget for *Queer Seeks Spouse* was heftier than most reality shows starting out.

Which meant the contestants' payments and the star's payment, too, were compelling reasons to come aboard.

"Okay, Luke, we're ready!" Andy called. "We're getting a later start than I wanted. So, Luke, stop fidgeting and make sure you hit your mark."

Andy hurried over to stand behind a cameraman a few yards away, and Luke stood up, moved to where they'd spiked the ground with T-shaped tape, and lined his toes up with the top of it.

Luke went into an introductory spiel while moving from one T-shape mark to another and gesturing at the pasture all around him. Then he laid out the setup for the audience, explaining the rules of the show and the expected outcome—"This handsome cowboy is seeking a husband, and he's not going to give up until he finds one."

Walker fought another roll of his eyes.

Once they'd wrapped Luke's intro, he took his position on the barstool next to Walker again. There was another round of discussion with Andy and more makeup for Luke since he was sweating after standing in the sun.

"All right, Walker," Andy said, walking up with a young woman at his side. "You remember Molly?"

Walker did remember her from their phone conversations, but he'd had no idea she was so young. Molly looked exactly like her name: youthful, farm fresh, sweet. If he had to guess, she appeared to be maybe seventeen—but surely she must be older; there were regulations or something, right? Her wavy hair was cut to chin length, and a smattering of freckles danced beneath her wide eyes.

"Good to meet you, ma'am," he said, standing up to take her hand.

"Nice to put a face with a name," she replied.

"Molly's gonna be your producer today," Andy said. "You need anything, ask her. Molly will take care of you." Somehow Andy managed to make that sound more like, "Molly will keep you in line."

She smiled up at Walker and gestured toward the barstool. "Go on and have a seat. We're going to get started soon."

Andy wandered off and the makeup artist turned to Walker, trying to put some sort of powder on his nose. He scowled at her until Molly nodded her assent, and the brush-wielding woman went away. He'd showered, shaved, and put his best shirt on. It'd have to do.

Luke gazed out across the field and muttered under his breath, like he was rehearsing lines. He probably was.

"So there's nothing to be nervous about," Molly said, reassuringly. "Just be yourself."

"As opposed to who?" Walker asked.

Luke laughed like he'd said something funny.

"As opposed to someone who doesn't remember why they're doing this?" Molly said with a sharp, too smart grin. "Remember, we chose you, Walker, out of thousands of candidates, because we know deep down you've got star power."

Walker laughed.

Molly winked. "That's it. Loosen up. Oh, and throw in some of that cute southern slang we love, okay, babe? Be charming."

"Be myself or be charming? Which is it?"

Molly wagged her finger at him like he was naughty and then walked away to stand behind one of the cameramen.

"Okay, get on with it," Andy called out. "This good light isn't going to last forever, and I'm already melting."

Luke plastered on a fake smile and began to talk into the camera straight in front of them.

"Without further ado, let me introduce you to our handsome cowboy looking for love," Luke said, and Walker's head snapped up, his cheeks heating. "What's your name?" Luke asked, eyes twinkling, his face angled toward the camera even though he was looking at Walker. It was like he'd turned on some kind of inner juice. It was weird.

"Uh, you know my name."

"For the camera, please," Luke said with a cheery grin.

"Oh, uh. I'm Walker Reed," he said.

"Molly!" Andy cried, and she darted forward.

"Walker, look. You need to say your name with a little more confidence, babe," she said in a whisper that was still loud enough that Luke could definitely hear. "You sounded unsure, like maybe your name's Jason, you know what I mean? Get it together." Then she scampered back to her spot behind the cameraman.

"Go again, Walker," Andy said.

"I'm Walker Reed," he said, lifting his chin and trying to imagine he was introducing himself to another rancher and not to the shiny eye of the camera.

"Perfect. Do it again," Andy said. "But this time look at Luke."

Walker said his name again, and it seemed like he'd done it the right way because Andy didn't have anything to say about it.

"Nice to meet you, Walker." Luke reached out to shake his hand. "How does it feel to be the chosen one?"

"Uh." He glanced at the camera with Andy beside it.

"Try not to look at the cameras," Molly called out. "It's okay if you slip, we can edit it out, but it's easier if you don't. Just answer Luke's questions as naturally as you can."

"Yes, ma'am."

Luke fanned his face before slipping back into his TV persona and giving Walker an encouraging smile. "So, how does it feel?"

"Oh. It feels pretty good, I guess." He glanced at Andy, who was now making frantic hand motions that either meant Walker had to do better or he was being attacked by mosquitos. It could really have gone either way this time of year when the mosquito eggs started hatching. "I mean, yeah, it feels like a great opportunity. One that doesn't come around every day?"

"Is that a question?" Luke asked, a bit harshly.

"No."

"Luke, stay on point," Andy said. "Molly!"

She stepped closer again. "What we're looking for here, Walker, is that you're excited to be on the show and eager to find the love of your life amongst our hunky and handsome contestants."

"Do I have to say exactly that?"

"Pretty much. Yes."

"Oh, God."

"I believe in you." She patted his arm and then it was go time again.

"I'm thrilled to be the first bachelor for *Queer Seeks Spouse*. It's going to be the adventure of a lifetime, and I'm eager to meet the handsome man I might share the rest of my life with." He felt a little dirty lying like that, but Reed Ranch was worth it, and Tessa had said it was okay for him to fib. Hadn't she? She certainly hadn't told him not to participate in the show after Marlon had secretly applied and Andy's team had initially reached out. She'd said, "Life isn't black and white, baby. You do what's right for you."

Luke smiled winningly again. "Why don't you tell us a little bit about yourself, Walker?"

"Right." God, this was torture. He ducked his head and rubbed the back of his neck, tipping his hat a little more over his eyes as he straightened. They'd brought him an awful fake cowboy hat he wouldn't be seen dead in, so instead he'd worn one of his own. "Well, like I said, my name is Walker Reed. I'm thirty-six years old, and I run Reed Ranch. It used to belong to Joe Reed, my father, but he passed it on to me two years ago."

"How exciting," Luke said. Walker raised an eyebrow at him. "It's been eye-opening already, filming on a ranch. Can you tell us a little bit about what you're going to expect from a potential partner? I know our eager contestants would like to know what you need in a husband. They all want to be the best for you."

Sweet Jesus. He expected to fake his way through this damn show and then send home whoever was left at the end with a pat on the back, half the prize money, and hearty best wishes for a good life. The best he'd hoped for was that he'd actually like one of the guys as a person, a pal, he supposed, but he hadn't really even let himself think that far ahead. Now he had to talk about what he wanted in a life mate, and he needed to make it sound good.

He squirmed in his chair until Molly cleared her throat. It was fine. This was fine. He could do this.

"Living on a ranch is hard work, obviously." He glanced at Andy again, then jerked his eyes away and tried to smile at Luke. He at least needed to act like he wanted to be here. "We've got about three hundred and seventy acres of land. We raise cattle for beef and at our peak have about 200 head."

"So your future man needs to be okay with you coming home dirty, smelling like hard work and sweat?" Luke joked.

Walker's throat went dry. He rubbed at his mouth and pushed his hat back again. Despite it being early, the sun was already beating down on their heads. Sweat slipped down the side of his face. The wind kicked up, and the scent of cut grass hit him, reminding him of the endgame. "He would. Yes." Then he tried a sly grin. It must have worked because Luke relaxed incrementally.

"What does an average day on the ranch look like?"

Walker wiped his palms on his jeans. "There's no such thing as an average day on a cattle ranch," he said. "There's always something unexpected we have to deal with. Anything from cattle tearing through fences to frolic on the highway, so that we have to abandon everything else to round them up, to a calf getting stuck out in the middle of a mudhole post-hurricane. But we do have regular chores. For instance, the cattle have to be checked several times a week. In calving season, we inspect them multiple times a day. In the spring and summer, we perform health exam measures, cut and bale the hay, do pasture maintenance. Then in the fall, we work the hayfields, plant winter forages, and in winter, calving season begins again. Around this time of year we also purchase more heifers, which we eventually breed—"

"Okay, hold up." Andy pinched the bridge of his nose. "Keep running," he said to the cameramen. "Molly!"

She walked up with a serious expression. "Look, I'm sure this is all really fascinating when you're actually, you know, into farming. But our audience watches this show for the romance, babe. Talking about breeding heifers is not romantic. Can we have something a little more 'cowboy in the saddle at sundown' or something?"

"You do realize," Walker drawled, "that a real cowboy's been in the saddle since sun *up*. Working."

Molly raised a brow, and she went from looking seventeen to looking terrifying.

He gulped.

"Yeah, whatever. No more talk about heifers." She gave him a reassuring smile that felt like a manipulation, but it was better than that eyebrow so he'd take it.

After she was back behind the cameras again, Luke sent Walker a little apologetic glance, and Walker studied the man for a second. He was fake-tanned, with fake teeth and a pretentious haircut, and Walker had judged him accordingly. But maybe he'd judged him too fast. He took a deep breath and smiled back.

"Okay, Walker, how about you tell us a little bit about what you want in a partner?"

Walker let a silent breath escape his mouth. Everyone he worked with knew he was gay, and either didn't care or had walked away when he came out as a teen. That didn't mean he found the idea of talking about what he liked in a man on national TV all that appealing.

"As a person," Luke prompted. "What would they be like?"

Walker relaxed again. "Oh! A good sense of humor," he said. "That's vital if you're going to live on a farm. And I love a man who makes me laugh. It's one of the things I'd never be able to compromise on."

"Tell us why you're looking to marry now."

Walker blinked rapidly. "I, uh, well, it's a lot running a ranch on my own, and I—"

"Hold up." Andy yelled again. Walker suppressed an irritated sigh. "Yeah, we're going to need more than this from you, Walker, darling. You can't just—"

"I've got this, Andy," Molly said, holding up her hand to stop whatever he was going to say next. "No one wants to hear that you're planning to marry a guy so he can help you run your ranch," she said when she was by his side again. "Marriage for the sake of free labor went out of fashion with the dark ages, or it should have. This is a show about romance. Tell us about how lonely you are, Walker."

"I'm not lonely."

She raised a brow, turned to Andy, and then back to him. Andy made a frustrated hand gesture, but Molly took hold of Walker's chin and directed his attention to her again. "Look, no one goes on a show like this if they aren't lonely, babe. No amount of money would make it worth it if you had a sweet man in your bed every night, would it?"

"I—listen, I'm not going to talk about things like that."

"Yes, you are."

"I'm not."

Molly's hand on his jaw tightened. "Walker, sweetheart, you're going to have to give on this one. You chose to walk this path. So walk it."

"What do you want me to say?"

"Tell me why you're lonely." She released him.

"I haven't had a boyfriend in a long time. It's been hard to even think about dating when my dad's health has been poor and my stepmom is holding everything together with her own two hands. Sure, I've got great pals and ranch hands, but there's a comfort that I'm missing."

"What kind of comfort?"

"Not what you're thinking. The kind of comfort that comes from knowing you've got someone to share it all with—the good, the bad, the ugly."

"Perfect," Andy said. "You got that?"

The man with the camera on his shoulder shouted back, "Yep!"

16

"You filmed that?" Walker whispered.

"Tricks of the trade, babe. But, don't worry. You didn't embarrass yourself. Half our contestants will be in love with you as soon as they see that clip." She patted his cheek. "You're a dream when you're honest."

Walker whipped his hat off his head and ran his fingers through his hair. He was vaguely aware the cameras were still rolling. Hilarious that she wanted him to be 'honest' when they were all setting up such an elaborate lie. "So anything's fair game? No conversation or space is sacred when we're filming?"

Andy pursed his lips, thought for a second, then shrugged. "Pretty much."

"No. I have a right to know when I'm being filmed."

"You don't," Andy said. "It's in the contract that when we're on set, you're ours."

"Forget this, then." Walker got down from the barstool. "I have work to do." He began to walk away, the grass crunching under his feet and sending up poofs of tiny gnats.

Molly called after him. "I'd like to remind you that if you break your contract, you'll be forced to repay the work already done on your barn and reimburse time and money spent by—"

Walker drew to a halt and slowly turned around. "You're an asshole."

Molly smiled cheerfully. "As long as you sit back down and give us something we can work with, you can call me whatever you want, cowboy."

"We don't need much more," Andy interjected quickly. He hurried over and started to put a hand on Walker's arm but apparently thought better of it and pulled back. "It's not that bad," he whispered. "Most of the work on the show will be done by the contestants."

Molly was there smiling nicely again. "You've got this, Walker. Don't destroy your chance due to a fit of temper."

"Listen to the lady," Andy encouraged, stepping back toward the camera monitors again.

"I hate this," Walker said, not bothering to keep his voice down.

"I know. You and every contestant will hate it even more before it's over," Molly whispered. "But, believe me, walking away isn't worth it."

Walker nodded once.

"Let's finish this up then, so you can get back to your cattle."

As Walker followed Molly back into the line of the cameras, Andy gave him a little smile but said nothing as he indicated Walker's barstool as if he was offering a throne.

Walker wanted to punch the guy in the face. Instead, he sat down.

"Let's do this then. I'll be charming as fuck."

"That's the spirit," Andy called out. "Roll."

The rest of the interview went as well as could be expected, given that Walker was now laying it on a little thick and the precious light was turning in a way that Andy deemed dreadful. But it was over before most people in the world had eaten breakfast, and it wasn't even noon before he was with Marlon and Dennis, spreading out the hay.

"WHERE Y'AT?" MARLON asked when they were done spreading hay and had headed over to the loading bay to await a straggling truck that was picking up the very last of the calves.

"I'm fine."

"Then why you making a bahbin, boo?"

"I'm not pouting," Walker said.

But Marlon tsked at him and shook his head. His hat hid most of his dark face but Walker could tell from the white glint of his teeth that he was grinning.

"It's nothing. I shouldn't complain. I knew what I was getting into."

He wanted to say, "I knew what *you'd* gotten me into" instead, but he understood Marlon had sent in Walker's application to *Queer Seeks*

Spouse out of sheer desperation and love for Reed Ranch, and Marlon had never, in a million years, dreamed that Walker would truly be chosen. Besides, no one had held a gun to Walker's head when he signed the contract—not Tessa, not his dad, and least of all Marlon, who'd been excited, sure, that his ploy had miraculously worked, but also skeptical from the start.

Marlon tipped his head back, and his brows drew down over his dark eyes. "Qui c'est q'ca?"

"For the next six weeks, I have no privacy. Unless I'm taking a shit, I'm fair game for them to film," he told Marlon, who stared at him, then whistled between his teeth.

"They can do that?"

"Apparently."

Marlon worried the corner of his mouth with his tongue. A faint sheen of sweat made his top lip sparkle. "I'm sorry."

"Listen, like I said, there's nothing to complain about. I knew what the contract said when I signed it. If the money on offer made me lose all common sense, then that's my burden to bear."

"Seems like you got plenty of those."

Walker straightened his back. Of course he did. But who didn't? After the last hurricane, all Louisiana farms were suffering. At least he wasn't a dairy farmer. With the price of milk dropping like a stone, dairy farms were going tits up all around him. It could be worse, and now he had this six-week-long opportunity to dig them out of the last of their recovery debt. It was worth it. Marlon had done a good thing by signing him up.

He slapped his friend on the back. "I just have to suck it up, is all. Don't *you* make a bahbin now," he said, teasingly using his friend's Cajun slang term for a pout.

They didn't talk much for the rest of the afternoon. Loading the calves was noisy business, and he tried unsuccessfully to put the show and all that went with it out of his mind. What had possessed him to sign up for this? Or worse, say yes to all the lies that went with it? Giving up his privacy was one thing, but pretending to be something he wasn't—namely, a wealthy cowboy of means—was another. A glance at the "lavish" changes to the old barn would have his neighbors howling with laughter. And when the show presented him as a catch worth keeping, they'd laugh even more. But in the end, he'd have three hundred thousand dollars to help all that scorn go down easy as his daddy's best whiskey.

It was worth it.

It had to be.

The last of the cattle were finally loaded up. The truck drove off with a deep rumble, leaving nothing but a cloud of dust and an eerie silence behind under the setting sun. Walker went to the stables and saddled Cormac, his old quarter horse. Most of the work happened with machines and trucks these days. Still, every once in a while, at the end of the day, he liked to saddle up and do his final rounds on horseback.

"Like a real cowboy," his step-mama always teased. And fuck it, that's exactly what it was.

At least, in this one particular way, he wouldn't be faking it. He was as All-American as he could get: a cowboy born and bred, and nowhere more free than in the saddle.

Contracts making him a slave to Hollywood be damned.

CHAPTER 2

"COPPERHEADS. WATER MOCCASINS. I thought moccasins were shoes. Wolf spiders? Oh my *God*." Roan Carmichael made an overly disbelieving face at his mom, who sat curled up on her chintz couch with a blanket over her legs. "Brown. Recluse. *Spiders*."

"Think of all the good food," his mom said. She closed her eyes. "Oysters. Catfish and jambalaya and boudin."

"I don't even know what that is."

"It's divine. Best I ever had was in Ville Platte."

"When were you in Louisiana?" Roan asked, quickly clicking away from the pictures of brown recluse spider bites, because holy crap. Nope.

His mom sighed softly. "A long time ago. When I was young." She didn't say anything else. He let it go.

"So the food will be good, huh?"

"It will be amazing. And they have great cocktails too, from what I remember."

"Mm-hmm. Basically you go to Louisiana to eat and drink and then horror-die from the bite of a venomous creature."

"Pretty much." His mom's smile faded a little. She reached for his hand, and he pushed the laptop aside. Her fingers felt brittle and cold. "You know you don't have to do this."

"Are you kidding me? This first season's theme is *cowboy* seeks husband. You know the dude is going to be hot stuff poured into a pair of jeans. I bet once I see him I'll be ready to battle a copperhead for a taste of that." He pursed his lips. "Or maybe a garden snake." His mom raised

21

an eyebrow at him. "Okay, a worm. Are you cold? I'll make some coffee."

"Thanks, honey."

Roan let go of her hand and stood. He found her coffee—instant—in the cupboard over the fridge in their tiny kitchen. He grabbed two mugs and put water in the kettle to boil. In his own mug, he measured a spoonful of sugar to mix in with the nearly black crystals of instant coffee and tried not to think about the Hawaiian Kona he'd gotten used to in college. Thirty four dollars per delicious pound, all courtesy of his rich ex-boyfriend-slash-former-roommate.

When the water was rumbling impatiently in the kettle, he poured it over the cheap coffee and made his way back into the living room. It'd taken a good few months to get used to living in his old childhood home again, but a year later grad school felt like a faraway dream.

"So don't forget, I taped all the emergency numbers to the fridge."

"I know, Roan. I'm not a child, you realize."

"And call Lindsay next door whenever you need something, okay?"

She squirmed in her seat a little with a pained look on her face. "I'll be fine."

"No," Roan said seriously. "If I think for a second that you're going to try to get by on your own when you shouldn't, I'm not leaving." The muted TV playing in the background cast odd lights on his mom's face, making her look even more jaundiced and gaunt. Roan wanted to cry. He wouldn't be able to stop if he started now, and he didn't want her to see him like that. Again.

"I'll call Lindsay every day," she whispered, even though he could tell it cost her. But it was a promise, and he knew she'd keep it. "What time will your taxi be here?"

"Six in the morning. You don't have to get up."

"Of course I'm getting up. I want to say goodbye. Six weeks is a long time."

Or no time at all when you're dying.

Roan's face twisted, and he lowered his head. Shit.

She gently stroked his knuckles. "It's okay."

"Call the producers if you need me. That's the number highlighted in bright yellow on the list in there, okay? They'll let me go if you need me to come back. I made sure that was in my contract. Don't try to be strong. If you need me—want me, even—I'll be on the first plane. I swear. I'll be here if—"

She smiled at him but her eyes were watery. "I promise."

He nodded. "Good."

His mom drew a deep breath and waggled what once were her eyebrows. "You know cowboys always have nice asses, right? It's all the horseback riding. Tight, fine asses."

"Mom!" Roan sputtered.

"I'm just saying!"

He curled up next to her and laughed, hiding his face in her neck and letting her hold him like when he was a little boy. He breathed in her scent and hoped all of this time away from her wouldn't be for nothing.

"Get on to bed," she finally whispered. "I'm going too."

He helped her to her room and then went to his own where he climbed into the twin bed he'd abandoned six years ago as a stupid kid with no idea of what the future would bring. He missed being that kid now.

After a long night of tossing and turning, a ride in a stinky taxi, and a five-hour flight from Ohio to Lafayette, Roan stepped out onto the tarmac and into a thick wall of wet air. He gasped for breath amidst the worst humidity he'd ever experienced. He immediately regretted his choice to wear skinny jeans, and not just for the five hours of crotch squashing thanks to an overly heterosexual dude's need to man-spread. No, the humid air made every place his clothes touched his skin feel damp and gross. He hustled up into the blissfully air-conditioned main terminal.

Roan was grateful he had one night in a hotel before the meet and greet with the cowboy bachelor because disheveled did not look good on him. And if this *Queer Seeks Spouse* program was anything like those other 'catch a rich husband' shows he'd obsessively watched over the past few months, the competition would be stiff. And good looking. But hopefully not all that smart.

He'd noticed that despite all the drama and ridiculousness that went on during these reality shows, the people who made it to the end were usually the ones with some measure of intelligence and who managed to keep their cool throughout. He did wonder what kind of people he'd be up against and how many really wanted to marry a cowboy and live on a ranch in Louisiana. Surely most were like him, in it for the money, right? Falling in love during a televised competition was a ridiculous objective for any sane person. But, man, if he could make it to the end, that would be phenomenal. The money would stretch so far.

Not that he needed to win to make this worth his while. He'd get paid five thousand dollars a week, so even if he lost out on the grand prize, twenty or thirty grand would be an amazing help toward getting his mom into an expensive, experimental drug trial that could be her only chance at extending her life. Not to mention making a dent in the pile of medical bills stuffed into his mother's kitchen filing cabinet.

And if he did win, well. That'd solve all of their financial problems. And it's not like he'd signed a contract to actually *marry* the cowboy. Not even Hollywood could compel that outcome. So, if he won, he'd politely thank Hot Stuff for his hospitality, explain that the relationship wasn't working out for him after all, goodbye and good luck. And if there was a smooch or two before that happened? He wouldn't moan about that either. It'd been a year since he'd gotten laid and *hoo-boy*. It was time.

Someone in a badly put together suit was waiting for him at the gate, holding up a sign that said Roan Carmichael.

"Hi. That's me. I'm Roan."

The guy gave him a nod, eyed Roan's two suitcases, and picked up the smallest one.

Ha. Joke was on him, because it was the heaviest.

"It's this way."

Roan had to hurry to keep up with him, and as soon as the automatic doors opened, the heat hit him again like a sledgehammer. "Jesus Christ. I can't believe how hot it is. Aren't you melting in that suit?"

The guy gave him a sour look.

Oh. Well that was probably why the suit looked a little badly put together. The guy said, "Guess you're not from around here."

"That obvious?"

Another look, this one starting at Roan's shoes and ending at his rapidly wilting hairdo. The guy snorted. "Yeah."

Okay then.

No other words were exchanged during the drive to the hotel, but Roan gave the man a good tip anyway. Anyone who was forced to wear a suit in this kind of heat deserved a decent tip. Or an ice-cream.

It wasn't the fanciest hotel, but the room was clean and the water pressure adequate. Despite not caring about winning the actual contest, Roan's stomach danced with nervous butterflies. What was ahead of him? Who would his competition be? What if he didn't have what it took to stay past the first elimination round?

I'm here at the hotel, he texted his mom. *It's hotter than Satan's balls outside. And more humid.*

Glad you got there safe and sound, she replied. *And maybe keep your sense of humor to yourself in the contest. For a little while at least.*

Roan sent an outraged-face emoji. *I am the funniest person you know!*
I don't know all that many people.

He rolled his eyes, grinning. *Big fish in a little pond. I'll take it.*
When does it all start?

In the morning. They'll grab me from the hotel and take me to wherever I'll be staying. No phones or outside contact until the show is done filming or I'm sent home.

He'd told her all that before, but he wanted to remind her.

So this is the last I'll be hearing from you until you've snagged that cowboy by his reins and lassoed that cash prize?

You're complaining about my sense of humor?

I'm the funniest person you know, she shot his words back at him.

He grinned again. *Yeah. You are.*

I love you, honey.

I love you too. It was midafternoon and he knew she needed her nap. *Talk to you in six weeks, Mom.*

I'll be waiting here with bells on.

Man, Roan was going to miss his phone. The contract he'd signed promised his mother access to a number where they could reach him within minutes in an emergency, but still. It made him nervous to part with his one straight line of contact to her when she was so sick. He'd never take this risk if the expensive drug trial wasn't her only hope.

To take his mind off things, he laid out his clothes for the next day so they could breathe a little, and then set out to explore the vending machine offerings of the hotel. After securing two Snickers bars, a packet of Zingers, and a Dr Pepper, he ate while looking through the tourist brochures tucked into racks in the wall by the front door to the lobby.

He wondered where the other contestants were. His understanding was that they were all staying in the hotel tonight, but he didn't see anyone in the lobby aside from an older woman with gray hair and a gaggle of preteen girls heading to the pool with their parents.

Hopefully his cowboy would have more to offer than a horseback-sculpted ass or else faking his interest might prove to be difficult. His gut tightened with nerves. He needed to stay on as long as he could. He was charming, he knew that much, but what else did he have to offer to a man who owned a cattle ranch? A pretty smile? A nice butt of his own?

Roan decided to head back to his room for a little one-on-one time with his hand. It'd be awhile before he had privacy to enjoy a long session of self-pleasure. Most of the reality shows he'd binge-watched in preparation required the contestants to room with each other, sometimes more than one in a small space. Even the showers would be discreetly filmed to catch or prevent guys from hooking up, so he wouldn't even be able to rub a quick one out in the bathroom once he was on set.

It was easy enough to pull up some porn on his phone and waste an hour.

Afterward, stretched out sweaty and panting on the bed, he stared up at the ceiling and willed time to pass even more quickly. He was anxious to get on with things. He got up and showered, but the steam just made the room feel like the inside of a giant's mouth. Pulling on fresh boxers, he climbed back into bed and waited for his heart to stop aching and his belly to stop flipping over anxiously. Neither did.

The AC creaked and complained beside him, blasting frigid air, but still the room felt sticky with humidity. He opened the apps on his phone, but a man could only scroll through Facebook and Instagram so many times before he wanted to stab himself and all of his friends who were living awesome, gorgeous, happy lives full of travel, wine, kids, and endless smiles. None of them had sick moms, it seemed. None of them were currently in Satan's butthole, trying to cool off. None of them were wondering if they were idiots to have made this desperate bargain.

He hated feeling like a crappy person, burning with envy for his friends' perfectly curated lives. But, man, what he wouldn't give to not have to worry about his mom being in pain, or where they were gonna get money for the medical bills, or whether he was going to lose her forever. He wiped at his eyes and groaned. Why couldn't his life be made up of trips to Fire Island, and swimming lessons for cute little brats, and picture-perfect gardens bursting with fresh vegetables enough to share around at the compulsory-yet-fun office party at his white-collar job? How did his friends get these lives, anyway? Where had he gone so wrong?

He'd give up all those normal life dreams, though, for his mom to be well. He'd give up anything for that.

He dabbed sweat from his forehead and decided to try to nap on top of the covers even though it creeped him out and left him feeling vulnerable. He clutched a pillow to his stomach to try to fool his brain into believing his vital organs weren't exposed to any knife-wielding maniac who decided to break into his room. The little boy in him had never stopped believing in the magic protection of pillows.

Sleep didn't come. Doubling up a pillow beneath his head, he turned on the TV. Five hundred channels of old-fashioned cable TV awaited his perusal. The summer sun blazed outside, and he passed his final hours as a free man flipping aimlessly through channels and marveling at the endless stupidity of humanity.

Pausing on *Naked and Afraid*, Roan stared at the screen. Whatever he'd gotten himself into, at least he hadn't tried out for that show. Talk about madness. Though right here, right now, in the heat of this hotel room, he felt every bit as vulnerable as those contestants looked.

He squeezed the second pillow to his stomach again.

"It's only six weeks. She'll be fine for six more weeks."

He prayed it was true.

WEEK ONE

FIRST IMPRESSIONS AND A FIRST DATE

Chapter 3

Roan loosed a pathetic groan when the alarm on his phone woke him at six am. The cover beneath him stuck to his skin, and the back of his neck was wet. When he sat up to turn the damn thing off, his hair flopped about on top of his head. Nothing like going to sleep with wet hair.

He was surprised to have slept at all, but after he watched four episodes of *Naked and Afraid,* consumed more vending machine treats, jerked off and showered again, he'd passed into a shaky, broken, sugared-up sleep. He was so tired now he considered rolling over for another ten minutes, but he needed to take extra care getting ready. Today was the day he'd meet his cowboy, and he aimed to make the best first impression he could. So he swung his legs over the edge of the mattress and stumbled to the bathroom.

He'd chosen his outfit carefully before leaving Ohio and mourned the fact that he'd have to leave the cardigan out of it. It was a little cashmere beauty, but the heat forestalled any further thought of it. Besides, the short-sleeved shirt with the bow tie and suspenders would work perfectly on their own too. His jeans were tight, but not too skinny, just enough to show off his long legs and narrow hips. He folded over the cuffs of his jeans once, then set about taming his black hair. It was longer at the top but cut close to his head on the sides, and he liked to create a puff of careful waves in the middle. The style made his cheekbones and hazel eyes stand out.

With his pinky finger he applied the faintest sheen of lip gloss, then smacked his lips with a pop, and smoothed his shirt down. Finally, he added the glasses he'd picked up the week before at a cute boutique. They'd cost a bundle, but they made him look adorable as hell, if he did say so himself.

The instructions for the meet and greet had suggested wearing a suit, but Roan didn't own one, and he figured he'd stand out more in his own clothes.

At seven thirty, he was all packed up and ready to go downstairs. His stomach churned with nerves and hunger, but it was too late for breakfast. He sent a quick, final "I love you" text to his mom, not knowing when he'd get the chance to communicate with her again. He assumed they'd be confiscating their phones that morning since they were headed to the filming location. With a quick prayer, he left the safety of his hotel room behind.

Downstairs, a bunch of people hung around the lounge. They were obviously connected to the filming of the show, given the bags of equipment laying around, but he wasn't sure if there were other contestants in the mix or not.

Where they'd all been the night before when he'd been eager for some entertaining company to keep his mind off things, he didn't know. They sure would have been a relief to see then. He could have chatted with them, charmed them, and maybe gotten some information about his competition in advance. Something that would have given him an edge. But oh well.

He joined the crowd now, shifting his bag on his shoulder awkwardly and plastering on a fake smile.

"Hi," someone said right in his ear, and Roan startled. He spun around to find himself face-to-face with a blond jock-type with a hyper-bleached smile.

"Hi." Roan surreptitiously eyed the guy. Was he a crew member? No, probably another contestant. He looked more like a professional model or something. What with his stupidly handsome face and his insanely even skin tone. Who even really looked like that outside of airbrushed pictures in magazines? This guy apparently.

"I'm Chad. You're here for the show, right?"

"Right." Roan took the offered hand. Chad's handshake was dry and firm. Shit, Roan was going to have to shake his cowboy's hand at some point, and by then he'd probably be all sweaty. He could already feel the humidity getting to him, making his jeans feel like they were plastered on. His gut rushed with butterflies, and his upper lip stung with sudden sweat. Great, here came the nerves again, too.

Chad lifted a brow at him and chuckled kindly.

Crap. He hadn't even introduced himself. Off to a great start already. So much for being the smart contestant who stayed cool under pressure. "Oh, I'm Roan."

Chad laughed. "Nice to meet you, Roan. Can I just say, you look confused?"

"I guess I am?" He was expecting things to be well-organized; instead, he got the impression he was leaving on a school trip. Everyone was on their phones, either talking a mile a minute or texting with irritation written all over their face. He supposed the grumpy ones were the crew members. A few other guys were obviously saying goodbye to whatever family might miss them over the next six weeks, and those must be his fellow contestants. Or at least some of them.

"It's a mess, from what I can tell," Chad said with a shrug. "But it always feels that way at the start of a project."

So Chad was familiar with this kind of thing. Maybe he was an actor then. Roan pushed at the glasses. They were very hipsterish, and he thought they made him look pretty darn sweet, but the moisture from the air was not his friend, and they slipped down again.

Chad smirked a little but wasn't unkind when he asked, "Are those glasses real? Like do you need them to see?"

"Uh. No."

"Friendly tip. Lose them. They're super cute, just like you, but they're very city slicker." He flicked an imaginary cap. "You're heading to a farm now, boy," he said in a strong twang that sounded nothing like the accents Roan had heard since stepping off the plane in Louisiana.

"Oh. Okay." Roan took the glasses off and stuffed them in one of his bags. "Thanks."

"No problem, man. I'm here to have fun. I'm not going to trample anyone on my way to the end of the race, you know?"

"Sure." Roan sucked his bottom lip and turned toward the group again.

Chad laughed. "Relax, you'll be fine. Come on, meet the others before Twinkle Toes shows up."

"Who?"

Twinkle Toes? Was that a gay joke? By a presumably gay man? Roan didn't know what to think about that.

"Andrew Towes." At Roan's confused expression, he went on, "Goes by Andy. He's the showrunner. This is his baby. Didn't you get any emails from him? Or phone calls?"

"No, I always talked to some lady."

Chad's eyebrows drew down a bit but the smile lingered on his face. "It's fine. I'm sure Andy delegates most of that kind of work. Anyway, he's a decent guy. For a Hollywood type. Come on, let me introduce you around."

"How do you know the other suitors?"

"We all met up in the lobby and then went out to dinner last night."

"Was that a planned activity?"

"No, just an impromptu thing. The producers were kind of mad about afterward, actually." He laughed. "We weren't supposed to meet each other until this morning. I'm sorry you didn't make it out with us, though. We had a good time. Did you fly in late last night?"

"No. I've been here. I guess it was just bad timing." Roan shifted from foot-to-foot. How had he missed everyone so completely? He'd have liked company last night, and getting to know some of the other contestants in advance would have been a nice boon, perfect for forming alliances and strategizing. Hopefully it wouldn't matter. The other contestants didn't make the decisions about who to cut and when. That was on their cowboy…whoever he was.

Roan followed Chad, dragged his luggage into a corner with everyone else's, and met his fellow competitors, promptly forgetting all their names.

Except for Ben's.

Ben was gorgeous. Holy crap. He was the only one apart from Roan who wasn't in some sort of formal evening wear, but unlike Roan he'd just thrown on a white T-shirt and a pair of tight jeans. And fuck, that was genius. They were heading to a working farm, not a party. Ben's tattoos clung lovingly to sculpted biceps, and Roan wanted to take a look at them up close. Very close. Possibly with his tongue.

Damn.

"You're drooling," Chad whispered in his ear.

"Can you blame me? I should just pack up and go home. What even is the point?"

"I don't know." Chad gave him a quick up and down. "You're not so bad yourself, cutie pie."

Roan blushed to the tips of his ears but couldn't help feeling a little pleased. He was about to say something nice to Chad too—please God don't let him accidentally mention the blinding whiteness of Chad's teeth—when someone clapped their hands. Loudly. Everyone in the lobby turned, including hotel employees and other guests who clearly had nothing to do with the show. An effeminate guy in tight pants and a floral top stood with his hands on his hips gazing intently at them all.

That must be Twinkle Toes then.

"Listen up, everyone. My name is Andy, and for the next six weeks—" he smirked "—if you're lucky enough to stay to the end—you'll do exactly as my producers and I say. Got it?"

Roan rolled his eyes and when he looked straight ahead again, he found Ben's gaze on him. *Oh hello, baby blues.* Roan licked his lips. Hell, he could get lost in those eyes if given a chance. Ben shot him a small but wicked grin, then turned his focus back to Andy.

Who was still talking. Roan got the idea he liked doing that. A lot.

"We're going to head out to two different filming locations today. First, we'll start filming the intros. We might not get around to everyone, but that's fine. We'll have more time after the meet and greet. There *will* be a lot of sitting around, people. So prepare to be bored. It's not going to be all fun and games around here."

Roan glanced at Chad, feeling more confused than ever. Chad just nodded along like he knew exactly what Andy was talking about.

"Before we leave, we'll divide you up into groups, and you'll meet your producer. Your producer is your lifeline, kids. He or she will be the one you go to with any problems, got it? Not me, not the AD, and definitely not the bachelor. Your producer is on your side and wants to help you shine. So if you know what's good for you, you'll do everything they tell you to do. If you don't like their suggestion, suck it up, and do it anyway." He raised a brow and said with a lascivious grin, "I know you're all pros at sucking it up, aren't you?"

"Nice," Roan whispered sarcastically, and Chad snorted.

"Let's get on with it," Andy said, referring to a clipboard. "Our first group will be produced by Rhonda. So that's Nick, Taylor, Davis, and Jaden," Andy called. Two hunks, a skinny dude, and a ginger guy all wearing cheap suits stepped forward. "Oh. And don't forget to hand in your phones, laptops, books, and any other forms of entertainment to Jillian," he said, motioning to a young woman wearing a Florence + the Machine tour T-shirt and a pixie cut. "She'll keep them until you're sent home."

"The next group will be produced by Molly." Andy tossed his thumb in the direction of a very fresh-faced woman with sharp eyes and even sharper smile. She wore a loose-fitting T-shirt and cut-off jean shorts but somehow looked dangerous as hell. And also like she might not even be out of college yet. Roan swallowed anxiously. Andy squinted at the clipboard. "Right, so that's Chad, Victor, Roan, Ben, and

Antoine."

Great.

He shook out his damp hands and tried to smile. Molly beckoned for everyone to gather around her. Handsome Ben, a muscled guy in a gray suit, and a mousy-looking fellow in a brown one all moved toward her. Roan took a deep breath. He'd wanted things to hurry and start, and now that they had, he wished he had a few minutes more to wait.

"C'mon cutie," Chad said, bumping his shoulder against Roan's. "Let's go get produced."

"Did they seriously lock us in?"

After they'd left the hotel, taken in separate SUVs by producer group to the first shooting location—an abandoned shopping center built in the nineteen-eighties, from all appearances—they'd been left hanging, cramped and uncomfortable, in the SUV itself. After telling them all to wait and locking the doors, Molly disappeared inside the building with all the other crew and producers. Their driver stood outside, leaning against the building, smoking a cigarette. The windows were blackened and made the world outside look gray and bleak.

"Yes, they seriously did," Chad said quietly.

"Protocol, I guess," Handsome Ben said from the very back of the SUV where he sat alone. His voice was a gruff rumble that made Roan want to squirm in a good way.

The men hadn't had any time to talk in the car on the drive over, what with Molly producing information about their cowboy—one Walker Reed, who was, from the photo she passed around, pretty decent looking. If by "decent" Roan meant "holy hotness wow." But now, after waiting for almost an hour, they were starting to get worried enough to talk.

"What if I have to take a leak?" the ridiculously buff one called Victor asked. His voice was deep and smooth, and he shifted uncomfortably on the bench seat ahead of Roan.

"Do you?" the mousy man next to him, Antoine, Roan thought his name was, asked quietly. He toyed with his skinny tie.

"Yeah, I kind of do."

"I guess we could roll down the windows and call for the driver."

It turned out the windows were locked too. "Fantastic," Chad said, running a hand over his hair and frowning. "This is a crap plan. My suit's going to look like shit before we even get started."

"I hope it's not indicative of how things are going to be run for the next six weeks," Roan said softly.

"How much longer do you think we'll have to wait?"

From what Roan could see out the window, they were taking guys one-by-one from the other SUVs in front of them, keeping them for a few minutes, and then sending them back. "Not long, I think? They've taken all four from the car in front of us. We should be next."

As if summoned, a guy in shorts and a T-shirt with dark bags under his eyes strode toward their SUV with a clipboard, some bottles of water tucked under his arm, and the key fob to release them from captivity.

"Roan!" the guy called as he jerked open the door. "You're up."

"Good luck," Chad said, patting his shoulder.

Roan had to practically climb over Chad to get out, but eventually he stepped into the fresh air and groaned at the heat.

"He has to pee," Antoine said, motioning at his seatmate.

"Yeah? Can you hold it?"

Victor nodded, and the guy said, "I'll get you next. Victor, right? Great. Don't piss yourself. It'll just be a few." Then he slammed the door, used the key fob to lock it again, and escorted Roan toward the rundown-looking building.

"Hi, my name's Dave, I'm taking you to your producer." T-shirt guy smiled wryly as they crossed the parking lot and then entered the air-conditioned cool of the main corridor of the shopping center. "I'd introduce you to the camera and sound crews, too, but there's no way you'll learn all their names today. Better to let that come naturally."

"Hi," Roan said. "Will I be seeing a lot of you over the next few weeks?"

"Probably. You'll get sick of all us soon enough. Through here." He led Roan down a narrow hallway jutting off the main one and into a small conference room. The table had been pushed to the side, as had most of the chairs, and in the corner behind a heavy-looking camera stood a barstool. A white sheet draped to look like a curtain hung behind it, billowing gently in an air-conditioned breeze. Molly sat next to the cameraman, tapping a pen against a file impatiently.

"Hi," Roan said, "I'm—"

"Yeah yeah, the kid with the sob story, I know. Sit down."

Roan gaped at Dave, who winced and shrugged apologetically before taking his seat off to the side of the camera.

"Excuse me?" Roan asked, rubbing his elbows in confusion. What was her problem with him?

"Look? Is there an issue? We need to get a move on; we have more of these interviews to do, and you're wasting time."

"It's just that—"

"No. Sit down. What did Andy say about following your producer's instructions?"

Roan blinked at her. She'd seemed like a hardass on the drive over, but she'd also seemed like she was on their side. She'd stated that it was her job to make sure one of them was in the finale and to always rely on her to do what was best for them.

But right now it seemed like she hated him.

She lifted a brow and smiled meanly. "I have about ten other potential contestants programmed into my phone, Roan. The higher-ups might've wanted you on this show, but that doesn't mean I can't axe you right now for holding up the schedule. Sit, so we can get this done."

Roan's heart thudded as he sat down and waited. Molly flicked through a file with harsh, jerky movements, mumbling to herself. "Okay, so it says here you requested your mom's illness to be kept from

Walker." She lifted her head. "Why is that?"

"I…it's personal," Roan said, his palms beginning to sweat in earnest. "I don't want to start this whole thing with everyone pitying me."

"Okay. Well, in a minute the camera's going to start rolling, and I'm going to ask you why you're here. What are you going to tell me?"

Roan had rehearsed this part. "I've always been drawn to farm life. As a kid—"

Molly held up her hand and pinched the bridge of her nose with the other. "Oh look, here's a story I haven't heard a million times already. No. This is what we're going to do, babe. Walker and the other contestants aren't going to see this clip until filming's long done and you're back in Minnesota or wherever you're from."

"Ohio."

"I don't care. Here's what your story line's going to be. You tell the camera everything about your mom, the real reason why you're here. Money. Then, over time, you're going to start to fall in love with Walker, and the money will become a secondary motivation. The public will eat it up. You'll be the underdog, here for the wrong reasons but out of desperation, so you'll have their sympathy. Then when you start to fall for him, they'll love you even more. It's perfect."

"I don't—" Roan shook his head.

"Don't get squeamish on me now, babe. Weren't you planning on acting like you were into him?"

Shame churned in Roan's gut, but he nodded. "Yes."

"Well then, this is no different."

"I don't want to use my mom—"

"You're not using her. It's the truth." She narrowed her eyes. "Isn't it?"

"Jesus Christ, yes. Of course it is."

"Well then." She nodded at the camera guys, plastered a fake smile on her face even though she remained out of the shot, then said, "Welcome Roan. Please tell me why you decided to take part in the inaugural season of the LGBTQ reality TV show *Queer Seeks Spouse*."

Roan took a deep breath, closed his eyes for a moment, and folded his hands tightly together in his lap. "My mom has stage four ovarian cancer. I was in grad school when we found out a year ago. I came home to be with her. It's…it's hard. Money's tight. And there's a drug trial we want to get her into, but if we can't then…" He spread his hands in frustration. Heat burned in his cheeks, and his eyes filled against his will. "So yeah, I'm here for the money." He stared at his white knuckles, and another flash of shame made him tremble.

He didn't believe for a second all the others were here out of true love aspirations and not for the big check at the end of the game, but they were probably not as ashamed about it as he was. Maybe they really intended—hoped—to fall in love. "I know I'm not here for the right reasons," he admitted quietly. "But I'm desperate. I didn't know what else to do." He fell silent.

After a long few seconds, Molly murmured, "Perfect. Nicely done. I'm glad to see you can be produced. There might be hope for you yet."

Roan wrapped his arms around himself. "Can I go?"

"Yes, please do. Don't tell any of the others what we discussed in here."

"Okay." Roan stood and turned to the door, then halted. "I was promised my mom would be able to reach you guys at any time and I could leave the competition if she got worse."

Molly didn't look up as she scribbled something in the file. "Yes, you were promised that."

When Molly said nothing else, Roan walked out.

"You okay?" Chad asked when Roan climbed back into the SUV again. "You look pretty bad. What happened?"

"Let's just say Molly is too sweet a name for that witch of a woman. We need something better."

"Mean Molls?"

"I was thinking more along the lines of bunch-back'd toad."

Chad lifted his head. "Shakespeare? Nice." When Roan gaped at him, Chad laughed. "English major," he said. "And just so you know…"

He pointed at Victor, who was being guided away by Dave with just enough hustle in his step to indicate he still really needed to take a leak. "Bio Chemical Engineer." Mousy Antoine turned around in his seat to see Chad and Roan more easily, and Chad pointed his way. "Account-ant. Ben back there's a mechanic. So we're not all dumbasses here."

"I never said—"

"No, but you assumed. And so did I. Don't worry about it. How about you? I'm guessing you're no dummy either."

"Me?"

"Yeah, what's your field?"

"Environmental engineering."

Chad stared at him in silence, then began to laugh. Loudly. "Holy shit, and you're going to live on a beef cattle farm for six weeks. I bet they're hoping for some environmentally charged drama between you and Walker."

Roan sat back, stunned. "You really think so?" Hours of psychological testing and interviews, but he was here because of his abandoned degree? He wasn't so sure of that. Molly hadn't mentioned it at all. She'd been much more into his so-called "sob story."

"Yeah, man. Now that we've figured that out, the producers are going to be disappointed, aren't they?"

"I don't know. I guess?" Roan frowned. "Cattle farms are important to the American economy, plus there are fair ways to run them that aren't as damaging to the environment. I have no grudge against them. You really think that's why they picked me? My…" He didn't want to bring up his mom. "My personality had nothing to do with it?"

"Ah, shit." Chad patted Roan's thigh. "Don't listen to me. What do I know? I'm just speculating, trying to feel more in control. You know how it is."

"Right," Roan said, a little miserably. It didn't matter why they'd picked him to be here—sob story or abandoned degree. He had to make sure he stayed through most of the six weeks.

He needed that money.

CHAPTER 4

"A SUIT? ARE those producers out of their damn minds? It's ninety-five degrees out there and—"

"One hundred percent humidity, I know. Stop complaining and let me straighten your tie." Tessa fiddled with the black silk thing, pushed on him by a woman from the damn costume department or whatever the hell they called it. "You know you're lucky to even be here in your own home. If it was up to some other director—"

"Showrunner."

"Whatever. If it was up to someone else, you'd probably be off somewhere in the middle of nowhere in a trailer or whatever. So be grateful to this Andy." She put her hands on his lapels and smiled up at him. "There."

"Thanks, Tess." Like he could ever go stay in a trailer somewhere for six fucking weeks. He had too much work to do.

Tessa put her hands to her rosy cheeks. "My beautiful boy. Look at you."

"I'm hardly a boy anymore." He winced. "Some of these kids coming out here to try to woo me are a decade younger than I am, though."

"They're all legal, and they want to be here, baby."

He snorted, checked the mirror one more time, and then gently put his hand on the small of her back to guide her out of his room. She barely reached his shoulder, his sweet step-mama, and he had to suppress the urge to pat her on the head. "They're in this for the same reason I am. The money." He hadn't realized he'd harbored some vague hope that maybe he'd actually meet someone real, someone worth knowing or caring about, until he heard how his declaration fairly rang in the air with its veracity.

Hope was ridiculous. No one found true love on these shows.

Tessa turned around and stopped him with a hand on his arm. "You never know," she said. "Keep an open mind. Life's a mysterious thing, Walker, and love even more so."

"I know, just look at how you and Dad got together."

"Never saw it coming," she agreed. "Now, come on. Show your father how handsome you are and then get out of here. The last thing I want are any of those horrible little peckerheads in my house again, telling us what to do."

Walker laughed and followed her down the creaking stairs. The farmhouse was old, but big enough that he had no problems still living here, under his parents' roof. The whole attic had been converted to a space just for him, including a bathroom and an office.

His dad was packing away lunch in the kitchen, and Walker saw him sneak the jar of jam—the sugary one—back onto the top shelf.

"You should be eating the sugar-free," Walker told him, and his dad spun around, a slight flush on his cheeks.

In the bright light of the country kitchen with the voile curtains and huge sink, range cooker and old style fridge, Walker was hit by how he might be looking at his mirror image in thirty years' time. Weather-beaten and wrinkled, his daddy was, with a hard, wiry body shaped by decades of hard labor. But his eyes were kind and at least half of the lines around his mouth were from laughing. Not a bad way to grow old.

"I'll eat what I damn well please," Dad said. "Now, what the hell are you wearing, boy?" He grinned at Walker. "Think that's how yer gonna hook a man? Dressed like that?"

"It's what they told me to wear."

"Will there be any women out there?"

"Not for me, no," Walker said in confusion.

"I meant in the crew, son." He wrapped his arm around Tessa. "Maybe I should take a look and see if there are any pretty ones." He brought a hand to his chin and scratched his jowls. "I've been thinking about upgrading."

"Joe Reed!" Tessa said, laughing. "If there's anyone who deserves an upgrade in this house, it's me. Maybe I'll take a look at the men on the crew and pick one for myself."

Dad pretended to stumble back, clutching his heart. "Now, Tess. Don't you go around saying things like that. My poor ol' heart can't take it." He hauled her closer. "And you know there ain't no woman for me but you."

"No one else would have you," she said, but she let him pull her closer and smiled, mollified. When they began to kiss, Walker spun on his heels.

"I still don't need to see any of that. Later, guys."

"Good luck," Tessa called after him.

"Snag one who's built like a horse," Dad yelled. "We can use the free labor."

"I'm not really marrying him, Dad," Walker threw over his shoulder.

"That's what you say now. But built like a horse is hung like a horse, and your—" The rest of the sentence was covered by the slam of the screen door as Walker headed outside.

It hadn't always been easy to grow up with two people so openly affectionate with each other and easy with talk of sex—especially when he was a teenager—but he wouldn't have it any other way. Most of the time.

The humid heat hit him like a ton of bricks, and the urge to tug at his tie was nearly overwhelming, but he didn't. He tossed the truck's keys in the air and caught them again, aiming for the battered old Ford, as a black Range Rover bounced up the black asphalt driveway. Which was in dire need of resurfacing. One of the jobs he'd get done once this ridiculous show was over.

A man with shaggy blond hair and a tired smile rolled the window down. "Afternoon," he called out. "I'm here to give you a ride."

Walker halted mid-stride, tugged his aviators down, and stared at him.

"I know the way to my own barn."

The guy winked. "Just following orders."

Walker didn't move. "You're serious? I can't drive to my own barn?"

"Sorry, man. Rules of the game."

Absurd. But not this guy's fault. Walker smirked a little, straightening his glasses. "Afraid I'm going to get cold feet and run for the hills, huh?"

"Not that I've seen hills forested enough to hide in around here, and you've got quite a few miles down south to go before you could hide in a swamp."

Laughing softly, Walker rounded the nose of the SUV and opened the passenger door. "When will they get here?" he asked when he sank in the seat. He had to push it back to make his legs fit.

"Nervous?"

Walker tugged at his shirtsleeves. "I want to say no, but I'd be lying."

The guy laughed and pulled away from the house. "I'm John, by the way. Your new producer. Let me offer my condolences for having to put up with Molly at the intro shoot." He winked and grinned. "She's a barracuda, that girl. Hope you weren't too attached to her. They've shifted her to produce some contestants, which means you're stuck with me now."

Walker gave him a wry smile. "Are you gonna manipulate me into saying and doing things I don't want to do? Because she was damn good at that."

John snorted as they bounced down the driveway. "Believe it or not, she's not all that bad once you get used to her. She just tends to treat the folks on the show as commodities, not people."

"And you don't do that?"

"I try not to." He smiled again, and Walker liked his relaxed vibe. "But I admit I've got a job to do, and I'm good at getting it done."

"Fair enough. So what happens now?"

"Lots of waiting around, I'm afraid. You'll get a gander at all the contestants really quickly while Andy explains what's going on—he's on set again today—and then, once the camera's rolling, you'll have to pretend you've never seen any of the guys before."

Walker cringed. "Sounds like a blast."

"You'll do just fine," John said and reached out to pat Walker's shoulder. "Everyone's nervous at first."

"You've produced on shows like this before?"

"A few."

"Any I'd know?"

John glanced at him. "Watch a lot of reality shows, do you?"

Walker averted his eyes and stared out of the window. "My step-mom does."

"Right…"

AGAINST ALL EXPECTATIONS, the barn had been finished in time.

Not that Walker could really get a good look at it with the dozens of crew members crawling all over the place, adjusting the set, the lighting, the fixed cameras. Walker took advantage of no one aside from John paying particular attention to him yet to try to see what all had been accomplished.

Gone were the straw-covered floors and spiderweb-adorned walls. It was also a lot more subdued than he'd braced himself for, if he looked past all the filming equipment and the hive of activity around him. He'd expected boudoir colors and decadent furniture, but instead it was modern and rustic at the same time, the walls painted in soft creams and

LETA BLAKE & INDRA VAUGHN

grays, while the wooden floor gleamed darkly under his feet. Comfortable white couches sat in a spacious living room, arranged in such a way that there was room for cameramen to move about. The kitchen was pretty big too, which made him curious about how much space was left for the bedrooms.

There were only two of them upstairs where the hayloft used to be, each with a bathroom that had a shower and a Jacuzzi. Tessa and Dad would love that when they finally moved in. He winced, laughing a little, imagining them in the Jacuzzi together. He'd have to remember never to use his own key when they were home by themselves.

Each bedroom had two sets of bunk beds and one queen-sized bed, and he didn't envy twelve men having to share those two spaces. He wondered if they were going to have to flip for who shared the queen beds and who got the top bunks.

Outside, he heard the banging of car doors, and his heart began to race. He sucked in a deep breath and slowly pushed it out of his nose again. He'd be fine. They were just men. Here to try to win his heart and get a cash prize for succeeding. That was all.

The AC came on as he made his way downstairs again, the cool air a relief against the sweat that prickled the back of his neck. He scrubbed his stubbled jaw, wondering if he shouldn't have shaved after all. But he wasn't about to pretend to be someone he wasn't.

Apart from the suit, that is.

And the remodeled barn.

And the pretending to be well-to-do.

Yeah.

Andy walked into the house ahead of another small army of shabbily dressed crew members. "There you are. So what do you think? No, never mind, I don't actually care. The contestants are taking a spin in the SUVs with their producers so we can grab some shots of their excitement at finally being here." He said all that in the most cheerful voice Walker had ever heard. "But they'll be back in half an hour. Want a drink?"

Without waiting for an answer, Andy aimed for the kitchen and yanked open the huge fridge. It was stocked to the brim with food.

"Wow. Who's going to be doing the cooking for these guys?" Walker asked.

Andy snorted and grabbed a bottle of water. He left the door open for Walker to help himself. "That's for them to fight out. The *ladies*, I assume." Andy made quote marks with his fingers, and Walker's eyebrows flew up.

"That's really offensive."

Andy had the slightest smirk on his face. "C'mon, Walker. I'm a filthy old queen." He motioned to his shiny, floral T-shirt. "I can say what I want."

"You're just trying to rile me up, aren't you? Is that what you people do? To get reactions on camera?"

Andy laughed, and it looked like his entire posture relaxed. He took a deep drink from his bottle and smacked his lips. "Congrats. Most people don't ever figure that out until they've been on the show for a few weeks. You're gonna keep me on my toes." He waggled his eyebrows. "The show needs drama, you see. The producers produce the drama, and I'm the showrunner, which means I'm a producer as well as everything else important. Aside from the star, of course."

"So underneath all that…" Walker motioned toward Andy's face and clothes. "You're also an asshole." Walker shook his head and then sipped the ice-cold water.

"Oh yeah, absolutely." Andy patted the fridge. "Wouldn't be able to do this job if I wasn't. Fresh food will be delivered every three days. The contestants can put in a list with their wishes, so you don't have to worry about that."

"I wasn't about to."

Andy grinned. "You're a bit of an asshole too, aren't you?"

Walker drank from his bottle again and shrugged. "Sometimes."

"That's what I thought. Okay, makeup is going to want to take a look at you again." He squinted up at Walker's face. "They'll do something about your hair and probably have a hissy fit over the fact that you didn't shave. Hell, I like it," he said when Walker began to sputter. "It gives you that authentic rancher look. Put a cowboy hat on, too." He gave Walker a sharp nudge with his elbow. "Got an extra I can wear home to my hubby?"

"I doubt it'd fit you," Walker said. "What with that big head of yours."

Andy laughed. "I'll send makeup in, and by the time you're ready, you'll get to meet your suitors. Or as Luke will put it, your future husband."

"More manipulation," Walker said.

"Oh, yes. And the best thing is, even when you know it, it still works."

Walker said nothing. He parked himself down on a barstool in the gleaming kitchen and waited. The whole place had been converted in a hurry, and he figured there'd be some problems with some of the construction sooner rather than later, but it was still an improvement. His parents would like living here after the show was done. And he'd have the farmhouse to himself. A little lonely, maybe, but maybe one day he'd find someone to share the old house with. For real.

A new make-up artist Walker hadn't met before, a girl with very short and very black hair burst into the kitchen, carrying a big white case on a strap on her shoulder. She was wearing a tank top and sported as many muscles underneath as he did.

"Ma'am," Walker said, rising to his feet and nodding politely. "How d'ya do?"

"Aw, aren't you a cutie? I'm Kylie." She held out her hand, and Walker caught sight of a tattooed sleeve that covered her entire arm.

"Walker. Nice to meet you. Now listen, I know you're here with makeup and all, but I really don't need—"

She held up one finger in front of his face. "One, I'm in charge of your face whenever it goes in front of a camera. I was about to tell you to go shave, but Andy likes it, so you're lucky. Two, it's hot as hell on fire out there. Half a minute in that heat and you'll look like a melting wax doll on camera. You're wearing makeup."

"Won't that make it worse?" he asked, eyeing the bag warily.

She grinned at him and patted the barstool he'd just vacated. "You just leave that to me." With one finger under his chin, she tilted his face this way and that, staring intently. He didn't think he'd been this close to a woman other than Tessa since Sarah Bordelon tried to kiss him in ninth grade. "Good skin," she mumbled, as if to herself. "I can work with the beard. Gonna have to pluck those eyebrows though." She tutted. "This should all have been done this morning."

"I was busy. And uh, what? What's wrong with my eyebrows?"

She fluttered her dark eyelashes at him. They were unnaturally long, and he wondered if they were fake. "Nothing is wrong with them. We're just going to get rid of that unibrow you've got going on."

"*Unibrow?*" Walker self-consciously touched the space between his eyebrows. It wasn't that hairy.

Kylie scrunched up her face and nodded. "Just a little one."

The way she opened her case and began to dig through it reminded him of the old doctor's visits to the ranch when he was a little kid. Walker tried not to gulp when she pulled out a pair of tweezers and what looked like lotion.

She waggled her eyebrows. "Don't you worry. It'll only hurt a little."

ODDLY ENOUGH, KYLIE'S brusque chatter and her intense attention to his face relaxed Walker a little, and he felt a lot more grounded by the time he heard the SUVs pull up and stop this time in front of the barn. He winced at the thought of being bounced for half an hour on the potholed driveway and ranch roads. Poor guys.

"I think you're supposed to wait inside," Kylie said as he stood up and started for the front door.

"Probably," Walker told her and grinned as he continued on. Andy was already out there, as well as John, talking with the camera crew.

"Okay," Andy was saying into the open door of the first SUV. "I want a shot of all of you climbing out and being super excited to be here. I know it's just a barn but for the next five minutes you're going to pretend this is a fucking fairy-tale castle, all right?" John, get the second-unit crew to catch some shots of the fields and any other romantic shit they can find. Fuck, why did I think a ranch would be a good idea?" He spun around and faltered for a second when he saw Walker standing there with his arms crossed in front of his chest. He recovered quickly though. "You should wait inside."

"I'll wait right here." Walker said. "I'll stay out of the way." For a second he thought Andy was going to bark at him, threaten him with his contract or whatever, but instead he just exchanged a glance with John and then shrugged.

"Okay," Andy yelled. "Start climbing out, ladies. Careful in your high heels."

Walker ground his teeth together at the "ladies" thing again and retreated a bit farther into the shade by the porch. He found Kylie by his side.

"God," she whispered. "He can be such a dick."

"Maybe. A product of his generation."

"Excuses."

"Yeah. Well, look, here they come."

Two guys had jumped out of the first SUV, one of them a spry little thing in a gray suit with a skinny tie. He was dancing up and down and clapping his hands in glee at the sight of the barn. Walker tried not to wince and think unkind, stereotypical thoughts about this little guy fainting at the sight of a cow. The dude next to him had his hands stuffed in his suit pockets and was grinning, more subdued but with a pleased twinkle in his eye.

A third man climbed out, and, hot damn, that was better. A brick of a guy in a white T-shirt and jeans, who hesitated for a second then reappeared holding the hand of a cute-but-geeky kid—and kid was the right word—in a short-sleeved shirt and a bow tie. Were those skinny jeans? Jesus Christ.

When the kid was out of the SUV, they quickly let go of each other.

"Personally," Kylie whispered, because cameras were on all over now, "I'm partial to the one in the white T-shirt. Look at those arms. Yum."

Walker was more into ogling the guy's ass, but he nodded his agreement.

In silence, they watched as all twelve contestants exited the SUVs, all squinting against the sharp sunlight before they faked their enthusiasm. Only Bow Tie and T-shirt Guy didn't put on any kind of a show. They looked around a little more carefully, and Bow Tie's eyes widened when he spotted Walker. Thinking he'd better step into his role, Walker allowed a small smile to break through, and he lifted one hand from where he'd crossed his arms over his chest to give a little wave.

Walker could see the kid blush from a mile away as he quickly looked away again.

Aw, shit. Bow Tie was *really* cute.

"All right, everyone inside before I die of heatstroke," Andy yelled. Then to John, he said, "Fetch me a cooling spritz of some kind and remind me next season to go film in Alaska or something. This is ridiculous."

John spoke into his headset and then rolled his eyes. "Spritz on the way. And this is why you should be inside with the monitors, letting the AD, Molly, and me handle this."

"I hate that bastard," Andy said, glaring at a guy in cut-off jeans and a Dead Kennedys T-shirt. "He thinks he knows what I want." Andy sniffed. "It's better when I do it myself."

"You hired him."

Andy shrugged and yelled, "Let's try that other take." Then stalked into the remodeled barn.

John caught Walker's eye and walked toward him. "That's Andy for you."

"Not the best delegator, huh?"

"No. But he's getting better at it."

"What's happening?" Walker asked as the suitors' producers herded them all back toward the SUVs. The men groaned and some gestured toward the remodeled barn with expressions of some urgency on their faces. "Why are they getting back into the cars?"

"Andy's new plan. He wants to try a different entrance. This could take some time to set up. Why don't you come inside?"

A half hour later, while Walker was chilling on the sofa, someone he hadn't been introduced to yet uncorked champagne bottles and filled twelve glasses. They left them standing on a silver platter in the middle of the giant coffee table and John pressed one of the glasses into Walker's hand.

"What?" John asked when Walker made a face.

"I hate champagne."

"Then just hold the glass without drinking it. Stand up. Try to look suave."

Oh God, this was so not him.

He didn't have time to think about it anymore, though, because someone yelled for action.

The front door burst open, and a dozen beautiful men tumbled in, talking loudly, most of them not noticing he was standing there. Bow Tie saw him, though, and so did T-shirt Guy. Now that he got a closer view, he recognized them both from the pictures he'd been sent the week before along with a little information about each of the contestants. Roan and Ben.

Andy clapped his hands, and the excitement dimmed a little. "Everyone, this is Walker Reed, your hot cowboy to woo. Walker, this is everyone." Walker opened his mouth to say hi, but Andy barreled on. "We're losing daylight and the bugs at night here are a menace so we need to get on with it. Here's what's going to happen. You can all grab a bottle of water—"

"But there's champagne there," someone piped up and everyone laughed. That had been Chad, Walker thought.

"That's for show," Andy said. "For now anyway. Grab some water, because you're going to pile back in the SUVs—"

Groans exploded, but Andy didn't care.

"Suck it up, darlings. Unless you want to wait outside? In the sun? And the heat? I didn't think so. So, like with the intros earlier, you're going to come out of the SUVs, one by one, and meet Walker for the first time in the shade by the porch."

"Then why can't we wait in the house?" some daring suitor called out.

"Because I said so," Andy snapped. "Afterwards, we'll come in here for a longer meet and greet, and Walker can pick and choose whoever he wants to talk to, but there will always be a camera present. After that, you'll choose your rooms. That's it. Kitchen's that way; you have two minutes."

No one seemed to be all that concerned with hurrying. They began to mutter amongst themselves again, some subtly and others not-so-subtly sizing Walker up. A small blond guy determinedly began to walk his way and Walker froze, but another producer intercepted him, spinning him adeptly around and sending him in the other direction. The look in the blond man's eyes had given Walker an idea of what a hunted rabbit must feel like.

"You're lucky," John said. "You get to wait in the AC without getting bounced around on those roads like a tennis ball."

"How long will this take?" Walker lowered his voice when a few suitors returning from the kitchen gave him a curious look. "I have things to do."

55

"For the next six weeks, your time is ours." John almost sounded apologetic but not quite. "You'll have to get used to it. And try not to look like you're about to murder someone. You're scaring your new little friends."

"They aren't my friends."

"You're right," John said soberly. "They're your future husbands."

Walker laughed against his will and watched the men file out of the renovated barn. He also wished he had put on stronger antiperspirant. His pits were hideously damp. And he was the one staying inside. He really felt for these guys.

"You're right," he said to John. "There's nothing to worry about. Just some man-eating, money-hungry, gorgeous men with their eyes set on my nonexistent fortune."

"Now, you're getting it," John said with a laugh. "Andy told me you were smart."

Walker rubbed a hand over the back of his neck and wondered just how smart he could be to have agreed to a ridiculous con like this.

CHAPTER 5

ONE BY ONE, the other contestants exited their SUVs, and the remaining men, including Roan, were sent on a loop around the property again. Roan sipped his water, but it churned in his stomach as they made a tenth turn past the old farmhouse and the newly renovated barn, bouncing off what felt like a million potholes.

"You okay?" Chad asked. It was just him and Victor left with Roan. They'd already taken Ben and Antoine inside.

"Yeah, fine." Roan swallowed back a burp and peered out of the blackened windows. They made the world look murky and dark, like he'd entered a dystopian sci-fi novel.

"He was pretty handsome, wasn't he?" Chad nudged him, and Roan looked over, a lurch of nausea accompanying the move. Fuck, he needed to lie down. "He was checking you out, you know."

"Probably just trying to figure out who was who." Roan glanced at Victor, who kept absentmindedly reaching in his pocket, probably for a phone that wasn't there. "God, is it hot in here?"

Chad shrugged. "Not really. It's hot out there though. That's going to take some getting used to."

Roan's head ached and his stomach lurched. He'd never been good in cars for long distances or on winding roads. After hours in this SUV, he was feeling green around the gills, to say the least. Desperate to think of anything other than how sick he felt, he turned to Chad. "Where are you from?"

"Michigan originally, but I went to college in Boston and never left."

"So you're not used to this heat either."

Chad looked out of the window. "No. It's intense. Oh, we're here again."

The car lurched to a stop and the door opened. Blinding sunlight spilled through and Roan squinted against it. A sharp pain spiked in his left temple. He almost wished the windows weren't so shaded. At least then they'd be used to the light.

"Roan, you're up," Molly said, leaning in with a clipboard in hand and a headset with a microphone attached to her ear. "Snap, snap."

"Thank fucking God," he groaned and clambered past Chad.

"Good luck," Chad said, but Roan didn't reply, too much in a hurry to get out.

And into the sickening humidity.

Instantly, his palms began to sweat and his shirt stuck to his back all over again, just like it had the first time they'd gotten out of the car.

Shit.

And there was Walker, standing in the shade of the porch, as calm and collected as before. Cool as a cucumber. Even in a suit he looked exactly like every cowboy fantasy Roan had ever had. No doubt thanks to that stubbled jaw, which was hot as hell no matter what, and the wide-brimmed cowboy hat. Roan hurried over to get out of the sun, not caring if it made him look anything but suave.

Surreptitiously wiping his hand on his jeans first, he thrust a palm in Walker's direction. "Hi," he said, his head spinning as his eyes tried to adjust themselves to the shade. "I'm Roan."

The noise of the bugs, the groan of the AC from the barn, and the skid of the tires from the SUV driving away became weirdly hollow. The sweat prickling his top lip turned icy. Somewhere to the left of them cameras were filming.

A warm, dry hand carefully folded around Roan's. "Walker. It's nice to meet you, Roan, I've been looking forward to—"

Oh, fuck.

Roan had no time to think; he simply bent over the porch rail and promptly puked in Walker's bushes.

And then he heaved a second time, bringing up water and stomach acid.

Walker let go of his hand in a hurry—not that Roan could blame him. Tears sprung to his eyes as he tried to get his retching stomach under control. When he was finally finished, he wiped his mouth with the back of his hand.

"I'm so sorry," he croaked. Someone patted him on the back, but the touch was small and light. He glanced up to see Walker's producer gesturing wildly and from somewhere behind him Molly yelled, "Medic! Now! And fly in some water for Roan, please!"

"Here, have a seat," Walker said, gesturing to a wicker sofa behind him.

Roan collapsed onto it, his knees and hands shaking. He couldn't even look at Walker. He squeezed his eyes closed. Walker stood next to him and put his hand on Roan's shoulder but said nothing more.

A woman in scrubs jogged around the corner of the barn, looking tidy and neat, which made Roan wonder if there were trailers for the crew back there.

"Are you okay?" she asked.

"Just car sick," he muttered, humiliation drowning him even more than the wretched humidity.

"Don't worry. It's not the first time this sort of thing has happened on a reality show set." She turned to Walker who had moved a few feet away upon her arrival and smiled wryly. "Although it's the first time someone nearly barfed on the bachelor. Haven't seen that before!" Roan stared into the nurse's face, refusing to look anywhere else, not wanting to see Walker's expression. "Here, have some water," she said as a crew member appeared with a bottle still wet with cool condensation.

He gratefully accepted it, stood to put his elbows on the porch railing, and rinsed his mouth. Then he pressed the cold bottle to his forehead and the back of his neck. Slowly the blood seemed to return to his brain. Trying not to let it show, he wiped at the tears that clung to his cheeks. Fuck. He'd be going home first, he was sure of it. All of this for nothing. He'd failed his mom.

"Thanks," he told the nurse belatedly as she watched him take a few sips of the water and then took the unfinished bottle from him.

"Don't worry, hon. Take a quick seat, and I'll check your blood pressure, make sure you don't have sunstroke." He did as he was told, trying not to notice the impatient activity of the crew around him. "At least you made a lasting impression."

Behind them, Walker snorted.

Well. He couldn't hide forever. Roan turned around.

"Sorry about that," he said, eyes on Walker's shoes. They were clean and shiny but not new. For some reason that made Roan relax a little.

"You okay? You need to go lie down or something?" Walker asked.

"No." He still felt a little woozy but he wasn't about to go to bed. "I just get a little carsick sometimes. I'll be all right." He quickly checked himself over but could see no puke anywhere on his clothes, thank God.

Walker leaned a little closer. "You look fine," he said with a small smile. "Here." He fished something out of his pocket and held it out. Automatically, Roan put his hand up to accept whatever it was, and Walker dropped a mint in his palm. "Don't worry about it. Once you've helped with a calving, you won't blink at a little vomit, either."

Calving? Him? As in, actually touching a cow? While it gave birth?

"Um, thanks," Roan mumbled. The SUV came around the bend again, and Roan popped the mint into his mouth. A welcome burst of freshness chased the last of the bitterness on his tongue away.

"If you're feeling all right…" the nurse said. He nodded, and she rose to her feet.

"Let's get ready people," Molly yelled. "We have what we need for Roan. Thanks for the drama, kid. Now it's Chad's turn." She waved him off. "Someone get Roan out of my shot."

Walker rolled his eyes a little, and Roan grinned weakly. "I should probably…" He pointed toward the door.

Walker nodded. "We'll talk more later. Not that this hasn't been interesting." He laughed a soft rumbly laugh, and Roan swallowed hard.

"Yeah, um. I'll try not to puke when I see you again."

"I'd appreciate that, sir." Walker made a move like he was about to tip his hat and then stopped himself. It was endearing. "I might take it personal if you do."

Roan ducked his head and laughed. "Nice to meet you too." Someone took him by the elbow, and Roan let himself be directed toward the nurse again. Once she was satisfied that he was fine, another producer took him inside. Over his shoulder, he could hear Molly coaching Chad and Walker through their introduction.

As soon as he entered the house, one of the guys from another producer's group—Peter, Roan thought his name was—strode up to him. "Did you seriously just barf all over Walker?" he asked, guffawing. He was pretty short but evidently made up for that by being very loud. Small dog syndrome, Roan thought with some bite.

"In the bushes," Roan said. "Not actually on him."

Peter laughed and swayed a little. Behind him the other contestants who had already been introduced to Walker and allowed inside were lounging around. It looked like they'd been digging into the champagne already. Deeply. Roan pushed the mint around his mouth and gave Peter a smile.

"I'm just going to grab some more water."

Peter shouted, "Hey, guys, Roan really did puke all over the bachelor."

A burst of laughter, then someone yelled out, "Ha! Retching Roan!"

What was this, grade school? He cringed and slunk into the kitchen, startling when he found it occupied.

"Don't listen to them," Ben said. Just standing there filling up his shirt with all his muscles and filling up his jeans with his meaty-looking junk. "They're assholes. And they're drunk."

"Yeah, I figured." Roan stood awkwardly in the bright white space, staring at Ben with his big paw wrapped around a can of Coke. "You don't drink?"

"No."

"Oh. Okay. I just wanted some water." Before he could move to the fridge, Ben was there, reaching inside and handing him a bottle. "Uh, thanks." Silence. "I should probably..." He pointed over his shoulder.

"Seems like it will still be a while before they get to filming the next part, if you'd rather hang out here." There were still cameras around, but at least Ben didn't seem to have the mentality of a twelve-year-old.

"Oh yes, please," Roan said, groaning with relief.

Ben shifted to the side a little and Roan went to lean against the counter next to him. "You feeling okay now?" Ben asked.

"No."

"I can find the nurse," he said.

"I mean, yeah. I'm fine. I'm just mortified as hell, that's all. Apart from that, I'm just peachy."

Ben gave him a small smile, his blue eyes warm and twinkling. His muscles bunched underneath the white T-shirt when he lifted his arm to drink from his Coke. "Glad to hear it."

God. Roan didn't stand a chance. The man was a dream.

And he'd vomited in front of the bachelor. Fantastic.

ROAN FELT INFINITELY better by the time Andy, Walker, and John finally trailed inside behind the final contestant. He didn't see how there could be much more filming tonight because everyone looked either sweaty or drunk or both.

Apparently Andy was of a different opinion. "Jesus Christ, are you all fucking wasted?" He grinned, clapping his hands giddily. "Excellent.

Usually we need to do a bit more coaxing than that."

"Bellamy went on a hunt for the champagne bottles," Peter piped up. "Found 'em!" He raised his glass high.

"At least Roan's the only one who's puked so far," Antoine said, clinking a toast with the man next to him, and Roan stared daggers. Who'd have thought the mousy accountant would turn out to be a little shit?

"Yeah, well he's the only one who still looks marginally decent," Molly called out, stepping into the middle of the room. "Here's the thing. It took so long to get the shots we needed tonight that the longer meet and greet is canceled." There was a collective groan from the suitors. Molly raised her hand for silence and went on, "In the morning, we'll have a full group date. That means Walker here is going to walk—heh—you around the ranch and explain what they do here." She glanced at Walker. "And make it sound interesting, cowboy. You'll all get a chance to talk to him in front of the camera so try not to behave like rabid dogs. Unless you just can't restrain yourself, and then go right ahead. We'll happily film it."

"Cheers to that," Andy called out, grabbing a champagne glass himself and taking a big swallow.

Molly rolled her eyes.

"Is he going to stay and party with us some tonight?" Peter asked, like Walker wasn't even part of the conversation.

"No," Walker said brusquely. Molly scowled at him, and Walker's shoulders crept up to his ears an inch or so. "This is a working farm," he explained. "I have to get to bed early and get up at the crack of dawn. Even with filming, there are things I need to see to."

"Aw." Peter pouted at him, and Walker gave him an apologetic little smile.

"As you know," Molly cut in, "the bachelor never stays with the contestants anyway. There's nothing new about that. Tonight will be your opportunity to size each other up and get to know your competition."

Andy clapped his hands together. "Right, so that means you princesses can go pick a bed upstairs."

"Hey," Walker said, sternly.

Andy grinned, obviously pleased to rile Walker up again. "Cameras will be running, guys. Sleep wherever you like. Duke it out. Make a good show of it. The toilets in each bathroom are in a separate, closed-door closet, and the only place off limits for cameras. But everything else, including the showers and tubs—and everything you say—is fair game."

So he'd been right. No jerking off in the shower, even.

"Behave yourselves," Andy said that like he meant the opposite. "And we'll see you tomorrow at seven a.m."

"Seven?" several people cried out. In fact, Chad, Ben, and Roan were the only ones who kept quiet. Roan didn't miss Walker's little smirk as he aimed for the front door.

"G'night, gentlemen," he said in that soft drawl of his.

Peter blew him a kiss, and Roan rolled his eyes.

When Walker had gone, a strange hush settled over the house. Then all at once, everyone scrambled for the stairs. Ben and Roan alone remained where they were.

"Do you feel like the odd ones out?" Roan asked him.

Ben laughed, a surprisingly cheerful sound from the big, broody guy. "You could say that again."

They gathered their bags and ambled up the stairs too. By the time they got upstairs, there was one bed left in each bedroom. Roan glanced at Ben, who shrugged. "They're both top bunks."

"Figures."

Ben went right, and Roan turned left. He ended up in a room with Victor, Jaden, Peter, Chad, and Antoine.

"Hey, it's Retching Roan," Antoine called out. "Dude you're not going to sleep above me, are you? What if you puke again?"

"Leave him alone," Jaden said before Roan could open his mouth. He was lying on one side of the queen-size bed and Victor was spread out on the other. "You can switch with me, if you want, Roan. You know, if you don't want to be on top of that idiot."

Antoine sputtered. "As if he tops anyone!"

"Thanks," Roan said, eyeing the queen bed. Victor took up about two thirds of it, and Jaden looked a little cramped. "But I'll be fine." He glared at Antoine. "And if I barf I'll make sure to aim for your head."

"Asshole," Antoine muttered, but his cheeks stained red and he turned away. Typical weak bully.

"So what do you think about all this?" Peter asked. "I have to say the houses on other shows I've seen were always a lot fancier."

"It's a farm," Victor said, stretching his arms above his head. "What did you expect?"

Roan tuned them out and hunted for a place to hang his clothes. There was plenty of closet space and a foldaway rack for each suitor to hang their clothes on. He'd brought enough stuff for two weeks all packed tightly in his two bags. It meant he'd be wearing the same things a few times, but that couldn't be helped. And the contract stated that whoever was left in the final two weeks would be dressed by the sponsors of the show, so that was pretty cool.

Final two weeks. Would he even make it? Everyone was so gorgeous. And ruthless. And they all got bonus points for not puking in front of their cowboy.

The sun was starting to set, and Roan didn't feel like hanging out in the house the whole evening. They'd have to talk about things as a group soon enough. About food, for one thing. Keeping the place clean, for another. Twelve people in one house wasn't going to be easy, even if they would start falling away next week. What if it was him? Maybe he was unpacking for nothing. He dropped his stuff and left the others talking amongst themselves. From the bedroom across the hall came raucous laughter and Roan was secretly glad he didn't have to be in there.

For now, he let it all go, went downstairs, and stepped out of the backdoor leading from the kitchen.

"You can go on the porch but no farther," someone to his right said. He was starting to get so used to all the crew milling around he hadn't even noticed the guy.

"Okay."

There were still people around but decidedly fewer. The lights of several cameras blinked at him as he made his way into the heat. A low hum of cicadas had been omnipresent all day but the lower the sun sank, the louder they seemed to become. He swatted at some unknown bug as he explored the big back porch, taking in the grassy and moderately rolling landscape. Less hilly than Ohio but not as flat as he'd imagined, either. The horizon was interrupted here and there by huge oak trees, their limbs spidering dramatically out of the trunk. A pond glistened in the not-too-far distance, and Roan's jaw clenched shut as his eyes widened. Were there alligators in there? Would they come up to the house? He hoped not.

"Oh, hey."

He spun around and came face-to-face with Ben. They were so in sync, it seemed, that he wasn't even surprised to see him. "Hi."

Ben's smile was sweet. "You escaped too, huh?"

"Yeah, it's been a pretty wild day. I just wanted some peace."

"I can go, if you want." Ben jerked his thumb back toward the house.

"Nah." Roan grinned and went to sit in one of the rocking chairs that overlooked the quiet fields with grazing cows. "I think you're kind of a peaceful guy."

Ben didn't smile again, but he did sit right beside Roan, who was suddenly a lot more aware of the cameras pointing toward them. "Yeah, I guess I am." A blessed breeze came from across the fields and they both sighed and then chuckled. "Where you from, Roan?"

"Ohio. You?"

"Florida."

"No way. So this heat is like home to you, I guess?"

He did grin then. "Pretty much."

Yeah, Roan stood no chance. Ben was a shoo-in. Why would Walker choose a lightweight like Roan over a gorgeous guy like him? He couldn't help but wonder why Ben was even here. Was he in it for the money, too? Was Walker? Hell, was anyone on this show really looking for love? If anyone was, it was probably Ben. There was just something about him.

Something kind of perfect.

Roan bit into his lower lip and hoped against hope that he could stay long enough to help his mom. That was all he needed. Let Ben and the others have Walker. Just so long as it wasn't Antoine or Peter. Or anyone who'd called him Retching Roan.

But, Ben, sure. He was a nice guy, and besides, he already seemed like he fit here on Reed Ranch.

Another part of the gorgeous scenery.

ROAN DIDN'T FALL asleep until three a.m. that night, thanks to the most violent electric storm he'd ever experienced. It frightened him to death at first, but when the barn didn't collapse, he settled in to listen. Once it moved on some distance, he found the rain pretty soothing. Less soothing was Antoine and his squeaky noises whenever a foundation-shaking thunderclap fell. It didn't help he'd gotten so used to listening for any kind of sound coming from his mother's bedroom that the slightest snore or whine woke him up instantly.

He got out of bed at six, groggy and disheveled, because he wanted to beat everyone to the bathroom, showering quickly out of considera-tion to the limited hot water. The red light of the camera caught his attention, but he noted it was positioned in such a way that it only recorded from the chest up. He hoped.

When he stepped out of the fogged up cubicle, he nearly squealed. Victor was sitting in the bathtub—covered in foam, thank God for small mercies.

"Sorry." A long, muscled leg appeared from underneath the bubbles and he rubbed soap all over it. "I figured we'd waste less time this way." Victor winked at him.

"Uh, I can come back to shave later," Roan said, shuffling toward the door.

"By then this place will be covered in steam and smell like a hair salon. Shave now, dude. Seriously. I won't stand up if it offends your sensibilities."

"Okay," Roan croaked, and he wondered if he could shave with his eyes closed. He maneuvered the towel around his hips without flashing anything more than Victor had already seen, and lathered up.

"Mmm, there's something so sexy about a man shaving," Victor said, and Roan froze. He laughed a rumbling laugh. "Don't mind me, I'm just going to objectify you from here. Jesus, you're pale, aren't you? No tattoos, not a one?"

"No," Roan said. He glanced at Victor in the mirror and noticed from his expression that he'd definitely seen the little barbells in Roan's nipples, but thankfully he didn't say anything about those.

Roan jutted his chin out to get the fiddly bit under his lip.

"You should think about getting a tattoo," Victor said. "Something pretty. Like you."

Roan ignored the flirting. "Do you have any?"

Victor grinned at him in the mirror, and Roan quickly turned his eyes back to his shaving. "One on each cheek." He put his hands on the edge of the tub. "Want to see?"

"Nope, thanks, I'm good." Roan wasn't usually shy about nakedness—he'd lived in a dorm—but something about this whole situation made him nervous. It didn't help that the red eye of the mounted camera seemed to pierce right through him. He shaved faster than he normally would, just wanting to get out of there. If he missed a spot, well tough luck. It wasn't like he'd be dancing cheek to cheek with anyone today.

When he shuffled out of the bathroom, Peter was there, waiting to get in. "Oh, hey, dude."

"Uh, you can't go in there," Roan said.

Peter looked at him like he was crazy. "What, why?"

Roan winced. "Because Victor's in there."

"But you—and he—" He went quiet and listened. "He's having a bath? With you in there? You horndog."

"No, that's not—he came in while I—" Too late. Peter gleefully turned away and stuck his head in their bedroom. "Roan just showered with Victor!" he yelled.

Roan pushed past him. "Whatever," he muttered when they all hollered at him. He wasn't going to get caught up in these petty mind games. He yanked on a pair of briefs under his towel, then hung it over the rung of the top bunk to dry.

Farm day today, apparently. So what should he wear? Jeans, but probably not too tight. He had a gorgeous pair of dark Calvin Kleins that were not too thick and made his legs look fantastic. He liked to pair those with a very thin pink Henley. So thin his nipples were visible to anyone who cared to look hard enough. It was a pretty flamingly queer outfit, but then it wasn't like he had anything to hide here. He pulled the jeans over his hips and the Henley over his head in a rush to get not-naked as fast as possible.

Which was when Walker Reed stepped through their bedroom door.

Antoine squeaked—again—and hid under the sheets. Victor wandered in wearing nothing but a tiny towel—somehow smaller than the one Roan had used. Maybe it was just all of his muscles. With his glistening skin on display, Victor gave Walker a long and appreciative once-over. Roan went hot to the tips of his ears and turned away.

Which put him and his open fly right in Walker's path. Roan wanted to zip up fast but was afraid that'd only draw attention to it, so he stayed still where he was.

"Morning," Walker said. When Victor walked past him again, brushing against Walker's body to reach into his wardrobe, Roan noticed Walker's cheeks were tinged a little red too. Victor's washboard abs didn't leave anyone unaffected, apparently.

Walker was wearing a cowboy hat, and he took it off. "Sir," he said, with a little nod in Victor's direction and then quickly looked away again. His eyes met Roan's, but he drifted on, taking in Antoine's lump under the covers. "I know I'm barging in unannounced, sorry about that." He said it like, *saw-ree*, and Roan died a little inside from the cuteness. "But like I said, we're making an early start this morning. You have half an hour to get ready."

Antoine sat up, the sheet still over his head. "I call next shower," he yelled, then he shuffled out of the bed, wrapped in the sheet, bumbled into a wall, then the open door, until Roan grabbed his shoulders and pointed him in the direction of the bathroom. "Peter," Antoine yelled, banging a small fist against the door. "Your time's up."

"You can come on in," Peter called out. Antoine hesitated for a second, then opened the door and disappeared inside.

"I'll see y'all downstairs." Walker's grin was downright evil. "On the tractor."

As soon as Walker left, Roan zipped up his jeans and smoothed his Henley down. He really hoped Walker hadn't noticed Roan standing there with his underwear hanging out.

But what was Walker expecting to see when he walked into their bedroom unannounced? And besides, witnessing Victor in all his glory had probably erased everything else from his mind. So unfair how hot the other guys were.

Wait. Why did Roan care? He wasn't here to actually win.

Victor caught Roan watching him shimmy into a tight pair of jeans and a sleeveless shirt. He grinned like he knew exactly what Roan'd been thinking.

Instantly, Roan understood something about the show. Even though it didn't matter who won or what the final outcome was, not in the scheme of his motivations for being there, anyway, it would be so easy to get swept away in the urge to win this thing. A part of him ached to beat out everyone else and just *dominate*. Either because he didn't like most of the other suitors much or because he was a competitive person at heart. It didn't matter.

His reasons for making Walker Reed want him to stay had already changed from needing to stick around for the money to wanting the guy to actually like him better than these other yahoos. If he couldn't beat his mom's cancer, at least he could beat backstabbing Antoine and sexually aggressive Victor. He could win *something*.

Maybe not Walker's heart, but one more week on the ranch longer than these jackasses?

Yes. That he could do. Barf or no barf.

He straightened his shoulders and lifted his chin. He was Roan Carmichael, devoted son to a fierce woman and a true fighter, and today, at least, he was going to *win*.

CHAPTER 6

WALKER YANKED THE fridge open, pulled out a bottle of water, and downed half of it. John, his producer who shadowed him everywhere, was leaning against the counter while a bunch of camera guys did mysterious things to their equipment.

"Of course you're welcome to that," John said. "But it's really for the contestants. There's food and coffee at the craft services table, if you want some."

"Oh, right. Sure." Walker looked at the water bottle a bit guiltily, but John just chuckled and slapped his arm.

"C'mon, cowboy. Let's get you fed and watered."

Walker rolled his eyes but followed John outside.

"You're looking a little out of sorts," John said, once they were parked under the big tent set up in the shade of an old oak with the vast and varied craft table spread out in front of them. Walker gave it a long once-over, pleased to see that whoever had set the food up seemed to take the heat into account. Nothing looked liable to spoil. "You all right?" John asked, tilting his head curiously.

"Yes, sir," Walker replied. He eyed the fruit, sandwiches, doughnuts, Gummy bears, and a ton of miscellaneous stuff. He grabbed a cereal bar. "I'm doing just fine."

"Yeah, okay. So we sent you up to the bedroom, and something's been bothering you ever since." John motioned at someone, and Walker knew the cameras were on him and that his body mic was picking up every word.

He shrugged.

"C'mon. Who was naked?" John laughed, and Walker rolled his eyes because he guessed it was all part of the act.

"Victor."

"*Ohhh,* the bio chem guy?" John waggled his brows. "Hot." He grinned.

Was John even gay? Walker wasn't sure. But this was obviously part of being "produced," having a guy all up in your business.

"You're the one who told me to go up there," Walker said.

"I know." John laughed. "Were they sizing you up, too?"

"Like sharks."

"Sharks. They'll want to rip you apart."

"They don't even know me yet."

John laughed, loudly, then turned around and poured himself a coffee.

"You're cruel."

"Eh. It's my job." He sipped his coffee and made a face. "Could be better," he assessed.

"Seems a little early in the morning to be stirring the pot," Walker said.

"It's after six thirty," John said. "They need to get used to it."

"Sure. It's my everyday life. But these poor schmucks…"

John grinned. "Your future husband's gonna need to be used the rigors of farm life. They might as well start now."

Walker rolled his eyes, but his ears grew hot. He wished they'd stop calling the contestants his future husband, even though that was the premise of the show. It was just so patently absurd that he couldn't believe the audience would ever buy it. "I think you guys just like to get people off-kilter. I think that's what you do."

John waved his mug around just as Luke joined them at the table, ready to film the opening segment of the day or whatever. "Yeah, yeah. Hey, Luke, take note, Andy says next season it's gotta be a nightclub owner in Alaska or some shit. He's over this heat."

"Noted, and I'm on board," Luke said. "The humidity is giving me cankles."

Kylie walked up to the table and poured herself some coffee too, while Luke started to do weird vocalizations.

"Is he gonna sing?" Walker asked.

John shuddered and sipped his coffee. "I hope not. I've heard him sing and it's not pretty."

"I'm expecting you in my trailer in five minutes," Kylie told Walker as she spun on her heels and left.

"Ugh," Walker muttered. "I think I'll need whiskey in my coffee for that."

John shook his head. "Showbiz, babe."

Armed with his mug and skipping the whiskey, Walker let Kylie do her thing. He didn't think he looked all that different after she was done. Just a little...smoother.

John was waiting for him when he stepped out of the makeup trailer. "Andy wants some shots of you greeting the contestants as they come down for breakfast. I wouldn't worry too much about these since they hardly ever get used. It's more for potential editing purposes later on."

"To make things look different than they really are."

John gave a little shrug and turned toward the house, so Walker followed him into the kitchen, still as much a mess of crew members as it was the day before.

Footsteps sounded on the wooden steps, and Walker turned to see who'd appear first. It was the kid who'd puked last night, wearing a pink shirt. Which shouldn't work but somehow did, especially with the way his jeans hung low on a pair of the narrowest hips Walker had ever seen on a man. Not to mention the plain-as-day pierced nipples.

He was staring, so he smiled. "Roan, good morning."

"Morning," Roan croaked, then his dark eyes lit up. "Is that coffee? I need coffee." He made grabby hands and aimed for the machine sputtering behind them. John stepped aside so the cameras could get a clear shot as Roan began to rummage for mugs.

Walker's eyes lingered on Roan's cute ass in his jeans and then, unable to resist, took a *long* gander, trailing up his slim torso to the pretty flop of curly hair on top of his head. When Roan found the mugs, he turned to Walker, his face flushing at Walker's obvious regard. "Um, would you like some?"

He'd left his mug in Kylie's trailer. "Yes, please." He licked his lips and said, "With cream." Fascinated, Walker watched as Roan's face turned a deeper shade of pink. Shit, he hadn't meant to load that with innuendo, but his tone had betrayed him somehow.

As Roan poured the coffee and added cream, Walker asked, "You feeling better this morning?" Because he just couldn't help himself. Yup, there the kid went. From red to puce.

"Uh, yeah. I'm really sorry about that. It was so embarrassing. But, yeah, I'm feeling a lot better. Thanks."

"I'm glad, sir. I'll take some sugar in that, too."

Roan nodded but wouldn't look at him. All his movements were careful, like he was trying to make as little noise as possible. He opened each drawer with the barest of sound, looking for a spoon, and made sure they didn't bang when they closed. When he stirred Walker's mug, the spoon never touched the sides or the bottom.

"Here you go," Roan said, still not looking at Walker.

"Thank you."

Roan glanced up then, and Walker gave him a small, lopsided smile. Roan's eyes grew brighter, and he kinda thought the kid was adorable. Exactly his type, if anyone asked. But he'd never tell.

"So…" Roan started and then stopped.

Footsteps thundered down the stairs, and Walker almost winced. He wasn't ready for this so called "group date," and he'd have liked the pleasure of Roan's cute company alone for a minute more.

The kitchen became a cacophony of noise, with people hunting for mugs and coffee and mutterings of, "Is there herbal tea?" and "I think I saw granola bars last night."

Walker looked at John and raised his eyebrow. John came closer and said, "I thought you were used to herding animals."

Roan nearly choked on his coffee.

"Oh no. He's gonna puke again," a small guy yelled. Walker remembered him from the meet and greet the prior night. Antoine. An accountant. From his bio and the photographs that came with it, Walker had imagined him to be a safe choice to keep until the end. Boring even. But he'd never met a dude this immature and bitchy in his life. He sent him a glare, and Antoine grinned at him cheekily. Walker put him firmly in the "send home soon" column. He wasn't interested in falling in love with anybody, but he didn't want to spend time with a jackass either. Life was too short for that.

A ginger guy named Jaden spilled orange juice on the counter and winced, cursing under his breath, but another guy, some brutish looking fellow that Walker thought was named Clark helped clean it up. And, heck, if the blushes and stares between those two were any indication, they were much more interested in getting to know each other than getting to know him. Perfect. He'd keep them both around a week or two, then cut them and send them on their way into each other's arms, assuming the attraction held out.

He ran his eyes over the other guys he hadn't paid much attention to yet.

There was Bellamy, a radio talk show host from Arkansas. He wasn't that much to look at, but he had the kind of voice that could fill a room, or clear it. The guy was currently booming on about a missing shaving kit, and, given the state of his patchy beard growth, Walker didn't doubt some kind of sabotage. Makeup would help him out. Probably.

Then there was Taylor, a tall, skinny guy wearing a tight T-shirt and comfortable-looking cargo pants. He was an elementary school teacher, if Walker recalled correctly, and he'd spent his one-on-one introductory time with Walker the day before talking about how nice it was going to be to hang out with adults all day instead of dealing with little monsters. Walker got the impression Taylor didn't much like his job and was probably hoping the prize money, if he stayed until the end, would help him out of a poor fitting career. Though he wasn't sure how adult this group of guys were, if Antoine and Peter were any indication of the maturity level. Taylor might have been better off with his classroom full of children.

Then there were Nick and Davis, two blonds who seemed to have already bonded as friends. They were huddled next to each other, sipping coffee and whispering, and seemed to be hatching a plan of some sort, given the way they gestured and nodded toward other contestants and then shot considering glances at him. Walker remembered they were both doing some boring office jobs. He wanted to cut them both early. He didn't have a good reason, other than the fact that he didn't find them at all interesting. There wasn't even an iota of desire to spend even an hour more of his precious time with either of those men.

"All right, producers," Andy yelled as he slammed into the kitchen like a hurricane, wearing a white short jumpsuit and holding a spritzing bottle. "Groom your men, please. Plant some seeds for drama. Get this show on the road. Molly, take the reins, babe." A vein began to throb in Walker's temple.

Molly stepped forward into the crowded kitchen, her young freckled face looking shrewd in the morning light through the windows. "Everyone, listen up! If you have coffee, drink it, if you don't have coffee yet, you're out of luck because we're leaving right now. Walker, pick someone to ride shotgun with you."

The annoying blond guy called Peter appeared out of nowhere and slid under his arm. "Hi," he said, fluttering his eyelashes at Walker. "Can I call shotgun?" Twelve pairs of eyes and just as many cameras regarded him. The silence was sudden and meaningful.

Not wanting to be rude, Walker said, "Yes, sir. Of course you can."

A lot of unhappy muttering erupted at that, but he didn't care. He just wanted to get this day—this whole show—over with.

"Aw, you're just the cutest," Peter said from beneath Walker's arm. He was wearing a yellow shirt with a matching hat and the most unsuitable shoes for farm life in Louisiana that Walker could possibly imagine. He'd be up to his knees in mud by the end of the day. Peter patted Walker's chest, his hand lingering a little on his left pec.

"This way." Walker took a step away and held out his hand like he wanted Peter to go ahead, but really he just wanted the man's hands off him. Peter gave him a bright white smile. *Sharks*, Walker thought. Maybe John wasn't so far off about them tearing him apart. He slammed his hat on his head.

The small row-crop tractor waited around the back of the barn to avoid messing up the driveway even more after last night's storm. The show had managed to find a red hay ride wagon somewhere, the kind of thing he'd never use on a real farm, and put hay bales around the sides for the others to sit on. Small blankets were placed over the hay bales. To avoid scratching the contestants' sensitive behinds, Walker figured. He snorted under his breath.

"Oh, how quaint," Peter said, clapping his hands. Walker helped him up onto the passenger seat of the tractor and then went around the back so he could give everyone else a hand up. He got a lot of meaningful looks and squeezes, but he remained distant and polite. Only the big guy, Ben, clapped him on the shoulder and heaved himself in without taking his hand.

Roan accepted Walker's help but kept his eyes on the step. "Thank you," he muttered and moved away.

"One producer will be sitting with you in the back," Molly called out as John hefted himself up into the wagon. "And there's a camera hitched onto the front of the tractor too, but most of the filming will happen when we reach our destination. Try to look excited and awake when we get there people. We'll be following behind in the cars."

Speaking in third person, Andy called out, "Have fun, girls. While you're out broiling, I'll be staying behind to monitor from the air-conditioned safety of the control room."

There were even more crew members today. They were crawling everywhere. And Kylie was there getting into one of the cars, too. No doubt to powder Luke's shiny face between takes.

Down near the pasture, Luke plastered on his fake smile and began to talk to one of the cameras.

Since no one had told Walker he needed to wait for anything, he climbed into the driver's seat, glanced over his shoulder to make sure no one was standing up, and turned the key so that the tractor roared to life.

Crew members scattered, Luke's face twisted into a grimace, and Walker pulled out from the front of the barn.

"This is so exciting!" Peter yelled at him. Walker gave him a polite smile and set off in the direction of the main house. Let the tour begin.

"THERE'S THREE I already want to send home right now," Walker complained two days later to Tessa. They were standing at the kitchen window overlooking the brunch picnic that was happening under a temporary party tent in the backyard. His parents had been instructed to stay out of the way, and none of the contestants were allowed in the house. Marlon, Dennis, and Dad were out working the hayfields, and Walker had gotten up at three a.m. to check the cattle. He was already tired and it was barely ten.

"Anyone in particular you want to stay?" Tessa asked, innocently sipping from her coffee. He poured himself another cup and sighed. She went on, "I mean, look at that hunk over there. He's awful gorgeous."

"That's Ben." And yeah, he was gorgeous. And he was also the only one who hadn't done any fawning over him yet, apart from Roan.

Unfortunately, after the vomiting incident, Roan seemed to want to stay as far away from him as possible. Maybe that was his strategy? To be distant and cool? To make Walker want to chase after him? Or maybe he just didn't want to draw any further attention to himself for fear of getting sent home.

"And what's wrong with Ben?" Tessa asked.

"Nothing. Ben's fine."

"He sure is."

Walker rolled his eyes. "I should get back out there. My producer wants to film me having private conversations with these people." He air-quoted the *private*. "I don't even know what to say to them."

"Make them talk about themselves," Tessa said. "Everyone loves to talk about themselves, especially the kind of folks who come on shows like this. And you'll learn a lot about them from what they say."

"Thanks, Tess." He bent down to kiss her cheek. She smelled like cinnamon and apple pie, and he gave her an extra squeeze.

"Have fun, baby," she told him and patted his back. "I'm serious, Walker. It's really okay to have fun with this."

"Yes, ma'am," he said and then headed out the door.

The humidity had dissipated a little bit with the prior night's storm, but the heat had already eradicated any kind of relief Walker felt when he'd checked his cows that morning. He tipped his hat at Victor when he walked up to the end of the table where Molly was talking to Luke.

"So should I just pick someone and start talking?"

"Yes, John's waiting for you by that huge tree over there." She pointed in the direction of a live oak where one camera's tripod rested on a piece of pressed wood so it wouldn't sink into the mud, while other cameramen and their Steadicams waited in the shade.

"There's drier spots than that one around," Walker said, but Molly waved him off and went back to her conversation with Luke. They were paying him nearly seventy-thousand dollars for the use of the ranch as a venue, so if they wanted to trudge around in mud, he was going to let them. He touched Ben's shoulder.

"Hey, man," he said, feeling incredibly self-conscious. "We need to go up there for a chat."

"Excuse me."

Walker turned around to be faced with John and a cameraman he'd never seen before. "Yes?"

"Can you ask him more romantically?"

"What?"

"You know, hold out your hand and ask if he wouldn't mind joining you for a talk alone, or something."

"Are you serious?"

John stared at him. "Yes?"

Walker huffed out a breath through his nose, and his cheeks heated up as he turned back to Ben, who watched the interaction with a twinkle in his eye. Walker would ask him nicely, sure. But he wasn't going to hold out a hand to a man taller than him, and he wasn't going to burden the request with innuendo. "Ben, would you like to join me for a chat under the oak tree over there?"

"Of course," Ben said. He swung his long, powerful legs over the bench he was sitting on and rose to his feet.

Damn. Walker felt a little frisson of *something* curl up his spine.

"After you," Walker said, but fell into step with him anyway.

"This is awkward, isn't it?" Ben whispered in his ear as they walked side by side.

Walker looked up at him in surprise. "Yeah, it is. I didn't really think of it from your side of things, but it's got to be worse for you. Especially dealing with all the others. How were your last few nights in the bunks?"

"Not bad. The smallest guy in the room snores the loudest, believe it or not."

Walker laughed quietly. "No way."

Ben nodded but didn't say anything else. Walker thought Ben

seemed a little uncomfortable, so he decided to take the lead and just pretend John and the cameras weren't there. He perched his ass on the low-hanging tree branch the camera was aimed at, tipped his hat back, and asked, "So you're a mechanic, right?"

"Right. In Florida. Born and raised."

Walker swatted at a fly. "So this heat doesn't bother you."

"Oh, it bothers me. But whining's not going to make it cool down any faster." He grinned, and his blue eyes twinkled. He shrugged his muscled shoulders lightly. "How about you? Did you grow up on this farm?"

"Yep." Walker shifted so the bark of the tree didn't dig through his jeans so much and patted the branch. Ben chuckled but joined him. Since they were sitting in the shade Walker tipped his hat back a little more so he could see Ben's stunning eyes better. "My family's owned this ranch for four generations."

"They still alive?"

"Yep. My parents live in the farmhouse with me," Walker said, nodding toward the structure in question. "Grandparents are gone. Pretty recently actually." He crossed his arms over his chest. "Hit my dad hard."

"I'm sorry."

Walker met Ben's eyes again and saw nothing but sincerity. "Thanks. So tell me, what brings you here? You don't seem to be a reality show type, if you don't mind me saying so." Molly wouldn't like that he'd said that, but whatever. Once all the editing was done this conversation would probably end up looking like it was about something else entirely.

Ben rubbed the back of his neck and the sleeve of his white T-shirt seemed about to give under the pressure. "I'm not, no. I'm—" He faltered and looked genuinely pained for a second.

"Hey, now." Walker shifted a little, putting his side to the camera for a modicum of privacy. Only to be faced with another one. "If you don't want to talk about something, just say so, okay? I'm winging it here. I don't know what I'm doing either."

Ben lifted his head and stared at Walker. He seemed to be at war with himself for a minute, then he sighed and looked away. "I knocked up a girl when I was sixteen. We married really young. My kid's twenty now, would you believe it?" He laughed humorlessly. "It wasn't until much later that I realized…"

"You were gay?" Walker prompted when Ben didn't go on, then remembered there were other options, too, and added, "Or bi?"

Ben winced a little. He had a small scar on his left cheek, a few pockmarks from long ago. Walker realized the original acne had probably still been there when he'd become a dad. Jesus. Poor guy.

"Bi, yeah," Ben said. "We got divorced a few years ago. It hasn't been easy. She was the one who suggested I sign up for this show." He shook his head and laughed again, sounding embarrassed. "She thinks I'm actually more into guys."

"And what do you think?"

Ben rubbed his neck again and stared into the pasture. "I don't know."

"Ben." Walker waited until he made eye contact. "Have you ever been with a man before?"

Slow, dark blotches appeared at the edges of Ben's jawline. "A few hookups, behind bars and in alleys. Man, am I a walking cliché or what? But that's it. I've never…had a relationship or anything." He looked at his hands and very quietly added, "Or kissed a guy."

Oh, *Lord.*

Walker tried to not find that idea appealing. And failed.

ALL THE OTHER one-on-one conversations were a lot less interesting, apart from Victor's, who intimidated the crap out of him. He had a whip sharp wit and a gaze that seemed to see right through him. *If he believes I'm in this to find true love for even a second*, Walker thought, *I'm a toad*. It made him feel a little ashamed and uncomfortable, and he wished he hadn't agreed to this damn show all over again.

His step-mama was right about one thing, though, the contestants loved to talk about themselves.

Everyone but Roan.

Walker didn't know why, really, but he'd kept Roan for last. By the time Roan joined him by the oak tree the sun had shifted and they had to lean against the other side to find some shade. It made the conversation awkward since they both faced the cameras full on.

"How old are you?" Walker asked. "I read your bio, but I can't remember everyone's details, sorry."

"Oh God no, don't be sorry. I can barely remember everyone's names and I've spent a lot more time with them than you have. Um. I'm twenty-seven."

Walker's eyebrows flew up. A disbelieving, "Really?" was out before he could stop it. Roan's jaw tightened.

"Yes, I know I look young. But really. I can show you my driver's license, if you like."

Walker tipped his hat a bit more over his eyes. "No, it's fine."

"Shit," Roan whispered so quietly Walker doubted the fluffy microphone hovering over their heads would pick it up. That's what the body mics were for, he supposed. "Sorry, I didn't mean to snap like that. I'm really hot, and I didn't sleep because of the storms the last few nights and—"

"You don't like thunderstorms?" Who didn't like thunderstorms? He loved them. They cooled everything off. "Because we get a lot of them. Really, a lot."

"No, I don't mind them generally, it's just that I never knew they could be so violent before." Roan shivered a little.

"Ah." Okay, that was kind of cute. Walker wanted to sling a reassuring arm around the kid and tell him it was all right. "You're from Ohio?"

"Yes."

Walker waited for him to say more, but he didn't. "And your bio said you're a grad student?"

"Yes." His jaw tightened again, the muscles in the sides flexing.

"Okay, then." Walker laughed under his breath. "Look, if you don't want to talk to me, you don't have to."

"It's not that." Roan straightened and moved away from the tree so he had his back to the camera. The Steadicam guys moved around to get his expression. "Listen, I don't know if it said this in my bio, or if they took it out, or whatever, but I'm—I *was* an environmental engineering grad student. But that doesn't mean that I'm here for the potential drama, okay? I know beef cattle ranches are important for the American economy and that you all work really hard. I've even learned about some of the things you ranchers do to help the environment, and I think that's really great." He snapped his mouth shut and looked away.

Roan had a really pretty profile. A sharp Adam's apple, strong jaw, but soft lips and long, dark eyelashes hiding hazel eyes. His hair gel had succumbed to the heat and the longer black hair on top curled frizzily. Walker wanted to bury his fingers in it, muss it up even more.

Roan had his hands stuffed in his jeans, making his narrow hips jut out and showing a strip of pale belly with a surprisingly thick line of dark treasure trail showing. His pink Henley had sweat stains under the armpits. Walker suppressed the sudden urge to step closer and find out what he smelled like. Or what those nipple piercings felt like.

"You said 'was'."

"Huh?" Roan was embarrassed by his outburst. Walker could tell. His hackles were up. It reminded Walker of a video he'd seen once about a baby lion trying to roar and he smiled inwardly.

"You said you *were* a grad student. I take it you didn't finish."

"No," Roan didn't expand on that, but he didn't look angry anymore either. Just sad. "No, I didn't."

Walker changed track. "Can you ever see yourself living on a ranch?"

Roan looked as startled as Walker felt. He hadn't asked any of the others that question. Because he didn't intend for any of them to move in. Not even sexy, pale, skinny boys with dark treasure trails who were exactly his type.

"Honestly?" Roan whispered, and Walker's surprise—and reluctantly, he admitted, respect—rose when Roan's eyes found his and he said, "No, I can't."

Walker let him walk away. When Roan's left shoe sunk into a swampy patch of grass and he stumbled, Walker nearly jumped out to steady him. But he didn't. Roan looked defeated by the time he reached the brunch table, where everyone was helping to pack up. That little shit Antoine yelled something about Retching Roan that made some of the others laugh, and Walker almost snarled.

He'd decided right from the start if there was anyone he felt seriously attracted to, he'd send them home right away because he couldn't afford to get distracted. But that asshole Antoine just had to go first. Walker got to choose two, though, to send away each week. Roan should be one of them. But Walker knew he wouldn't be. He wasn't through with the kid yet.

The camera and sound guys began to pack up too, and John caught Walker's eye. "I like that one. Roan, I mean," John said, glancing around to make sure Molly wasn't anywhere near. "Don't dismiss him too fast."

"I won't," he said, tugging his hat further over his eyes and making his way over to the house. He had a good deal of daytime left and the winter forages needed to be planned out and ordered.

"Hold up. Hey, Walker!"

He rolled his eyes but stopped and turned around. Several SUVs were driving toward the house to pick up the contestants and take them back to the barn. "Molly," Walker said, nodding his head once.

"Loving the look today, cowboy. You've dressed the part and it looks great in the shots. Anyway, I need to talk to you for a minute, and I'm dying in this heat. Can we go inside?"

"Sure thing," he said, groaning inwardly. "But I don't have a lot of time."

"Your time—"

"Belongs to you, I know." Walker aimed for the house and didn't look back to see if Molly followed. He had no doubt she would. "Would you like something to drink?" he asked when they entered the kitchen, cursing the hospitality that had been ingrained in his bones by generations of southern living.

"Do you have any ice tea?"

"Sweet tea? Yes, ma'am." Walker reached in the fridge, and then poured two glasses of sweet tea. "So what's up?"

"I know we said you had to send two people home tomorrow, but we're changing that to three."

"What? Why?"

Molly gave him a feral grin. "I wouldn't want to spoil the surprise." She took a sip of the sweet tea and grimaced, but then lifted the cool glass to her forehead.

Uneasiness stirred in Walker's stomach and he sat his sweet tea aside untasted. "Send three home. Okay, I can do that."

"Right, the ones that have to stay are Peter and Ben."

He narrowed his eyes at Molly and let out a slow breath through his nose. "Fine. Care to tell me why?"

"Nope. Also, would you consider keeping Antoine?"

Walker's mouth dropped open. "What? No, absolutely not. He'll be the first to go. What an asshole."

Molly laughed. "Exactly, makes for good TV. He's certainly going to be more lively than Roan. I had high hopes for that one but he's turned out to be a limp washrag. Alas, he's one of mine. Ah, well." She sipped her tea again.

Walker tried not to bristle on Roan's account. "Is that all?"

"No. One more thing. You're taking someone on a date tomorrow morning, and I strongly suggest you kiss them. So choose wisely."

"What the hell? Are you going to tell me when it's time to bone them too?"

"As a matter of fact, yes."

"You can't do that."

"Of course not." Molly blew out an exasperated breath, placed her tea glass next to his on the counter, and crossed her arms over her chest. "All we'll do is film a door closing behind you and whatever man you're going to quote-unquote bone, play some cheesy *bow-chicka-wow-wow* music, and we're set." Molly did a sweaty little shimmy Walker hoped to God he'd never have to witness again.

"That's disgusting."

"Nature of the beast. Now go do your cowboy thing and think about who you want to smooch tomorrow."

"What's the date?"

Molly smiled slowly. "The noodling one."

Walker couldn't help it. He began to laugh, throwing his head back. He knew exactly who he'd be taking on that date. And the kiss…eh, he'd deal with it.

CHAPTER 7

"WE'RE GOING *WHAT*?"

"Noodling." Walker looked far too calm. And smug. Roan figured this probably heralded danger in brooding southern cowboys.

"And I need these?" Roan held up the waterproof bib overalls.

Walker smirked. He had his arms folded over his chest and was leaning against the doorjamb of the kitchen. Roan had been cornered there by Walker and John while making sour apple tea. "Technically you don't, but I'm sure you'll want to wear them."

Roan narrowed his eyes. "But that means we're going into the water. I know what lives in your water down here. Alligators. And venomous snakes. I googled."

"Now, why would you do that?" Walker dramatically slapped his forehead, then leaned in closer as if to share a secret. Roan leaned in too, drawn to Walker's firm, muscled body and cheerful brown eyes, despite his probable imminent death on this so-called date. "Here's the thing: gators aren't that aggressive really. You probably won't even see one. They want to stay as far away from you as you do from them."

"Really?"

"No. But it makes it easier to get in the water if you tell yourself that."

Roan stared at him.

"But, seriously, I'm not scared of the gators, and if there was a real, true danger, you know they wouldn't let us anywhere near the water."

Roan swallowed hard. The morning light from the kitchen window highlighted the little wrinkles at the edges of Walker's eyes. Probably from squinting into fields all day. The man even smelled like fresh-cut grass and fresh air.

"As for the snakes, yeah…well." Walker shrugged. "You just have to make sure you don't wander into a nest of moccasins. I'm sure the set nurse has antivenom on hand."

"Water moccasins. The shoe snakes."

"They don't look anything like shoes."

Roan put the waterproof overalls on the counter. "Oh my God, I'm going to die."

Walker straightened, and the attractive, teasing grin fell from his face. "Seriously, though, if you don't want to do it, just say so. I won't hold it against you."

"If you say bless your heart, I'll know exactly what you mean," Roan grumbled. Walker laughed, and *God*. He was so damn handsome. Feeling his face heat, Roan looked down at the dry bib overalls. They were pretty thick. Maybe the fabric would stop the snake bites. "Fine, I'll come."

"I'm mighty glad."

"You should be."

Between the threat of biting critters, the thrill of Walker's sweet drawl, and the headiness of his eager attention, Roan's head was awhirl. Leaving his tea behind untasted, he stomped away for some privacy to get changed, ignoring John who said, "That's got to be the most reluctant acceptance of a date I've ever seen. Andy's going to love it."

"NOODLING, BEN," ROAN moaned to Ben who sat on the big, empty queen bed in Roan's room reading a magazine to escape his annoying roommates. "Do you even know what that is? I miss Google."

"I *do* know what that means," Ben said, flipping a page. "But it'll be much more fun for you to just find out on your own."

"Rude." Roan pulled from the closet a pair of jeans and a T-shirt he didn't mind getting ruined. Then he glanced at Antoine, who lay asleep on top of his covers on the bunk below Roan's. He lowered his voice, despite knowing the mic attached to his chest would pick up every word regardless. "I'm kinda nervous. He's so handsome, I keep tripping over myself and saying all the wrong things."

Ben looked up from his magazine. "You like him, huh?"

"I don't know." Roan groaned and slapped his own forehead. He stripped off the cute jeans he'd put on that morning and hopped into the fresh, expendable pair. "It's just that he's got that stereotypical cowboy walk and his accent is just so…" He waved his hands around. "Fuck me, it's adorable."

Ben chuckled. "You'll be just fine. Go impress him with your gator-wrangling skills."

"God, I hope you're joking."

Roan changed his shirt, turned around, and saw Walker standing there in the doorway, holding the waterproof overalls and looking mildly perplexed. "That was a private conversation," Roan said, heat rushing from his chest up to his cheeks.

Ben's brows shot up, and he buried his nose in his magazine, steadfastly minding his own business.

"I didn't overhear much. You forgot these."

"Don't they go over my jeans?"

"No, they'd be way too hot. Just wear them like pants."

Roan grabbed the waterproof pants, unbuttoning and unzipping his jeans. He paused before shucking them again. "What all did you hear?"

"Well." Walker gave him a lopsided grin. "That apparently I'm handsome and adorable." The smile faded a bit as he looked down at the carpet. "And you think you're saying all the wrong things. But you're not."

Roan blinked when Walker spun around and hurried away.

"Sounds like he likes you, even if you don't like him," Ben muttered.

Roan loosed a little confused noise and then got on with kicking his jeans off again. The waterproof overalls creaked and screeched as he tugged them on and he sighed. He was going to squeak his way through a date. Fabulous.

By the time he rasped his way downstairs, Walker and John were already outside. Most of the others had been gathered up in the SUVs and taken into town for supplies, so Roan basked in the quiet for a minute before he stepped out into the humid heat. Which was ten times worse in the dry bib overalls. And he could *feel* his hair frizzing up.

An old Ford truck stood rumbling in the driveway, the camera and sound guys sat in the back with their equipment. The fact that all the windows were open didn't bode well for potential AC presence.

"Sexy," Walker drawled when Roan squeaked his way around the front of the truck, and Roan wrinkled his nose at him.

"You're the one making me do this." He opened the door, climbed into the truck, and slammed it shut. Walker got into the driver's side.

Walker's fingers curled around the wheel. The skin of his hands was dark and weatherworn, more so than his face, and Roan figured the cowboy hats should be thanked for that. Hell, he should probably be wearing a hat too. The factor fifty he lathered on his face every morning might not be enough. "You still have time to back out," Walker said quietly. "Just say the word."

"I'm coming with you," Roan said, crossing his arms. "But no promises about actually entering the water."

Walker hesitated. "You can swim, right?"

"Yes, he can swim," John said from where he was crammed with a sound guy into the truck's cramped backseat. "That was all in the questionnaire when he applied."

Walker grinned, gunned the engine, and off they bounced.

Roan's pants creaked every time they hit a pothole—which was a lot. And it got worse the farther they went. Roan had expected actual asphalt at some point, but instead they remained on dirt roads that turned into little more than tracks through cattle-dotted fields. He glanced over his shoulder to see if John was filming, but it must've been too bouncy, or else the mounted cameras on the dashboard were enough to grab his every grimace for now.

"So," Roan began, deciding to take control and break the ice between them, "what made you agree to do this show?"

For a second, Walker said nothing. His eyes flicked to the rearview. "My step-mom watches all the reality shows. She particularly likes the romance ones. So when she and my head ranch-hand heard there was a reality TV show looking for a gay man with an interesting job to be the main love interest, they talked about how fun it would be if I applied. I left it as a joke. But then Marlon, my hand, went and actually did it. Applied for me, I mean."

"Wow."

"Yeah, it was kind of an overstep. But, well…" He shrugged.

"Here you are."

"Yeah. Here I am. We were all surprised when they chose me, to be honest. And I didn't intend to do it at first. Not when the first producer called, anyway. I wasn't interested in meeting someone on TV." He flicked his hat up and glanced at Roan with a smile, but it looked a little self-deprecating.

"But you obviously changed your mind. Why?"

Walker frowned briefly but then sighed. "It's not easy meeting a person to build a life with when you have a ranch to run, never mind when you're gay. So I thought, why not? What do I have to lose?"

"Nothing but a bundle of money if you say no."

Walker cleared his throat and shrugged. "Right. But it all got a little more real than I'd anticipated when you gentlemen actually showed up on my doorstep. It's been an adjustment."

"Do you ever have to fight the urge to slam the door in your producer's face?"

Behind them John laughed, and Walker's mouth pressed together. "Every damn day. How about you? What made you decide to go on the show?"

Roan opened his mouth, but John leaned forward and cut him off. "If you don't mind, that's a conversation I'd like to catch outside of the car."

THEY PULLED INTO a patch of...mud. That was pretty much all Roan could think of to describe it. Dirt with a few trees and a murky-mirror river meandering around it. The pervasive green of the landscape was more sparse here but picked up where the river met a thatch of forest.

"Pretty," Roan murmured dubiously, peering out of the window. He twisted in his seat to ask John if the nurses really did have antivenom when he found Walker watching him. The gaze was powerful. Roan felt it penetrate into him like the sun, deep into his flesh. With a slow whoosh, he let out the breath he'd taken to ask his question.

"You really think so?" Walker whispered.

Roan smiled. "Yeah. I do." Maybe he wasn't talking about the land, though. Maybe he was talking about the rugged beauty of Walker's face and the cut of his jaw. Pretty meant a lot of things, and Walker could be part of that definition for sure.

Walker gave a firm nod toward the water. "This is the best spot for noodling in the area because the catfish don't live too deep."

Roan opened his mouth. Closed it, then said, "Catfish?"

Walker grinned, his teeth white like a flash of lightning. "Yes."

"So...we're fishing." Roan's shoulders dropped a little in relief. He used to go fishing with his neighbor Lindsay's ex-husband Roger. And while he was sure the fish here would be different, he wasn't completely incompetent. He strained his neck to see over Walker's side of the pickup. "Where's the boat?" He frowned. "And the gear? I didn't see any in the back of your truck. And aren't catfish, like, huge?" Walker's grin just kept on growing. "I'm going to regret feeling relieved, aren't I?"

"Do you want to tell him John?" Walker asked. "Or should I?"

"I wouldn't mind getting that on camera outside too, actually. Maybe with the river in the background." John nudged the sound guy beside him and they climbed out of the car.

"Is this some ancient hazing ritual or something?" Roan asked.

Walker stopped looking like the cat who got the canary. Or the catfish, rather. "No, it's a tradition actually. The Native Americans were the first to do it, but during the Great Depression a lot more ranchers and other folks began noodling, because it brought free food to the table. It's the kind of thing that gets passed on from father to son around here."

"Oh." Now Roan felt kind of bad for sounding so pissy. "Is your dad still around?" Roan blurted, and God why. Why?

Walker's eyes searched his face. "Yes," he said slowly. "He lives in the farmhouse with my step-mom and me. He's retired but still helps out. What about your dad?"

Roan shook his head but didn't say anything more. Another car pulled up behind them. Roan hadn't even noticed they'd been followed by more crew. Though he should have guessed they would be.

"We're set up, guys," John called out from near the winding water. "Ready when you are."

Roan reached for his door handle but Walker stopped him with a hand on his arm. "Really, if you don't want to do this—"

"I'm fine," Roan said. His overalls made a funny *pfft* sound as he slid off the leather seat. They already stuck to his skin like a layer of clingfilm. He hugged his arms around himself and walked over to where the crew waited. "Here okay?" he asked.

"Perfect," John said. Roan felt a zing as Walker stepped up behind him, and he shuffled to the side a little, unnerved by his body's response to the man. "And we're rolling."

"So, noodling." Walker flashed him another breathtaking smile and began to unbutton his shirt.

Roan blinked. Was he hallucinating now? The sun was hot, but, God, he wasn't having heat stroke already, was he? "Why…are you taking your clothes off?"

"Because we're going into the water to catch catfish." His grin turned rakish. A flash of heat went through Roan's body in response. "With our bare hands."

Roan gaped and did a comedic double take. "Say what now?" He glanced out toward the murky, dark water. It had an oily layer on it. "We're actually going in there?"

"Yep." Walker couldn't have sounded more excited, and while that was cute as hell, it was also terrifying. "Catfish burrow into holes, and when we stick our hand in a hole, the catfish will bite it." Walker pantomimed the whole thing. It was the most animated Roan had ever seen him. "Then we'll hook our fingers into one of its gills and yank it out."

Roan had no words. None. His jaw dropped open again but there were so many bugs around he snapped it shut pretty fast to keep from swallowing a mouthful.

"Say something Roan," John called out.

"Do they have teeth?" Roan asked, his voice high and reedy.

Walker's eyes glinted with excitement. "They have bony bits in their mouth that can scrape a little bit, but no real teeth."

Roan nodded and swallowed hard. Okay. That didn't make the idea of sticking his hand in a *living fish's mouth* any more appealing. "So people don't like, lose their hands or anything?"

"The odd finger maybe."

Roan's eyes grew wide.

Walker chuckled, obviously delighted. "Not because the fish bites it off," he clarified. "At least, I've never heard of that happening. But in rare instances, maybe, because of an unexpected bacterial infection from a scrape or something. The real danger in the water is the snakes and snapping turtles."

"Snapping turtles?" Could this get worse?

"Yeah. Sometimes they make their nests in abandoned catfish holes, so we'll have to choose wisely."

"You're joking now, aren't you?" Roan's heart pounded and he put his hands on Walker's arms to steady himself.

Walker's eyebrows flew up. "No," he said, dead serious, and pulled his undershirt off too.

"Oh, wow," Roan whispered before he could stop himself. His hands hung right in front of Walker's chest, which was all taut skin over hardened muscles, but he didn't touch. Walker's forearms and neckline were tanned, but the rest of him was startling, almost fragilely pale. A bead of sweat ran down the center of his breastbone.

Roan's eyes snapped back up to Walker's face to find him looking surprised, and just for a fraction of a second, a little vulnerable. Roan bit into his lower lip and wished the overalls had pockets to shove his hands into. Instead, he dropped them to his side.

"You ready for this?"

Roan swallowed hard. "Shit. Um. Okay. What...what do we do now?"

"We go in. I'll go first, and you can spot me."

"I don't know what that means." He watched as Walker stepped into a pair of wading boots he'd brought out from the back of the truck. "And why aren't you wearing overalls like me?"

"I figured you wouldn't want to mess up your designer jeans." He motioned toward his faded Wranglers. "I don't care about mine."

Roan's face heated. "Oh. Okay." He knew his clothes looked expensive, but if it hadn't been for Philip, his ex-boyfriend, he'd never have been able to afford them. They were all he had left of his college life, and he cherished them. "So how do I spot you?"

"You just make sure I don't get pulled under if I catch a big one. No big deal."

Roan felt faint. "Right, no big deal." He pulled his V-neck T-shirt over his head and tried not to feel self-conscious about his scrawny, white chest. He deliberately didn't look at Walker as he tossed his shirt aside, not wanting to see what he thought of his lack of real muscles either. God knew he was no Ben.

"You ready?" Walker asked, handing him a pair of gloves before putting on his own.

Roan took a deep breath and donned the gloves. "Nope. But after you."

Walker laughed a soft, rumbly sound that made Roan smile despite his nerves and headed for the river. When he'd waded carefully in, he held out his hand to Roan and beckoned, eyes twinkling. His chest gleamed in the destined to be short-lived sunlight. Dark storm clouds were drawing together in the distance. Walker had left his cowboy hat in the car, and while his hair was flattened a little bit, it still looked soft and thick. His eyes were like gold. Leonine.

"I don't like this," Roan said under his breath, hitching the water-proof overalls back on his bare shoulders. "I don't like this at all. Don't I need a fishing license?"

"All taken care of," John said.

Jesus. Was that an ambulance pulling up behind the second car?

John saw him watching. "Just a precaution."

"Right." The water was so murky Roan couldn't see the bottom. He had no idea what was swimming underneath. His mind flipped through all the images he'd seen in his pre-show internet research endeavors. And, really, why had he ever looked up all that stuff? He met Walker's eyes again, steadied himself, and stepped off the swampy bank. His boot sank into the moist, slushy river bottom. "No gators?" he asked.

"Just stay close," Walker softly answered. For a second he hung on to Roan's hand and squeezed it. "Try to have fun."

Roan's mouth went dry as he nodded. "Okay."

His second boot joined the first and when he tried to move, the ground sucked at him before it let go. He shivered violently despite the sweltering heat.

"There," Walker encouraged. "You're in. The worst is over."

Roan laughed a little desperately and said, "I highly doubt that."

JOHN AND THE sound guy followed them along the river bank with their handheld camera and microphone, while the second set of crew members came behind in a small boat they'd brought along. Another guy waded in front of them with a shoulder camera.

A very deeply buried part of Roan found the whole situation hilarious, but he was too busy watching the river and trying to keep his torso and arms out of the water to give in to the humor of it all. But it was interesting, that was for sure, being strung between panic and hilarity.

Walker didn't seem to care in the least about their potential imminent deaths by snake or alligator bites. He walked confidently through the water like it was a chlorinated swimming pool, a god of a man who, every once in a while, made sweeping gestures with his arms, looking for catfish homes. His skin glistened with the water.

Roan wished he wasn't too scared to really enjoy that.

"Here," Walker called out eventually, keeping his voice low. Despite all his grinning earlier, Roan could tell adrenaline was thrumming through Walker now. He was all tense, bunched muscles, searching, brilliant eyes, and his breathing came rapid and deep. A camera guy on land climbed as close as he dared, leaning over a sturdy tree limb hanging above the water while John called directions and a second sound guy hovered behind them on the boat with his giant fluffy microphone.

"There?" Roan asked. "How do you know?"

"Shh, I just know. Get ready to grab me if you need to, and if it's a big one you'll have to help me carry his weight."

"Fucking fuck, we're going to die," Roan gasped. Then he threw his chin up. "All right. Let's do this."

Walker laughed and gave him a playful little shove, catching his arm before he could topple over with his feet stuck in the mud.

"Ready?"

Roan rolled his head on his shoulders and took a two-point football stance he remembered from his high school days. "Yeah. Noodle me, baby."

Walker laughed hard, patted Roan's back, and then took a deep breath. He plunged his arm into a darker abyss of the river and went tense all over, his back muscles roping along his spine. Then he gave a startled shout and lunged forward. Without thinking, Roan grabbed him around the waist and hauled. Walker stumbled back, weighing ten times more than he should.

"Grab its body!" Walker yelled, which was when Roan noticed Walker had his hand buried in the ugliest fish Roan had ever seen. Grabbing the beast around the head, Walker told Roan to grab its body again, and so Roan shoved his arms under the monster's belly.

"Omigodomigod, it's so squirmy, *argh*." He was breathing so hard his lungs hurt, and the thing weighed an absolute ton as it struggled and fought, slapping Roan with its tail. Walker worked his hand out of its mouth.

"Did you get that, John?" Walker called out.

"Got it!" John hollered.

"Okay, let go!"

"Wait, what?"

But it was too late. Walker had already released his hold and the fish gave an almighty lurch. It caught Roan in the ribs, hard, and just like that he went under. Water rushed over his head and down his throat.

He wasn't under for long, though. Walker hauled him up almost immediately, but it was enough to scar him for life. He gagged and sputtered, spitting out the most unfiltered water he'd ever had in his mouth.

"Oh Jesus, this water is probably full of salmonella. And e-coli. And vibrio. I'll probably die from it." He hadn't noticed he was leaning against Walker until he felt a warm, calloused hand explore the curve of his lower back. It made his knees go a little weak. He grinned up at Walker. "But we caught a fucking catfish."

Walker laughed and his hand stayed where it was for an extra second even when Roan had regained his balance. Then he asked, "You want to try next?"

"Me? Do the fingers in the hole thing?"

Walker's eyebrows shot up, and his smile took on a whole new shade of amused. "If you feel like it."

Wiping the water from his face, Roan slung his arm around Walker's shoulder and gave the camera a thumbs up. "Never let it be said I shy away from sticking my fingers in dark, wet holes. I'm a real pro at that."

John cracked up, and Walker snickered against him. It'd been a bit unexpected, but he and Walker were actually nearly the same height, which was nice. Walker was much more muscular, of course, but he didn't tower over Roan like he'd thought he would.

Standing there with him felt pretty good, even though he'd probably have nightmares about this damned date for the rest of his life. He didn't care. Right that second, he felt elated and invincible, and the world and its worries fell away.

He propped his fists on his hips. "Show me a nice hole, cowboy."

Walker shook his head, laughing at the ongoing teasing, but his cheeks pinked a little. "Found your courage, little lion?"

"It only lasts 'til midnight so c'mon."

Walker located another catfish hole less than five minutes later. "I'm pretty sure there's one in here. Nothing else. Hopefully…" He grinned, and Roan rolled his eyes. "Just plunge your arm in and wiggle your fingers. The catfish will attack and bite, then feel around fast for his gills to hook your fingers into and yank. I'm right behind you, and I won't let you be dragged under."

Roan nodded and took a couple of deep breaths. He flexed the fingers of his right hand. "Here goes nothing," he muttered, and plunged his hand into the darkness. "Oh jeez, oh jeez, oh jeez, I feel something, oh my GOD!" Something slimy wrapped around his hand, and his first instinct was to yank his hand away, but Walker was shouting encouragement behind him and more shouts came from the river bank.

John better be filming this shit because his mom would never believe him. He gritted his teeth, oh hell, and hooked his fingers around a small opening he found, and yanked.

The catfish yanked back, and he felt something scrape his hand. Before he could even open his mouth to shout for help, Walker was already there, arms around Roan's waist. "Did you get it?"

"It's huge! I can't get it out." The mud was fighting him too, sucking harder the more he pulled.

"Don't let go," Walker said, "I've got you. Jesus, what—John, get in here!"

Roan didn't look up to see what was going on, but he heard John say something to the sound guy and then a splash.

"Make sure he doesn't go under," Walker said, then his touch was gone. Roan's muscles screamed in protest as he strained. "Rock with it a little bit. Give and take. I'll help."

Roan gasped when Walker disappeared under the water completely. He rocked with the movement of the fish, which was gnawing at his fingers. He startled when something else touched his leg, until he realized it was Walker. The fish continued to struggle and then suddenly it gave way.

He stumbled back, and Walker resurfaced with a gasp. He shook his head so a large arc of water sprayed through the air, and he was swearing loudly. John yelled something at the crew, but Roan didn't hear him. Because right there in his arms was the biggest fish he'd ever seen.

CHAPTER 8

"THAT THING MUST'VE weighed sixty-five pounds, if not more," Walker said, following Roan as he scrambled inelegantly onto the bank.

"Isn't that a little big to fit into such a tight hole?" Roan looked pained when Walker snorted and he realized what he'd said. This damn kid was just too cute. "Still, I'm glad to be out of that water, oh my God."

John stayed behind to go over the footage, but an assistant and camera guy tracked back toward the truck with them. "I have some towels in the back, and a spare pair of jeans."

"Great. And thanks for lending me these. I think I would've had to burn my jeans otherwise." Roan pulled the bib of his overalls down, letting it hang low.

Walker chewed his lip, a thrill awakening in his stomach. "It wasn't that bad, was it?"

"Bad?" Roan looked at him, eyes wide. His black hair hung plastered to his face and his pale shoulders were turning red. Roan's chest wasn't muscular, but it had an enticing line of hair running right down the middle of it, and his dark brown nipples were circled by faint dark fluff too. Walker didn't even allow himself to think about those damn piercings flashing in the sun. But the one thing Walker had the most trouble keeping his eyes away from was that dark trail of hair disappearing into the waterproof pants.

"It was horrendous," Roan went on, drawing Walker's eyes back up.

If he'd noticed that he'd been ogled, he didn't let it show. "And awesome."

"Yeah? Glad to hear it." They reached the truck and out of the corner of his eye, he saw John give him a little encouraging nod. Walker's stomach contracted as he turned away from the camera. "Let's get changed."

"Gladly."

Walker reached into the truck, handed Roan a towel, and watched as Roan vigorously dried his hair. When he resurfaced it was a poofy mess he tried to smooth down to no avail. Walker unbuttoned his jeans and stepped out of them, then dried himself off before easing out of his boxers too. Roan made a little startled noise, but Walker paid him no mind, just toweled off quickly and pulled on his dry jeans. Commando.

Roan's face had turned as red as his shoulders, and he hadn't gotten any further than hooking his thumbs in the top of the overall pants to tug them down. Walker kept his eyes studiously on Roan's.

On the periphery, John waited. Fuck, he had to get this done and now.

"Hey, listen." He hesitated, then cupped Roan's face with one hand and leaned close. "I had a great time. Thanks for the date."

Roan gazed at him, wide-eyed and silent, and, dammit, he couldn't do it. Not just for show. He gently kissed Roan on the cheek, lingering a little longer than he meant to, pressing his nose against Roan's cheekbone. Somehow it turned into something even more intimate than a simple kiss on the mouth. Roan smelled good. Like the water and sweat and something fresh and spicy underneath, like cilantro.

Shit.

Roan stood nailed to the ground, his eyes squeezed shut. Walker froze, wondering if he'd overstepped. His heart thudded in his throat. "Roan? I'm—what's wrong?"

"There's something," Roan whispered, voice thin. "On my belly."

Walker grabbed Roan's shoulders and looked down. Right there, attached to the soft skin next to the jut of his sharp hip. "It's a leech."

"Oh, God." Roan swayed on his feet, going deathly pale, and Walker held him tighter.

"They're still filming so try not to pass out." He gently patted Roan's shoulder. "John? We have a problem."

"What's up?" John came up to them, and his eyes widened when he saw what Walker was pointing at. "What's that?"

"A leech."

"Is that a problem?"

"It needs medical attention."

John nodded and yelled, "Medic!"

The guys leaning against the ambulance made their way over. "Oh cool. Leeches. I haven't ever dealt with... alcohol, right?" The taller one looked at his co-worker. "Can you remember? I've never had to get one off of anyone."

"It's okay," Walker said. "I've got this. I've done it before." He gently touched Roan's cheek. "Open your eyes, baby. There you go. Listen, I'll get it off, it's no big deal. But you're going to have to strip naked so I can check if there are more. I'll tell the others to go away."

"Nope. We're going to film it," John said, and Walker sent him a dirty look. "It's in the contract that we get access to everything except genital shots."

"Fine. Whatever, but give him room to breathe, for fuck's sake."

They did move back a bit, but the cameras stayed on Roan despite Walker wanting to shove them even farther away.

"Why didn't I feel it?" Roan asked, his voice wobbly. Little lion had lost his courage, and Walker didn't blame him. Of all the critters in Louisiana, leeches grossed him out the most too.

"They inject some kind of anesthetic so you can't feel their bite. And that's why you won't know if there are any more on you. How are you with blood?"

Roan's gaze went faraway for a second. "I can deal with blood."

"Okay, good, because there might be a lot of it." To the medics he said, "I just need some cotton balls, rubbing alcohol, and a bandage."

Roan looked pale. His hands trembled, and Walker squeezed one of them briefly.

"Aren't you supposed to put salt on them? That kills them, right?" the medic asked.

"Yes, but you can't do that when they're still attached to you. They might regurgitate blood back into your body and cause infection."

"Oh, Jesus." Roan closed his eyes, and Walker dropped to his knees.

"You'll be okay. You won't feel a thing, I promise." He lifted his head and grinned at Roan, who was staring down at him. "Remember, leeching was a medical practice for hundreds of years."

"So was trepanation."

Walker laughed, then looked down at the leech again. He gently rubbed his hand over Roan's stomach. "Ready?" he asked.

"No, but do it anyway."

"Little lion," Walker whispered, then gently felt around the leech, looking for the narrowest side. He eased his nail underneath it, taking his time to work the sucker loose. Blood began to drip down and he held a wad of cotton balls drenched in alcohol at the ready. As soon as the leech came off he flicked it away so it couldn't reattach on his hand and pressed the cotton to Roan's hip. It soaked through almost immediately.

"Can you hold this for a second?" he asked the medic.

Roan looked down as the nurse pressed his hand against the wound while Walker readied a new tuft of cotton with rubbing alcohol. "Here, let me." He rubbed the alcohol into the wound, pulled out more cotton with his free hand and pressed it against Roan's hip. "Now hold this, press it tight. I'm going to see if there're anymore, okay?"

"Okay."

"You know," one of the medics said conversationally. "They still use leeches these days in medicine. With reconstructive surgery, aftercare following reattachment of severed fingers, and other circumstances where the removal of congested blood from a wound is required."

Walker eyed the guy. "Right. This is none of those things. I need more pressure over here please," he said, and flicked another leech back into the water.

"Second crew," Walker heard John call out. "Go see if we can spot any gators." Then to the camera guy zeroing in on Roan, John added, "This is some seriously good stuff."

"I'm feeling the love, John," Roan muttered.

John ignored him and spoke into his mic, "Set up an interview spot over by the boat with the water in the background. We'll grab an In-the-moment interview with the medics after this. That way we'll have it in the can. No need to trek back down here or round them up in post."

Walker rose to his feet and checked Roan's chest, his back, and his hairline. He really did have a bit of a sunburn, Walker noticed. Roan would want to apply some aloe to that. Then he checked Roan's ears, and went to stand in front of him again. He tipped Roan's head up, pushed his fingers into his thick hair to feel his scalp, checked his nose, and then, "Open your mouth."

Roan blinked at him. "Are you serious?"

"Very."

"Really?" one of the nurses said. "I wouldn't have known to check there."

Roan looked away and opened his mouth. "Lift your tongue. Okay, you're good." He waited until Roan could look at him again. "I know this is embarrassing. And we can wait until we're back at the house so you can do it yourself, but—" He waved at Roan's lower half.

"Just do it," Roan whispered and closed his eyes.

THE COTTON HAD saturated with blood again, so the nurses changed it while Walker gently eased the waterproof pants over Roan's narrow hips.

Roan steadied himself on Walker's shoulder when Walker checked over his feet and his calves.

"I need to take these off too," Walker whispered, his heart beginning to thud in his chest as he indicated Roan's underwear. "You can check your groin. I'll do the back."

"Okay," Roan said again, sounding a little strangled.

Walker already knew what he was going to find by the time he eased Roan's underwear down over his ass. He'd seen the shape of the little sucker through Roan's soaked white briefs. "There's another one here," he said, feeling winded.

Shit.

Roan's ass was gorgeous. Tight and round, the perfect punctuation to the long, long line of his beautiful legs.

"Is it bad?" Roan asked with a note of panic in his voice.

"No, it's smaller than the other one. It'll bleed less." He reached up and the nurse handed him more cotton balls with alcohol, then he removed the leech like he had before.

He held the cotton against the bleeding wound until Roan said, "This isn't what I usually have in mind when I think of having my ass eaten."

Walker laughed, startled, and a rush of affection soared through him. He pulled some fresh cotton out of the bag, then stuck it in place with a tight bandage. Roan looked over his shoulder, looking sheepish.

"Sorry. I say embarrassing things when I'm...well. Embarrassed."

"Nothing to be embarrassed about," Walker said. "Nothing at all. How's the front?"

"Nothing there. Thank God."

Walker was relieved, too. He didn't really relish the idea of removing a leech from Roan's balls or cock. "Good. Here, put on these jeans," Walker got to his feet and reached into the truck while the medics put bandages over the other little wounds. "Those bites might keep bleeding for a while, but I'm sure there's a first aid kit at the house if you need to change the bandages."

"I'll get blood on your jeans."

"That's okay." Walker looked down at the old Wranglers. They were both holding on to them, and he was about to let go when he noticed a few scrapes on Roan's right hand. "This from the catfish?"

Roan lifted his hand. His cheeks were pink, and Walker realized Roan was still stark naked. He kept his eyes on Roan's hand. "Yes," Roan said. "I think so? Something scraped me through the glove when my hand was in its mouth." He started to laugh giddily, and Walker realized the adrenaline was wearing off big time. He needed to get the little lion home.

"I'll clean that up," one of the nurses said. "And put some antibiotic cream on it to be sure."

"You'll be going home with war wounds from this date." Walker risked a glance up to find Roan's eyes on him. He winked. "You did great today. I have to be honest, I didn't expect you to."

Roan laughed but he sounded tired. "No, me neither."

"Okay guys, get dressed and ready to go," John said.

"Sorry, but I have to check Walker out first," the medic said. "Take your clothes off, please."

Walker nodded and watched Roan quickly dress before John lead him off for an In-the-moment with the other medic. He was almost disappointed that Roan wasn't going to see him naked, too. Tit for tat, and all of that. Within minutes, the medic confirmed that he was leech free. Roan must really taste sweet to have attracted so many of the boogers, when Walker had been underwater a hell of a lot more than he had.

When Walker joined Roan by the river again, the kid seemed exhausted.

John checked the time and said, "We'll interview you later, Walker, back at the house. We're losing this light, anyway, and the storm is coming in. I'll go find our gator hunters."

"I'll come with you," Walker said. He turned to follow, but found himself oddly reluctant to leave Roan's side. He pushed himself on, though, and only looked back twice to watch Roan walk back to the truck with the rest of the crew.

By the time they returned with the second crew, Roan was sitting in the passenger seat, head leaning against the rolled-up window.

"Aw, your boy's tired," John whispered. "You need to look after him."

Walker rolled his eyes.

John grinned. "We got some good stuff today, well done. Andy will be pleased."

"With the noodling? I hope so. That was one badass fish he pulled out."

"Well, that too. But the two of you snuggling and making sexy eyes at each other after one date is going to make Andy salivate."

Walker's mood darkened. For one thing, it felt wrong to share little moments like that on television, and for another, he *had* been making sexy eyes at Roan. He couldn't help it. He also couldn't afford to fall for any of these men, but sending Roan home after all they'd shared today would be harder than he thought. He still had to pick a third for tomorrow.

"Hey." Roan straightened when Walker opened the driver's-side door and offered a soft, sleepy smile. "Did the gators eat them?"

"Nope!" John said, drawing Roan's attention away, and Walker took a breath of relief. "You can stop filming now," John said to his crew, indicating they should load up. "We got the good stuff. Mounted camera in the car stays on, of course."

Walker kept his eyes on the road the whole way home because the potholes were brutal on his old Ford, which wasn't an excuse exactly, but he used it gladly.

They drove in silence, and Walker didn't get out to open Roan's door when they arrived. He stayed in the driver's seat and waited. Roan's knees seemed to nearly give out when he jumped down to the ground, and Walker automatically jerked, ready to reach for him.

Roan closed the door and leaned in the now-open window. "Despite the leeches, I had a really good time. Like, really good."

Walker nodded once and when he didn't say anything, Roan turned away, looking confused. His shoulders hunched up as he made his way inside. The set nurse must've been given a heads up that there'd been a medical incident, because she appeared almost instantly and followed him into the renovated barn. The ambulance guys were gone.

Before Walker could drive off, Molly appeared. "Date with four people tomorrow," she said without preamble. "Ben and Peter have to be two of the ones you pick, apart from that you have free choice. Except not Roan, since he went today. And what was up with him just now? He looked like a kicked puppy on his way in."

Walker ignored her. "Are you going to tell me why I have to take Ben and Peter?"

Rolling her eyes, Molly said, "Fine, Jesus! We'll be picking one of them to go on into the next season, okay? So they need to make it to the final rounds or thereabouts, but not all the way to the end."

"Oh. Okay, that makes sense."

Molly snorted. "Glad to have your approval. Not that I need it. You know who you're sending home?"

"Yep."

"Gonna tell me who?"

Walker grinned. "Nope."

Molly's eyes rolled back in her head so far Walker figured she could see her own brain. "Fine, whatever. Wardrobe has a suit for you. Wear it for the ceremony. And you're giving everyone who stays a horseshoe."

"A horseshoe?"

Jesus.

Molly clapped her hand on Walker's shoulder and her youthful face broke into a wide grin. "This show is cheesy, in case you hadn't noticed.

111

Deal with it." She slapped the top of the Ford and walked away.

THE WARDROBE ASSISTANT looked harried when she delivered a suit for Roan after he'd sheepishly admitted he didn't own one. He apologized about a hundred times before she rushed out of the door again.

"I don't know why you bothered," Antoine called out after her. "Retching Roan's going to go bye-bye tonight."

"Shut up Antoine," Peter said, startling Roan a little. He hadn't expected any support from that quarter. "So far he's the only one who's gotten alone time with him, so he's miles ahead of the rest of us." He glared daggers at Roan.

Huh, not support then.

Antoine scoffed as he tied on a horrid red skinny tie. "He probably was ordered to take him by the producers to make it more dramatic when he gets cut tonight." He drew a finger across his throat dramatically.

Roan remembered Walker on his knees before him, easing off the leech, then the gentle caresses that had followed as he'd checked him over. The ghost of a stroke against the underside of his ass. The tenderness in Walker's eyes, and the protective way he'd warned the camera guys off. Heat rushed to his face, and he realized he didn't want to go home. And not just because he needed the money.

Dammit.

He hung the suit on his little rack, and began to get dressed. Would Walker send him home? There had definitely been a good vibe between them. And he'd called Roan "little lion." But maybe that was a southern thing and everyone got nicknames? Maybe he had one for all the contestants already. Had it all been for the camera? At the end of the day, Walker had been distant and strange.

Roan pulled on the crisp white shirt and went in search of an unoccupied mirror to turn the tie into a handsome knot. His mom had taught him a long time ago. God. He missed her.

"You okay, Mom?" he asked his reflection. Her hazel eyes in his own face looked back at him. "I shouldn't have left. I mean, I like it here. It's kind of fun. But I'm worried about you…"

Would she be sleeping? Surely Lindsay was stopping by every day. And if things got worse, someone would let him know. Wouldn't they? The show wouldn't be *that* evil.

He closed his eyes and imagined telling her about noodling. She'd be simultaneously horrified and terribly amused.

His eyes burned with tears. She had to be okay. And not just now. She had to be forever-okay and be his mom for a long time to come. He had no one else. "I love you," he whispered, sending the emotion to her over the miles.

Roan shook himself and opened his eyes only to find Walker standing behind him.

"Again," he said, pointedly, "with the private conversation."

Walker gave him a bewildered look. "It's just you. And your reflection."

"Well. Yeah. I was giving myself a pep talk."

"Right. Well, it's good to love yourself. So…okay then."

A cameraman appeared behind them, but since they were being watched by two ever-present mounted cameras as well and didn't seem to be doing anything really interesting, he left again.

An awkward silence fell, and Roan remembered he wasn't wearing any pants yet. He gestured at his lower half. "I guess we should stop meeting like this, right?"

Walker's eyes danced with amusement. "Oh, I don't know, I kind of like—"

"There you are. We need to film some preliminary scenes." John glanced at Roan, then did a double take. "Ah, the good old accidental nakedness strategy. I like it, Roan. Well, I'd personally like it more if you were a woman, but whatever works for Walker here is good for the show." He turned to Walker. "I told you, sharks, all of them. Even the cute ones."

"That's not—" Roan began, but John was already leading Walker away. Roan snapped his mouth shut. It didn't matter one bit what Walker thought, as long as he kept Roan on the show a little longer. He needed the money for his mom's treatment and nothing else was important—not their "vibe" earlier, not the flipping sensation in his stomach whenever he saw Walker, and not how Walker made his palms sweat. Nothing mattered but his mother's health.

Stewing madly, he had to redo his tie three times. The suit was nice though, a soft charcoal gray with the faintest pinstripe. And you know what? Chad could go suck a lemon, Roan was wearing his fake glasses. They could be like armor. Something to hide behind.

He had the feeling he was going to need it.

HE NEEDED IT all right. As an armor against boredom. He suppressed his millionth yawn of the evening as Andy, Molly, and John conferred about more reaction shots.

"Attention!" Molly called. "Everyone look this way, and on three you clap your hands and cheer! One…"

"God, I want to be eliminated before I die from this inane crap," Chad muttered in Roan's ear. Then he let out a whoop, while Roan floundered on the "three."

"Now," Molly said, sounding like her teeth had been glued together. "Let's try that again, without the gaping fish impression." She glared at Roan.

"Thanks a lot," Roan mumbled, elbowing Chad softly in the side. Chad only grinned.

"…Three!"

Roan clapped his hands and cheered. A little. He hated this. Beside him Ben seemed to hate it even more. He'd fist-pumped once, then stuffed his hands back into his pockets, ruining the lines of his suit.

"Okay, let's continue with the eliminations. Can the final three step forward while the others go back to their marks please," John called out.

Roan, Antoine, and Bellamy took their spots in the center of the room, while the others formed a semi-circle behind them. Makeup fussed a bit with Luke's hair and then Andy gave the go-ahead.

"Yes, we've already said goodbye to one contestant tonight, and while it's only our first elimination night, I have to make an important and unexpected announcement," Luke said, like he was picking up in the middle of a sentence—and for all Roan knew he was. They'd been filming back and forth so much he had no clue what time it was, how much champagne he'd had, or why he was even there anymore. "...*Extra elimination tonight.*"

"Wait, what?"

The words rang hollow in Roan's ears. It had to be him. Why else would they bother? Maybe Antoine was right and the entire 'date' with Walker had been a setup for drama when they eliminated him tonight. Maybe there'd been no 'vibe' between them at all. This was a fucking TV show. It was all a game. He tried to wipe his sweaty palms surreptitiously on his pants, but the cameras were aimed relentlessly on the final three awaiting their fate. There was only one horseshoe left and the only thing that gave Roan any hope at all was Antoine's dumbstruck face beside him.

"That was a good reaction," Molly called out. She smiled that barracuda grin that looked so strange on her sweet face. "But I want to do it again. On three, everyone react. One…"

Roan didn't even have to try. He couldn't seem to get the horrified look off his face. Go home in the first week? Oh, God. Not only would he have nothing to show for it monetarily, but the humiliation…

"Great. Some solidarity amongst the final three contestants, please?"

Molly said, motioning at them. "Hold hands or hug or something."

Roan swallowed hard, and he didn't even shudder when he felt Antoine's equally sweaty palm slip into his.

"Perfect. Go on, Walker," Molly ordered.

Walker looked terribly uncomfortable as he drew out the required ten seconds before lifting up the final horseshoe. It was adorned with a red rose and a bow.

Roan wondered if everyone could hear his whooshing blood and his ragged breathing. He could barely hear anything else.

I don't want to go home tonight, he thought. Walker's eyes hung on his, and Roan felt faint. *And not just for the money.*

He knew that had to be the show talking. Being here in this house with all these people vying for the same man's attentions was a mindfuck making him feel things that weren't real. But dammit, standing there sweating under the lights, it was hard to remember that. He didn't want to go home yet.

Walker walked straight for Roan, his expression all solemn apology.

"Hey, little lion. Will you stick around for another round of noodling?" he asked, and a burst of giddy laughter left Roan's mouth before he could stop himself and try to play it cool.

Beside him Antoine cried, "What the fuck? That's not fair! I never got my chance!"

Walker didn't even look at him. He leaned a little closer to Roan and murmured, "They made me keep you for last for the tension on the show. I'm sorry."

"Okay, you can't say that," Molly cut in. She put her hand to her earpiece and listened to whatever Andy was saying from the "control room" set up in a van outside. "Andy likes the little lion bit, so you can say that again. Also, Antoine, while we're loving the pissy look on your face, please keep the swearing to a minimum. Let's go again."

Roan felt a lot more cheerful this time around.

"I'd love to stay," he said when Walker asked him a second time.

"But I'm not so sure about the noodling."

"That's fine with me." Walker grinned the lopsided smile that was beginning to look awfully familiar and dear. "I've got plenty of ideas for exciting dates."

"Oh yeah? Why am I scared?" Roan asked, and they both laughed.

Beside them, Antoine seethed. Roan went to join the others while Walker tried to exchange some polite words with Antoine. But the dude obviously wasn't having it. Walker turned to the other eliminated contestant, Bellamy, instead, who'd taken it a lot better.

"Hey, man."

Roan tore his eyes away from Walker to see Ben standing beside him. "Oh, hey."

"Glad it's them going home and not you."

Roan smiled up at him. "Thanks. Me too."

Ben slung his arm around Roan's shoulder and shook him a little. "You're the only one here who doesn't make me want to punch their face in."

Roan chuckled, and a guy with a camera on his shoulder was there getting everything. "Chad's okay."

"Chad would throw you under the bus in a heartbeat."

Roan shrugged Ben's arm away and said, "I'm going to grab a drink."

Almost everyone got pretty drunk that night, including Walker when he decided to show off his cocktail-making skills. It was pretty funny to watch, especially since Walker's grin grew dopier with every glass he drank. After a while people seemed to forget why they were there, and it turned into a really fun evening. Roan held off from drinking too much because he didn't like that feeling of losing control, but it was great to watch everyone else throw caution to the wind and have a good time. Everyone but Ben, it seemed.

Walker was required to have a little staged chat "in private" with each of the people still standing. Antoine had packed his bags with ill grace and was being driven to a local hotel. When Walker wandered off toward the back porch with Ben, Chad pulled Roan outside and plonked them both down in the rocking chairs out front.

"So come on man, spill the beans. What really happened when you guys went 'noodling,' or should I say *ca*noodling." Chad cracked up like he'd told the funniest joke ever. Roan just stared at him until he calmed down. "No seriously, what happened? Walker can't keep his eyes off you."

"Antoine would say he's probably afraid I'm going to pass out or throw up or something."

"Dude, come on." He put his arm around Roan's shoulder. "Tell Uncle Chad."

Roan sniggered and shrugged him off. Fine, Chad probably wouldn't remember tomorrow anyway. Though the cameras would. "Okay well, everything I told you happened. We really did catch catfish with our bare hands." He wiggled his fingers to show the abrasions he'd earned even through the gloves. "But after that, well. He kissed me on the cheek."

"Ohhhh," Chad mocked, but it was friendly enough. "On the *cheek*."

"Yeah, but then I completely freaked because I noticed something vile and slimy was stuck against my stomach."

Chad gaped at him, then began to laugh again. "Are you sure you're gay?"

"No, I'm serious," Roan said, laughing too. "It was a leech."

"Oh, fuck no."

"Yep. Walker had to peel it off me. I swear that wound kept bleeding for like half an hour. And then…" He was glad for the dusky porch because he felt his face warm. "He had me strip completely naked to see if there were more."

"No. Fucking. Way. The perv."

"It wasn't like that. He found another, so it was good he looked."

"Oh gross. Where was it?"

"On my ass," Roan admitted, and Chad began to howl with laughter. He was bent over clutching his stomach while wiping tears from his eyes when Walker came outside.

"Why did I know I'd find you out here?" he said to Roan. "Come on, not-so-private chat time." He jerked his head in the direction of the house and Roan rose to his feet as Walker disappeared inside. Chad stopped laughing and grabbed hold of Roan's wrist.

"None of the rest of us stand a chance," Chad said. "Jesus, the way he looks at you."

"You're drunk," Roan said, but he couldn't suppress the little butterflies awakening from their long dormant sleep in his stomach.

"WOW, THIS IS…COZY." Roan took in the small covered and screened-in porch tucked away to the right of the barn. It had been off limits before now. It held a comfy couch and a nice view of the farm in the distance, but three cameras were aimed at the couch, with a microphone hovering above it. "I feel like I'm about to be interrogated or something."

"Close enough," Walker said, gently taking his arm and steering him toward the couch. "This is where you tell me all your darkest, deepest secrets."

He said it with the cutest little eye roll towards the four crew members sticking their noses and cameras in their business. "Ha, funny," Roan croaked and sank down into the deep couch. He wanted to reach for a pillow and hold it against his stomach but didn't. Instead, he pulled one leg under his ass, and twisted a little so he could face Walker and only one camera instead of all three of them.

"So how was the first elimination?" Walker asked. "You happy you're staying?"

"It was pretty nerve-wracking," Roan admitted, then gently swatted Walker's arm. "Thanks a lot for making me stand there until the end with Antoine, of all people. I mean, Bellamy was a fine guy, but Antoine? C'mon."

Walker blushed and spread his palms. "It wasn't my choice, believe me. It's all for drama or whatever. I knew I was going to keep you." He didn't smile when he said it, and his brows drew together in a small V for a second.

"Don't sound too thrilled about that," Roan teased.

Walker laughed under his breath and rubbed at his face with his hands, holding them up in disgust and looking at them like he expected them to be dirty. "Sorry, it's been a long day. They make me wear makeup, did you know that?"

"Yeah. Kylie has chased me with lipstick too." Roan chewed on his cheek as he tried to think of something interesting to say. He felt put on the spot, like he was being interviewed for a job. He suppressed the urge to share his typing speed and the details of his up-to-date Mac skills. "I read in your bio that you went to college," he finally fetched out of thin air. "Where did you go?"

Walker looked startled for a second, then shifted in his seat so he could put his hand along the back of the couch. "I went to LSU. Geaux Tigers! I studied agriculture."

Roan was distracted by Walker's hand gently rubbing back and forth over the couch. His imagination supplied him with a vision of them here on the couch alone, sans cameras and hawk-eyed producers. He would put his own hand over Walker's, thread their fingers together, kiss those tanned knuckles and drag him closer. He cleared his throat. "I bet they couldn't teach you anything new."

"Oh, you'd be surprised. I didn't know much about the financial aspect of farming. Or marketing or anything. And I learned a lot about bringing our ranch up to date, adding in sustainability features and changing the way we handled the fields."

"Was your dad okay with that?"

"Sure." Walker's eyes found his and they twinkled with amusement. "He pretends to be a grumbly bear, but he's on board with me taking over and improving things."

"Was it fun to get away to college for a while?"

Walker's smile turned a little wicked. "You could say that." He cleared his throat. "But enough about me. Tell me a little about you. Have you had any long-term relationships?"

"Wow, jump straight to the point, why don't you?" Roan laughed and looked away, forgetting the cameras were standing there. He faced Walker again in a hurry. "I had a boyfriend when I was an undergrad, but we didn't last. We lived together for a while, though. His mom was a fashion designer, and they dragged me to a bunch of fancy parties. It was insane. His mom used to dress me up in her clothes, and I modeled a little bit for her. I, uh." He felt himself go red, but barreled on. "I liked the clothes, I admit. The rest of the relationship? Not so much."

Walker's hand dropped down to Roan's knee, touching the fabric of his pants. "I noticed your clothes were really nice. That's a very different life from living on a farm."

"I live a very different life from that already," Roan whispered. "The clothes are all that's left." Walker's hand lingered, and Roan reached for it, gently touched the veins visible through the skin. He had nice, blunt fingernails and thick, long fingers. His palms were broad and sturdy. Hands you could count on. Walker caught Roan's fingers when he tried to withdraw and turned his hand palm up.

"How are your injuries? Did the leech bites stop bleeding?"

"Yeah, they did."

He traced Roan's lifeline. "Not getting infected?"

"No, I don't think so."

"Good," Walker whispered as shivers of attraction traveled up Roan's arm. It was like Walker's hands were magnetized, and Roan didn't stand a chance of resisting his pull. "That's good." When Walker met his eyes, his pupils were dilated. "This situation is so weird, isn't it?"

"So weird," Roan agreed. "I wish we could just get some time alone and…you know."

Walker's eyebrows rose comically. "I don't believe I do know," he said, and Roan's face went hot. "Please enlighten me."

"That's not what I meant," he protested, and Walker smirked. "I wish we could just talk without feeling so put on the spot, you know?"

"Yeah, I know what you mean." Walker fell silent for a second, studying Roan like he was trying to think. Then he leaned forward, let go of Roan's hand and brought it to the back of Roan's neck instead, drawing him near. "We could try to arrange a meeting alone somewhere if you want," Walker whispered directly into his ear, and Roan shuddered at his hot breath.

He had no doubt the camera could hear them anyway, but maybe this was all part of the game.

"Is that allowed?" Roan asked, turning his head lightly. His lips grazed Walker's stubble, and he closed his eyes.

"No," Walker whispered. "Do we care?"

Roan shook his head. The moment clung and hung, time slowing to nothing more than their breaths and eye blinks as they pulled far enough away to gaze at each other. Roan's stomach flipped wildly.

"Good luck with trying to meet up, guys," John said, cheerily, ruining the moment. "Not gonna ever happen. But thanks for the footage. We got some great stuff. The audience is going to eat you two up with a spoon."

Roan's face went even hotter, but Walker squeezed his hand.

John turned to a member of the crew and called out, "Next!"

Then Roan was hustled away from Walker, and the intimacy of the moment was lost for good.

WEEK TWO

MUCKING OUT THE MESS

CHAPTER 9

FAST ASLEEP, BEN had one arm slung over his head, the other tucked across his chest. He was breathing deeply, and his eyes danced under his lids. His feet stuck out from underneath the covers, and he was clearly far too big for the bed. Snuffling sounds came from the bunk above him, and the room was cast in the faded grays of early dawn.

"You are really not supposed to be in here."

Walker's heart skipped a beat as he spun around to be faced with a bleary-eyed John complete with haywire hair.

"I need help fixing a tractor. He's a mechanic."

"Sorry, man. It's the rules. You can't just come in the house without telling us. But I can have a mechanic here for you in—" He pursed his lips. "Hold on, let me call Andy." He moved to step out of the room, then turned back to Walker. "I can't leave you in here with the contestants, sorry. Can you follow me into the hallway, please?"

Walker rolled his eyes. What did they think he was going to do? Jump one of them and have all the off-camera hot sex in the two minutes they were out of the room? Of course, no room was actually off-camera, so even then they wouldn't miss anything.

John gestured for Walker to follow him.

"Fine."

He stood leaning against the wall, one foot propped up, not caring if it left a mark, while John held one furious phone conversation after the other. He checked his watch. The morning was getting away from him now, and he had a lot to do before this ridiculous TV show took up the rest of his day.

"Right," John finally said. "There's a sound and cam crew on the way. We're going to wake Ben, wire him up, and then tell him to pretend to go to sleep again. Then you can do your thing."

"What?" Walker stared at him.

"Andy agrees this will make a great mystery date."

"You're joking."

"Afraid not."

"I think I'll take the other mechanic you have on call."

"Funny. Ah, here are the sound guys." John turned away and pointed the men toward the bedroom. "Yeah, get Ben wired up, please."

Walker heard a lot of grumbling and complaints coming from the bedroom, and he cringed inwardly. He was certain Ben would've happily helped him with the tractor. But as a date? Before dawn?

John clapped his hands. "Now everyone, quiet please! Pretend to be asleep again, especially you, Ben." He waited a few seconds until the rustling of sheets and pillows fell silent. "Okay, Walker. You're up."

He felt like the biggest idiot on the planet.

"Ben," Walker whispered very quietly. Ben opened his eyes and sat up immediately, clearly wide awake now.

"No, look more asleep," John ordered. "Like when we first woke you up."

"You mean when he asked for his mama," someone said from another bunk.

"Shut up, Clark," Ben said, but he grinned and lay back down, giving Walker a little wink. "Sleepy. Got it."

"Okay Walker, if you could step back outside and come back in," John said.

This was going to be a long, long morning.

This time, Ben blinked sleepily and mumbled a little bit when Walker said his name. "It's only me. I'm sorry I'm waking you up but I need your help with something."

Ben blinked slowly a few more times before he focused on Walker. "Oh. Sure, yeah." He swung his legs out of bed, ducking his head so he didn't hit it off the top bunk, and pushed the blankets aside. He grinned a little bashfully as he rearranged his dick in his boxer briefs. "That's what you get for surprising me so early. Sorry."

"No apologies needed on my account," Walker said, taking a step back to give him room to stand. "I'll be downstairs."

"Five minutes," Ben told him, and Walker nodded before leaving the room.

Damn. Ben was packing some heat.

Walker wandered into the kitchen to wait and made coffee to give himself something to do. The camera crew had followed him down so the guys at least got some privacy showering, it seemed. He'd have to ask Roan. If he got a chance to see him later, that was. He hadn't been able to stop thinking of Roan all night—remembering his sweetly perfect black brows, wondering what they'd feel like beneath his fingertips, and the lightning-strike memory that came again and again of Roan's nude body, nipple piercings, and sweet ass. He'd spent too many hours the night before imagining what might of come of both the post-noodling nudity and the tender scene on the couch without cameras or witnesses. His balls still ached from coming so hard.

He cleared his throat and sipped his coffee, directing his mind away from such images before *he* started packing heat, too.

"Hey, man. Ah, thanks. Can I grab a coffee?" Ben cracked a huge yawn, patted Walker on the back and reached for a mug. "What's the problem you need help with?" he asked, then peered at the clock on the microwave. "At five-fifteen in the morning."

"Sorry about that. One of my tractors isn't starting." He glanced at John. Fuck it. They could edit. "I can usually tinker enough to get it going but not today. I was hoping you could take a look. But then John caught me sneaking in to ask you for help and made me turn this into our mystery date."

Ben didn't say anything for a long moment, then started to laugh. "Whatever, man. I haven't worked on heavy gear in a long time, but sure, I can take a look." He poured a dainty cloud of milk in his mug, which made Walker smile. He glanced at Walker, then stirred the coffee. "So if you weren't doing this show, what would your day look like today?"

"Feeding and checking the cattle, getting the fields ready for the winter forage, preparing for fall calving season. Sometimes we're still baling hay at this time of year, but we got that out of the way thankfully. We'll have to cut hay again in July, mind you, after all this shooting is over." Walker shrugged. "A lot depends on the weather, especially in Louisiana."

"Who's doing the work now that you're so busy?"

Walker stared out of the kitchen window. A thick fog clung to the brightening horizon but Walker figured it wouldn't stay bright for long. "My dad still helps out, and I've got two full time farmhands. I hire in more folks when I need to."

"So a permanent extra pair of hands here would be nice, I bet." Ben's face was half hidden behind his mug but there was a touch of wariness to his blue eyes. Walker wondered why he was worried.

Weighing his words, Walker said, "If I ever find someone—on this show or otherwise—I'd like them to do what they love. If that's working on a farm, great. I'm willing to teach them whatever they want to know. But if they've already got a job and they want to keep doing that work, that's fine by me. I ain't gonna make no one quit doing what they love. Why are you smiling?"

"Your drawl got stronger."

Walker laughed reluctantly, reached for the hat he'd left on the counter and planted it on his head so he could pull it over his eyes. "Yeah, well you put me on the spot."

"I didn't mean to." Ben hesitated, then gently nudged Walker's shoulder. "Let's go fix that tractor."

"This way." Walker directed Ben toward the Ford. One of the crew was fiddling with the mounted camera in the car, and John was already climbing in the back. Privacy. Walker never realized how much he used to have and how much he'd loved it.

Ben had appeared in another one of his white T-shirts and a torn pair of jeans, which was a good thing because he was covered in grease within ten minutes. Somewhere in the background cursing broke out. One of the crew had discovered what a cow patty really was the hard way, and Walker tried not to laugh. Ben kept muttering to himself while he handled Walker's tools. After asking three times if he could help but getting waved away, Walker just leaned against the tractor and settled in to watch. Judging by the angle of the cameras, John was making sure he got an optimum shot too.

"What kind of engine do you usually work on?" Walker asked.

"Luxury cars mostly, these days. But I worked as a heavy truck mechanic for years, if you're worried about what I'm doing." He straightened and grinned at Walker.

"Just making small talk," Walker grumbled.

Ben's smile widened. "What about you? Did you always want to take over the farm?"

"I'm an only child, so it wasn't ever something I questioned. But I'd have chosen this life regardless. I love it."

Ben reached for a rag and wiped his hands. "Hard work."

"So's being a mechanic."

"It's different though. I still have my set hours and I mostly get to work inside. You're out there in all kinds of weather. Not to mention the animals." His smile dimmed a little as he chewed his lip and fell silent. Then he said, "I heard you had to remove a couple of leeches off Roan."

Walker's head snapped up in surprise. "He told you about that?"

Again, Ben hesitated. "I heard him tell Chad about it after the horse-shoe thing. He wasn't bragging or anything," Ben added quickly, rubbing the back of his neck and leaving a smear of grease there. "Chad was digging for details. Shit, I should've kept my mouth shut."

"No, it's okay." Walker laughed although he wasn't amused. "I guess nothing's private on this show anyway, right?"

Ben winced. "Right."

"Guys," John called out. "This isn't exactly making for good TV. Either act more jealous, Ben, or talk about something else. And Ben if you want to lose the shirt at any point, please do."

"Lose the shirt?" Ben looked adorably confused and a little embarrassed. "Why?"

Walker rolled his eyes at John. "Because he's a jerk. And because you're supposed to be seducing me."

"Oh." Ben went red to the roots of his hair. "Um."

"I'm joking, and ignore him." Walker slapped the tire of the tractor. "So what's your verdict?"

"You're going to need to order some parts I'm afraid, but if you get them in I can replace them for you." He grinned even though his face was still bright red. "You can pay me in kisses."

Walker laughed, startled, and looked Ben over deliberately. He sure filled his clothes out nicely. He was taller than Walker. Broader too, with a face that wouldn't go amiss on a male model. Sharp cheekbones. Full lips.

"I don't think that'll be a hardship," Walker flirted, but he felt a twinge of apprehension.

This was for the show, he realized. This flirtation. But last night with Roan? That hadn't been for the show at all.

Fuck. He was already in too deep.

OUT OF THE whole damn ridiculous show, John was probably the only person on the crew he liked but right that second Walker wanted to throw something at him. He was sitting on the large wraparound porch of his parents' farmhouse, thunder rumbling in the distance while the cicadas buzzed louder than any car alarm. There was a sound guy present but Walker guessed they'd have to edit over the noise later anyway. They'd given him a stack of the contestants' photos to consider for a potential one-on-one date.

"You look like you're searching for your next murder victim, not potential date," John said. "I know you don't like this, but Andy told me to stand here until we get a shot of you looking whimsical or some shit." He sighed. "Okay, who are you definitely not taking?"

"Davis," Walker said instantly.

"Okay, who else?"

Walker flicked through photos of a few others he could barely remember, and eliminated Victor and Chad for date consideration. When he came across Roan's picture—a frankly ridiculous shot of him looking into the distance while holding on to a pair of fake glasses—he paused. He'd snorted at the picture the first time he'd seen it too, but now that he knew Roan, knew the line of his thighs underneath those silly red velour pants…

He abruptly turned the picture over, realizing John was filming him almost fondling it.

"Okay," John said, "I got what I need. Now we have to talk about your morning date with Ben and then your decision to keep Roan over Bellamy at the first elimination."

Walker groaned and pushed himself up to his feet. "Fine. But I need a drink," he said, and disappeared inside.

As he wandered down the narrow hallway, he peered into the living room. Dad was lying on the couch, feet propped up on the opposite end, snoring softly. Every once in a while, his fingers twitched against his chest.

Walker sighed, headed into the kitchen, and opened the fridge. He reached for the pitcher of sweet tea, caught sight of his dad's insulin pens, and gently closed the fridge again. He leaned his forehead against it for a second, but then he straightened, poured a tall glass, and went back out to meet John.

"What do you want to know?"

"How'd it go with Ben this morning?"

"Fine."

"C'mon, Walker, we have an audience to entertain. Give us something."

Walker rubbed the back of his neck, and finally said, "Ben was useful as hell with the tractor. Obviously, with a ranch to run, having a man around who can pitch in when needed would be great. Ben's a good helper. A team player."

"And hot, too."

"He's a looker. That's for sure." He sipped his sweet tea and sighed.

"Sexy."

Walker shrugged and pressed the cold glass to his hot cheek.

"Oh? Not sexy?"

Walker sighed again. "He's objectively a very handsome man. Killer guns. Fills out his jeans. Can't complain about his looks."

"But he's no Roan."

Walker flushed.

John smiled. "Tell us about Roan now."

Walker rubbed the back of his neck and gazed out toward the fields. "What do you want to know about him?"

"Everything."

Walker groaned. "Look, give me some guidance at least."

"All right. At the horseshoe ceremony, why'd you let Bellamy go?"

"I'm sure Bellamy's a great guy. I admit I didn't spend much time with him, but I didn't really want to. See, my first impression of him wasn't bad, per se. I just didn't feel any sort of connection." He sounded like an idiot. He *felt* like an idiot. He squinted at the sun setting against the trees. "I didn't see us having much in common."

"Unlike Roan? With whom you have *so much* in common?" John

teased.

Walker's ears positively burned. And here he'd thought Molly was the evil producer. Apparently, John was just as awful. He was just not as obvious about it. Kept it hidden until he pulled out the stops and made you say stupid shit for the cameras. Producers…demons. Hard to tell the difference sometimes. He sipped his tea again.

John winked. "Come on, admit it."

"Admit what?"

"You think Roan's cute."

Walker shrugged. "Yeah."

John rolled his hand encouraging him to say more.

"Yeah, fine, okay. Roan's cute as hell."

"And?"

"And braver than I expected." Walker leaned against the porch railing and swallowed more sweet tea before wiping some sweat from his forehead. "Nice ass, too." Then he cringed imagining Tessa watching him say that on TV. "Sweet personality."

"A little prissy," John offered.

Walker broke into a helpless grin. "Yeah. Definitely a little prissy."

John chuckled. "I guess you like that, huh?"

Walker shrugged. "I reckon I do." He ran a hand over his hair. "He makes me feel manly. Not like in comparison or anything. Obviously, he's *all* man." He thought of that sexy line of chest hair and Roan's treasure trail. "But in the way he's so…" he trailed off. The word that came to mind was vulnerable. But it seemed wrong to say it, like he'd be telling the whole world a secret Roan hadn't even shared with *him* yet. His ears grew hotter. "Hell. I don't know. He's cute."

"Perfect." John motioned for the camera to move back farther. "Thanks, and, hey, for what it's worth, I don't think Roan's faking being into you. Not like some of the others. If anything, I'd say you've really taken him by surprise."

Walker swallowed down any urge to ask what exactly made John think that by taking another big gulp of tea. He had to keep in mind that John's interests were not Walker's interests. Making him think that a suitor was truly into him was good for the show. Easy emotional manipulation for drama later. But still...

John and the cameramen gathered their gear, and by the time the sun was low enough in the sky for Walker to head inside and investigate dinner, he'd made up his mind that he should send Roan home at the next horseshoe ceremony. He was already too attached to the guy, and nurturing a fantasy in the middle of all this bullshit wouldn't do anyone any good. This show was about the money—for everyone.

Walker washed his hands at the kitchen sink, still thinking about Roan. He let out a long sigh. Walker tucked into his dinner alone, glad that Tessa and his dad had already eaten and gone to their rooms for the night. He didn't want them asking questions about the show and his feelings, too. John's had already been disturbing and enlightening enough. Yes, he needed to get rid of Roan.

That ass, though. And that smile. Those nipple piercings. Jesus.

By the time Walker finished up his plate of Tessa's chicken and dumplings, he'd changed his mind again.

Roan wasn't going anywhere. Not yet. Walker needed to know more about the man first. Like why he was really here, and whether or not what John had said was true.

And maybe what Roan's mouth tasted like.

And if he'd moan when Walker kissed him for real.

Maybe Walker was a bad man, but he really wanted to know how Roan liked to fuck or be fucked.

No, Roan couldn't go home yet.

ANDY WAS MAKING Walker interact more with the contestants he hadn't had as much contact with before now. Not because Andy cared about their participation but because he needed them to have some screen time for "dramatic tension." Emphasis on the dramatic aspect, since no natural tension existed between these other men and Walker.

Still, he did what he was told. Not only because it was expected of him, but also because he felt bad they'd come all this way and he'd been all but ignoring them.

So he spent some time showing Nick, Jaden, and Davis how to milk the dairy cows he kept for personal farm use. Tessa usually dealt with it, since she sold unpasteurized milk, cream, and butter at the local farmer's markets. But Walker took over the job for the day, and everyone seemed to enjoy it once they got the hang of it. Apparently there was "good TV" in grown men squirting each other with milk from a cow's teat, and a few buckets of spilled milk wouldn't be too much of a loss to Tessa. Though it really was a crying shame.

Then, later in the week, he'd taken Peter out on a "date" to the feed supply store and to grab a milkshake in town. The guy was nice, handsome enough, but truly nothing compared to Roan. Walker had to fake his interest the entire time, and when they'd shaken hands at the end of the date, he thought Peter was glad to be done with it, too.

To be honest, Walker was looking forward to the next elimination round, dying for it, actually. Not because there was anyone he especially disliked since sending Antoine home, but so that there'd be even fewer contestants he was required to spend time with. He'd never considered himself an introvert, but the constant interaction with people was starting to wear him down. Every night he went to bed exhausted, drained in a soul-deep way that the hard physical labor of farming had never once left him.

Only four and a half more weeks to go.

Walker had been joking when he'd suggested mucking stables as a group date, but the producers had loved the idea. Dirty farm work made for good TV, they claimed. He didn't get to choose the group, either. At least Victor, Peter, Clark, and Jaden gave the traditional cowboy work of shifting horse shit their best shot, none of them holding back despite the stink. Even though Walker could've done the whole thing a lot faster by himself, it probably did make for entertaining television, what with the gagging and all.

With the cameras rolling, and John, Molly, and another producer constantly issuing instructions that were more like orders, Walker barely got to lift a shovel to muck. And, worse, whenever they were alone for even a second, Peter tried to grope him. He was surprisingly determined to get a handful of Walker's ass. Walker suspected Molly was behind this sudden fixation, since Peter hadn't seemed that into him on their milkshake date. But he couldn't know for sure, so he tried to avoid him as much as possible.

Spending time in the stables reminded Walker that he needed to confer with Marlon about the winter feed. He ducked into one of the clean stalls to clear his mind and make a mental list of all that he was getting behind on. He was thinking about how soon they'd need to castrate the remaining calves when a flash of blond hair over the side wall made him jump in fear that Peter had cornered him again, but it was only Tessa's sweet palomino's tail.

Victor and one of the show's hired animal handlers led the mare back into her clean stall.

"Any chance we can ride these sweethearts?" Victor asked, spotting Walker watching from the empty stall.

"You ride?" He went over to pat Callie's neck. She nosed at him, and he laughed softly. "Sorry, doll. I don't have any apples on me."

Victor smiled, the most genuine grin Walker had seen on him yet. "I used to ride. It's been a while."

"Did you grow up on a farm?"

"No." Victor shook his head, running his hands along Callie's flanks. "But I took riding lessons as a kid. I was obsessed with horses back then." Victor stared at Callie with longing in his eyes, and Walker suppressed a laugh.

"You falling in love there, cowboy?"

Victor grinned again. "A little bit."

Walker looked at him. Victor studied him in return, but with none of the predatory vibe he'd given off before. "You'll have to ask Andy about liability and whatever, but as far as I'm concerned, sure, you can ride."

"Is that a date?" Victor teased, and Walker laughed again, holding up his hands.

"No promises," he said, and slipped out of the stall before Victor could pin him down to any specifics. He went over to John to float the idea, though. He hadn't spent nearly enough time on his horse Cormac recently, and taking Victor out on a ride would be a lot less of a burden than having to actually have a conversation with the man.

John thought it was a great idea. What's a cowboy romance without taking his potential lover out on a horse? But, alas, Andy said they didn't have the insurance to cover the contestants actually getting on the horses. However, Victor's request to ride *did* give Andy the idea to squeeze in a second group date in the afternoon. This time with all the contestants.

The idea was to let them play around with the horses for a while—petting them, feeding them apples, and learning how to put a saddle on and take it off. Walker was fine with all of that because his horses were as calm as the animals could get. He trusted them with the contestants. But most of the guys didn't have Victor's experience and needed guidance on how to behave. At least that meant the conversations went easily enough for the most part.

Molly tugged him aside right at the start and said that Andy wanted another kiss today. Preferably a couple of kisses. With a couple of different guys.

"And none of them can be Roan. Or Ben."

"Why not Ben?" Walker asked.

Molly's left brow arched. "Oh, you'd like to kiss Ben?"

"No."

Yes? Maybe? Hell if he knew what he wanted with Ben. He liked the guy, but he didn't send sparks flying through him just by smiling the way Roan did.

"No? Well, too bad. Kiss someone today, Walker. Even though Andy said not to kiss Ben, I'll let it slide if you do. I think it'd be good TV. And if you can do it so that the other guys can see, let them all pretend to be jealous for the cameras, all the better."

Then she walked away before Walker could say anything more. He turned to observe what was happening with the four horses he'd brought out for the men to play around with.

Victor, true to his word, could obviously be left to his own devices. He was helping Chad with the saddle. Ben was also good with the horse he'd been assigned. Apparently, his family had owned some land in Florida, along with horses and goats, when he was a kid. Walker folded his arms over his chest and watched as Ben taught Roan the basics.

Frowning, Walker noticed the way Ben kept touching Roan unnecessarily as he showed him what to do. The closeness and comfort between them made Walker's gut knot up. But it was clear Ben knew everything there was to know about saddling up a horse, so Roan was in capable hands.

Peter had abandoned playing grab-ass and was paying a lot of attention to one of the camera men, which Molly wasn't liking by the looks of things. Clark and Nick seemed fairly okay with the horses once Walker gave them a little instruction, but Davis and Jaden acted like they were dealing with wild tigers or something, what with the way they kept grabbing each other and squealing whenever the horse moved. So Walker spent quite some time reassuring those two.

When things started to wind down, and the pressure to get on with it and kiss some of the men was coming down hard, given the intense looks Molly kept sending his way, Walker decided to corner her again. By the shade canopy the crew had set up for the monitors, she was staring at her clipboard with a mighty deep frown for her little, freckled face. Leaving the men with the horses, he headed her way and took up a position by her side. He had to help her understand it from his point of view.

Rubbing the back of his sweaty neck, he gazed uncomfortably down at her from beneath the brim of his hat.

"Yes?" she prompted, rolling her hand to get him going, but not looking up from her clipboard.

"I don't know how I feel about this whole 'kissing a few different people' thing," he ventured. "Is it really necessary? I thought Andy wanted to promote this show without the usual LGBT stereotypes. Doesn't that include avoiding the oversexed stereotype? Or promiscuity?"

Molly signed something and punctuated so hard she tore the paper a little, then waved the guy holding the clipboard away. Her bright eyes met his, and they were sharp. "If I recall correctly, Andy said he wanted this show to be treated just like any heterosexual version already out there. Am I right?"

Walker swallowed and nodded. He already knew where she was going with this.

"And you know what the straight shows have their contestants do? Kiss. Make out. Steal blow jobs. Fuck. I'd say we're already well distanced from the stereotypical oversexed gay man trope. You've kissed one guy on the cheek. Another you've promised to kiss and not delivered—you giant tease—and a few others you've manfully clapped on the shoulder. We're downright prudish to be asking you to lock lips with a couple of guys at this point, at least in comparison to the heterosexual shows."

Walker shuffled his feet. It still didn't mean he wanted to kiss anyone but Roan, and he balked at being forced to do it against his will. He opened his mouth to say just that, but Molly beat him to the punch.

"Hey, I can't make you actually do anything at all, like I said be-

139

fore." She glanced around, but the only person nearby was a lonely sound guy and Molly seemed to dismiss him. "You're in this for the money, babe. This show is going to be a cash cow for you, if you work the drama the right way. I know what you need, Walker. I know your situation here and how much the storms from the last hurricane cost you and your ranch. Not to mention your father's diabetes and the medical expen—"

"Don't talk about him or that." Who the hell did she think she was prying into his parents' lives? How did she know that about Dad?

"Fine. But all that together means you need money. You'll want to be able to score future magazine interviews that will shell out cash to speak with you, maybe you'll want a book deal. Whatever. My point is, you want to milk this thing."

"I really don't."

Molly rolled her eyes. "Then you're not the right person for this show, which I actually told Andy at the start. But it's your choice." She shook her head, frowning. "You want to know why else you aren't right for this show? You want people to like you too much."

"What? I never gave a shit what anyone thought of me." Walker bristled. His ego chafed at the idea that he couldn't carry this show, that he wasn't enough.

"But you do care, though. Yes, you want to be charming. It's the southern way." She punctuated that with another eyeroll. "But you know what's more important than being liked? Making the viewing audience come back to watch the next episode. You want to make them feel torn up about who they want you to be with. You want to make some viewers root for Ben, some for Roan, and some for Victor or Chad. You want them to *feel* things, Walker. You don't want to be known as the queer bachelor who was so determined not to be seen as stereotypical or promiscuous that he bored the public to death. We're selling emotions here. Trust me, the media is ruthless."

"You are the media."

Molly grinned. "My point exactly." She waved her hands in the direction of the contestants milling about the stables. "Look, we're not asking you to do anything wrong. You realize people everywhere in this country—straight, gay, bi—date different people at the same time, don't you? They even kiss them, and—gasp—sometimes have sex with them."

"Yes," Walker said. "But generally not on TV."

Molly waggled her eyebrows. "Depends on what you're watching. Okay, so let's get real. What's the problem here? You like one of the guys too much already? You only want to kiss Roan's pretty lips?" Molly smirked. "Fine. At least it's one of my boys."

Walker frowned.

Molly went on, "I produce Roan. So obviously, I'm happy if he wins. But, look, I get it. Hearts can't be reined in and all that shit." She put her hands on her hips. "But you still kiss your mama, don't you?"

"I guess."

"You don't have to slip anyone tongue. Just make the kisses *look* good. Fake a little passion for it. Sell some emotions, Walker." Her grin turned feral. Louisiana sunshine highlighted the freckles on her young face. "I think you should kiss Ben soon. And Roan would probably be up for real smooch, too. Hell, they *all* would. That's what they signed on for. It's what they and the public expect. Why don't you just ask them?" Her phone began to ring. Without a backward glance at him, she pressed it to her ear and walked away.

Walker tipped his hat down a little and glanced around. Chad, Victor, and the others were brushing down two of the horses. Ben had his arm slung over Callie's neck as she lipped at Roan's hand. Roan laughed delightedly and when he pulled his hand way, Walker saw he was holding an apple. He suppressed a smile. He'd taught Callie years ago to take dainty bites of an apple rather than eat the whole thing in one go.

Ben's eyes ate Roan up like he was a piece of candy, and Walker got that. He really did. But the irrational spike of irritation building in Walker the more he watched the two of them together he didn't understand at all.

What was he jealous about? He barely knew either man. But they knew each other, didn't they? That was pretty evident in the comfort they took in each other's presence and the easy smiles and laughs between them. They had time to develop that, didn't they, cooped up with the other suitors in that barn all the time?

Walker kept watching until he realized the look on his face was probably being filmed in such a way that it would be easy to manipulate and use out of context. And, yep, there were two cameras aimed particularly at him. Walker knew who he wanted to kiss out of those two. But that didn't mean that he shouldn't take Molly's advice. Who knew if his feelings were even returned? And he didn't want to be a failure as a bachelor, ruin the one of the first reality gay romance shows with his stubborn inflexibility, and not even end up with Roan in the end anyway. Molly was right—he was in this for the money. They all were. His feelings for Roan were out of proportion and ridiculous.

He took a deep breath, the salty-sweet air filling his nostrils, and breathed out slowly. Steeling himself, he made up his mind. He'd go bust up their little one-on-one to ask Ben out for a date tomorrow. And he'd kiss him real fast. Not on the mouth, maybe, but...yeah.

"Hey, man." Walker flinched in surprise to see Chad at his elbow.

Molly caught Walker's eye and raised her brows as if to say, "Do it. Kiss him."

When Walker had grown to read her facial expressions, he didn't know, most of the time he worked with John. But Molly had a way of radiating what she wanted a guy to do and enough bite in her glare to make even a grown man like him think he ought to do it.

Chad put his hand on Walker's forearm and tilted his head as he asked, "Do you think we can talk for a sec while everyone else is occupied?"

"Sure, what's up?" Walker nodded in the direction of the empty pen and they began to walk. Chad was a handsome guy, but a little too artificially so. Walker hadn't hated the time they'd spent together so far, but he hadn't really enjoyed it either.

Cameras were on them like white on rice. Three to be exact. Plus the one wired up in the corner of the pen. Jesus, they'd really covered every inch of his ranch in cameras. And they were all body mic-ed, too.

"I just want to be honest with you," Chad said, peering up at Walker with an earnest expression.

"All right." Walker studied him for a second, hooking his foot over a slat on the fence and resting his arms over another one. He tipped his hat farther down. "I'm listening."

"The thing is, I'm an actor. I'm on this show in the hopes it'll kick-start my career." He darted a look toward Molly. "I'm not supposed to say that. She'll probably murder me in my sleep tonight for it, but I thought it was better to be honest. I thought it might actually help things move along."

Walker wrinkled his brow.

"Don't get me wrong, if I'd met a great guy in the process, that'd have been a bonus, obviously. And you are a great guy! But this life—" he indicated the ranch "—just isn't for me. No offense."

"None taken," Walker said, a bit bemused. "It's not like the two of us are bleeding chemistry."

Chad's face brightened. "Right? That's what I mean. I wanted to come clean with you, so you knew what was up. You can send me home any time you want, and don't feel bad about it."

Walker smirked. "But it'd help you out if I let you stick around a little longer?"

"It would, yeah. And if you interacted with me more often. But I'm not going to ask that of you. If you don't like me, you don't. And that's fine."

Walker nodded slowly, biting his bottom lip. "You're a decent guy, Chad. I have the feeling you're the only one so far who's been complete-ly honest with me."

143

Chad's eyes grew a little sad. "That doesn't mean they're all hiding awful secrets," he said. His eyes shifted toward Roan and Ben, and then he met Walker's gaze again. "Or that they don't really like you."

"I know." Out of the corner of his eye he saw John rushing over, shaking his head with a big frown on his face. Probably about to yell at them that none of this was usable material. An idea began to blossom. "So an actor, huh?"

"Yeah. Trying to be at least."

"You any good?"

Chad gave him a curious look. His white teeth gleamed despite the overcast skies. "I like to think so."

Walker tilted his head to the side. John was almost here. "Play along with me?"

"Okay." Chad grinned, eyes twinkling like his curiosity had been piqued.

Walker flicked back his hat, looked down, and toed the ground in an *aw shucks* kind of way. Then he reached out and touched Chad's arm, sliding from shoulder to wrist, and took hold of his fingers.

Chad scooted closer, tilting his head invitingly. "You've got callous-es," he said, flipping Walker's hand over and touching them softly.

"Farm work," Walker offered.

"I like that."

Walker grinned. This could work. He felt nothing for Chad, no excited flip of his stomach and no racing heart. But he could flirt a little.

"So I was wondering," he said, once he was sure John was close enough to hear. He glanced up at the camera in the corner and made sure the camera guy in the pen with them also had a clear shot. "How about we go on a date? Just you and me. And my calloused hands."

To his credit, Chad really was a good actor. Flattered surprise washed over his features, and then he cast his eyes down, looking a little bit shy. "Gosh," he said, pretending he was trying to suppress a smile. "I'd really love to."

Ah well, in for a penny.

"Good," Walker said. Then he caressed the side of Chad's face and leaned in to press a very chaste, dry kiss to his mouth. Chad blinked in surprise when Walker pulled back but then grinned. He touched his fingers to his lips and grinned even bigger as he backed away. "Excited for our date, big guy."

"Likewise."

There. Molly had her kiss, and Walker had a date without having to worry about who to ask, and without acting on his jealousy by asking out Ben just to put a stop to his flirting with Roan. He finally felt like he had a handle on this thing. Maybe he could keep Chad and Roan until last and send everyone else home.

Automatically his eyes searched out Roan, who was still beside Callie, his fingers in her long mane and his gaze on Walker. Ben was there too, his expression conflicted but stoic, while Roan's wounded hazel eyes told the whole story. He looked absolutely devastated.

Walker yanked his hat down again and walked toward Davis and Jaden to help them with grooming the horse again. Thunder clapped in the distance, and just like that his plans for the immediate future changed. Rain was coming and the horses—and more importantly their tack—needed to be inside. He ignored the guilty churning in his stomach as he showed everyone what to do next.

The crew hustled, too, to prepare their equipment for the sudden storm.

When Ben walked Callie inside, Roan wasn't with him. Walker stepped out the stable door and looked around. The rain started to fall in fat drops, making rings in the dirt. Roan was nowhere to be seen.

THE DRESS CODE for the second horseshoe ceremony was a lot less strict. They were told to look nice, but no suits would be needed again until the final elimination. Roan had worn his favorite pair of jeans that made his ass look great and a red button-up that he knew made his pale skin and dark hair shine. Walker looked amazing in a dark pair of Wranglers and a green shirt that set off his eyes. Roan wondered if they were his own clothes, or if they'd been provided by wardrobe.

The ceremony was being held on the front porch of the farmhouse as the sun was going down. Andy was on the set again, running around like a headless chicken, screeching that there would be no room for error tonight. They had to catch the light. Not that they didn't have artificial light, too. Six huge ones that made the swampy air even hotter.

Roan tugged at his collar and looked around at the remaining contestants. They all looked anxious, but it was clear some were more invested in staying than others. As they stood on the grass beneath the porch, awaiting their fate, Roan felt torn about what he hoped for the most. He wanted to stay, if he was being honest with himself. But he also wanted to be with his mom, because who knew how much time they might have left together. Muddling his clarity was the fact that they really needed the money for the clinical trial. How he really felt and what he really wanted was all mixed up in what he was supposed to feel and do.

He chewed on his lip and let his gaze settle on Walker, who was enduring another round with Kylie's makeup brushes before they started filming again. He huffed a soft laugh as Walker grimaced and squirmed.

Then there was Walker to consider.

Roan liked Walker a lot. More than he'd ever expected when he signed up for the show, but Roan was also very aware how emotions were easily manipulated in situations like this. He'd read an article about these kinds of shows in preparation, explaining the psychological principles and biological forces at play that made it impossible for him to see Walker as anything other than desirable. He knew he was being manipulated, just from being around others who also wanted to get into Walker's good graces, but it didn't make it feel less real.

And even if in some crazy world they somehow ended up wanting to be together, how would it ever work? Walker obviously couldn't leave his farm, and Roan wasn't leaving his mother. Not until—

He winced and pushed the thought aside, concentrating instead on the clouds above. One looked like a frog. Another a bunny rabbit. There, that was better. One step at a time, that's all it took. And an awareness that what he felt was artificially created and wouldn't stand the test of time.

"Places! Let's do this people!" Andy cried.

Molly was instantly in motion, cracking her whip, and the contestants lined up at their marks. Up on the porch, Walker did too.

Luke faced a camera and did his thing as a host, but Roan had trouble paying attention to it all. He struggled not to tug at his tie, feeling hot and weak in the humidity. He could hear the faint buzz of the cicadas in the trees. He knew they'd only grow louder as the evening wore on. He hoped Andy's sound guys had a plan for that. On the horizon another thunderstorm threatened, making the air stifling with humidity. His fake glasses kept sliding off his nose and twice Ben leaned over to ask him if he was okay.

"I'm fine," Roan told him, wishing it was all over so he could go inside. Win or lose, he'd at least be in the air conditioning again. "Just hot."

Ben nodded, not saying anything because finally the moment was there. Walker was about to announce his first choice for a horseshoe. Roan's stomach churned with anxiety and indecision. He didn't know what he wanted to happen. He just hoped Walker didn't leave him for last again. His nerves couldn't take it.

But Walker walked up to him immediately and thrust out the first horseshoe. "I have a date in mind for next week that will beat the noodling," he said, looking oddly bashful. As if anyone in this room would refuse him anything. "You in?"

"Yes," Roan said, accepting the horseshoe. "Thank you." He swallowed hard and Walker's dark eyes narrowed a little, his brows drawing down. He opened his mouth to say something else when an almighty thunderclap sounded and Jaden let out a screech.

"I told them to check the Doppler," Walker said. "They didn't listen."

Another thunderclap came and it sounded so close everyone jumped, even Roan.

Walker's fingers found his and held tight. They were both still gripping the horseshoe with their other hands, like the wishbone of a turkey.

"You okay?" Walker whispered over the worried gasps of the others. The big lights flickered again and stayed on. Mics crackled, and Andy groaned. "It's okay. Just thunder."

Roan nodded.

"Meeting!" Andy cried out, and a confab began between Andy, John, Molly, and some guys from the crew. "Doppler says this storm is moving in faster than we expected," he yelled after a few tense minutes of discussion. "But we're gonna risk it. Do it all in one fast take. Roan move away from Walker. We have what we need from you."

Walker's eyes searched Roan's face for another moment, but then he let go of the horseshoe.

Roan went to stand in the designated "winners" spot, and wondered at the way he could still feel a tingle where Walker had held his hand. He watched as the rest of the horseshoes were handed out post-haste.

He wasn't confused about what the hoped for anymore. There was just something about Walker…

His pulse raced a little faster, and his cheeks heated. Yeah. He wanted to stay.

Just as he admitted that to himself, the gathering clouds overhead burst open, and rain poured down on them all.

"GODDAMMIT."

Walker's voice made Roan startle awake. They'd all been hustled back into the remodeled barn after the rainstorm broke. There'd been so much going on, and Roan had been soaked through. The producers hadn't let them change, though, insisting that there was more they needed to film inside. So, Roan had stumbled back out to the little covered porch where he and Walker had shared that first cozy interview, and, finding it blessedly unoccupied, he'd curled up on the sofa with a warm blanket and listened to the rain on the tin roof. He'd watched it grow dark outside, and drifted off to sleep while waiting to be called back in for filming.

Now he winced as he straightened up, his neck stiff from the un-comfortable angle. He still felt shivery from getting soaked by the warm rain, but the body-warmed blanket helped. "What's up?"

Walker was scowling back through the door into the main part of the house. John was waiting there with a sound guy. And Andy.

Roan rubbed at his eyes and said, "Oh. I guess they want you to wake me up to film some scene or whatever?"

"Yes." Walker looked mad.

"Um. Sorry. That I fell asleep and, you know," he waved his hand toward the John. "Did I miss my cue or something?"

Still not looking at him, Walker said, "No. We just couldn't find you. No one thought to check the camera feed to this room for some reason, and everyone's hunted all over the house. Molly was getting ready to flip her shit. Thought you'd done a runner."

Roan cleared his throat. "Um, yeah. No. I wouldn't do that. Like I said, sorry." He started to stand up but Walker stopped him. Roan could see that John and the camera guy were recording everything. As were the cameras wired in around them. This room was definitely being watched on the feed now.

"No. I didn't mean to sound mad. It's not you. It's them. All of this."

John cleared his throat. "C'mon now. Let's film something we don't have to edit to pieces."

Walker frowned at him, but then stepped into the room, sitting next to Roan on the sofa. His muscled thigh pressed against Roan's and his mouth twisted like he was trying to get words out. Finally, he turned to Roan almost urgently, took hold of his hands and said, "Thanks for staying."

Roan squeezed his fingers. "It's no hardship."

Though it should be. He could be with his mom right now. He should probably want that more. And he did want to be there for her, but this, whatever it was, was pretty exciting, too. He wasn't ready to be sent away yet. He wanted to get to know Walker. *Really* know him. And if it meant all the trappings of the show, then he was willing to deal with that, too. For money. For the opportunity to help his mom. To know a man he'd otherwise have never met.

"You had every reason to turn the horseshoe down," Walker said, frowning at their clasped hands. "I wouldn't have blamed you after what I did."

Roan tilted his head. "What did you do?"

"Kissing Chad like that in front of you."

Roan laughed softly, and then harder. The ridiculousness of their situation overwhelmed him, and he couldn't catch his breath from giggling so hard. He hunched over as the laughter shook him, and he pressed his forehead to their joined hands.

Walker was chuckling now, too, but not nearly as hard. He seemed more than a little confused when he said, "What's so funny, little lion?"

"You. This. That kiss."

"Yeah?"

Roan sat up and pulled his hands out of Walker's grasp to wipe at his laughter induced tears. "Yeah."

"You were acting then? When you looked upset by it?"

Roan shook his head and smoothed his fingers through his hair.

God, it must be a mess. He cleared his throat and tried to explain. "I didn't like it. It bothered me. A lot. But, now, right here with you? It's absurd. That kiss meant nothing to either of you."

"Hey now," John said. "Let the home-viewing audience decide that."

They ignored him. Walker stared into Roan's eyes. "No, it didn't."

Roan shrugged. "It's the way it works. This show, I mean. You have to do it."

"But I don't want to. I only want to—"

Roan looked up at Walker then, not sure if he wanted him to finish that sentence or not. "It's not a big deal, Walker. And I'm sorry if I made it seem like one."

Molly popped up behind John and muscled her way into the room. She crossed her arms and glared at both of them. "This is yawn-inducing. Give me something good."

"Roan and I had something we needed to clear up."

"I don't care if someone was dying and you needed to plan their funeral," Molly said, and Roan winced.

Walker went red with anger. "You watch your mouth," he snarled and Molly backed away a little.

Wait, did Walker know about his mom?

"Cough up some fucking romance," she barked. "You guys are the best thing this show has going for it, and you're acting like little old ladies at a church social. You realize what's at stake here? If we can't make a good show out of all this footage, the studio will yank this entire project, and make you pay for the whole deal."

Walker's jaw clenched tight as Roan gaped at him and Molly slipped behind John again, still waiting for them to do something 'romantic.'

"They can do that?" Roan whispered.

"If I breach the contract in some major way." He glanced at Roan and quickly looked away again. "But she likes to throw threats around. Don't worry about it. We'll deliver a good show."

Shit. It looked like everyone had something to lose on this show.

Except for the studio. "So what do they want us to do out here?"

"I'm guessing," Walker said, "they want me to kiss you."

"Uh." Roan stood up on shaky legs, his damp clothes feeling weird and uncomfortable against his skin.

"Wait, wait." Walker grabbed Roan's wrist. "Trust me?"

Roan blinked. He thought he did, but he was also very aware they were already being filmed. God knows what they'd edit this into. He sat down beside Walker again on the couch.

Walker gave him a small smile and rubbed his back. "C'mon little lion, just follow my lead." He twined his fingers together with Roan's and the zip of that connection jolted up Roan's arm.

Molly smirked at them. "Finally. Your guy rolling, John?"

"Rolling."

"We'll edit some shit in with Luke later," Molly said. "So tell me, what have you lovebirds been doing back here all alone?"

"Earlier we had a bit of a downpour, and Roan here got good and soaked. Naturally he was a cold and wet, and probably tired. I think he came out here to be alone."

Roan nodded.

Walker went on, "Now usually on a farm we love some rain, but too much of a good thing can interfere with haying. So that was where my mind went when the rain started. I wasn't thinking about where Roan was or any of the other suitors, either. I was mainly wondering about the hay fields, and if my farmhands have everything under con—"

"Skip the boring farm shit and get to the good part."

Roan bristled and squeezed Walker's hand. "Does being rude to people make you feel better about yourself?"

Molly laughed. "Oh, look at that, our little lion's got teeth."

Roan's breath caught in his lungs and he tried to pull his hand away but Walker held fast. "She's just trying to push your buttons. Produce a reaction. It's her job. She watched the footage and got that I'd called you that a time or two, and now she's trying to poke you with it. Guess if she can't get the kiss she wants, a huffy fight will do."

Molly laughed softly. "Look out, Cowboy Mastermind is on to me."

"Okay, you want the good stuff?" Walker turned a little so he could look at Roan head on. "If I had to do all this over again, I couldn't have wished for a better guy to meet on a rigged reality show."

"Do it again. Without the 'rigged'," Molly said.

Walker ignored her, leaning closer, eyes darting from Roan's mouth to his eyes and back again.

Oh my God, Roan thought. *He's going to kiss me.*

And he wanted it, but without the audience. Out of the corner of his eye he saw Molly give them a thumbs up. Walker took hold of Roan's face, and then pressed his mouth to Roan's cheek sweetly.

"I want to kiss you," he whispered, probably hoping the boom pole wouldn't still pick the words up. Or maybe he didn't care. "But not in front of these jackasses."

"Same," Roan whispered.

Walker straightened, winked at him, and left.

"All I care about," Molly said to Roan as he stood up from the couch feeling flushed and irritated all at once. "I repeat *all* I care about is that the first time you make out? It's on camera."

"Whatever." Roan went to push past her, too, wanting to follow Walker inside, but Molly stopped him.

"Not whatever, Roan. You guys are our money makers, got it?"

Roan wiped a hand over his mouth and glared at her.

"One more question. Get a close up of his face," she said to the camera guy. Roan thought he saw John roll his eyes, but he didn't say anything. "How are you feeling about your situation now, Roan? Are you still just here for the money? You and Walker seemed to be getting pretty cozy in here before we busted in."

"I hope Luke will be rephrasing that into a decent question," Roan said.

"He'll ask whatever I tell him to ask, depending on your answer.

We'll make it look good, don't worry. We've already got plenty of shots of you watching Walker when he's not looking. Oh." Molly laughed. "And a fantastic one of your face when he planted that kiss on Chad. You can say whatever you want, Roan, baby, but you were jealous as hell. We'll edit it to make sure it sounds the way we want it to sound." Then her eyes softened and she said the next bit almost like she was proud of him or something. "The public is going to eat you up."

Roan sighed, feeling bone tired all over. "I like him," he said, looking down at his hands. "I like him a lot. And he deserves someone who can be here with him. On this beautiful farm. Someone who will be able to share this fascinating life with him wholeheartedly. And that can't be me. I have to go back to Ohio when this is over no matter what happens here."

"Aw, little lion," Molly said softly. "You're gonna make me cry."

"Don't call me that," Roan snapped and pushed his way into the house. He hated that woman so much.

Everyone else was already asleep by the time he stumbled out of the bathroom and into his bed. The advantage of five people leaving was that he'd managed to grab a bottom bunk for himself. As he wedged his toes between the wooden end and the mattress, his final thought was how he coveted Victor's giant queen bed that he had all to himself now.

No, that was a lie. His very final thought was how he wished he'd turned his face at the very last moment and kissed Walker's soft mouth. Cameras be damned.

WEEK THREE

SNAKE BITES AND HORSEBACK RIDES

Chapter 10

WITH THE STUPID group date of the day out of the way—an excursion out to a lesser field for a haying lesson—the producers seemed happy with the footage they'd gathered and Walker planned on making an easy escape to get some actual farm work done. He gathered his cell phone from the crew member who claimed it during filming and headed off toward the sun, eager for an afternoon getting sweaty and dirty. And for a few hours of thinking about anything other than Roan's smile, listening for his laugh, and sweating bullets over his closeness with Ben. What *was* going on between those two? Just friendship or something more?

He pushed his hat up and then tipped it low again when he saw John coming his way. *Oh, no you don't, buddy. I'm getting out of here.*

"If you have some time I'd like to go over next week's schedule," John said, intercepting Walker before he could get away. "And we need to talk about the next horseshoe ceremony."

Walker's cell phone rang and he lifted it out of his back pocket, frowning, surprised but also relieved to see the name on the screen. "I have to take this." He walked away toward his truck, leaving John standing there.

"Marlon, what's up?" He knew it had to be bad because Marlon had agreed to only call Walker's cell for the duration of the show in the case of a true emergency.

"You need to come to the East pasture, boss. We've got a snake bite."

"Ah shit." He pinched his nose. "On the muzzle?" He already knew because if it was just a leg bite, Marlon would've dealt with it himself.

"Yes. And…it's Hannah. She's got trouble breathing, too. And I'm here all by myself."

Walker's jaw clenched so hard his teeth ached. "Call the vet. I'm on my way." He rang off, and sprinted toward his Ford. He kept various first aid kits in all the barns and within seconds he started the truck and pulled away, tires skidding.

His phone rang. Molly. Walker gritted his teeth again.

"What?"

"Where are you going? You can't just drive off set without our go ahead! It's in the contract!"

"One of my cows got bitten by a snake. Cottonmouth, most likely. Usually they manage pretty well, but she got bit on the muzzle, and she's got trouble breathing, which means there's swelling and she might suffocate."

"Wait until I get a camera crew—"

"No." Walker hung up and glared at the mounted cameras on the dashboard as he raced to the East pasture where Marlon's battered old pickup waited. Walker grabbed the first aid kit and an old blanket off the backseat and was out of the truck in a heartbeat.

He found Marlon and Hannah a little way from the rest of the herd, in a patch of shade under an old oak tree. Marlon must've coaxed her there, and Walker sent him a silent word of thanks.

"How is she doing?"

"She's stressing." Marlon ran his hand over her neck. "Aren't you, cher? The Serpent Congo got her good."

Walker looked into her sweet, long-lashed eyes and felt a twinge of fear. "It's okay, Hannah," he crooned gently as he stroked her nose. He could see the swelling around her left nostril. Yellow pus oozed from a puncture wound. "Must've happened a few days ago."

"Yep. She'd have been fine if it hadn't gotten infected."

Hannah stood calmly but her flanks were heaving and the air whistled through her nose.

"Everything will swell shut," Marlon said.

"I know. The faster we can help her, the better. Vet's on the way?"

"Will be here in twenty," Marlon said. "But I don't think we got that kind of time."

"No," Walker said grimly. "Marlon, you'll have to keep her still while I intubate her."

"Won't be my first time, boss. And won't be the last. You sure you're up for it, though?"

Walker didn't say anything, he just bent down and opened the first aid kit, pulling out a huge jar of Vaseline and an eight inch piece of hose.

"This ain't just any cow."

"Marlon," Walker warned, but he knew it'd be no good. Marlon was going to tell the story like Walker hadn't been there in the first place.

"Hannah's the first cow you ever brought into this world."

"Twenty-two years ago. I know, Marlon."

"You've always been real sentimental."

"All right, grab the blanket and cover her up. We're wasting time." He slathered the tube in Vaseline, then murmured softly to Hannah as he began to ease the tube into her nostril.

He knew it was sentimental, but it couldn't be denied that he could do just about anything to Hannah, and she'd let him. He'd never been able to get rid of her, and he didn't look forward to the day she didn't come to him when he called.

"It's in. I'm going to disinfect the wound." Walker worked in silence for a while but felt Marlon staring at him and wasn't surprised when Marlon asked, "How you doing?"

"Fine. If Dr. Collins brings some DMSO, she'll be all right. She might need some antibiotics though."

"That's not what I meant. How you doing with that show?"

"I've regretted it a thousand times already."

Marlon pursed his lips and nodded. "Any of them sweet on you?"

Walker sighed and paused to look at his longtime ranch-hand and friend. Hannah let out a low sound, and Walker ran a soothing hand over her. "They're all here for the same reason I am. Money."

"Hmm. You sweet on anyone?"

Walker rolled his eyes and looked down so he could gently rub Hannah's nose, rucking up the blanket a little so she could see him better. "This competition messes with people's heads. I'm pretty sure none of them would look at me twice in everyday life."

"Ah, don't sell yourself short, boo. Who wouldn't want you? Heck, you know I'd snap you up if I could." He made a sad noise. "I can deal with what you got between your legs, but I like breasts."

"Shut your mouth," Walker said, laughing. He wanted to slap Marlon upside the head like he'd usually do, but he didn't want to startle Hannah. He hated that Hannah had been bitten, but he liked the normalcy of this moment, away from the cameras, his life back in his own hands.

Marlon gently stroked her neck. "But seriously, you don't feel anything for any of them?"

"I know you're a romantic old fool, friend. But you know that's not why we're letting this charade happen here."

"True, but that don't mean you can't meet someone." Marlon peered up at him meaningfully. "How long has it been since Mike?"

"Don't," Walker said. He heard a woman call out, and he looked over his shoulder. "Doc's here." Under his breath he added. "And you know exactly how long since Mike because we hired Dennis when he left."

Marlon smirked at him. "Just reminding you of the years that've passed, boo. Long, lonely years with no arms to hold you tight."

"Who says my years have been lonely? Temporary ranch hands get horny too."

"Who you talking to here? You expect me to believe the boss man is taking advantage of his temporary help? No, boo. You've been holding back a lot of years. You need a man in your life."

Walker shrugged, pleased to be interrupted by the vet trudging up to them in her jeans and plaid shirt, a look of determination on her face. Marlon might be right. He might need a man in his life, and maybe he had found a guy he wanted to know more about. But there was nothing normal about the circus they were in right now. In a way, he was just going through with the act, hoping to get through to the end and wondering if he might have the chance to really know Roan then.

He knew it was pathetic. But he hoped he did get that chance with Roan.

He truly did.

THE REST OF the third week was torture for Roan. Chad got chosen for another date with just Walker, then everyone *but* Chad, Roan, and Ben got to go on a special group date too. Which meant Roan hadn't spent any alone time with Walker at all since they'd talked about that kiss with Chad and then been interrupted by annoying, reaction-producing producers.

The stupid kiss with Chad still rankled a little, especially since Walker hadn't kissed *him* on the mouth yet. But…it was all part of the game, right?

Still, the next horseshoe ceremony was tomorrow night, and he hadn't spent any real time with Walker to impress upon him just why he shouldn't leave. Maybe, despite what was said the last time they'd talked, Walker wasn't really interested in Roan at all, or maybe production had decided to force Roan to go home since he and Walker weren't following their cues the way they wanted.

"We're screwed," Roan sighed, bored out of his mind and tired of all the loops of second guessing in his head. It was raining like the apoca-lypse and he petulantly hoped they were all stuck out in a field somewhere. But he also worried about the rain, too, because Walker had said something about too much rain making problems on the ranch. Roan didn't want Walker trying to deal with troubles during the chaos of shooting.

"We're not screwed," Chad said, lounging around with feet propped up on the coffee table like the incredible boredom didn't faze him at all. Ben was doodling on a notepad. The pen looked ridiculously dainty in his large paw. "Especially you guys. You're definitely not screwed."

"What?" Roan sat up a little straighter, and while Ben didn't move, Roan noticed his pen wasn't dancing across the paper anymore. "Why do you say that?"

"This whole thing today is a pity date. It's pretty clear he's most into the two of you."

Ben finally lifted his head. "Pretty clear how?"

Roan gazed at Ben speculatively. Of course Walker would be into that. Who wouldn't be? And Ben was a great guy, so it'd be good to have him around for another week, but… Roan swallowed down the weird lurch of jealousy at the idea that Walker might be more interested in Ben than in him.

"Well, let's see." Chad held up a manicured finger. "Out of every-one, you two are the only ones he's ever sought out on his own." He held up a second finger. "He stares at the two of you constantly, and—" he held out a third finger "—the producers are always warning him away from you both so his preference doesn't become obvious too fast." He grinned, and Roan shifted a little uncomfortably in his seat. Ben, on the other hand, looked downright mortified.

"I think it's wrong," Ben mumbled. "Love isn't a competition."

"No, it's not," Roan said. But they'd all come on this show voluntar-ily, so they had no room to protest.

"No? You don't date people, weed out the ones you don't like, stick around with the ones you do, and see how it goes?"

Roan sat up straighter, elbows on his knees. "Yeah, but that happens over time, not in the span of six weeks This whole situation is artificial and unnatural."

"Well, you knew that going in. And in this case, trust me. You two are the only ones actually in the running."

"You seem okay with that," Ben said, dropping his gaze back to his notepad.

"Yeah, well." Chad hooked his arms behind his head. "We all have our reasons for being here."

Roan mulled that over while he went into the kitchen to grab some dinner. They'd made huge lasagnas the night before and he plated some leftovers, shouting toward the living room, "You guys want some?"

"No, thanks," Ben called back, as Chad yelled, "Maybe later."

While the microwave did its magic, Roan stepped out onto the covered, screened porch and stared at the pouring rain.

"You'd love the sound of that, Mom," he murmured. "Louisiana rain on a tin roof."

She adored thunderstorms, and he wondered if this was where she'd learned to love them, back when she'd visited here as a young woman. Was she okay? He wanted to hear her voice so badly it hurt. She'd probably be cozied up in front of the TV right now with her favorite blankets. Maybe with a cup of tea. He couldn't remember the last time she didn't have rings under her eyes, her skin sagging and sallow.

God, what was he even doing here? His chest ached. He stumbled forward, catching himself on the screen. "Mom," he croaked. The rain splashed against the screen, getting him wet, but he didn't care. "I should go home." He said it to no one, forgetting the mounted cameras and the wired mic on his body.

He buried his face in his hands. He didn't allow himself to cry very often. They'd both shed oceans of tears when she'd first been diagnosed, but recently he felt like giving in to the pain was like giving up. If he allowed himself to think the worst or be anything but optimistic about her chances, he smudged her fate. He didn't dare to give in to the hopelessness, because without hope he had nothing. It'd been him and his mom for as long as he could remember, and if the drug trial didn't take her on, or they didn't get the money to enter it, he didn't know what he'd do. Without her the world was a dark place, and the future a predator waiting to devour him whole. He had no one else, and the idea of being completely alone made his blood go cold.

Roan straightened his back and sniffed, wiping his nose on the back of his hand. He couldn't think like this. He had to stay strong enough for both of them. He pushed against the kitchen door, startling when he found Ben at the counter in there.

"Hey, I wondered where you'd gone. You left your lasagna in the...are you okay?"

"Yeah I'm fine. I'm—" Roan winced as the pain in his chest hit him again. He pressed the heels of his hands in his eyes until colors danced behind his lids, hoping to hold back the tears.

"Roan? What's wrong? It's okay, c'mere." Ben tugged at him until he sat down on one of the barstools. Behind him, the living room was ablaze with noise. Shit, everyone was back from the date.

"I need to get upstairs," he croaked.

"Yeah, okay. You sure you're all right, though?"

"I'm fine."

Ben hesitated for a second, then leaned closer and put his arm over Roan's shoulders. "They're all too distracted to notice if you slip upstairs now, but listen. If you want to talk, I'm here okay? Aside from all this bullshit, I care about you."

"Okay," Roan whispered. Ben pulled him a little closer, and Roan went with it, finding comfort against a strong body in a pair of arms willing to hold him up, even if it was only for a second.

"Thanks, Ben. For everything. You're a good guy."

Ben nodded once, lips tightening until they went pale. Roan steeled himself, then slipped upstairs to go hide in the bedroom. He couldn't take it anymore. The whole reason he'd wanted to stay on was to get to know Walker, and he'd barely seen him the whole last week.

He did some calculations in his head. Yes, if he went home tomorrow night, he'd have enough. Not as much as they really needed, but enough to get his mom into the drug trial, hopefully. And he could be with her again, making sure she was okay, keeping them both going with the power of his love and hope.

Closing his eyes, a tear slipped out and down his cheek and he made up his mind. Tomorrow night, at the next horseshoe ceremony, he'd volunteer to leave. He'd save it for the last minute. It'd be good TV. His original reasons for being here had been satisfied and his secondary reason wasn't holding up.

It was time to call it quits and get back to his mama. It was time to say goodbye to fantasies and butterflies in the stomach. It was time to give up the pretense that he could ever be anything real to Walker.

ROAN, WILL YOU stay here with me another week?

Roan stared down at the horseshoe in his hand and tried to figure out how his plan to quit the show tonight had gone so wrong. Maybe it had been the twinkle in Walker's eye when he asked or the way he'd leaned so close, smelling of a refreshing aftershave, and whispered his apology.

Sorry about this week, little lion. Next week will be better for us. I promise.

Or maybe it had been the way Walker reached out and thumbed his chin gently, gazing at his mouth with a hot look of longing before smiling wickedly and backing away. Whatever it'd been, Roan had sputtered out a, "Yes, of course," and now here he was blinking into the bright lights of his post-ceremony, one-on-one interview with Luke.

"We're nearly ready," the producer, John, said, nodding at them.

Kylie came and touched up Luke's face, then looked at Roan. "Oh, you're all shiny. Hold on." She pulled out more brushes, fluttered them over Roan's face until he sneezed, and left again.

"Ready." Luke cleared his throat. The camera guy gave him a nod and said they were rolling. "Roan, how are you doing tonight?"

"Great," Roan said, feeling awkward. "Happy to still be here."

Was he? He didn't know anymore. He'd been so sure he should volunteer to go home, but now he couldn't help being dazzled, thrilled even, to have been Walker's first choice.

"How does it feel to be given the first horseshoe again this week?"

Roan reached to scratch his face, but Luke shook his head minutely, and Roan put his hand back in his lap. "It was a complete shock. But good, I guess?"

"You guess? Aren't you happy to be here still?"

"Yeah. Of course. I just—" He heaved out a sigh and squirmed. "This is all just…a lot, you know?"

Luke smiled kindly.

John said, "Just relax, you're doing fine. We're going to talk a little bit here, deepen the storyline on you a bit since you've made it to the halfway point now. Luke will ask you some personal things. Of course it's up to you if you want to answer them. We know you're going through a tough time."

"Right." Roan narrowed his eyes suspiciously.

Luke launched into it then. "How's your mom?"

Roan clenched his fists but kept his voice steady. "She's hanging in there."

He hoped she was, anyway.

Luke nodded, his eyes soft. "I'm glad to hear that. You found out she had cancer a year ago?"

"We did." He gave in. What did it matter that he talked about this on the show? It wouldn't air for a long time. By then his mom might not even—

He closed his eyes. "It was pretty advanced by the time they caught it. She went through a few rounds of chemo and radiation, but it didn't help for long."

Luke looked sincerely sad. Roan wondered if he truly was. It made his own throat tighten. "But there's a drug trial that might help her, you said?"

"Yes. It costs a lot of money. Plus the medical bills from the past year have added up. She can't work, and I…" Roan cleared his throat. He would *not* cry. "I need to help her."

"And that's why you're here."

His gaze slid down to his hands and he whispered, "Yes, like I said before…that's why I'm here. For the money."

Luke paused for a moment, then asked, his voice equally soft, "Where's your dad, Roan?"

Ah jeez. Roan wanted to walk away. To tell Luke and John to shove this whole interview up their asses. But if he stayed a few more weeks, it would be more than enough for the trial; it would cover the stack of bills, too, and maybe leave enough to take his mom on a vacation somewhere nice and warm when she got better. Maybe bring her down here to Louisiana and let her have all that food she'd loved so much again. And the cocktails. Yes, definitely cocktails, too. To celebrate her return to health. And he could introduce her to Walker… He wanted to stick around for all of those reasons now, but Jesus. This wasn't easy.

"Your dad?" Luke prompted again.

"He left."

Luke held up a hand to stop him. "My dad left…"

They'd all been trained, before filming started, to use complete statements instead of obvious responses so the show could use those clips with or without airing the question.

"Sorry. My dad left when I was two years old. I never knew him, and my mom doesn't talk about him."

"And you're an only child?"

"Yes. I'm an only child."

Luke smiled. He seemed so friendly. "Just like Walker. He's an only child, too."

Roan realized he hadn't known that. He'd assumed, but the topic of siblings—or the lack thereof—had never come up.

"This is important to you, isn't it? Winning the show. So you can take the money home and help your mom get better."

Roan hesitated, getting annoyed. Hadn't they just gone over that? He sighed. It made him seem like an asshole, but it was the truth. He cringed at the thought of Walker ever seeing this, of him thinking Roan had faked everything just to get the cash, but by then everything would be done, and Walker would either understand or he wouldn't. "Yes. I just want my mom to get better."

"How do you feel about Walker?"

Color rose to his face, and he couldn't do a thing about it. "Under different circumstances, I think he and I could have really hit it off. I'd love—I'd love to know him better. He's fun, he's sweet and kind. He cares about his ranch and his family and all the animals. And, obviously, he's hot." He laughed self-consciously. "In a lot of ways, I don't want to be here," he admitted. "I don't want to be away from my mom this long. But…" He trailed off, feeling the strain of so much unspoken.

"But?"

"But I really want to know Walker better."

"And Walker? What do you think you could bring to him as a partner if your heart's with your mom?"

"I don't know. But who's to say what makes a good relationship?" He might as well throw it all on the table. "I do like Walker a lot. And I think he likes me pretty well, too. This is a weird way to have met, and God knows we both have a lot going on in our lives. But so what? So what if I'm a grad school dropout picking up shifts at the local coffeeshop to put food on the table, and he's a successful farmer? So what if he's older than me? Or whatever? If we can get through being on this show, and we can get through my mom being sick, then we could probably make it through anything. And isn't that what a good relationship is about?"

God, he sounded ridiculous and desperate.

"Thanks, Roan. That was great." Luke patted Roan's hand. "And I know that wasn't easy. For what it's worth, I truly am sorry for what you're going through, and it's not fair that these are the steps you've got to take to get your mom the care she deserves."

Roan didn't look him in the eye. He smoothed his hand over the counter until he bumped into his water bottle and opened it. "Can I go now?"

"I think Walker might want to talk to you before you do."

Roan winced and nodded. "Okay. I guess I'll wait here."

Why was it that just the mention of Walker's name made his heart thump?

CHAPTER 11

"**I** WANT TO ask you something."

Walker sank back in the deep couch of the screened-in porch and uncrossed his arms. The horseshoe ceremony was over, and Walker wanted nothing more than to find Roan and make some kind of plan to be alone with him. He wanted to know the guy better, and the damn cameras weren't helping anything at all. He thought he'd figured something out, but before he could find Roan and float the idea, he'd been corralled by producers and dragged to shoot a private conversation with Ben.

Ben, who was fidgeting with the cuff of his shirt, a dark green thing that seemed to be on the verge of succumbing under the strain of Ben's muscles, and who now wanted to ask him something. The way Ben's voice quavered, it sounded ominous. "Shoot," Walker said.

"It's a weird question."

Walker's brows drew down a little. "Okay, weird is fine."

Ben glanced at the cameras and grimaced. If he was wishing for them to not be there, Walker could relate. "What's it like? Being with a guy?"

Walker's eyebrows flew up, and he leaned forward trying to catch Ben's gaze. Ben sat beside him on the couch but they were both tucked away in opposite corners, and now that he'd asked his question, Ben's eyes were anywhere but on Walker's. "I thought you said you'd hooked up before."

The edges of Ben's jaw began to turn a blotchy red, like paint mixing in water. "A couple of times, but—I don't know. It always left me feeling…" He shrugged, looking so uncomfortable Walker felt sorry for him.

"Unsatisfied?" Walker tried. "Maybe a bit unsure if that was really what you wanted?"

Ben slowly nodded. "Yeah, I think so. Maybe."

"Look, I don't know you very well. But you got a girl pregnant and did the right thing, didn't you?"

"I don't know about that," Ben mumbled.

"Well, you could've left her to deal with the baby herself, and you didn't. No matter how your marriage ended, I'm sure she was grateful for the support when she needed it most."

"Yeah, okay."

"And you stayed and tried to make the marriage work for as long as you could. I don't know anything about your family situation, or how your relationship was while you were together, but that takes a dedication and commitment I don't think you'd find in the kind of man who's okay with hookups in a dirty alley. My guess is you're not feeling it because you need to have your heart involved for the sex to be good."

Ben turned so red Walker had to suppress a laugh. "Jesus. I thought you cowboys were all supposed to be repressed and shit."

"What can I say? I grew up with hippy parents who taught me very early on to listen carefully before bursting through any closed door." Walker paused. "In the house or any of the barns."

Ben gaped at him. "I'm so sorry."

Barking out a surprised laugh, Walker patted Ben's leg. "It wasn't all bad. I've seen some guys struggle with being gay, and it ain't pretty. Listen, you need to date a guy for real a few times, have that first kiss, date a bit more, then think over how you'd feel about sleeping with him. You deserve someone who treats you right."

"Usually I'm expected to do the treating."

"It's a two-way street."

Ben nodded slowly. "So how many dates would you recommend

before that first kiss?"

Bless his heart, Ben the hunk was so naïve and so nervous. "It depends on the situation. If you have a really good first date, and you're both feeling it, go for it. I tend to wait until the second date." He paused, remembering his first date with Mike where the dinner had been a thrum of sexual tension from the very first minute, and they'd barely made it to one of the barns before Mike had knocked his hat off his head and kissed him breathless. "But yeah." He cleared his throat. "Whatever feels right for the both of you."

"How many dates have we been on?" Ben asked quietly. He scooted closer.

"Oh. I—"

Ben's big paw traveled up Walker's leg. His hand was shaking, and he looked terrified.

Walker put his own over it and stopped its ascent. "Ben, you don't have to."

Ben let out a shuddery breath. "I do," he whispered.

"Hey now, give yourself a break. One step at a time, okay?" Walker gently cupped his face. It felt rough against his palm, the scratch of stubble a subtle tease. "How about a hug instead?" He was so close, Walker could see the gray striations in Ben's blue eyes.

Ben's shoulders drooped with relief, and Walker hauled him closer. Something protective surged in him. The poor guy. Ben gingerly let his forehead rest against Walker's shoulder and Walker moved a little closer, letting his hands trace the curve of Ben's back. "Okay?" he whispered.

"Okay," Ben agreed.

When he stopped shaking, Walker let go of Ben. "You'll be just fine," he said, and Ben nodded but didn't reply.

"That was excellent!" Molly cried out, and Walker startled. He'd forgotten about those damn cameras and hadn't even seen Molly come in. "No, really! That was great. Tortured gay man finding his feet. It's a dream come true. This show is going to be so awesome." Ben quickly rose to his feet and left, and Walker wanted to go after him but figured he needed a minute to himself.

"Why are you so relentlessly unkind, Molly?"

Molly waved him away, clearly still envisioning golden scenes. "First, you and Roan pretty much eating each other up on that fucked-up fishing date, then that kiss with Chad and Roan's jealous face, and now this. And right now Roan's pouring his heart out to Luke." She smiled gleefully. "I hope he cries."

Walker stood up, ready to leave. "That's heartless."

"Yeah, well, don't judge before you have all the info, cowboy. And you won't have it until the show airs."

"Whatever." Walker pushed past her and stomped through to the living room. He didn't even pretend like he wasn't looking for Roan. And shit. This was exactly what he'd initially wanted to avoid. These feelings.

He liked Ben, but he didn't feel that tug beneath his breastbone like he did whenever Roan's name was mentioned. There'd been something right from the start. From the very first moment he'd seen Roan get out of the SUV, he'd thrilled to him at a cellular level. Maybe the show was playing tricks on him, maybe not. He knew two things. One, he needed to make sure Roan was okay, and two, he needed to get him alone so he could figure out what was real.

Next week, I'm getting him to myself if it kills me.

"IF YOU'RE LOOKING for Roan, he's in the kitchen," Luke said while Kylie attacked his face with wet wipes. They came away orange.

"Thanks," Walker said. "And by the way, I like you better in your real color."

Luke laughed. "You and me both."

Walker pushed his way into the kitchen and found Roan at the counter in there, hunched over on a bar stool with his back to the door.

"Hey, little lion," Walker said. Roan glanced over his shoulder, and Walker stopped in his tracks for a second. He looked awful. "What's up?"

Roan let his forehead drop back into his palm and he stared desolately at the counter. "Do you ever do or say anything in front of those damn cameras and instantly regret it?"

Walker laughed softly. "All the time." Roan's shoulders hunched further, and fuck, it was really hard not to walk over there and put his hand between those sharp shoulder blades, then slide around him, and tug Roan into a big hug. "What did Luke pry out of you?"

Roan was quiet, and Walker took the barstool beside him. Eventually Roan said, "Luke asked about my dad. I never meant to bring it up here. It just caught me off guard, I guess."

Walker smiled gently. "Yeah, they're good at doing that. My mother calls it the show's trauma trick. They want the home audience to think that someone's character should be weighed by what horrible things they've gone through and how well they've responded to it. But it's no basis for a healthy relationship in real life."

Lifting his head, Roan smiled at him a little. "That's a good point, actually."

"That doesn't mean I don't care about what you've gone through, or that I don't want to know. It's just that it doesn't matter in the long run. Day-to-day life isn't determined by childhood losses."

Roan shrugged and ran his hand through his hair, or tried to at least, but the product keeping it stylishly bent to his will didn't budge. He stuffed his hand between his knees. "It was nothing special. It's not a sob story. My dad and my mom weren't married, and one day he just left and didn't come back."

"How old were you?"

"Two."

"I'm sorry," Walker said. "That must've been hard."

Roan shook his head. "It really wasn't. I never knew any different."

Walker reached for him, putting his hand on Roan's thigh. The muscle bunched beneath his palm, then slowly eased. Roan swallowed hard, his Adam's apple dancing up and down. God, he was so pretty, his profile an artwork of contradictions. Sharp nose, full, luscious lips, strong jaw but long, thin eyebrows. Dark hair and pale, pale skin. He had a beauty spot on his cheekbone, and Walker wanted to taste it.

A week he'd spent admiring that beauty from afar. Too much time and no time at all.

"You want to go for a stroll?" Walker asked. Someone cleared his throat behind them and they both looked up. A camera man stood there, looking uncomfortable. "Let me guess, you go where we go?"

"It's okay," Roan said. "I'm tired. I just want to go to bed, to be honest."

"Five minutes," Walker said. "It's really windy out, so less bugs. Come on, little lion."

Roan smiled reluctantly and rose to his feet. His dark eyes met Walker's, and their gazes snagged, held. Walker hesitated, then threaded his fingers through Roan's.

The sound of the cicadas hit them as they stepped outside, and Walker hoped it'd ruin the sound for the filming. The wind was hot and tugged at their clothes. He led Roan down the steps and to a small trail that ran between the fields. He used to come here with Mike before his parents knew they were dating. It'd been a while since he thought about his ex, and he wondered how Mike was doing with his veterinary practice in the city.

"How are you holding up in there with the others?" Walker asked, squeezing Roan's hand lightly as he tilted his head toward the barn behind them.

"This whole thing is so surreal," Roan said. "It's a total mind fuck to be honest."

"Hey, slow down some, guys," the camera guys behind them called out. They both slowed their pace but didn't look back.

"It is. It makes me wonder if anyone here would even look at me twice under normal circumstances, you know?"

"Yeah, I know what you mean. It's an artificial environment. And they create this situation where you can't do anything but think you're falling in love. With the 'dream dates' and whatever." He made a face. "Not counting the noodling."

Walker pressed his hand to his heart. "That wasn't a dream date?"

"Fuck you," Roan murmured, laughing softly. "I have nightmares I'm going to die of salmonella poisoning."

"How are the bites?" Walker gently pulled them both to a halt and lifted Roan's hand. It was hard to see under the moonlight, but he could make out that the scrapes against the flesh of his thumb were gone.

"I used the antibiotic cream the nurse gave me and they healed right up."

"Hmm. Good." He traced the lines on Roan's palm, making his fingers curl slightly. "What do you think would've happened if we were just two guys who ran into each other out in the world?"

Roan's tired eyes lit up a little bit. "Well, that depends. Where do you run into guys around here?"

"Oh, I don't know. The feed store."

Roan laughed and then pretended to think about it, mouth pursed. "I'm not sure. I'd probably be in the alpaca feed section. Or the llama feed. Maybe those special sheep, whatever they're called. Something furry and fancy. I wouldn't be anywhere near the cow feed section."

Walker wanted to laugh, but he held it back. "Cows not good enough for you, huh? Yeah, I can see that. Okay. I got this. Maybe I spotted you from a mile away. Maybe I followed you to your deserted alpaca feed corner of the store."

Roan's lashes fluttered. "Yeah? What would've happened then?"

Walker ducked his head and grinned. He loved that Roan was playing along. "I'm a gentleman, so I'd have pretended to be interested in your silly alpacas. Then I'd ask you for a drink. Dinner maybe."

"Wait, wait. How would you even know I was gay? Isn't it pretty dangerous to assume something like that in the South?"

"Oh, baby," Walker murmured. He dared to let his hand slip up Roan's forearm. His sleeves were rolled up, and damn. He might be on the verge of skinny, but he had strong forearms, like he'd played a lot of tennis at some point. His broad wrists were covered in dark hair, and his skin was surprisingly soft over that muscle. "In those jeans? I'd know."

"Then what would happen?" Roan asked, sounding a little breathless.

"Would you say yes to dinner?"

"Duh."

Walker laughed under his breath. "I'd take you someplace nice. For oysters. Do you like oysters?"

"Never had them."

Walker's jaw dropped. "You are fucking kidding me."

"Nope. Raw oysters? I'm not convinced. I'll try anything once, but I'm silently judging you for liking slimy things."

They were still standing close, and Walker had cupped his hand under Roan's elbow. Walker eased his thumb into the hot, slightly damp crease and his mouth went a little dry.

"Oysters," he said, voice husky. "You'll love them, I promise you. I'd even mind my manners on our date and not stuff my face. I want to make a good impression, after all."

"So you can get into my pants?"

Walker lifted his head, suddenly dead serious. "So you'll want to see me again."

"Okay." Roan whispered, swaying closer. "Then what?"

"I take you home. I debate whether or not I can get away with kissing you, but I decide against it. It will be so much better after the second date when I take you dancing. There's this bar where they play a mix of Latin and local music. We'll get swept away in the heat of it. It's sensual and intense. Everyone's hot and the energy in the air tastes like sex. I'll want to taste *you*." Walker's voice dropped to a whisper and he was lost in the moment, almost seeing Roan's skin glistening with sweat, clothes sticking to his body, narrow hips undulating against him. "It'll be torture to watch you and feel you and not touch you the way I'm dying to."

"Jesus," Roan groaned and jerked back, the spell broken.

"Too much?" Walker whispered.

"No, it's just..." Roan stepped close again and brought his free hand to Walker's chest. His pinky slipped between the buttons and touched the center of his breastbone. The point of contact radiated heat all through his chest, down his arms where goosebumps rose, and straight through his stomach into his dick. "I wish that was how we'd met. I wish this wasn't—"

"A show."

Roan looked down and nodded. Slowly, Walker trailed his hand up Roan's arm, over his shoulder and applied some gentle pressure. Roan came easily, stepping up against him, and Walker stared into the night. As they hugged each other tight, the cicadas sang loudly, the night hung close and warm against them, and stars spanned out all the way to the horizon.

With Roan's breath fanning his neck, Walker wished it could be true too.

And then the camera guy whistled under his breath and said, "The producers are going to love this."

WHEN WALKER AND Roan wandered back inside, most of the others had gone to bed already. John hung out on one of the couches, talking to Victor and Peter, but that was it. Most of the crew was gone.

"Night, little lion," Walker said. Roan began to back away, hands stuffed in the back of his tight jeans. The effect wasn't lost on Walker.

"Sweet dreams, cowboy," Roan murmured, grinning, then turned away and took the stairs two at a time.

Walker waved at the others as they called out their goodbyes. He dug his keys out of his pocket and was about to unlock the Ford when he heard suppressed, heated voices. Walker frowned and quietly made his way to the side of the house, where he spotted Ben and Molly stuck in some kind of standoff. Part of him wanted to interfere, but he figured it wasn't his business, so he went back to his car.

He opened the door, but turned around when footsteps came running up behind him. The porch light had gone out, but Walker recognized Ben's big body and ever present white T-shirt.

"Hey, where y'at?" Walker asked, slipping into Louisiana slang. "I mean, what's up?"

"Hey, I'm glad I caught you. I was wondering if we could talk for a second."

Walker glanced around but Molly was nowhere to be seen. "You okay?"

"Yeah, I—yeah." Ben ran a hand through his hair and let it fall. He reached out and gently hooked one finger through Walker's belt loop but wouldn't look him in the eye. "Do you think we could talk inside for a second? I'm being eaten alive out here."

Did Ben want to go home during the next horseshoe ceremony or something? Maybe that was what the argument with Molly had been about. "Sure, come on."

All the lights in the living room had been turned off apart from one small table light in the corner. John and the other guys were nowhere in sight now. Walker reached for one of the big switches, but Ben stopped him.

"What is it?" Walker asked. Ben gripped his hand tighter and stared at their entwined fingers.

"I just wanted to say…" Ben took a deep breath, and his big chest expanded. "I really like you. And I want...I want to kiss you. If that's okay. I mean... I know you like Roan. It's pretty obvious. And who wouldn't? But this is a...a safe place to try it, do you know what I mean?"

"Ben..." Walker began, a little dumbstruck. He wanted to say this wasn't right, that Ben should wait for a real date and man who really cared about him. But Ben was a grown-up and he could make his own decisions. Walker didn't really want to kiss Ben, not like he wanted Roan, but he felt for the guy. Still, he hung back.

The decision was taken out of his hands when Ben stepped up, cupped his large hands around Walker's face and kissed him.

It startled Walker so much he didn't instantly react. But it felt nice, and Ben was so tentative, he didn't have the heart to shove him away. He gently touched Ben's arm when he pulled back a little. Ben moved in again, eyes squeezed closed, tense all over but ready to try again. "Shh," Walker said against his mouth. "Relax. It's okay."

Ben stepped away and still wouldn't look at him.

"Look, if that still didn't feel like you were expecting, it doesn't mean—"

"That's not it," Ben whispered and took another step back.

Walker blinked at him, confused, and then saw something move at the edge of his vision. He leaned aside a little to look behind Ben and saw Roan standing there. He had his hand pressed to his mouth, his eyes wide.

"Roan," Walker said.

Roan shook his head and fled upstairs.

A red, ugly rage curled up hot in Walker's stomach. "Did you set me up?" he said very quietly. "Did you arrange that? You and Molly?"

"She made me," Ben said. "I'm really sorry. I didn't really want to do it. But she said—"

"Save it," Walker told him and pushed past Ben only to find Molly standing in his way.

"Not now, Walker."

"Get out of my way, Molly."

Molly shook her head, and Walker vaguely noticed how she didn't look like her cocky, assured self. "Not this time. I mean it, Walker. Leave him alone."

Walker balled his fists and glared at Molly. He wanted to make a scene and storm up the stairs to Roan, but everyone would hear, and Molly would probably find a way to film it. He'd talk to Roan tomorrow. As he spun on his heels and passed Ben, he said, "I'm sending you home. I don't care what the producers want."

"Don't worry," Ben told him. He looked disgusted and beaten. "I don't want to stay."

CHAPTER 12

ROAN WANDERED INTO the stables and spotted a bunch of apples in a bucket just inside the door. He grabbed a nice one and peered in every stall until he reached the end and found Callie. She neighed softly when she spotted him and walked forward, head bobbing. She nosed his hand and he gently stroked her blonde mane out of her eyes.

"You want this?" he murmured. "No? You don't want an apple?" She lipped at his hand with more insistence, and he grinned, opening up so she could take a bite. "It's been a boring day, Callie," he said. "I bet you had lots of fun frolicking around in the fields earlier this morning, huh? You better watch out because there's lots of dangerous animals around who wouldn't mind taking a bite out of you."

Callie blew air out of her nose, and he offered her the apple again. Technically, he wasn't supposed to be here, but Chad had been asleep all day, Peter had been working out for hours now, Ben was hiding on the screened-in porch, and everyone else was on a mystery date with Walker. He'd been too antsy to sit inside, the sight of Ben kissing Walker the night before burned on his eyelids whenever he closed them.

For the millionth time he told himself he didn't care whom Walker kissed. It wasn't like Walker had taken Ben out on a walk and said all that stuff to him. The kiss was for the show. He knew that. But the sight of Ben's hands on Walker's face, the intimate darkness, no big cameras, no nothing... Just Ben and Walker, kissing so softly it was as if time itself had held its breath.

He'd hated it. And he hadn't been able to bring himself to confront

Ben.

So after a day of working himself into all kinds of knots, he'd taken the opportunity of a distracted, skeleton set of crew to slip out of the house and wander alone in the general direction of the farm. He wasn't supposed to, and he could get in trouble for it, but there were cameras all over the property. It wasn't like he would be unobserved. Though he'd disconnected his mic, and that would probably get him in a load of shit, but so what? What were they gonna do? Send him home? He doubted it very much. He and Ben and Walker were the romantic triangle they wanted and all the drama they had going right now.

When he got close to the farmhouse he'd spotted a woman with gray hair hanging out laundry in the backyard, so he'd slipped into the barn before she could see him. Now he was talking to Callie like she was his therapist.

"Where do you think he took them on the group date? I know I shouldn't be jealous or anything, but God. This is such a weird situation to be in. I kinda like him, you know? More than kinda. But everything is so fucked up."

When the apple was gone, Callie nudged him with her nose so he stroked her face and kept away an insistent fly. Her eyes fluttered closed after a while, and Roan just stood there, taking in the comforting horse scent wrapped up in clean stables.

"Your life isn't complicated at all, is it?" he murmured to her. "Sleep, eat, go outside. Ride around with silly humans on your back. Unconditional love for your owner, and he loves you unconditionally back." Callie stepped forward a little more and hooked her head over his shoulder. A little surprised, Roan hugged his arms around her neck and held on. "I wish someone would love me like that," he whispered, burying his nose in the scratchy but still soft hair of her neck.

"Keep feeding her apples and she will."

"Jesus!" Roan startled, and Callie stamped a hoof, backing away a little. He spun around to find Walker leaning against the opposite wall, one knee bent, boot propped up behind him. He had his arms crossed and his cowboy hat tilted over his eyes, but Roan could see his smirk. "Again with the private conversation," he said.

Walker burst into a laugh and tilted his hat back. His tawny eyes shone brightly with amusement. "With a horse?" he asked. He pushed himself away from the wall and ambled up to Roan, taking his time. He came to stand right beside him, shoulders brushing. "I shouldn't laugh. She's a good listener." He stroked Callie's nose, and she nodded her head, giving a satisfied blow. Walker glanced at Roan from under his cowboy hat. "About last night…"

"You don't have to explain," Roan quickly said, knowing he sounded mulish but unable to help it. "You can kiss whoever you want."

"That so?" Walker sounded even more amused, so Roan glared at him.

"Yes."

"You didn't care at all?"

"Of course not."

"What if I told you Ben surprised me?"

Roan tried to keep his face blank and reached for Callie again to give himself something to do. "Intellectually, I know it was all a set-up, but seeing you kiss him bothered me. I guess I can admit that."

Walker sighed. "I didn't want that kiss, little lion."

"I know. It was just…" Roan shrugged.

"You said it was a set-up, and you're right, but how'd you come to be there to see it?"

"Peter lost a favorite cufflink, and we were looking for it in the bedroom when Molly wandered by and told me she'd spotted it downstairs. I came down to find it when I found you instead."

Walker's eyes widened. "You mean Peter was in on it too?"

"I doubt it," Roan said. "He was still looking for the cufflink this morning. I think Molly needed an excuse to get me down there, and used the moment to produce drama." He rubbed his face sheepishly. "I guess she got it, huh?"

Walker looked around. "What are you doing out here, Roan?"

"Needed to get out. I couldn't take it anymore." Roan smiled, a gleam in his eye. "Guess I've got a bad boy streak. Hope you don't mind."

"I noticed and I like it."

"You did?"

"Those nipple piercings gave it away, baby."

Roan flushed. "Speaking of…what are *you* doing out here? I thought you were on a group date?"

"It's over. Thank God."

"Yeah?"

Walker smiled slyly, and Roan shivered a bit despite the ever present humid heat.

"Where are John and Molly? And the camera guys?"

"Off with Andy looking over the footage they got. I'm free for the rest of the day. Not even mic'ed. Thought I might take a horse out for a ride."

"Wow. So you're not mic'ed right now?"

"Nope."

"Me either." Roan's stomach danced wildly. "Took mine off too."

Walker tsked at him. "You'll get in trouble for that."

Roan shrugged. He nodded up at the motion-detection cameras above them. The red light showing they were filming…but the question was who was watching? "They'll probably be here any minute to scream at us and record everything we do and say."

Walker tipped his hat back. "Maybe. And maybe not. The horses set off those cameras all the time. I think they've stopped paying much attention to the stable feed." He considered Callie with a smile. "I have an idea. You want to go for a ride?"

"Oh." Roan cocked his head. "Like for a date?"

"Yeah. Just you and me."

"I thought we didn't have the insurance for that? Won't Andy mind?"

"Andy's not here. Yet."

Roan swallowed thickly. "I'm not very good on a horse."

Walker's smile widened, his eyes burning with intensity. "We won't go fast. Just fast enough that they can't catch up to us until we want them to."

"What will Ben say about you sneaking off with me?" Roan asked, hating that he was showing his cards just by asking.

"Ben's not here either."

Oh. So if he was here, then what? He'd be the one asked on this impromptu rule-breaking getaway? Roan took a step away from Walker and crossed his arms. "I don't know. I don't think we should risk—"

Reaching out, Walker put his hand on Roan's shoulder and rolled the tight muscle between his fingers, effectively pinning Roan in place. "That didn't come out right. I don't want to be here with Ben. And I certainly don't want to be here with Andy, or Molly, or John. I want to be here with you. Alone. Let's go for a ride. Talk a little. Just you and me."

"It's getting dark," Roan said, his throat feeling dry.

Laughing a little, Walker said, "Not for a while yet. You afraid to be alone with me, Roan?"

Oh, God. Roan shivered a little again. "Yes."

"And why's that?"

"Do you need to ask?"

Walker stood so close Roan could smell him. He was just wearing jeans and a shirt with its sleeves rolled up, but he smelled sophisticated, and Roan wondered if he'd changed out of a suit from his mystery group date before he came here. Or maybe he was smelling of one of the other contestants. Roan shook the jealous thought aside.

Walker let go of his shoulder and softly moved his knuckles along Roan's jaw. "No," he said. "I don't need to ask." Then he abruptly turned away and went into the tack room. Needing a minute to get his breathing under control, Roan stayed behind.

When Walker returned, Roan helped him saddle Callie up, and then did the same with a big black horse that wouldn't stand still.

"Just so you know, I'm not riding this one," Roan said, and Walker laughed.

"No, you're not. Whiskey would run circles around you within a minute. He's my ranch hand Marlon's pride and joy. Normally, I ride Cormac, but he's out in the pastures today. Don't worry. Whiskey tolerates me well enough, don't you, boy?"

Whiskey stamped his hoof, danced to the side, and jerked his head up and down. Roan jumped and stepped back. "I'll just wait over here," he said, and Walker grinned at him.

"Go ahead and take Callie outside. I'll be right there. No time to lose."

"Um. Okay." He gripped Callie's reins like Ben had shown him last time and led her out of the stable, relaxing a little when she followed sedately.

The woman was still out there, doing something to the flowers attached to her windowsills. At the sound of Callie's hooves, she turned and froze for a second when she spotted Roan. He gave her a sheepish little wave and even from where he was standing he saw her beam a smile at him and wave back.

"That's my step-mama," Walker said, stepping to his side with Whiskey. "Want to meet her?"

"Uh, I thought we weren't allowed to talk to your family."

Walker smirked. "Convenient."

"Also, we don't have time. They'll probably be here any minute."

"Even more convenient. Here, let me give you a leg up." He slipped his arm through Whiskey's reins, then cupped his hands together and bent down a little. Roan hesitated, then steadied himself on Callie's saddle and put his knee in Walker's palms. A little heave, and he found himself on the horse. Walker maneuvered his foot into the stirrup.

"I got the other side," Roan said as Walker checked the cinch.

When they were both saddled, Walker pointed toward a dirt trail that led behind the farm. "We'll go down there. It's a little loop that's very pretty and they can't follow us in a car. We can walk side by side. Don't slip behind me, because Callie's a good girl, but with Whiskey she can get a little competitive, and she might want to have a little fun racing.

"Oh." Crap, maybe this wasn't such a good idea after all.

"You'll be fine, little lion," Walker said, smiling. "Hold your reins gently, squeeze your legs to go, lean back to stop. That's all there is to it."

"Right," Roan said dubiously, but he squeezed his legs when Walker started off, and Callie obediently fell into step with them. They were out of the farm yard and down the path without any sign of producers in pursuit. His heart pounded. Were they really doing this? And were they going to get away with it?

"TELL ME A little about your family," Roan said. "I feel like I don't know anything about you that hasn't been fed to me by a PR person."

Walker glanced at him under his hat. "I hope that's not true."

"Well." Roan pretended to think about it. "I know you like to stick your hands down fish throats and that you like to eat slimy things." He flashed Walker a cheeky grin. "But I'm going to need more than that to decide whether or not I want to stick around."

"Oh yeah?" Walker eased Whiskey closer, reached out and traced his fingertips along Roan's thigh. "I can think of something to convince you, and it ain't talking."

Roan gulped and fixed his eyes on the trail ahead of them as Walker laughed and moved Whiskey a little away again. Did he say things like that to Ben? To any of the others? Roan took in the rolling landscape, the cows peacefully grazing in the distance, and tilted his face toward the setting sun, relishing in the diminishing heat, even though it was still humid enough to make him slide around in his clothes.

"You're very easy with all this, aren't you?" Roan watched Walker's thigh move under his worn Wranglers and wished he had the courage to reach out and touch the rolling muscles too.

"With what?"

"Being gay. I thought that wasn't a picnic around these parts."

"It's not." Whiskey did a little dance like he sidestepped something and Callie reared her head but otherwise didn't startle. "Oh hush now, it's just the sun reflecting in a puddle," Walker said to them. He glanced back at Roan. "It's not easy. But it helps that my family's been here for generations. We owned a lot more land back in the day than we do now, so my family's well known. We kind of didn't make a big deal about it, and if someone doesn't want to deal with me because they care about who I sleep with, there's plenty of others who need my business."

"A take it or leave it kinda guy, huh?"

Walker grinned at him. "Oh, I wouldn't say that."

By the look on his face, Roan knew he was walking into something, but he asked anyway. "What do you mean?"

"I've been known to take it on occasion." He looked Roan up and down. "If the offer's right."

Roan laughed, going red to the tips of his ears. "Does it ever get cooler around here?" he asked, not caring how blatant he was about changing the subject.

Walker snorted but didn't call him out. "In winter, yes. Summers are brutal."

Callie swayed beneath him, and Roan felt the odd urge to close his eyes, so he did. It felt a little unsettling at first, but he eased into her rhythm, feeling every movement of her muscles beneath him.

"You look good on a horse, little lion," Walker murmured, and

Roan's eyes snapped open. Heat traveled up his throat.

He took in Walker, riding one handed, hat tipped back, his hair slightly sweaty underneath. He owned that saddle like he'd been born in it. "So do you, cowboy."

Walker ducked his head and settled his hat a little lower over his eyes. "You want to know more about my family, huh?" he asked.

"Well, about you really. Growing up here. What was that like?"

"There's a lot I loved about it, and a lot I hated. Sometimes it came down to the same things."

Roan waited, and when Walker didn't go on he said, "Wow, you're an open book, aren't you?"

Walker laughed. "About some things." Then he scratched at the stubble on his jaw, and Roan was the one to laugh. "It was hard work growing up on a farm," he eventually said. "Early starts and late nights and sometimes I hated it, especially when I was a teenager and I had friends who went to movies and on dates and hung out together all the time. I didn't have much of that. But then when I figured out I was gay…those years in high school were real tough and this place became a refuge."

"Did you get bullied?" Roan asked softly.

"No, but I felt isolated and worried I might get beaten up if anyone found out. Going to college changed all that, and then when I came back I found out the odd temporary ranch hand was sometimes willing to give a different sort of hand too."

Roan rolled his eyes.

"I had a boyfriend for a while, too, and I stopped messing around with the hands since I took over from Dad, though. It's not fittin'."

"So how did you make the leap from handsy ranch hands to a reality show like this?"

Walker leaned back in his saddle, and Whiskey slowed to a stop. Roan flailed for a second, then did the same, although he suspected Callie only stopped because she wanted to.

"Meeting people when you're gay down here isn't easy. Meeting them when you're a farmer is pretty much impossible. No one wants to do this kind of backbreaking work for hardly any pay anymore." He looked away, took his hat off for a second, ran his hand through his hair, and plonked the hat back on his head. "I honestly never thought they'd pick me as a candidate. Hell, to be honest, I never even applied. My ranch hand did, and Tessa, my step-mom, she was all for it when he told her."

"Are you two close?"

"Yeah. My mom died when I was a baby. Never knew her."

"I get that. Like I said, my dad left when I was two, and I never knew any other way."

"Tessa came along when I was a kid, and she's been like my mama ever since. She's amazing, really. Helps around the ranch and keeps up with all the office work around here." Walker rubbed his neck and shot Roan a sideways look. "I want to be honest with you, Roan."

"I'd like that, too."

"Okay, well, everything isn't what it seems here on Reed Ranch. We've got debts here. The wealthy, successful rancher they've played up on camera isn't real. A couple of hurricanes hit us hard, and we've had a lot of losses. So when the call came that they wanted me to be the bachelor for the show…" Walker's jaw looked tense and his shoulders rounded.

"I'm not judging," Roan said, risking his balance by reaching out and patting Walker's thigh. He wobbled precariously when Callie did a little sidestep and righted himself quickly. "It's all bullshit, this show. Every last one of us knows that. And you're doing it all for understandable reasons. It's okay, Walker. I get it."

Walker gave him a quick smile and nudged Whiskey forward again. The cicadas' song began to thicken in volume as the sun dropped nearer to the horizon. The air smelled sweet and humid, like some herb he recognized but couldn't quite pinpoint. "What about you?" Walker asked. "What made you quit college?"

191

Roan chewed on his lip and stared at the red and orange horizon. The fading sunlight glistened in what must be various ponds in the distance, and Roan wondered if they were full of gators. The truth was on the tip of his tongue, and he wanted to share it with Walker, but he also didn't. He never wanted Walker to think he'd given him the 'sob story' as Molly called it just so he could win.

"I ran out of money," he said and tried to smile. "It's no big deal. I'll just have to work for a while until I have some more funds and then I'll go back to finish it."

Walker nodded at him. "You should do that. You're a bright guy, Roan. If more school would make you happy, you should pursue it. Is that why you're here? For the funds to go back to school?"

Roan blinked at the sunset and nodded slowly. He thought of his mom's proud smile when he got the acceptance letter to his first choice university back when he graduated high school. He thought of the guilt lurking in her eyes when he'd left Grad school to work at a coffee shop and help out after she got sick. "Yeah. That's why I'm here."

Walker's eyes softened when he looked at Roan. "Like you said, that's an understandable reason."

Roan wished he could turn back the clock by half a minute and tell Walker the truth. But now that he hadn't, he didn't know how to take it back. "We should head back before we piss the producers off so much that we blow both of our chances at getting the money we need."

Walker nodded and opened his mouth to say something more, but then he closed it again. "Home now," he said to Whiskey, turning him around.

Roan was grateful when Callie followed.

ANDY, DRESSED IN pink shorts and sleeveless tank, stood outside the barn with John, Molly, two camera guys, and with his hands on his hips.

"Anyone going to tell me what you two were thinking?"

"We wanted to go on a ride," Walker said.

"I see that. Just what were you off doing together?"

Roan plastered on his most innocent face. "Who says we were together?"

Andy snorted. "Right. Like you saddled that horse all by yourself. For fuck's sake." He shook his head and wagged his finger. "If I didn't have so much time and energy invested in this thing already, I'd put an end to this right now. We could be sued by the other contestants, you realize, for allowing this. Giving Roan an edge."

"He already had an edge," Walker said.

Andy ignored him. "Whatever. I swear I'd put an end to this entire thing, and I should after what you've done here today. But my husband would kill me! He's wanted me to do a gay *Bachelor* for years and this was going to be my anniversary present for him! You—and you—" he said, pointing at them hysterically. "Don't fuck this up for me. Understand?" Then he stomped off, screaming at John and Molly to follow him. The camera guys stared off after them in confusion, having apparently never been ordered to start filming. Probably Andy didn't want evidence of what had happened in case his worst-case scenario came about.

"You think we're going to be okay?" Roan asked.

Walker nodded but kept his eyes on the ground and his hat pulled low. "Seems like it. Without me and you, he doesn't have a show, and I think he really wants one."

"Yeah." Roan's stomach churned. He hadn't considered the implications of how the other contestants might react to him sneaking time alone with Walker.

They took the horses into the stables and the camera guys followed, filming, but there was no boom mic and they still weren't wired up with body mics. One camera guy stepped into some shit that Whiskey had dropped while Andy was yelling, and the other stopped to steady him.

Walker pulled Roan closer and said, "Look, my dad's going to be in the hospital later this week."

"What?" Roan gasped, surprised. "I'm sorry. What's going on?"

"It's okay. He was diagnosed with diabetes not so long ago. He hasn't been sticking to the diet or taking his meds like he should. He had a scary episode earlier this week," Walker said, frowning. "The diagnosis has been tough on him because he's never been sick, and now suddenly he has to adapt his whole life around it."

"I bet it's tough on you and your step-mom too."

Walker didn't say anything to that. He glanced back to where the camera guys were still struggling with the horse shit. He leaned in closer and went on quietly, "The point is, my folks will be out of the farm-house for a night while my Dad has some tests done at the hospital in LaFayette."

Roan's brows arched up.

"So maybe while they're gone you could slip out and—"

Roan's throat went dry. "Why, Mr. Reed, you haven't even taken me out on a proper date yet."

"Roan, we don't have time to joke." He looked pointedly toward the camera guys who were steadying themselves, wiping their shitty shoes in the dirt, and starting toward the stables to resume shooting, sound or no sound. "Will you meet me?"

Roan stared at Walker's sun-lightened brown eyes and tried to say no. After what Andy had just said, the legal potentialities for them all if the other contestants found out... "Yes, okay. What time? Where?" His heart thundered with excitement.

"I'll leave the farm house kitchen entrance open. Ten o'clock late enough?"

Roan nodded. "They're usually out of the suitors' house, except for a skeleton crew, by nine. What day?"

"Wednesday."

The camera guys were on them then, so Walker led Whiskey into his stall and pointed toward Callie's. "Just lead her in there, I'll be with you in a sec."

"Can I take off her saddle already?"

"Sure."

Roan ran his hands down Callie's neck and peered at her saddle. His blood was pounding at the thought of what they'd planned. Excitement? Trepidation? He wasn't sure. But he was going to do it—sneak out, meet with Walker again, and throw caution to the wind. Because there was something in him that couldn't say no. Not to Walker's earnest eyes and hopeful smile.

Remaining very aware of where Callie's hooves were, he lifted a flap with shaking hands and found the buckles he'd seen Walker fiddle with before. It took a little strength but he managed to undo them, and he pulled the saddle with its little blankets over her back. The strap hit her side and she stomped her back hoof, but otherwise didn't move. "Sorry," Roan whispered. "I guess I did that wrong, huh?"

"She can be a bit of a diva in her stable," Walker said, smiling at him. "Here, give me that. I'll put it away."

Roan hung on to the reins until Walker returned to take care of them. "Can she have another apple?"

"Sure. Bring one for Whiskey too or he'll get jealous."

"Okay."

By the time Roan came back, the camera guys dogging his every step, Walker was closing Callie's stable. He took one of the apples, bit into it himself, then fed it to Callie.

Roan grinned at the happy crunchy noises coming from the horse.

Walker turned around and regarded him intently. Then he took hold of Roan's hand and rubbed his thumb over his knuckles. "You're a good guy, little lion," he whispered and let go.

"Goddammit, they still aren't wired!" Molly's voice sliced through the air, and she stomped in with an enraged expression on her face and body mics in her hands.

Their privacy was over for now.

WEEK FOUR

Encounters of the Hot Kind

CHAPTER 13

WALKER FIDDLED WITH his phone, obsessively checking the weather, while his parents talked to the doctor.

They'd invited Walker to come with them to the hospital so that Tessa wouldn't have to repeat everything the doctor said later. He'd been happy to go, getting out of filming a "date" with Ben, which would have been awkward as hell after the kiss. One of the few loopholes in the contract was for immediate family illness, specifically a hospital stay. So there was nothing Andy, John, or Molly could do about it. They'd had to rejig their whole schedule, but, in the end, Walker got his day away with his parents, and the suitors endured playing board games like Twister and Monopoly in between special interviews.

Walker was grateful his parents had let him come along. It helped to know what was going on, but he also knew how much it pained his dad to be seen like this. In the hospital bed, wearing nothing but a gown, he looked like the old man he was, not the fighting fit cowboy he'd been his whole life. It was an adjustment for all of them.

They'd already corrected his insulin, and, despite the scary episode that had prompted these tests, his condition was stable. He'd been lectured most of the day about the importance of his diet and actually taking his meds, and he looked properly chagrined. Tessa, for her part, had been taking copious notes.

After replying *yes* to the latest wave of frantic text messages from John and Andy asking if he'd be back for filming tomorrow, Walker turned off his phone and told Tessa he was going for a soda. A few minutes later, she joined him by the vending machine in the waiting area, sinking into the plastic chair beside his. He stood and thumbed some more quarters into vending machine slot, selecting a Dr. Pepper for Tessa, and opening it for her before he plunked back down in the creaky chair. He took another sip of his Coke and let her be the one to break their comfortable silence.

Tessa shook her head and sighed. "That man."

"He needs to stop trying so hard to get back to his regular work routine."

"He needs to stick to his diet and check his blood sugar regularly." She took a pull of soda, obviously relishing the taste. "I've been eating better than he has. They've given us a lot of new websites to look at, though, and forums with support groups. Not that he'll use them."

"Nope."

"And hopefully these tests will show that he's not done too much damage to himself in the last few months."

Walker nodded.

With an irritated sigh, she pushed herself upright. "Stubborn ass, but I think the doctor and this latest episode made quite the impression on him. He swears he's going to pay attention to his diet and insulin. At least until the next time all goes well for a while and the tough cowboy thinks he's cured."

"He does realize there is no cure, right?"

Tessa lifted a square shoulder. "You know what he's like. I love him to death, but he's so stubborn he could quarrel with a wall and win."

Walker couldn't argue with that. He glanced at the time. He should be leaving soon to get things ready for his meeting with Roan. His stomach did a little dance like his horse Cormac in the sunshine. Clearing his throat, he asked, "So Dad's still spending the night here, right?"

Sipping her coffee, Tessa nodded. "Yes. There're still those tests to run, and he's still under observation until tomorrow afternoon. They want to see what his blood sugar does after he's eaten a couple of meals."

"You're staying with him?" he confirmed, his pulse racing. It was ridiculous, but he felt like a teenager trying to get away with sneaking a boy into the house while his parents were out. His foot jiggled as a pulse of excitement throbbed.

"Yes, I think so. I hate to leave him alone. Unless you need me at the farm?"

"No," Walker said. He ran his hand through his hair and glanced at his phone again. Already six o'clock and he hadn't eaten anything yet. It was a long drive back to the farm. He needed a shower too. If he planned to meet Roan at ten…

"I should go on home, Tess. You gonna be okay for the night?"

"Oh yes, you have a cast of thousands waiting for you back there." She winked. "Was that why your phone was all lit up? They need you back there?"

"Something like that, yeah." He pulled his phone out and turned it on out of habit, then regretted it once he saw more new messages. "Andy's on the warpath right now. Not about my being here tonight, but about, uh…people not following all the rules." He played with a thread on the knee of his jeans, glad he was facing away from Tessa and she couldn't see his face.

"Was that someone you?"

"Little bit."

She laughed. "I see. Are you playing by the rules being here?"

"Yep. It's in my contract. Parent in hospital means a get out of jail free card."

She looked him over speculatively. "And tonight? You planning on playing by the rules tonight?"

He felt his cheeks grow warm. "The show's rules could use some breaking."

She chuckled. "I see. You got a hot date, baby?" Tessa asked, smirking. "I thought you weren't allowed to see the contestants without cameras present."

"Yeah, well...I'm not."

Tessa laughed and patted his arm. "Don't let that stop you."

"And, again, I'm not."

She started laughing but then grew serious again. "So, you and that boy I saw you riding off with?"

Walker wanted to roll his eyes, but suddenly he was grinning too hard. "Yeah. Roan. He's fun."

"I was wondering who was making you smile like that lately. Nice to see, baby." Tessa peered at him intently. "Is it more than fun?"

"Maybe." Laughing, Walker covered his face, scrubbed at it, then dropped his hands. "I don't know? I really like him. But this show messes with your mind. If I'd met him anywhere else..."

"But you didn't. And you never would've. This show has been a pain in the ass for all of us, but that doesn't mean it can't bring good things."

"Money."

"Ye-es," Tessa said slowly. "But maybe Roan too. It's good to be cautious, I agree, but don't let something wonderful slip through your fingers because you're afraid."

Walker wrapped his arm around his step-mama's shoulder and gave her a squeeze. "Thanks, Tess,"

She gave him a little wave as he stood and sauntered away. He slowed at the corner and blew her a kiss before braving the evening heat to go find his Ford.

If he drove a little faster than the speed limit dictated all the way back to the farm, it was probably because thinking of seeing Roan alone made his heart jump and his guts wriggle like wild things. He hadn't felt this way since Mike. And back then he'd been in love.

He aimed the Ford for home and didn't dwell on that thought too much.

AT TEN OH five, the kitchen door opened and Roan ducked inside. Walker's heart leapt to see him, and his blood raced with excitement at the risk they were taking, too. If they got caught tonight, Walker wasn't sure Andy's desire to see the show finished could compensate for the way the outcome had obviously been compromised. Because there was no way he was going to choose any other suitor as the winner now.

"Hey," Roan breathed. "Sorry I'm late. It was harder to slip out than I thought it would be."

"I'm just glad you're here."

Roan leaned back against the kitchen door, the long, pale line of his throat shadowed by his jaw in the low light.

"Gotta keep the lights out," Walker said. "Or they'll see us moving around in here. And I'm not actually supposed to be here. I'm supposed to still be at the hospital."

"Ah." Roan looked like a skittish horse, and Walker wanted to soothe him.

He stepped forward, reached for his hand, and twined their fingers together. Roan relaxed a little then, but he kept his eyes down, not meeting Walker's gaze. "Nervous, little lion?"

"Yes."

"Me, too."

Roan's mouth twitched with a small smile then, and Walker was satisfied.

His hands were soft, with none of the scars and calluses Walker had. He stroked the skin until he caught sight of the one scar on the back of Roan's wrist. "What's this?"

Roan winced and pulled his hand away. "Just a burn." When Walker waited, he went on, covering the scar with one hand. "From a coffee machine."

"That must've been some coffee machine."

"Yeah, in a coffeeshop. That's what I do since leaving school. Serve coffee to people." His fingertips went white. "Nice career, huh?"

Walker reached out and gently pulled Roan's hand away. He eased the white marks on his wrist until they went red, then faded. "A job's a job, Roan. The idea that in order to be happy your work has to be your life's calling is a myth. Your job doesn't diminish you as a person. At least you're productive. And you can set your mind to finding something different whenever you're ready for it."

"Yeah. Maybe."

Walker rubbed Roan's hand a little more. "I have a plan for to-night."

Roan peered at Walker. "That's your noodling face. Oh my God, what are you planning now?"

Walker invaded his space and grinned, pecking him quickly on the cheek. "Now, why would I go and spoil my fun by ruining the surprise?"

He'd realized that he wouldn't be able to have Roan in the house for long, not without lights and movement alerting any observing crew or producers to the fact that Walker was home and not alone. With just his Ford out front, and Tessa's Jeep noticeably missing, that would bring up a ton of questions in the morning.

So he'd texted Marlon with a favor and now he hoped Roan would go along with it.

"Wait here," he said, tugging Roan out to the kitchen porch. "I'll be right back. Try not to let anyone see you."

"Be quick then," Roan whispered, gripping his own elbows like he was cold, even though the air was still warm.

"I will."

It only took him a moment to jog around the side of the house and climb up on the animal Marlon had left hitched there.

Walker rolled his shoulders as he sat astride Cormac. His skin tingled with nervous excitement, and he tried to shake it off. "Get a grip," he mumbled, and Cormac shook his head. "Sorry, pal. Not talking to you."

It'd been forever since he went for a bareback ride, and the fluid movements of the old quarter horse felt so soothing he promised himself to make more time for this in the future. But first he was going to take Roan out with him.

When he rounded the barn, he found Roan pacing anxiously on the kitchen porch and gave him a little tip of his hat.

"That's just not fair," Roan whispered, quietly climbing down the steps.

"What isn't?" Walker looked down at Roan and grinned.

"You on horseback with no saddle. Jesus."

"Ready to go for another ride?"

Roan's eyes flew wide, and he actually clutched his chest. "With you? Now? On one horse?"

"Obviously, when else, and yes." Walker jumped down and made a cup out of his hands. "Take a good handful of his mane."

Roan looked between Walker, the horse, and the driveway leading to the renovated barn, as if judging what was more dangerous. Finally, he put his hand in Cormac's mane. "I don't want to hurt him."

"You won't." He nudged Roan with his shoulder.

"But we're too heavy."

"He might look small, but he's very sturdy. C'mon."

"I didn't say he looked small—"

Walker straightened. They almost stood nose to nose, and Roan fell silent. "Why are you resisting when we both know you want to go?" he whispered and trailed his fingertips along Roan's jaw, rough with the day's stubble. "It'd be so much easier if you just gave in."

"I give in," Roan said. "Sometimes." His thick eyelashes fluttered down as he looked at his feet. They were long and fanned across his cheekbones, casting shadows.

"Wow," Walker whispered and barely resisted a low, admiring whistle.

"What?" Roan looked up with a coy smile.

"You're an irresistible temptation," Walker murmured. "Like the smell of that first cup of coffee before the sun's even up. Or the feeling of fresh sheets when you go to bed exhausted. I just want to...relish you."

Roan stared at him, the coy smile all gone. His eyes were wide and his lips parted. His chest heaved a little, like he was breathless. He lifted his hands and put his palms flat on Walker's chest. Slowly he rubbed his hands up, then down, thumbs pressing a little when they passed Walker's nipples.

"You can't say things like that and expect me to keep my hands to myself," he whispered.

A faint bang came from the road toward the suitor's barn, and they both startled but didn't move. No one came.

Walker cupped Roan's jaw, moved closer until he could feel the heat of Roan's mouth. His eyelids went half-lidded as he breathed him in, moving his head side to side a little, like he was inhaling fine wine. But Roan was better than wine, better than anything he'd ever smelled before, his scent intoxicating, sweet and spicy all at once. He wanted to taste him everywhere.

"Let's get out of here," he whispered. "Before someone comes outside."

A shuddery breath left Roan's lips, and he swallowed hard as he nodded and stepped away. "Up?" he asked, nodding toward Cormac.

Walker cupped his hands again to help. "Yes, up." He waited until Roan was settled, then reached to grip Roan's hand. "Brace yourself so I can pull myself up."

"Um. Okay." Roan loosed a surprised noise when Walker's weight nearly dragged him down again, but he compensated fast enough that Walker could swing a leg over Cormac's back.

"All right, little lion," Walker whispered in Roan's ear, taking advantage as he reached for the reins to press close to his back. "Sit back and relax." He eased Cormac into a walk, and gradually Roan sank against him until he sat cradled in Walker's arms.

Night had fallen in earnest but the moon was full and bathed the trail away from the house and out across the more forested parts of the property in plenty of light.

"This is nice," Roan murmured, letting his head rest on Walker's shoulder. He had a soft smile on his face as he eased completely and moved fluidly with the horse. Walker pressed his nose to Roan's temple and breathed. Roan turned his head a little and rubbed his cheekbone to Walker's jaw. Like an affectionate cat, Walker thought.

He gave Cormac his head, letting him move as he wanted, the undulations of his sure steps soothing.

"You smell good," Roan murmured, and Walker felt a jolt of lust spark in the pit of his stomach.

"I was just thinking the same." He moved his mouth over Roan's neck, not kissing exactly, but definitely teasing, a slow torturous promise of what might yet come to be.

Roan made a little noise, something awfully close to a moan. Walker moved against him, guided by the horse's gait, but pressing closer than he technically needed to.

"You're driving me insane," he whispered as his dick grew hard. Roan closed his eyes and the sound came again, a little more desperate now.

Cormac knew the ranch's trails as well or better than Walker did, so he didn't hesitate to pass the reins to one hand, lift his other palm and press it to Roan's stomach. He felt Roan hold his breath, then expel it in a rush. Walker's dick throbbed.

He moved his hand up Roan's chest, feeling the ridges of his muscles and bones dance as he squirmed a little. When Walker's thumb brushed one of the piercings, he couldn't stop himself anymore. The temptation that had teased him from the start became undeniable. Roan's nipple peaked beneath his touch. He took hold of the barbell and twisted gently.

"Ah." Roan arched against him, ass digging against Walker's groin and his head pressing harder against Walker's shoulder. So he did it again, twisting a little harder.

"When did you get these?" He moved his hand and tweaked Roan's other nipple.

Roan was already breathing with his mouth open in a small O, and Walker wanted to feed his thumb into the wet heat.

"I faked my way into a tattoo parlor when I was sixteen." Roan's voice sounded hoarse.

"Yeah? And did you like it?" Walker pressed his palm flat against Roan's sternum to feel his heart thud rapidly in his chest.

"The pain?" Roan laughed softly. "No. Do I like them played with now? God yes. It can make me come if I'm hot enough for it."

"Jesus." Walker pressed closer to Roan, mouth still open against his temple. He was breathing hard with arousal but couldn't stop. He flicked one of Roan's nipples and rode in against him, rubbing his erection against Roan's ass. "And are you? Hot enough for it right now?" He let go of Cormac's reins and pressed his hand to Roan's groin. He was rock hard and moaned when a shudder tore through him.

"God. Yeah. But these jeans are really tight."

"Then undo them."

Roan's eyes flew open. "Now? On this horse?"

"Yeah. I want to see. Don't you want to show me?" He pinched Roan's nipple a little harder as he pressed his mouth to Roan's ear.

"*Fuck.*" Roan keened against him, gripped Walker's thighs hard, and for a moment Cormac tried to speed up, but Walker sat back and slowed him down.

"You have to relax though," Walker murmured, "or Cormac will run off."

"That's easier said than done," Roan whispered. His iron grip on Walker's thigh eased and he ran his hands up and down, leaving tantalizing trails of heat behind. He twisted his head a little and looked at Walker. "You're serious about this."

Walker took the other barbell between thumb and forefinger and twisted. "What do you think?"

Chapter 14

ROAN SQUIRMED AS the zing of electricity shot straight to his balls. Walker couldn't know, but if he kept that up Roan's body would begin to jerk and shake uncontrollably with over-stimulation. It was a response he'd always been self-conscious of and he wasn't sure if he wanted Walker to see him like that right off the bat. On a horse of all things.

Walker let go of his nipple and eased the pressure off his dick. "Baby?" he asked. "If you're not okay with this, we don't have to."

"It's not that," Roan whispered, because, God, now that Walker's hands were gone he needed them back. Now. "I'm just…"

"Shy?" Walker murmured. His breath rushed hotly against Roan's cheek and he closed his eyes again, relaxing slightly. He rubbed his hands over Walker's thighs, enjoying how the muscles rolled beneath those worn jeans. His cowboy exuded strength and confidence, and Roan wanted nothing more than to just give in to him and think of nothing else for a while.

"Okay." He squeezed Walker's thighs. "Okay, yes. I just need you to know—"

"What? You can tell me."

"It can get pretty intense."

Walker's breath faltered for a second, and then his mouth pressed against Roan's cheek. "I got you," he said, and rubbed Roan's belly. They had neared the ranch but Walker's muscles bunched underneath Roan's palms and Cormac changed direction, aiming for another trail disappearing around the back of the house.

After a last moment of indecision, Roan closed his eyes and reached for his jeans. When he popped the button and unzipped, he moaned with relief, then hesitated again with his fingers hooked under the elastic band of his briefs.

"Don't tease me," Walker whispered, his thumb drawing absent-minded circles around Roan's nipple.

"I'm not—oh screw it." He pulled his briefs down, tugged them over his cock and nestled them under his balls. The air hit him like a humid kiss and he shivered with the goosebumps trailing all over his skin.

"God, look at you." Walker slid a hand up Roan's thigh, all the way to the seam of his groin, almost but not quite cupping his balls. Then he skirted around and tweaked both Roan's nipples at the same time.

"*Shit.*" Roan trembled and shook until Walker let go.

"Oh, it's like that." Walker's words rang thick with anticipation, and he didn't hesitate to ruck up Roan's T-shirt and palm his stomach. "I love how you look under your clothes," he whispered. "So unexpected." He rubbed the hairs on Roan's belly, up to his chest, but his T-shirt kept falling down and spoiling the view. Walker tugged at it, testing the stretch, then pulled it over Roan's head so it sat tucked behind his neck. Roan looked down at his dark nipples and straining, leaking cock, and hid his face in Walker's neck.

"Shh, you're amazing."

"I'm on a horse. Half-naked and hard. And we haven't even kissed yet."

"But we will," Walker promised, and then his fingers were back on Roan's nipples, and he couldn't think anymore. Walker rolled the left one lazily between his thumb and his forefinger, agonizingly pleasurable circles that made Roan's legs jerk. Cormac danced underneath them for a second, but Walker did something with his legs to make him stop. "Hold on."

He pulled Roan's left thigh up and settled it over his own, then did the same with his right. "I'll fall," Roan croaked.

"I won't let you. Is this comfortable? With your jeans, I mean?"

Roan gripped Walker's thighs tightly, but nodded. "Yeah, they have a lot of stretch."

"Good," Walker whispered. "This way you can go wild and not kick Cormac accidentally."

"Oh, God."

Walker laughed low in his ear, his mouth trailing hot after the words, lingering on Roan's earlobe, but still not kissing. He rubbed Roan's belly, his chest, all the way up, back to his nipples. Roan couldn't stand it for a second, he had to grip his cock to ease the elusive ache that made him squirm against Walker's groin. He was hard too, Roan could feel it, and it settled him a little. He wasn't alone in this.

"Let me see you work yourself," Walker told him. "Just a little."

Roan squeezed his eyes shut. "Got a bit of a voyeuristic streak, do you?"

To his surprise, Walker was silent for a second, then quietly said, "Yeah, I do."

He let his head thud back again, then jerked himself slowly, letting Walker see it all. He pushed the head of his uncut cock into his fist, making it pop through the ring of his fingers, then pulled up again, the heat of his palm swallowing his dick. Precum coated his hand and the next slide was easier, wetter. He squirmed and his breathing deepened, until Walker pressed two fingers against his left nipple, and he stopped breathing altogether.

"You can stop touching yourself now if you want," Walker whispered, and Roan obeyed. He dug his fingers into Walker's thighs even though his palm was wet and sticky, because he knew what was coming next.

Walker took his time, pressing his palms against Roan's skin wherever he could reach, but he never touched Roan's cock. Like it was okay to watch, but nothing more. He ran his hands over Roan's shoulders, then down over his chest, circling his nipples with light fingertips, then harder. The movements became smaller and smaller until Roan thought he'd jump out of his skin with anticipation.

When Walker finally rubbed his nipples, hard, Roan jerked, then began to shake. It started as a tremor in his legs that became a twitching tremble, until his whole body was shuddering as his stomach clenched and unclenched, cock jumping while liquid beads seeped out, one after the other.

Roan hid his face against Walker's neck again, unable to help the little moans and gasps as Walker's fingers sent bursts of fire and heat straight to his cock and asshole. He wanted something in his mouth, wanted to suck on Walker's tongue or his fingers, but was afraid to ask.

"You shy?" Walker asked and Roan shook his head, but splotches of heat burst all over his face and a strangled cry escaped his mouth when Walker twisted his nipple. "Let me ask you that again," Walker murmured. "You shy, little lion?"

"No one's ever—" He broke off when Walker sucked on his own fingers, then massaged Roan's stinging nipple with spit so the humid breeze cooled the oversensitive nub.

"No one's ever what?"

"Watched me like this."

"Do you like it?"

Roan squeezed his eyes closed, and his breath hitched. He wanted a hand on his cock, to put an end to this almost unbearable shivery pleasure, too much and too little, but he knew he wouldn't touch himself until Walker was good and ready for him to. Walker wasn't touching him either, not counting where Roan leaned against him, but his breath puffed against Roan's ear and his heartbeat was a steady, comforting thump. Roan's skin felt tight and tingly all over, and his asshole kept clenching in anticipation of a still elusive orgasm.

"I do like it," Roan admitted, turning his face away, but Walker stopped him from hiding, gently stroking his cheek, thumbing his open mouth.

"I love it," Walker whispered, his voice hoarse. Needy. "Jesus, Roan. I love watching you. You're so…" He trailed off like he had no words for it. He rolled both barbells, twisting them side to side, but not pinching. Hot fire bolts of frustrating lust shot through the pit of Roan's stomach, making his balls contract and his legs twist. Walker didn't ease up this time, and within seconds Roan was a shuddery mess, unable to hold his own balance. If it wasn't for Walker's strong body keeping him rooted, he'd have fallen off the damn horse ten minutes ago.

"I can't," he gasped when Walker didn't stop. "Oh God, I— *hnnnngh.*" He squirmed and panted, rolling his hips, unwittingly searching for any kind of relief. "I can't do it." To his mortification, a tear rolled down his cheek.

"Shh, baby. What do you need? What can I do for you?"

"I need to touch my cock," Roan said, voice quivering with the electrifying thrills leaping from his nipples.

"I never said you weren't allowed to."

"Ah, God." Roan's breath hitched when he realized he'd been sitting there waiting for permission like a good little boy, all because of a simple suggestion.

"Do you want me to do it for you?"

Roan shook his head and squeezed his eyes closed. His palm was already slick with sweat so his cock slipped easily through his fist, even though his fingers shook so hard he couldn't have gripped a pen. The movement of the horse beneath him fed into his rhythm.

"I feel like I'm in a dream," Walker whispered against Roan's neck, pressing little kisses to the skin. Roan tightened his grip on his cock, gritting his teeth against another onslaught of shudders when Walker flicked his barbells. Even over the clop of the horse's hoofs he could hear the slick noise with which his cock was coating his hand.

He felt a tug at the fabric around his neck and realized Walker was biting into his T-shirt, eyes transfixed on Roan's cock. Heat spiked when

Walker rolled both nipples simultaneously. Roan began to shake again, so hard his breath shuddered out of his mouth.

"It's too much," he cried out. "I can't—" Walker let go of his nipples and Roan made a devastated noise, squirming so hard Walker wrapped one hand around his waist to hold him steady. "No!"

"Okay baby," Walker cooed. "Whatever you want. I just don't want to hurt you."

"You're not hurting—*ohhh*." And just like that the evasive orgasm grabbed him by the nuts.

"Jesus," Walker whispered, barely audible.

Roan mindlessly searched for him, nuzzling and turning his head until his mouth latched on to the underside of Walker's jaw. He mouthed and sucked as he spasmed, spurting cum all over his own stomach, and knuckles, and—*oh, God*—the horse. Walker didn't seem to care where it landed. He grabbed hold of Roan's hand still jerking his cock and Roan let go, allowing Walker to take over, going boneless as aftershock upon aftershock squeezed his balls. He closed his eyes and let the motion of the horse calm him down until he became aware of Walker stroking his belly, his chest, gently circumventing his nipples.

"You okay?" Walker asked, and Roan nodded, afraid to say anything at all.

Roan bit his lip hard when tears sprang to his eyes, and he looked away.

"Hey, it's okay. That was intense. Just like you told me it would be. I loved watching you." Walker gently eased Roan's legs down, straightened his T-shirt and pants out, then wrapped his arms around him and enveloped him from behind. He let Roan hide his face against his neck as he steered Cormac back to the stables.

WALKER HELPED ROAN off the horse like he was something to be handled with care, and he wanted to bristle, but the moment Walker's arms closed around him, all he could do was bury his nose in Walker's neck and hold on.

"I need to take care of Cormac. It won't take a minute," Walker whispered in Roan's hair. "You okay on your own for a while?"

Roan wanted to laugh but the sound stuck in his throat. He nodded but Walker didn't immediately let go. "I'm fine," he said, in case Walker didn't get the message.

"That was really amazing, you know?" Walker whispered. "I have the worst blue balls ever."

"Oh." Roan straightened with a jerk. "Do you want me to—"

"No. Not this time."

Walker's eyes shone with promise, and Roan started to feel self-conscious all over again. His gaze darted to Cormac who stood patiently waiting, but Walker gripped his shoulder and rubbed it, thumb traveling up to trail along Roan's neck. He ducked his head a little, lips parting, and Roan couldn't do it. After everything else, a kiss seemed like too much, like he'd fall apart, burst wide open, and wouldn't be able to reassemble himself again. He turned his head away, and Walker stroked his hair.

"It's okay," Walker told him. "I understand. I'll be right back."

Roan leaned against the side of the farmhouse as Walker took care of Cormac. He felt weirdly floaty and had no idea how much time had passed by the time Walker touched his arm and drew him in another hug.

"How are you feeling?" Walker asked.

"Fine."

"Okay. How 'bout the truth this time?" He drew back a little to look at Roan, and his eyes were kind.

Roan sighed and leaned his forehead against Walker's shoulder. "Weird," he admitted. "Embarrassed."

"Ah, shit, Roan. What can I do to make you feel good about this? I meant it. That was the sexiest thing I've ever seen. And I want to do it again."

Roan lifted his head, giving Walker an incredulous look. He laughed.

"Well, maybe not on a horse."

"And maybe without blue balls on your part," Roan said, cupping his hand over Walker's cock, and wow. He was still more than half-hard.

Walker groaned and his eyes fluttered closed. "Ah shit," he whispered, face going slack, and for some reason that made Roan feel a little steadier, so he decided to push it.

"Next time I get to make you lose your mind," he murmured. Walker ducked his head, but Roan reached with his free hand and tipped Walker's chin back. "And no hiding under cowboy hats."

Walker laughed hoarsely and under the rickety stable light, Roan noticed a faint pink sheen on his cheeks. "Promises," Walker said.

"Say when."

Walker gave him a regretful look. "I wish it could be tomorrow. But my folks will be back and my excuse to shake off my producer will be gone."

Roan stepped back, drawing in a deep, much needed breath. "I understand. This was risky."

"But fun?"

"Yes," Roan said, his throat oddly tight. "Fun."

"I wish I could drive you back to the suitors' house. Give you a proper good night at the door." Walker wrapped an arm around Roan's shoulder and kissed his temple. It was sweet, a gesture Roan could get used to fast, but it lacked all the heat from before, and his shoulders relaxed a little.

If Walker had invited him inside, he would've gone, but he was actually glad for the reprieve. He'd only rarely let go like that with anyone before, and he needed some time to process.

"I should get back."

"Be careful. Don't get caught."

Roan nodded, adrenaline shooting through him at the thought. He remembered Andy and Molly's lectures the day after their last horseback adventure. He didn't want to push his luck. The cameras probably caught him coming and going, but so long as he got back inside, he could claim claustrophobia and that he'd gone on a night walk alone. They'd still be mad, but maybe they'd believe him.

When Roan looked back over his shoulder as he took the dark path home, he saw Walker's shadow waiting by the farmhouse watching him go. He held back the urge to lift a hand and wave.

WALKER WAS SITTING on the porch with his feet propped up against the banister and surrounded by camera crew by the time Roan and Peter stomped outside.

"Really?" Roan called out the minute Walker's feet hit the ground. "Another date that requires rubber boots? I'm not sure I like this, cowboy."

Peter peered over Roan's shoulder at the cameras and scrunched up his face. "I'm with Roan on this one. I'm going to look like a twelve-year-old in those."

Walker ducked his head and tugged his hat closer over his eyes. "Date?" he drawled, and hot damn that went straight to Roan's balls. He shifted on his feet, flushing red. "Who says this is a date?" Walker stuffed his hands in his pockets and ambled closer to where Roan was wrestling with a pair of dark green rain boots. "I'm going to put you to work."

"Oh." Roan stopped tugging at the boots and looked up at Walker looming over him. His face was cast in shadow, his outline sharp against the sunlight. "What kind of work? Are we going to be mucking stalls again?"

Walker pressed his lips together but a small snort made it through anyway. "No. I think the producers got their fill of that already."

"Cleaning the chicken coop?"

"Nah, my step-mama doesn't like strangers around her chickens. Says it disturbs them so they won't lay."

He pulled his hands out of his pockets, reached out and tugged Roan to his feet, then gave him a firm clap on the back. Twisting around to face his truck he gave one sharp whistle. The head of a gorgeous, spotted, black-and-tan dog appeared over the rim of the bed. It yipped once, jumped out of the truck, and came bounding toward them, ears flapping.

"Ohhh, who's this?" Roan asked, crouching down to greet her. But the dog sank to her haunches by Walker's side, head tilted curiously to stare at Roan.

"Release," Walker said, and the dog immediately went over to investigate. She sniffled Roan's fingers, then his boots, his jeans, working her way up to his face. He fondled her ears and cooed at her, but she eased back before he could really start petting her.

"She's so cute." Roan said, taking his cues from the dog and straightening. "What's her name?"

"Her name's Dana. And she's going to help us today."

Roan peered at him. "Help us do what?"

Walker grinned. "Hunt snakes."

Roan reached for the banister. "What did you say?"

"Snake hunting. We've had another cottonmouth bite in the same field as my favorite cow Hannah, but luckily just a leg bite. But that means we need to cull the population a little."

"Okay, I'm going to leave aside the fact that you have a favorite cow—"

"Which is adorable, by the way," Peter interjected.

"And go right to the fact that you took Victor to New Orleans last week. And two days ago, you went on a ride and a picnic with Chad."

Walker's eyebrow rose when Roan mentioned a ride, but he said nothing, thank God. "A truck ride," Roan clarified, blushing harder. "Yet, the minute I get involved, we go snake hunting? I take it back, I don't like you at all."

Walker's stupid grin widened, and he leaned a little closer. Roan was very aware of the cameras zoomed in on them too. "I didn't know you liked me to begin with."

Roan huffed. He bit back the retort he wanted to make, which would reveal way too much truth about his "claustrophobia-relieving night walk". "Whatever. Let's just get going so I can complain the entire time."

Walker turned toward John. "Are we taking my truck?"

John thought for a minute. "We can't all fit with the dog. You, Roan, and Peter take the truck; the rest of us will follow. The mounted cams will do the trick, and the two of you don't require much producing at this point," he said meaningfully. "Just don't tell Andy."

"Yes, sir."

Roan sighed and stomped after Walker and his stupid cowboy hat and his stupid Wrangler jeans, and why? Why did he deserve this? He helped Peter into the cab, then climbed in after him with a huff while Walker let the back of the bed down so Dana could jump back in.

"Snake hunting?" Peter hissed at him as he settled in the small backseat. "Oh, hell no." He plastered on a smile when Walker opened the driver's-side door.

"Same goes as every time we go out to do something like this," Walker said as he fastened his seat belt. "You don't have to do anything you don't want to."

"Will there be guns?" Roan asked, more than a little apprehensive. He hated guns.

"No," Walker said, and Roan relaxed a little in relief. "We'll be using sharp shovels. And you need to watch out because the detached heads can still bite."

"What?" Peter gasped and lost what little color he had in his face.

"You are insane," Roan whispered, staring out of the windshield. "This whole state is insane. Why would anyone want to live here?"

Walker was quiet beside them, and Roan glanced over. Clearing his throat, Walker finally asked, "Do you mean that? Do you hate it here?"

Roan blinked rapidly and went back to staring out of the window. The ranch spread out before them. Cows grazed in the distance. The sun rose red and yellow above the horizon, turning the sky pale blue and chasing the last of the stars away.

"No," he whispered. "I don't hate it here."

"Good."

"Lord, the two of you are gonna kill us all," Peter muttered and rolled his eyes.

Walker's hand twitched on the steering wheel, but he left it where it was, started the truck, and began to drive. He glanced in the rearview. "In New Orleans and during the date with Victor, the cameras were on us the entire time. Andy was there. He made me reshoot the same conversation with Victor three times. I figured he wouldn't join us for this, especially since it's out in the heat. Andy hates heat." He grinned, including Peter in the joke with a quick glance, but Roan knew what he really wanted to say. Another chance for privacy if they could escape the watchful eyes of Molly and John.

They drove up to a gate, where Walker parked the Ford, and Roan was grateful for the boots at least because the field was swampy.

"What if they bite us?" Peter asked when Walker let Dana out of the truck bed. Two guys Roan had never seen before ambled up to the truck.

"There's an ambulance over there," Walker said nodding to where the others were coming up in the SUVs with an ambulance bouncing around behind them. "They have antivenom stocked. But don't worry. You just have to be faster than them."

"You're kidding, right?"

Walker looked at him. "No. But don't freak out. Dana knows what we're doing, and she'll show us where to find the snakes." He grabbed two shovels, passed one to Peter and one to Roan. "This is Marlon and Dennis. They'll help out today. Don't stray too close to the water unless one of us is with you."

"Okay." Peter eyed Marlon up and down and smiled winningly. "Hi, there."

Walker smirked when Marlon put on his own charming smile and said, "Sorry, but you're barking up the wrong tree, cher."

Walker then tugged on Roan's arm. "What's up? You look like death."

Roan gripped the shovel in two hands, knuckles going white. "I don't think I can do this."

"Okay." Walker glanced over to the camera guys piling out of the SUV ready to roll. He stepped a little closer. "What do you have a problem with? The snakes? Or the killing?"

"Both." Roan looked at him, then quickly away. "I've never killed anything. I don't think I can."

"I understand. We don't do this lightly. And we have a license for it, like we did for the noodling. It's not against the law as long as you don't do it at night. Normally, I don't worry much about them, but Hannah and a second cow being bitten is evidence that there are probably too many cottonmouths this year, so it's encouraged. For the safety of the herd. And check this out." Walker bent down and lifted the cuff of his jeans. Roan gasped at the scar on his calf. "That's tissue damage after I was bitten by a cottonmouth in a field when I was ten."

"Oh my God," Peter breathed, hand pressed to his mouth.

"Yeah." Walker straightened. "It's not pretty." He fiddled with his shovel, and Roan put a hand on his arm.

"I don't care about pretty. That must've hurt."

"It wasn't a party, no. But all I meant is that we're doing this for a reason. Not just because we're a bunch of illiterate rednecks who enjoy killing things."

Roan frowned. "That's not what I think of you."

"Good," Walker said. "And like I said, you don't have to do anything you don't want to."

"Suck it up, guys," Molly called out when the others joined them. "And let's go kill some damn snakes." She grabbed a shovel off Walker and cheerfully set off with Dennis by her side. Peter trailed behind them until he fell into step with John, and then stayed there.

They all walked the perimeter of the field, always aiming for the ponds, and Dana alerted them to two snakes. Roan looked away as Walker dealt with them, the shovel feeling like an awkward weight in his hand.

"I'm sorry," Walker said when the silence dragged on. "I admit I had second thoughts about this date earlier. You know, after..." He cleared his throat.

Roan's head snapped up, and he stared at Walker, who had a sad smile on his face. "You had second thoughts about a date with me?"

"No. About taking you snake hunting. After the noodling, it seemed like fun to rile you up again, but now I wish..."

"What?"

Walker stepped a little closer, and Dana danced around them once before running off to explore the field. A couple of cows stared at them like they were watching a soap opera. Their first audience for the show. Apart from the crew, anyway. "I wish this whole circus was over."

"Yeah?"

"Yeah. Come on, let's head back."

"Already? But the snakes," Roan protested.

Walker shrugged easily and smiled. "Marlon loves snake hunting. He'll happily finish up." He hesitated for a second, but Roan smiled and held out his hand. Walker gave a little laugh and threaded their fingers together. Roan loved the callouses brushing against his palm.

Walker scanned the field, and Roan joined him, surprised to find that the others spread far across the pasture. Strangely, no one was paying attention to them. All the camera people and other crew were unusually distracted, too preoccupied with making sure they didn't step on any snakes. It was everything that wasn't ever supposed to happen on a show like this.

It was a sign.

Walker pointedly lifted his shirt and turned off his body mic. Glancing around to make sure no one observed, Roan did the same.

"Are we running away together again?" Roan asked after they were both clear of being recorded, his stomach dancing giddily. What was wrong with them? They shouldn't be doing this. But he couldn't bring himself turn the opportunity down either.

Walker grinned, tipping his hat down. "Little bit."

Roan's heart did a giddy hop. "Okay."

Walker whispered, "Stay," at Dana, then grabbed Roan's hand again. Without a word he tugged him along to the side of the field where a huge tree offered a hidden patch of shade. All fear of snakes left behind in the excitement of being alone with Walker again, Roan followed.

Once on the opposite side of the massive trunk, Walker pushed Roan against the bark. The air hung humid between them, and Walker's tawny eyes smiled lazily.

"Can I kiss you?" Walker asked. "No cameras. No show. Just you and me."

God, did Walker really think he had to ask after last night? But Roan had refused to kiss him then, hadn't he? He'd been afraid. He was scared now, too, but for a different reason. This was a good kind of fear. A thrill.

"Yes," Roan croaked, his mouth going instantly dry. He licked his lips to generate some saliva. "Fuck, yes."

Walker's eyes sparkled happily. He pushed his hat out of the way, and the light hit his face. He was so gorgeous Roan's knees went weak, and he was glad of Walker's grip on his shirt. Walker grinned, tilted his head to the side, and kissed him.

A BEAD OF sweat left Roan's temple and slowly made its way down the side of his face. When it reached Roan's ear, Walker closed his eyes and fell a little deeper into the kiss. It felt restrained, chaste almost, but with a burning urgency underneath that told him Roan was putting on the brakes.

Knowing those piercings were there was a big temptation, but this wasn't the time, so Walker let go of Roan's shirt and shifted his hands lower, settling on his sharp, narrow hips.

Roan moaned a little, slipped his fingers in the loops of Walker's jeans, and tugged him closer. And just like that the brakes gave out. A fierce heat swallowed Walker whole, and he licked at Roan's mouth, tasting sweat, then pressed his tongue inside. Roan shivered, knocked Walker's hat off his head, and buried his hands in his hair as he pressed closer.

On and on, the kiss went, until the sound of the bugs and critters and birds became white noise. He went lightheaded, though not from lack of air. Walker had never been kissed like this. Had never felt it to the tips of his fingers where they tingled against Roan's stomach when he slipped them underneath Roan's shirt. And still the kiss lasted. Walker's mouth throbbed, but stopping didn't even enter his mind. His heart thudded hard against his ribcage, and he felt Roan's respond in kind, rattling his chest like it wanted out. Roan's breath hit his cheek in little panting bursts, and he felt like he was flying, untethered and weightless.

Finally a noise penetrated the fog that had descended on Walker's mind. Roan must've heard it too because he slowed the kiss, ending it with a soft peck, then another one like he couldn't help himself, and Walker felt his smile before he pulled away.

"Jesus," Roan whispered.

"You can say that again."

"Jesus."

Walker laughed and eased away a little so he could look at Roan, but their hips remained pressed flush together. "Does that make up for the terrible date?"

"I don't know," Roan said, smoothing a wrinkle out of Walker's shirt. "I think you need to take me on another terrible date, this one without any need to hide, and kiss me again so I can compare."

Walker grinned. "I think that can be arr—"

"Very nice work, boys."

They startled apart to find Molly with her arms crossed and an amused expression; the camera crew ranged behind her. A boom mic was dangling to catch their conversation now since they'd turned their body mics off. Walker still had his hand wrapped around Roan's hip, but it fell away when a second figure stepped up beside Molly. Roan frowned at him, confusion clouding his face, but Walker saw red.

"What the fuck." A sense of déjà vu unbalanced him. "Mike? What are you doing here?"

"Hey, babe." Mike flicked his cowboy hat up and strolled toward Walker like he still belonged here. That easy lope as he neared was still so familiar. His wide and dimpled smile and bright blue eyes shone in the pretty sunlight. "Did you miss me?"

Walker glanced at Roan, who looked completely blank. Walker wanted to say something but didn't know what. Instead, he bent down, picked up his hat, and dusted it off before tugging it over his eyes. *Hiding myself away from the world again*, Walker thought, disgusted. *From Roan.*

"Who's this?" Roan whispered. Two more boom mics lifted over their heads.

"This is—"

"Mike Defalco." Mike held out his hand, and Roan automatically took it. "I'm his boyfriend."

A vein began to throb in Walker's temple as he stepped into Mike's space, forcing him away from Roan. "Hey now, you haven't been my boyfriend in years. What are you up to, Mike? What the hell are you doing here?"

Mike grinned. "Your good friend here"—he patted Molly on the shoulder, and she arched her brows savagely with a nasty gotcha grin—"she invited me. Thought it might be fun."

"Fun? You mean—" Walker's jaw clenched. He turned to Roan. "I'm sorry, I had no idea that—"

"That's okay." Roan put up his hands, which were obviously shaking, backed away. "You two clearly need to catch up. Um, I'll see you later. And thanks for the date."

"Roan…"

Shaking his head, Roan waved him off as he stepped more or less carefully back toward the gate and the parked trucks.

Molly had a shit-eating grin on her face as she called out after Roan. "Didn't I tell you I'd get you two making out on camera? I always win, Roan." Her eyes went blank as she spoke into her headset. "John, pull a team together and intercept Roan for an in-the-moment about our new contestant."

Walker decided to ignore her. "What the hell, Mike? What'd you say you were my boyfriend for?"

Mike laughed and slipped a hand around his shoulder, but Walker pushed him off. "Aw, c'mon, man. It was just a little fun. Molly wanted some drama." He nodded her way. "She seems like an interesting person."

Molly tuned back in to the conversation. "Please try not to address the crew directly or mention them when on camera."

Walker glared at her, then back at Mike. "She's an asshole."

Mike's blue eyes twinkled. "Yeah, I figured. Look, are you really mad? Don't tell me you take this whole thing seriously. Everyone knows you're doing this for the money, which is pretty much the only reason you're not being laughed out of the parish."

"Been talking behind my back, have you?" Walker aimed for his truck, barely noticing when the camera crew followed.

Mike shrugged easily and fell into step beside him. "I'm a vet. People talk. What am I supposed to do? Plug my ears?"

Walker ripped his hat off and tore a hand through his hair, gazing to where a producer and two camera guys had cornered Roan. "You don't get it all. You have no idea what you've done."

"So tell me."

They'd reached the truck, and Walker was itching to go bust into Roan's in-the-moment with an apology and explanation, but he couldn't. That would play into Molly's desire for drama. He didn't want to let her win. "This show messes with your mind, and now Roan thinks I'm messing with him too."

"Roan, huh?" Mike propped one hand against the truck and smiled down at Walker. He was still the same brick of a guy he'd been when they started dating, but now crowfeet and laugh lines around his mouth gave his face the depth and maturity he'd missed when they were in their early twenties. "Looks like a little twink to me. You always did have a wandering eye for guys like that."

"I never wandered," Walker snapped, instantly regretting it. He didn't want Mike to think he was getting to him. And he *really* didn't want Molly or the other producers to think Mike was getting to him.

"Neither did I, honey," Mike said softly.

Walker let out a deep gust of a breath and whipped his hat off his head. "No," he said, resigned. "But you wanted to."

"That was a long time ago. I was young and stupid, and I wanted to explore."

"And what are you now? Why are you here?"

Mike's easy smile faded a little. "Molly's been calling me, asking me to come on the show. I got the feeling I wasn't the first person she called, and I figured if I kept saying no she'd call someone else. And then who knows who'd have shown up here. I figured I'm better than some random ranch hand."

Molly groaned. "That isn't what we talked about, Mike. You're really going off script here. We're going to have to reshoot, and Walker's terrible at that, so can you try to focus?"

Walker winced. "This whole thing has been a mistake." He ran a hand through his hair. "Goddammit."

"It didn't look like you felt that way five minutes ago."

Walker snorted.

"But everything's okay now. Take a breath." Mike tapped the roof of the truck. "I'm here as a contestant, honey. All you have to do is keep me to the end, and you're free of all the conniving, money-hungry shits."

Walker's head snapped up, and he stared at Mike in disbelief. "What are you saying?"

"Suzanna's taking over my practice for the next few weeks. I might have to go in a couple of times if there's something she can't deal with by herself, but other than that." Mike spread his arms. His checkered shirt stretched over his broad chest, and Walker knew exactly what he looked like underneath. "I'm all yours."

"WHAT'S THE MATTER, baby? You've been walking around with a thundercloud for a face all morning." Tessa massaged his shoulders as he slumped back in his kitchen chair. The coffee in front of him danced with tantalizing wisps of fragrant smoke, and Dad slid the sugar in his direction.

"Just what you need," he said with a wink. "A little something to sweeten you up."

"You're not allowed any sugar," Walker said, scowling.

"We're not talking about me, are we? We're talking about your sour face."

He narrowed his eyes. "What are you up to today?"

Dad looked innocent as he stirred his coffee, adding a good dollop of full fat milk. Walker glanced at Tessa, but she gave him an apologetic smile. She never could deny his dad anything. "I thought I'd go take a look at the south pasture. It's been a while since I got on a horse."

"Because you're not supposed to," Walker said, sitting up straighter. "When's the last time you checked your sugar since you got back from the hospital? Actually, when's the last time you took your insulin?"

It was rare for his dad to get mad, and when he did he never shouted, never banged the table. Even when Walker had been a kid, all he'd had to see to start behaving was his father's stern look. That look was there again, and Walker tried not to feel ten years old. He knew he was in the right.

"I feel fine," Dad said. "Better than I have in a long time, boy. And it'll be the day when you tell me whether or not I can ride my own horses to check on my own ranch."

Walker ground his teeth together. There was nothing he could say to change his mind, and he sure as hell wasn't going to remind his father that the ranch wasn't his anymore. The man deserved some dignity. "At least take Marlon or Dennis with you."

"I'll go with him," Tessa said. "It's been a while since I was on a horse too." Walker wasn't happy about that either; just his luck they'd both fall off and break a hip, but he nodded once. Tessa touched his arm. "Now, tell us what's got you in a funk this morning."

"Mike showed up on set," he said, and Tessa gasped. "The producers dragged him into this in order to, I don't know, to produce this kind of response in me, I guess." He dragged his hands through his hair in agitation. "I knew there was a reason why I had to send three people home at the very beginning, and I figured they'd spring someone new on me, but Mike? Goddammit."

"Language," Tessa said.

"Sorry, Tess."

"I can't believe he agreed to it," Dad said, shaking his head with a frown. "You think he's trying to get back with you?"

Walker made a face and lifted his mug. "I doubt it. He says he's here to offer me an out. I can keep him until the end, send everyone else home, make people think I got my happy ever after, and be done with this." He sipped his coffee, avoiding Tessa's eyes.

"What about Roan?" she asked.

"Is he that skinny kid she saw you with?" Dad asked. "I thought I told you to pick someone with some—" He made a gesture indicating size. Tessa smacked the back of his head. "Hey! I was gonna say who can work hard."

Walker snorted. "Yeah, right." He sighed and put his mug down, leaning back in his chair as he ran his hands over his face. "He's great. But something doesn't feel right."

"What do you mean?" Tessa reached across the table and refilled his mug.

"Thanks, Tess. I don't know. I don't think Roan actually wants to be here."

"Why?" Dad reached for the sugary jam, and Walker pushed it out of the way, giving him the sugar-free one instead. "What makes you say that?"

"He's never tried to convince me he's always wanted to live on a farm, like everyone else has been doing. Seriously, if I hear one more time from one of these men how farm life seems so romantic, I'm going to throw something."

"Not in my kitchen, you're not." Tessa patted his hand. "Maybe that means he's more sincere than anyone else. Does he have a job? Family? Something else tying him down?"

Not the job, Walker thought. "I don't know."

Tessa raised an eyebrow at him. "Well then maybe you oughta find out, Walker Reed. Before you dismiss him off the bat."

"I'm not dismissing him," Walker mumbled, knowing he was turning red.

"Ohhhhh," Dad crowed. "Did you get laid?"

"Joe, you're embarrassing the boy." Tessa's twinkling eyes turned toward him. "Well? Did you?"

"Oh, please, get your minds out of the gutter."

Tessa shrugged, reaching for her own coffee. "Well, the way I see it, it's simple. You either want to keep Roan in the running until the end, and see how it goes, or you go along with Mike's charade. Both are perfectly fine, baby. You just need to make up your mind."

"Simple as that, huh."

"I didn't say it would be simple." She smiled. "So who are you sending home next?"

"I don't know." Walker pushed away from the table and kissed his step-mama's forehead. "Thanks for breakfast. I'm going to go for a ride."

"Wait." Dad held on to his arm when Walker patted his shoulder. "You like him? This Roan guy?"

"Yeah, but liking someone wasn't the plan. I just wanted to get the money and get out unscathed."

"Love very rarely goes to plan, Walker. I'd say just go with it. If he's the one you want, you owe it to yourself to try." His bushy gray eyebrows drew down, but Walker could see the teasing glint in his eyes. "Did I raise you to be afraid, boy?"

"No, sir."

"Did I raise you to do the right thing?"

"I think that was Tess," Walker said, grinning. Dad puffed up his chest and growled at him, but Walker just laughed. "Yes, you both did."

"Trust your feelings, Walker. You'll know if it's right."

Walker ran his hands over the rough, wooden kitchen table. The knots and cracks were as familiar to him as his own face. "But I don't know if I can trust his feelings," he admitted very quietly. "I don't want to get hurt."

Tessa touched his shoulder, and he looked up. "That's something you can never know, baby. No matter when or where you meet someone. It's a chance you have to take. All you have to do is decide whether or not it's worth it."

Walker sighed and patted her hand. "Don't mind me, I'm just being moody."

"Nothing new there," Dad said.

"Whatever you decide, be nice to the boy," Tessa added.

"But not too nice," Dad interjected. "Make sure he'll want to make an honest man out of you before you let him put his dick—"

"I can't hear you!" Walker yelled, cupping his hands over his ears as he left. God, his parents were insane.

He ran by the stables and quickly talked to Marlon about what needed to be done for the day, planned the rest of the week with him, and then saddled Cormac and rode off into the sleepy dawn. Grateful for the cool, light fog still blanketing his cows as they slumbered.

The heat of the day would be on him soon enough.

CHAPTER 15

"LEAVE ME ALONE."

Molly hummed and tapped her charming little chin. "No, I don't think so. Luke is going to sit down with you and ask you deep and meaningful questions about your feelings on Walker's ex turning up."

Roan stopped with his hand on the fridge door and glared at Molly. He'd managed to evade John the day before, but Molly was more persistent. "How long have you known this was going to happen?"

Molly laughed. "Since before we started filming, babe. What did you expect?" She was still laughing as he turned walked into the weirdly quiet living room.

There had been a horseshoe-throwing contest earlier that day with the winner and runner-up being allowed to stay home, while all the losers went out to camp in a field—without Walker—for the night. Somehow, Roan had gotten extremely lucky, and managed to come in second after Ben. He didn't think there was any way for the producers to have rigged the outcome of the game, and yet it was clear they were pleased with it. Things had been awkward between the two of them ever since Roan had seen Ben kiss Walker, and the camera crew had been all over their very quiet, very tense dinner together.

After turning his back on Molly, he went upstairs to change into a pair of sweat pants. He saw Ben in the other room as he walked by, lying on one of the bunks, staring at the ceiling like it had offended him. As Roan pulled on his sweatpants, he decided to also put on his big boy pants, and address the elephant in the room.

He took a deep breath and then crossed the hallway, leaning against the doorjamb. "Hey," Roan said awkwardly. "I thought maybe we should talk."

Ben's face twisted in a grimace. He said nothing for so long that Roan was about to give up and walk away when Ben suddenly sat up. "Yeah, okay. You're right. Let's do this."

"Yeah?" Roan hesitated. Now he wasn't sure the he even wanted to.

Ben turned to him, his handsome face lined with sadness. "I wanted to say I'm sorry. About the other day. It was all—"

"A set-up. I know."

"Yeah, but that's just it. I agreed to go along with it for the worst reason." Ben buried his face in his big hands, and Roan blinked at him, surprised at seeing the big guy so vulnerable. Ben looked up again, blue eyes rimmed with red. "I'm not even into him," he softly said. "Molly put me up to it just to fuck with you, to get a reaction out of you, the way they're always doing to us. And I didn't want to fuck with you, Roan, because I…." His voice caught. "I really care about you."

Roan froze with his hand pressed to his mouth. What was Ben saying here? That he was into Roan? Like *that*? Or was this just a set-up, too? They were still being recorded after all. The blinking red lights of the cameras all over the room made that clear. And they were body mic'ed. He didn't know what to believe. "Oh my God," he managed eventually. "They have to create a dramatic storyline for everyone, don't they? Does Walker know the truth?"

Ben shook his head, eyes dark and wide, like Roan hadn't said the right thing, but he wasn't going to correct him. "No. I haven't talked to him since."

"Maybe you should tell him the truth. He has the right to know." Guilt twanged in his chest. Maybe he should listen to his own advice.

"Yeah," Ben said, lying down again and covering his eyes with his arm. "He does."

At a loss, Roan wandered to his own room and gathered up the dirty clothes he'd piled neatly in a corner. He should do some washing, really, now that everyone was gone and the machines were open. Maybe have a long, hot, private bath. But he didn't feel like indulging. His heart and mind were racing and not in a good way. He should never have come here.

It was raining again, so he made himself some hot herbal tea and went to sit on the back porch to watch it pour down from one of the rocking chairs. The water battered on the tin roof above him. He wished he could snap a few pictures of the view and send them to his mom. He closed his eyes and imagined a text conversation with her instead.

So pretty. How are you doing, darling? she'd reply to his text of the pictures.

I'm okay, he'd send back.

You sure?

Because she would know. Somehow, from the other side of the country and through just a few words, she would know. He sighed and imagined his reply. *No. I'm not okay.*

Why, honey?

I think I really like him.

Oh, Roan.

She wouldn't send anything else. She wouldn't need to, and she'd know he wouldn't want to talk about it and that trying to convince him to make a go of things here—because that's what she'd suggest, he just knew it—would get her nowhere.

Roan missed his mom so damn much.

He stayed on the porch until his butt went numb on the hard wooden rocking chair. He realized he was half-hoping Walker would show up, but chances of that were slim in this kind of weather. With the producers away, Walker was probably out with his cows, doing the work he needed for the ranch even in the rain. Because he was that kind of man. Dedicated, hard-working. A true cowboy. Roan let his head thud back against the chair and rocked gently back and forth.

LETA BLAKE & INDRA VAUGHN

Flashbacks of what they'd done on the back of Walker's horse kept assaulting him at the most inopportune moments, but now he relentlessly pushed them away. He didn't know how to feel about what they'd done, and, when he was at his most insecure, all he felt was shame. During the day he could put it in perspective, knowing Walker had been really into it, but in the darkest, sleepless hours of the night, surrounded by other men vying for Walker's attention, he kept reliving the whole thing, unable to shut off his brain. The squirmy feeling the whole thing gave him wasn't the good kind.

At least he could be sure Walker wasn't out with Mike right now either, since Mike had joined in on the horseshoe game and been sent out to the tents, too. Roan covered his eyes with his free hand, clutching the cold and empty mug against his chest. He didn't want to feel this jealousy, didn't want to feel attracted to Walker, and didn't want to feel ashamed of how he was wired sexually. He hadn't counted on *liking* Walker and couldn't give in to it. They had no future, no chance, and it was unfair of him to make Walker think they did. He took a shuddery breath.

He had to get home to his mom.

He suddenly missed her like she was already gone with an intensity that made him put his mug on the porch deck and hunch over his arms wrapped around his chest. Raw, gaping, empty pain filled him up inside. He needed to go home.

He couldn't do this anymore. He shouldn't. Walker deserved better.

Roan waited until the next morning, after everyone came back from what had proven to be a miserable overnight in the tents, then cornered Molly who was going through her phone in the living room. Mike gave him a curious look, but Roan completely ignored him.

"I want to go home."

Molly raised an eyebrow. "Say what now?"

"I want to go home. I need to be with my mom."

A flicker of uncharacteristic concern flashed over Molly's gaze. "Is she worse? Has there been a call I don't know about?"

"No. But I know she's not getting any better, and I haven't talked to her in so long." He scratched at his arms anxiously. "I need to go home."

Molly's expression hardened, and her eyes narrowed. "How about this—we let you make one phone call to her. On camera, obviously. With Walker listening—"

"No."

"No? That was a incredibly generous offer."

"One you made because you want to use my mom's illness for drama, and I'm not doing that. I want to see her. I want to go home."

Molly took a long, slow breath, and then said tightly, "Then let me put it plainly, hipster boy. This is week four. It clearly states in your contract that if you leave voluntarily before the fourth week, and/or on any terms Andy and I don't agree with, you don't get paid." Molly pointed a pen at him. "We don't agree with these terms. Got it?"

Roan gritted his teeth.

The Bluetooth device began to blink red in her ear. "Think carefully, Roan," she said, then walked away, tapping her earpiece and barking, "Make it quick."

He stared after her, his gut churning. Rubbing his hands over his face, he headed back out to the porch to stare into the fields, dread pouring through his veins like the rain from the sky.

"I don't know what to do," he whispered. "Tell me what to do, Mom. I'm so confused right now."

The sky opened up and the rain came down in sheets, clattering against the tin of the porch roof and shooting out from the gutters. A few tears slipped down Roan's cheeks. He wiped them with the back of his hand, lifted his chin, and turned to go back inside.

ROAN FINGERED THE long part of his black hair into shape, giving a curl

237

a tug so it flopped over his forehead. He smoothed his shirt down and tugged at the Bordeaux velour jacket. His black pants looked pretty much painted on. He'd brought this outfit in case he made it to the final couple of episodes, but…

Well.

"Showtime ladies!" one of the crew yelled down the hall.

"Ready?" Chad asked him.

Roan tried to smile. "Sure."

"Hey. You nervous? You know you have nothing to be nervous about, right?" Chad looked good. He wore a V-neck cashmere sweater in baby blue and it made his smile sparkle. It was a bit weird to be honest, because he was the only one who didn't seem to care whether he got to spend any time with Walker or not. Roan had seen him play it up for the camera a few times, but Chad was different—like with that weird kiss Walker had given him. Why was Chad really here? They'd never talked about it.

"Actually, I've been thinking—" Roan began, then clammed up when Mike wandered into the bedroom from the bathroom wearing only a towel. Why on earth did he have to be staying with them? And why had he chosen Roan's room, instead of the one across the hall?

"Hey, y'all," he said, giving Roan a big wink. Like he knew all his secrets. He did that constantly, and it drove Roan insane. He gritted his teeth as he fought down an embarrassed flush. Mike went on, "If it isn't my stiffest competition. Looking good, Roan."

"You too," Roan grumbled.

"Hey, man," Chad said when Mike greeted him too, like Mike wasn't dripping wet and showing off his big, muscled chest. Walker's ex showing up hadn't thrown Chad for a loop at all. Chad turned his attention back to Roan. "You were saying?"

"Nothing," Roan mumbled and made his way out of the room so he didn't have to see Mike's perfect arms, and his perfect face and abs, or the pert ass he kept showing off. Dammit. Why was he jealous? One more week and he'd be gone. Probably.

"Word is you and Walker kissed. Like, *really* kissed." Chad followed Roan downstairs. When he was met with nothing but silence, he gave Roan's arm a soft squeeze. "It's not all fake, you know."

Roan nodded but couldn't get any words out. Automatically he scanned the room, and at the exact moment Roan spotted him, Walker looked up. Damn, Walker looked hot. He wore a pinstripe suit that accentuated his muscled chest and clung to his thick thighs. It made Roan want to strip the whole thing off his body—hang it up neatly—then have his wicked way with that cowboy.

On his terms this time.

Their eyes met across the expanse, and Roan felt the jolt of whatever it was that coiled tight between them. It grabbed him and tugged at his guts. Walker made a small move, like he was going to come over, but Roan averted his gaze.

Everyone milled around for a while, trying to make polite small talk, but the room thrummed with anticipation. Roan figured the vibe would only get worse as the night continued. Eventually he couldn't keep up his pretense of not wanting to look at Walker, and his eyes strayed in his direction. Now Mike was standing right beside him.

In a fucking matching suit. They looked like two grooms ready for their wedding.

"Dick move, huh?"

"What?" Roan turned to Victor.

He nodded at Walker and Mike. "Having the ex turn up? Assholes. And then they put him in the same suit."

Roan's gut churned.

Victor went on, "You're not buying that, are you? They want some good footage of you green with jealousy so they can make everything seem more dramatic than it actually is." Victor squeezed Roan's arm. "But trust me, those two aren't getting back together."

Roan looked back over at the two of them. Mike plucked something off Walker's tie, and it was clear they were easy with each other. Familiar.

"I don't know," he said dubiously. Not that it mattered to him. Not at all. *One more week.* Then he'd be home with his mom, where he belonged.

Victor shrugged a strong shoulder. "I'm wasting my time here anyway."

"What do you mean?"

Victor turned to him and gave him a disbelieving look. He looked gorgeous in an emerald shirt that clung to his tanned skin and shoes that made him even taller than he already was. "I didn't expect to feel anything for the guy, and I don't. Not really. But he's a good person, and he deserves a good man. That's not me."

"It's not?"

Victor laughed. "No. For me, it's all about the money."

"But it's all about the money for me, too," Roan confessed. "So I'm no better than you are."

"Maybe it started that way for you, but…" Victor looked toward Walker pointedly. "You're fooling yourself, kid, if you think everyone here hasn't seen how into each other you guys are."

Roan swallowed hard and rubbed at his arms. Victor wandered away, leaving him to his thoughts. Did he dare to hope? Was it ridiculous to think that anything real could come out of something as fake as this show? His heart beat quickly, his pulse thrumming with restrained excitement. His eyes swung back to Walker, who was looking at him, too. He lifted his hand to wave, and Walker's lips tweaked up at the edges, a small smile.

Roan's heart soared. Okay, yes, maybe he didn't need to go home right away. Maybe he would stay around for the full six weeks if possible, and not for the prize money. But for the way his stomach flipped, and his blood pounded, and his soul felt like it was taking to the sky just from that small, sweet smile Walker had sent his way.

A heavy hand gripped his right biceps and pulled him into the less crowded kitchen. "Hey, what…?" Roan bit back the rest of his question when he got a good look at who had hold of him.

John's expression was grim, but his voice was steady when he said, "Roan, it's your mom."

His stomach flipped again, but not like it had when Walker had smiled at him. No, now it flipped with a cold, sick terror. "What's going on?"

"Don't panic, but we got a call—"

Roan's pulse pounded, and he couldn't make out the rest of John's words. They sounded like they were coming from far away, in slow motion, under water, and not in English. He blinked rapidly, acid lurching into his throat.

They got a call.

They got a call.

His mother would never have allowed that unless…*unless*…

Roan darted toward the nearest door. He shoved through a few crew members to the edge of the porch. It was hotter than the devil's armpit out there, but he didn't feel it. Shaking all over, he leaned over the banister and puked into the bushes again.

Then suddenly John was there, saying, "Man, oh, crap. I need a medic around back and, oh, hell, someone fly in some mouthwash for Roan."

"I knew something was wrong," Roan whispered, wiping at his mouth with the back of his hand. "I felt it. In my gut. Last night. All morning." He puked again, heaving and heaving. John's hand steadied him, and then someone shoved a bottle of water into his hand.

"Look, calm down," John said, watching him drink with kind eyes. "It's going to be okay. Just breathe." He handed Roan the mouthwash another crew member had brought over, and Roan swished, the alcohol burning his tongue. He spit it into the bushes, too, and then turned to John, pleadingly.

"I need to talk to her. Now. Please. *Please.*"

John darted anxious looks around, but then he tugged out his cell phone and handed it over. "Okay, but buddy, we gotta film this."

Roan didn't give a shit anymore. He took the phone and bolted from the porch, pacing out in the heat, sweat pooling in the small of his back and slipping down the side of his face. The camera guys dogged his heels and walked in front of him. He hated them, but he didn't have time to tell them to fuck off, and he knew they wouldn't anyway.

First, he dialed the landline at the house. Nothing. He then dialed his mom's cell number. Nothing. With shaking hands, he dialed their neighbor Lindsay, grateful she hadn't changed her number in the last twenty years, not since he'd had to memorize it as an emergency contact for school.

"What's going on?" he asked as soon as she answered. "How's Mom?"

Lindsay sighed. "Oh, baby."

Roan crumpled to his knees in the mud of the yard. He vaguely felt the wetness soak through his favorite black pants. He couldn't give a shit though. "Lindsay? What? Tell me."

"She's not doing well, Roan. You need to get to the nearest airport and come home as soon as you can."

"Oh my God." He bent over, pressing his forehead into the mud, his gut trying to turn inside out again. Cameramen squatted next to him. He squeezed his eyes shut and whispered, "What happened?" He felt the cameras more than saw them, like a claustrophobic hell surrounding him.

"She collapsed sometime this morning, baby. I found her unconscious on the kitchen floor in the afternoon. The EMTs thought she'd been down there for at least a few hours."

"Fuck." He clenched his fist against the wet grass.

"She's at the hospital, but they don't have any news for now. She's having trouble breathing, Roan."

"No. No, no, no." His face twisted in agony. Drowning in her own lung fluids was her worse nightmare. "I'm on my way," he whispered and sat up slowly, handing the phone over to John who had been hovering just out of range of the cameras. Roan's breath seesawed in his lungs, his ears rang, and the world spun. He allowed himself one moment to sit there with his eyes closed, the heat and humidity stinging his face. Sweat beaded everywhere on his body, but he ignored it, willing the last five minutes to never have happened.

He startled when someone barked, "Andy! Stay back!" from the porch. Roan looked up to see a crowd of people standing up there watching him—all the remaining suitors, the other producers, and half the crew. Andy himself was frozen halfway down the steps in response to that strong order.

Then Walker was there, on the ground next to him, his hand on Roan's back. "Oh, Jesus, little lion. What's going on?"

"I have to go home," Roan whispered. Tears leaked out of his eyes, and Walker cupped his face, catching them with his thumbs.

"Okay. Whatever you need, Roan. What happened? What can I do?"

"I...just need to go. My mom is sick. I never told you, Walker. But she's really sick. And she's the only reason I'm here. She...she has cancer. I came here for the money. It was never about you. I needed it for her treatments. But she's not okay. And...she's at the hospital. It's bad. I need to go."

Walker's face became carefully blank. "Okay," he said. "Someone's going to book you a flight and take you to the airport, even if I have to do it myself." He shot a hard glare at John and then at Andy, still on the stairs, watching with an odd expression. "And Roan, I really don't—oh for fuck's sake, are you kidding me?"

Roan's head snapped up to see the other suitors crowding around them now, all wearing cloying, sad faces. "Fuck this."

Jerking away from Walker, he stood up, pushed passed them all, and ran into the house, leaving a trail of tears and mud behind him. He didn't have time for false sympathy or words of comfort for the sake of this fucking show.

His mom was dying, and he had to get home.

CHAPTER 16

"T HE CONTRACT SAYS if he leaves before the end of week four, he doesn't get a penny," Andy said, slowly flipping through the pages of the contract. "Though he did have a clause stating that he could leave for his mother's illness at any time without actual penalty. That's not the same as paying him the per-week fee."

"I don't fucking believe you!" Walker yelled, not caring who could hear. "You heartless bastard."

Andy wiped a hand over his face and grimaced. "Them's the rules, cowboy. I can't just go around breaking contracts or they lose their power."

Walker stared at him. "What about the power of some human grace and kindness?"

"Look, this was all pre-agreed."

"But Roan was here for that money."

"Right. Just like Chad and Ben and even you, for fuck's sake." Andy's brow rose, and he nodded toward where Ben hovered with an anguished expression. "Though I think Ben's been here for a bit more the last few weeks, haven't you, babe?"

"And what's Ben here for, exactly?" Walker snapped.

"I'm in love with Roan."

Walker spun on his heels. Ben stood there with his hands stuffed in the pockets of his jeans, white T-shirt stretched tight over his broad chest.

"What did you say?" Walker asked very quietly.

"Didn't mean to fall in love with him, but it happened. I hoped I'd be a soft place for him to land in the end. But it doesn't matter now. Because you're in love with him too. And you're the one he wants."

"Oh, love is a many splendored thing, cowboy," Andy said, but he sounded sad. "And totally unpredictable, no matter how we try to produce it."

"I'm going home," Ben said. He looked painfully embarrassed, and Walker wanted to feel a shred of pity for him, but his mind was reeling.

Andy planted his hands on his hips. "You're not going anywhere or you don't get paid either. It's in your contract too. Jesus Christ, this whole production has turned into a shit show. I've never worked with a bigger bunch of ungrateful contestants."

Walker seethed. He wanted to smash Andy's face in. "If you try to tell me Roan out there earlier was an act—"

"No, his mom's really sick," Andy said, and his irritable expression fled to be replaced by what looked like genuine remorse. "Like the kid said, she was why he was here to begin with. They can't afford a new, experimental treatment. Looks like they might not need it now."

Walker covered his face. "Oh my God, what is wrong with you? How can you not pay him when you know this?" He flung his hands out, and glared at Andy. "Did your mother not love you or something? I want this whole thing to be over. Now."

Andy picked a piece of cheese from the platter on the kitchen counter and took a bite, chewing with a thoughtful expression. "No, we can't cut the show short. But there is a solution. Now, you can have your boyfriend Mike save you. We won't have an eviction tonight. We'll use some sad shots of Roan crying and leaving, and Ben crying and leaving, if he insists on sabotaging his life, too. And then some of you looking all maudlin and sad, and a little bit torn about finding out that Roan wasn't here for your heart after all."

Walker blinked wildly. Was this guy for real?

"Then next week, you can send Victor or Chad home." Andy nodded firmly. "The week after that you choose Mike, propose to him on one knee, with a brilliant smile on your face. That's it. We're done and out. My husband gets his queer dating show that ends in true love. I get out of here alive. And next time, if there even is a next time, I'm choosing a more grateful bachelor."

"Unbelievable," Walker said.

"No, *you're* unbelievable," Andy snapped. "You signed on for this. There are no surprises here, but you act like this is so unfair to you. It's not. We're paying you handsomely and saving your insolvent ass by making you the star of this show."

Walker wanted to argue, but he really couldn't. What Andy said was true.

"But don't worry your little cowboy head about anything. We're going to leave this farm with a sellable product, for fuck's sake. All you need to do is pretend you don't know about Ben, show some interest in the others for the next week, and rekindle your flame with Mike. It'll be over before you know it."

Walker gritted his teeth. None of that mattered. "What happens with Roan?"

"Show must go on, baby," Andy said. He motioned toward the stairs leading up to the bedrooms. "He's packing up, and he'll be leaving while we still have some decent light."

"So you can catch everything on camera?"

"That's the name of the game." Somehow he sounded both determined and sad at the same time. Andy lifted his chin at something behind Walker, and asked, "Cameras rolling?"

Walker spun around to find Roan waiting at the bottom of the stairs. He was wearing his typical skinny jeans, but this time with a comfortable sweater over it, the neck too stretched and slipping over one shoulder. Something ached inside Walker. He would've wanted to get to know this comfortable Roan, the one out of his designer clothes. From the corner of his eye, he saw John nod at Andy that they'd started filming, but he didn't care.

"I'm so sorry about your mom," Walker said, taking Roan's hands in his. "I really am. I hope she's okay when you get there. If there's anything—" Walker shook his head. What could he possibly do from a thousand miles away. "For what it's worth, I understand. Why you came on the show, I mean. And I don't blame you. Like I said out on that trail, we all had our reasons. I agreed to this whole ridiculous circus because we need the money too. I just hope…" He trailed off, afraid to put it out there. He didn't need to.

Roan's dark eyes were shimmering and a little puffy, like he'd been sobbing upstairs, but he wasn't crying anymore. "That it wasn't all fake?" he whispered. He squeezed Walker's hands. "It wasn't. Not for me."

Walker opened his mouth to say it wasn't for him either, but the words wouldn't come out.

"Car's here," someone said from the doorway, and Roan took a step back.

Walker let go.

"Let's get this over with," Roan said to Andy and turned toward the living room. Walker watched as he said wooden goodbyes to the other suitors while the cameras looked on. The only ones who got a bit more time were Chad and Ben. But he shouldn't have been surprised, he supposed. The inter-contestant love story between Roan and Ben was no doubt going to be edited in and sold to viewers as added drama. He followed Roan out of the door, and when they reached the porch, Roan put his bags down and turned around. Someone stepped up and took the bags to the waiting Range Rover.

"So," Roan said, clearing his throat as he stared at the wooden slats under his feet. "Thank you. For everything. It was great getting to know you. And you have a beautiful ranch here."

Walker stared at him, and the ache that had begun to bloom in his chest spread like all over. "Roan," he whispered, but Roan moved away from him, shaking his head infinitesimally as he created distance between them. Physically and emotionally. Walker faltered. "I…it was good to have you here." He drew a complete blank, not knowing what to say while his brain screamed, *I don't want you to go, and I want to come with you.* "Let me know how you're doing? And about your mom?"

"I don't know if that's a good idea," Roan whispered. His bottom lip trembled a little, and he quickly stepped into Walker's space, hugged him fast, and was gone. Walker wanted to yank him back, to kiss him breathless, to say whatever Roan needed to hear, but he didn't. Roan obviously didn't want a goodbye like that, and the least Walker could do was respect his wishes.

"Bye," Walker said softly, even though Roan was long out of earshot. Vaguely aware of being filmed the whole time, Walker stood on the porch watching until the Range Rover disappeared into the sunset.

Andy had wanted a lonesome cowboy pining for love as his star, hadn't he?

Well, he'd gotten what he wanted after all.

WEEK FIVE

Black Moments

CHAPTER 17

"CAN YOU AT least pretend you're into this?"

"Hmm? Oh, sorry." Walker grimaced at Mike and sent an apologetic glance to John. He couldn't help but grimace a little again at the ridiculous table set-up the crew had put together in one of the barns. They were supposed to be having a romantic dinner in the straw with sparkle lights twined all around for a starry-eyed mood. He guessed it looked good on camera, but his idea of a romantic dinner didn't mesh with the smell of horse manure. "Sorry, I'm distracted."

"I can tell. Have you heard from him?"

Walker focused on the wine glass he'd been fiddling with. "From who?"

Mike said nothing, and Walker sighed. They were in the final week of the show. Ben had gone home last week after he "came out" during the elimination ceremony as in love with Roan. Walker had pretended to be shocked, didn't give him a horseshoe, and that was the end of it. Ben had packed his bags and left, after apologizing to Walker again. He couldn't even bring himself to care enough to be angry, especially since he understood completely what Ben might see in Roan. He just wished he knew if it had been reciprocal at all. Some wretched, jealous part of him was afraid Roan and Ben might be together right now.

"No," he said. "I haven't heard from Roan since he left. The producers wouldn't have let me talk to him even if he'd tried to call. Rules. Contracts. All of that. And when I've asked them about him, they don't have any real information for me."

"Cut!" the assistant director called. A gaffer darted into the shot to deal with a wire leading to one of the lights they'd set up for the shoot.

"Guys, you should be focusing on each other, not another, already-eliminated contestant," John hissed.

Mike ignored him, asking, "Have you tried to get them to pass on a message from you?"

"I gave them a letter. Asked them to mail it, but I don't know if they did or not. Regardless, he's gone, and there's no word from him at all. I think, if he wanted to get in touch with me, the producers would have passed on at least that much. That he'd tried. Don't you think? Maybe the truth is he really was in it for the money?"

Walker could take a hint and this one was about the size of Texas. Roan was gone, and Walker was the furthest thing from his mind. Never mind that he was all Walker thought about these days.

"That doesn't matter. Everyone is in it for the money."

"Except you."

"Except me." Mike's eyes glinted. "So you're stuck with me. Are you going to propose this weekend? Go down on one knee for me? I've heard the ring is real nice."

Walker snorted. "Maybe I want *you* down on one knee for *me*," he said. He pushed his wine glass away, barely having touched it.

John groaned and rubbed his face. "Hurry up," he snarled at the gaffer. "We're missing the actual good stuff here."

Walker said, "I'm thinking of just saying I pick no one."

Mike clutched his chest. "Ouch."

"Oh, come on. Don't tell me you want to continue this charade?"

"Why not?" Mike ran a hand through his blond hair. "Give the viewers their romance. It doesn't have to be fake, you know. The romance...or proposal."

Walker burst out into a startled laugh. A few boxes down, Callie or Cormac stamped their foot. "Doesn't have to be fake? What does that mean?" To his surprise, Mike's face heated. In all the time they were together, Walker hadn't seen him blush once.

"Obviously I'm not saying that we'd get married right away. You need some time to get over…to get over things," Mike said. He reached for Walker's hand, who was too stunned to pull it away. The gaffer crawled out of the shot. Across the barn, the AD called for the cameras to roll again. "I've really enjoyed spending these last few weeks with you. It made me realize what an idiot I was to walk away from you. Anyone who's lucky enough to be loved by you would be stupid to ruin it by insisting on dragging an unwanted third into the relationship."

"What are you saying?" Walker asked, his voice coming out hoarse.

"I guess what I'm saying—no, what I'm *asking*, is if you'd consider giving us another try? For real?" He looked up into Walker's eyes. "I've missed you."

"But it's been years. I—" Walker's eyes narrowed. "Are you playing this up for the cameras? Is this all for show, because I'm telling you right now, Mike, this isn't funny."

"No show," Mike whispered. His hand tightened convulsively on Walker's for a second, and then he leaned forward in his seat and kissed him.

It was just a brush of lips. Warm, dry, sweet contact. So familiar Walker felt a jolt to his stomach.

He'd missed Mike too. Once he'd missed him like something'd been ripped out of his chest. But that was years ago, and now…

"I can't," Walker croaked. "I'm sorry."

Mike sat back and nodded. "Is this because of Roan?"

"Partly, but not only."

"He's not coming back, Walker."

"I realize that." Fuck that hurt to say out loud, but the truth was he had no reason to believe that Roan would ever come back to him. He'd been on the show for the money, and even if something real had started between them, it'd been a hothouse love, grown in forced conditions, and killed by exposure to the outside world. "But that doesn't mean I'm just going to jump into something with you as a replacement. That wouldn't be fair to anyone."

Mike's jaw clenched, and he reached for his wine, draining half the glass. "Replacement," he said softly. "We were together for *years*. You only knew Roan a few weeks. I know you loved me once. You can't compare that to whatever little crush you have on Roan."

"Yes, Mike. Loved. Past tense as in years ago. You broke my heart when you left, but I picked up the pieces and carried on. I'm flattered you'd be willing to try again, but it's not going to happen."

"Okay." Mike reached for the wine bottle to refill his glass, but changed his mind and pulled back. "Okay," he said. "I know when I've lost. I'm just…sorry."

"Yeah," Walker said. "Me too."

"You're still going to pick me this weekend, right?"

Walker pushed away from the table. He didn't care what John, or Molly, or anyone else said, this date was over. "I don't know, Mike," he said. "I guess it depends on what I'm told to do. It's not like any part of this hasn't been a giant sham anyway."

Mike gave him a shrewd look. "But not all of it." Walker opened his mouth. Closed it. "Give the kid a call when this is all over, Walker. Who knows what he's going through? Have patience with him. If you care about him this much, you owe him a call."

Walker touched his hat and stalked from the barn. When Mike was wrong, he was spectacularly wrong, but when he was right, he was entirely right. Walker wanted nothing more than for the show to be over so he could reach out to Roan.

He did owe him that much. There was nothing he wanted more than to make sure Roan was okay. He just hoped Roan wanted to hear from him.

THERE WERE A lot of things that Roan wished he could go back in time and do differently. He wished he'd made more time for his mother the years he was in college and grad school. He wished he could somehow have known before she did about the cancer in her ovaries and gotten her to seek help sooner. He wished he could have been there to catch his mom before she'd hit the kitchen floor. He wished he'd been able to tell her goodbye, because the doctors said there was no hope for her waking up. The only way out for her now was the permanent exit, and his last words with her would always and forever be his last.

Roan sat beside her hospital bed. The darkness outside her window fading to the navy that heralded dawn. He had his fingers twined with her frail ones, and he talked to her quietly, wondering if she could understand him at all wherever she was now.

"I don't regret meeting him, though, Mom," he whispered. "I regret that I missed that time with you, but I'm glad I met him. I wish you could have met him, too. You'd have liked him." He paused, huffed a small laugh. "He has a fine ass."

The machines bleeped and buzzed, and he looked up at the numbers. Her respiration rate was way down. Each breath like pulling through water. Roan squeezed his eyes closed and took a slow inhale himself to keep his panic at bay. Anything to keep from screaming or sobbing again. He'd done that already. It didn't help anything at all.

Ben had somehow ferreted out which hospital his mother was staying at and had come to visit after leaving the show. It'd been awkward and strange. Like a part of a dream—and not even the best part—had come to life and stepped into his hospital room reality. He had wanted to shield his mother from Ben's gaze. He hadn't wanted her to be seen that way, not by someone who'd never met the real her. The vibrant, funny, smart-mouthed, beautiful woman she had been.

Ben hadn't stayed long. He'd been kind enough, but ultimately he'd sensed that he was unwanted. If his professed feelings for Roan had been real, maybe they were the product of the circumstances of the show or they'd fizzled in the face so much painful reality. But Ben hadn't brought up his so-called love, and he hadn't called or come back after that first visit. Roan didn't blame him, and, frankly, was relieved.

In all likelihood, Walker would be the same way. A forbidden romance during the filming of a reality TV show was a lot hotter than the reality of a broken-hearted man who hadn't eaten in a week, and was wearing stained jeans and the same old T-shirt for the third day in a row.

"It was a fantasy," he whispered to his mother's sunken face. "All of it. That I could bring back enough money to save you. That Walker could care for me. I always did have a good imagination, Mom." He laughed sadly. "And you encouraged me. You always encouraged me."

The darkness outside the window ripened to a lighter blue. The sun was coming up. Another all-nighter by her side, but he knew deep down it would be the last. He put his lips to his mother's hand, kissed the roughened skin.

"It's okay, Mom. I'm all right."

Her straining breath hitched.

"You go on now. I love you. But you…it's time for you to go on."

The machine's noises didn't change. Not for another hour or so. But by dawn, Roan was alone when a nurse came in to confirm.

His mom was gone.

WALKER STOOD ON the porch of the farmhouse and stared up at the early dawn sky. A falling star trailed into the moody blue of the rising sun. He closed his eyes, sent up a prayer, and then adjusted his hat.

It was time to start the day. It didn't much matter how much he yearned to talk to Roan, to find out how he was doing. The only way out was through. One more day, one more elimination round, and then he would be free of all of his contractual obligations, and the ranch would be finally out of debt.

Come Monday, Reed Ranch could be back to normal, and about time too since there was a lot to do in preparation for hurricane season. Now, if only he could convince his heart to stop aching with every beat, reminding him constantly of what he already knew: Roan was gone.

He set out toward the barns, feeling heavy-hearted and helpless. In the end, what good was the money if he wasn't the man he wanted to be? What good had come out of doing the show at all? If Roan lost his mother and was out there hurting alone while Walker was 'courting' the final men, he'd never forgive himself.

Even if he wasn't wanted, even if Roan's feelings had all been for the show, Walker wanted to do whatever he could for Roan to ease him through. Digging his phone out of his pocket, he pulled up the internet and searched for flights.

Cincinnati. Four hundred and fifty-eight dollars.

He paused by a big tree, pulled his wallet out of his back pocket, and dug his credit card out. He bought the tickets without hesitation. The sun crested the horizon. No matter what happened tonight, he had a plan.

WEEK SIX

The Final Horseshoe

W ALKER TUGGED AT his tie. All those weeks of filming, and it had never felt more constricting than it did now.

"So who are you going to choose?" Tessa asked as she leaned against the counter. All innocent like he didn't know she was hiding something behind her back. He glanced at the table where Dad sat bent over a plate.

"Whoever Andy tells me to pick," Walker said, trying not to sound too dejected. It was the last week.

Tessa pursed her lips and hummed innocuously as she pulled a stack of papers from behind her back. "Actually, I went through this last night. Just scanned it quickly." She walked over to him and shoved a particular page under his nose. He peered at it, recognizing the contract. "It clearly states the show can't force you to choose a certain person once you're in the final week."

"Oh." Walker shrugged and slipped into his shiny dress shoes. "That doesn't really help since I don't want to pick either of them."

Tessa grinned, eyes twinkling. "Ah yes, but it also says they can't actually force you to choose anyone. As soon as the show ends, your time is your own again, and only if you choose someone would they require you to film a few extra segments of your life with them. If you choose no one, you're free as a bird."

"Thanks, Tessa. I knew that already, but it sort of makes for a crummy ending to the show, doesn't it?" Walker said glumly.

Behind him, Dad grunted. "Can you do an old man a favor and come eat some of this heifer food? I swear to God if I have to eat another carrot I'm going to turn orange."

"It's good for you," Walker said. Out of solidarity, they'd all been eating healthier, and he didn't mind it, really. Dad gave him the stink eye. "I gotta go." He kissed his worried-looking step-mama on the forehead. "Time to go be fake one last time."

"Think of the money," Tessa said, but she sounded as sad as he felt.

"Yes, the money," Walker agreed. "It'll be good to go into hurricane season in a more secure place financially. And then there's the barn you guys will be living in. You'll like it once it isn't crawling with suitors and cameras. And me? I'll have this whole place to myself." He swallowed hard. Strange. When had he ever thought that someone might live here with him? He'd never really imagined he'd find a husband, had he? On reality TV? But then he'd never imagined meeting Roan. He cleared his throat and winked at her, then turned to Dad and squeezed his shoulder. "Enjoy your dinner."

Dad grumbled something unintelligible, but Walker knew it was more posturing than anything else. He'd been taking his insulin and paying more attention to his diet recently, and choosing his chores more wisely. Walker couldn't ask for much more.

When Walker stepped onto the porch, he sent a brief thought to Roan, wondering how he was getting on. If his mom was okay. "Last time," he muttered to himself. "This is the *last time* I have to sell my soul, and then I'm coming for you, little lion."

Then he stepped into the humid evening and aimed for the Range Rover waiting for him.

Walker suffered through the last of the interviews with Luke, pretended to be pensive on the back porch as he stared into the setting sun for the cameras, and finally came face-to-face with Chad. They'd set up a fake stage beside the barn with lots of plants that wouldn't survive a week in Louisiana, but Walker nearly swallowed his tongue when Chad appeared in an honest-to-God white fucking wedding suit. Oh God, Chad was really working his last opportunity to be on the show. Trying to make an impression, Walker supposed.

"Chad," he said as the tanned man beamed up at him. He eased a tense breath through his mouth. Thank fuck Molly had given him a speech to rehearse. "You are a wonderful person, and I feel so honored to have met you. You were a bright light throughout the whole show, and I enjoyed every minute I spent with you, but I can't ask you to marry me."

"Oh." Chad brought a hand to his mouth and ducked his head. His shoulders shook a little, but Walker noticed there were no actual tears. Not a bad actor, then, but not the best either.

"You'll find someone who deserves you," Walker told him sincerely. "And whoever he is, he'll be getting a really special guy."

When Chad looked at him, his smile was genuine, and his eyes did shimmer a little. "Thank you," he whispered. "That means a lot. You're a great guy, Walker. You deserve to be happy too."

"And cut. Well done."

"Thank God. Someone get me out of this suit. It's torture." Chad turned the emotion off like a faucet. But Walker couldn't help but agree with him about the suit. Unfortunately, he still had Mike to deal with. Chad began to walk away, but turned around suddenly to look up at Walker. "Have you heard from Roan?"

"No," Walker softly said. "I haven't. I mean, I'm not allowed—"

"I know, I just thought… He really cared about you. It wasn't fake, you know."

Walker swallowed hard and nodded. God, he wanted to get out of this suit, get into his car and on that plane. Soon. *Soon.*

Chad gave him a small smile. "If you ever do talk to him, and I'm betting you will, please tell him we're all thinking of him. It wasn't the same after he left."

Walker smiled. "It wasn't, was it?"

Chad gave him a shrewd look and was on the verge of saying something more when a producer came up to him to help him out of the dreaded suit.

"You need a break?" Andy called out. He was on set for the final shoot, wearing a shiny, silver T-shirt and matching gray and pink floral shorts. He was obviously feeling generous now that the show was wrapping up.

Walker rolled his shoulders. "Let's get this over with."

Mike looked good. His hair had been swept back from his handsome face, the corners of his eyes crinkled as he smiled, deep dimples inviting kisses. He wore a suit that looked made for him—and maybe it was— but not even the most stylish clothes could take the cowboy out of him. Just like Walker, he'd been born and raised to farm life, but his older brother had taken over the farm, so he'd gone on to study veterinary medicine. It hadn't taken the swagger out of his step, and when he climbed the little stage, Walker felt a rush of affection for his ex.

They'd been good together while it lasted. He was familiar and kind and a good man. Once upon a time, Walker had thought Mike could make him happy.

But now Mike had nothing that he wanted.

"Hey." Mike grinned at him, then swooped in for a quick, dry kiss. Then he looked Walker up and down and whistled between his teeth. "You're something else," he whispered. There was a slightly feverish light in his eyes, and Walker could see his pulse jump in his throat.

"Walker," Mike began, reaching out and taking hold of his hand. His fingers and palms were just as calloused as Walker's and in a flash of sense memory he could almost feel them on his skin. "I know you said we missed our chance. But I can't stop thinking about you. Even over the years, I've always thought I made a mistake. Being here with you, it's…" He laughed softly, a little disbelievingly. "It's been wild."

He sank to one knee, and Walker's heart skipped a beat.

"No," he whispered. "Mike, please don't do this."

Mike's smile faded a little. "Won't you hear me out?"

"You're on one knee. I think I know what you're about to do, and it's crazy, Mike. I can't. I'm sorry."

Mike didn't let go of Walker's hand, but he ducked his head and stayed where he was. Walker squeezed his eyes closed and tipped his head back to the sky as his insides contracted in agony. There was only one man he'd consider such an impulsive proposal from, and he was in Ohio. Walker fell to his knees and hugged Mike tight.

"I'm really sorry," he whispered. "But it would be a mistake."

"You're probably right," Mike said, sounding choked up. He clung to Walker, hard, his breath wet against Walker's throat. "I've just been so damn lonely."

Walker swallowed and hugged him closer. "I know."

"And cut," Andy called. Even his voice sounded subdued. "Beautiful."

Walker pulled back and looked at Mike, assessing for a moment to see if it had all been an act. But no. Mike's eyes were red. He wiped the back of his hand across his nose and wouldn't look at Walker as he clambered to his feet. Walker was about to say something when he saw someone run up to Andy, whisper something, and Andy covered his face.

"Oh, dear Lord, that's horrible," he murmured, then lifted his gaze and looked at Walker.

"What is it?" Walker asked.

Andy climbed the stage and reached up to put a hand on Walker's shoulder. "It's Roan. I had Molly call to check up on him so we could arrange a follow-up bit for the show." He squeezed Walker's shoulder gently. "His mom died."

Walker jerked away from Andy. "When?"

"A few days ago. The funeral is tomorrow."

Walker swallowed hard, glanced around in a daze, and then jogged off the stage. He didn't call out, he didn't explain. He didn't even care if filming was done. He just knew one thing. He had to go.

Roan needed him.

CHAPTER 18

ROAN SMOOTHED HIS hair back as he stared in the mirror. The charcoal suit wasn't black, but it was the only one he had. He took a shaky breath and straightened the black tie around his neck. There was a fine layer of dust clinging to the hallway mirror.

When was the last time this house had been cleaned top to bottom? It didn't matter. Nothing much did. All that mattered now was his mom's funeral. And for that, he needed to walk out the door.

And go.

That was how he'd get through it all. One step at a time. Alone.

"You ready, hon?" His mom's neighbor Lindsay stuck her head around the front door. She wore a black dress underneath her coat that looked a little too tight, and her gray hair was pulled back into a subdued bun. He'd seen that hair in every color of the rainbow despite Lindsay being in her sixties, but not today. "The car's here."

"Thanks, Lindsay. For everything."

She pressed her lips together and gave him a sad look. "I wish I could've done more. I'm just glad you were with her at the end."

"Yeah." Roan slipped his wallet into his pocket but left his phone home. Somehow it felt wrong taking it to the graveyard. And it wasn't like he needed it for his mom anymore anyway. He was glad he'd been here too, even though the end had been brutal.

He was just so tired.

"Come on." Lindsay slipped an arm through his and tugged gently. "Let's get going."

An nondescript black sedan sat waiting in front of their humble front yard, and Roan was glad the undertaker provided this service since he'd gotten rid of their car over six months ago. As they stepped off the porch, Roan noticed things he hadn't paid attention to in over a year. The paint on the stairs was chipped, the flowerbeds overgrown with weeds. The grass was cut though, and for the first time in a long time he wondered who'd been cutting it.

It was cold outside, and he wished he had an appropriate coat, but he didn't, and he wasn't about to stand at his mother's grave in one of his flamboyant designer jackets.

Even though his mom would've liked it if he did. Tears pricked behind his eyes, and he breathed carefully. He thought he was done with crying but apparently not.

When they reached the sidewalk, the driver got out and opened the passenger door for them. He nodded his head respectfully, waited until they were both seated, then gently closed the door. The drive to the graveyard wasn't long, but it was spent in silence, so Roan stared out of the window. He'd lived here his whole life but the landscape felt alien to him. What was he going to do now? He could go back to school to finish his master's, but then what? He didn't feel motivated to work as an environmental engineer at all. He didn't feel motivated to do anything.

Lindsay reached out and patted his hand. "We're here, hon."

Roan blinked. He hadn't even noticed they'd stopped. The parking lot was full. Here and there, people made their way into the cemetery, heads bowed, respectfully silent.

"I can't do this," he whispered. Watching his mother's coffin sink into the cold, dark earth? No. Never.

"Yes, you can," Lindsay said, her voice soft but firm. Behind her, Roan could see the driver waiting to open the door. "You can and you will. You'll regret it if you back out now."

Roan's heart twisted in his chest. Its thud rang hollow. He felt dark on the inside. Dark and sluggish and, God, so tired. "Okay," he whispered.

Lindsay nodded at the driver, and he opened the door. With one hand, he reached out and helped Lindsay from the car. When he did the same for Roan, a flashback so vivid hit him that he gasped. He'd been about to climb on the hay wagon when Walker's hand had gripped his, those calluses a delicious contrast to the warmth of his skin.

Now, he let the driver help him out of the car. The heat and sunshine of that day on the ranch was a stark contrast to this one. It wasn't raining, but it looked like it might. The grass surrounding the graves was damp. His mom had hated the cold. He wished he could've taken her away from here to somewhere warm. To Louisiana, maybe. She would've been happier there. Roan let the pain and regrets assault him, and he thought he'd buckle under the weight of it. Nothing mattered anymore now. She was gone, and he was free to do what he wanted. Only the freedom felt like a scary weight, a frightening abyss of the unknown. He didn't know what to do now that he was all alone.

Lindsay didn't say anything, but she slipped her arm through his again, and together they walked down the path.

At least the cemetery was pretty. His mother's grave lay at the crest of a soft, green hill, right beside her parents. Roan wondered if he'd end up here too one day, still alone.

The pastor nodded at him and began to speak. Roan didn't pay much attention to the people around the grave. There were more of them than he expected, but it wasn't a crowd by any means. He focused on the words, on the prayers, even though he didn't know if he believed in a God anymore. How could he when there was so much suffering, so much loneliness. How could a God be benevolent and almighty and allow Roan to helplessly watch while his mother drowned in her own lung fluids?

His mind flinched away from the memories, and Lindsay squeezed his arm, moving a little closer.

The pastor went on and on as Roan's feet went icy cold and he lost all feeling in his fingers. He didn't care. The wind made him shiver as it bit at his ears, and still the pastor kept talking. Roan kept his gaze fixed on the flowers on the coffin. They were pretty and more extravagant than anything he'd ordered. For the first time, he frowned. There was a card attached to the largest wreath, and he wanted to step forward to read it.

Before he could, a large, heavy warmth enveloped him. The coat that landed on his shoulders might've been unfamiliar, but he knew the scent that came with it instantly.

Oh my God.

Roan closed his eyes as tears dropped from their corners. He didn't look up, but Lindsay let go of his arm, and the comforting weight of a man's strong arm gently settled around him. Roan allowed himself to be pulled closer, and he gratefully leaned against Walker, suddenly too tired to even carry his own weight.

ROAN WOKE UP with a start and the horrible feeling he was late for the funeral, then he remembered it'd already happened.

"Jesus." He sank back in his bed, waiting for his heart to calm down and the sick dread in his stomach to ease. He hated waking up halfway through an anxiety attack.

When he settled down a little, he frowned, wondering why he was in bed with his shirt and pants still on.

Walker.

Swinging his legs out of bed soundlessly, Roan held his breath as he listened but heard nothing. He closed his eyes and swallowed down the disappointment. Roan hadn't tried to reach out to Walker at all the last few weeks; he couldn't expect Walker to stick around now. With a sigh, he levered himself out of bed, considered changing his clothes, then remembered most of his stuff was piled up in the downstairs laundry room.

As he stepped out into the hallway, he automatically strained to listen for any sounds from his mom's bedroom, but of course there were none. He shivered, thinking he should probably turn on the heat, but he should first find himself a new job before he began to spend more money. The funeral alone would cost enough, and while Andy had paid him against all expectations and contract requirements, it wouldn't last long after the cost of the funeral and other final expenses.

The house felt strange, the small, old-fashioned living room all wrong with his mom's blankets neatly folded on her chair. He averted his gaze and stepped into the kitchen as he unbuttoned his shirt, ready to rummage through the laundry in search of a warm sweater.

"Oh, hey, you're awake."

Roan froze in the doorway, shirt half-unbuttoned, and stared at Walker sitting on a rickety kitchen chair. A mug of coffee curled with steam in front of him, and he put his phone down as he rose to his feet.

"I thought you were gone." Roan's voice sounded rusty.

Walker frowned a little. He'd taken off his suit jacket and tugged the tie loose so it hung over his shoulders. The top two buttons of his white shirt were undone, and his hair was a mess of ridges drawn by repeatedly shoving his fingers through it.

"You asked me to stay," Walker said carefully. "When I brought you home after the funeral… But I can go if you want."

"No! I—" Roan watched him warily. "I forgot. I'm not thinking right. I'm confused." He suddenly felt self-conscious about their small, old house in the rough part of town where all the yards were tiny, divided by peeling fences. Somewhere in the distance a dog barked incessantly. Compared to Walker's farm, this place was a shit hole.

"You want some coffee?" Walker asked. "I hope you don't mind I made some."

"No, of course not. Um, if you're hungry, there are a lot of casseroles and lasagnas in the fridge and freezer."

Walker gave him a small, careful smile. He was watching Roan intently, as if trying to figure him out. "I wanted to wait and eat with you."

"Oh. Thanks. Um, I'm just going to change out of my suit." He looked at Walker. "I'd offer you something more comfortable but I don't think my skinny jeans will fit you."

Walker laughed softly. "It's okay. I have a suitcase in my rental car out front. I just didn't want to assume…" He looked uncomfortable for a second.

"How long are you staying?" Roan asked.

"I have an open ticket. I can be gone tomorrow, or next week. Whatever you want."

Roan blinked at him. "Whatever I want?"

Walker nodded solemnly, and Roan cracked his first smile in what felt like forever.

"I want you to go get your suitcase, cowboy."

By the time Walker came back, Roan had changed into a pair of sweatpants and a hoodie. He kind of felt like he should've dressed up since Walker had never seen him like this, but he was too drained and too vulnerable. He wanted to wrap himself in layers upon layers, comfortable like a hug. He was pulling on a pair of thick, woolen socks, when Walker reappeared.

"I wouldn't mind a pair of those," Walker said. "I didn't realize it was already going to be so cold here."

"Really? Because I have some."

Walker smiled. It wasn't his usual grin, like he didn't know if he was allowed to smile his full smile while Roan was hurting. "Sure, why not."

Roan grabbed another pair of the thick socks. "I should turn on the heat," he said, feeling his face flush. "It's just that I have to be careful right now."

"Careful how?" Walker pulled off a thin sock. His toes wiggled, and

Roan's eyes were drawn to his long, slender feet. He had high arches and surprisingly beautiful toes for a man who worked in boots all the time.

Roan's gaze snapped up. "I need to find a new job," he said. "And I have to be careful with the money Andy sent me. It will definitely help for a while, but until I have some prospects..." Roan trailed off and shrugged, uncomfortable discussing his financial situation.

"Wait. Andy paid you?"

"Yeah, he even paid me for an extra week. I hadn't expected it either."

"That little shit," Walker said under his breath.

"What?"

Walker shook his head as he pulled the thick socks on. "He told me he wasn't going to pay you because you were leaving early."

"He's been great, actually. He paid for my ticket home and there was a car waiting when I landed. He even called to find out if I needed help paying hospital bills."

Walker's lifted his eyes and watched him carefully. "And do you?"

"No. The hospital stay was included in her health insurance. She'd reached her lifetime max while I was gone. Thank God." That was one thing he never had to worry about, but it was messed up, wasn't it, to be grateful about that? "They didn't cover the new treatments she would've needed. But she didn't hold on long enough for those."

"I'm so sorry, Roan."

He nodded and grabbed a mug, taking a moment to get himself under control. As he poured coffee, he said, "So you want me to put a lasagna in the oven? It's past lunchtime."

"I'll do it. You sit down."

"You don't have to—" Roan fell silent when he turned around and Walker was right there.

Walker reached out and dragged his hand down Roan's arm. "I want to. Let me."

Roan nodded and held his mug in both hands, clutching it to his chest. "Okay."

"HOW DID THE rest of the show go?" Roan asked. They were sitting in the small living room, curled up on the sofa barely big enough to fit them both. Roan had laughed when Walker made them hot chocolate, but he was grateful for it now. Each hot sip was like liquid comfort warming his belly.

"Predictably terrible," Walker said, making a face. "It was Chad and Mike in the end. Ben left after you did."

Roan cleared his throat. "I know. He came to visit me."

"Did he?"

"Yeah." Roan frowned. "Just once. It was weird. He didn't come again."

"And how did you feel about that?"

"Glad. I didn't have the space for him."

"And if he showed up now?"

"No space for him now either."

Walker tilted his head earnestly. "Roan, you don't have to let me stay if you need—"

"I have space for you," Roan said. "Space. Feelings. Whatever."

"Feelings?"

"Yes. Real feelings."

"That's good to hear. That's great."

"What happened with Mike?" Roan played with a loose thread on his sweatpants.

Walker reached out and covered his hand. "Mike is firmly in my past." He squeezed once, then let go. "He and I are over."

Roan nodded. "Did you—" He faltered and fell silent.

"Did I what?" Walker gently prompted.

Not looking at him, Roan said, "Did you hook up with anyone else on the show?"

"No." Walker waited until Roan looked at him. "And I don't consider what we did a hookup."

Ridiculously, Roan's eyes began to sting again. He couldn't deal with this right now. He set his mug aside and reached for the remote of the old TV. "Want to watch a movie?"

Walker watched him for a second, then said, "Sure." He reached for one of his mom's blankets, but before touching it, asked, "This okay?"

"Yeah," Roan said, surprised to find it was. "Yeah, that's okay." He flicked the channels until he found something that looked halfway decent, then went with it when Walker gently tugged him closer and arranged the blanket over them both. Roan sat stiff and uncomfortable for all of one minute, but Walker's heat and familiar smell were like a drug, and inevitably Roan eased against him, muscles relaxing one by one.

CHAPTER 19

WALKER TRIED TO breathe as evenly as he could while he paid the barest attention to a soppy romance develop on the small TV. The living room was cozy. In fact, it reminded him a little of home, with its worn chintz couches and the slightly faded curtains. Their new barn might look like it belonged in a magazine, but the farmhouse still was the way it had been when his grandma lived there. Maybe now that his parents had their own place, he'd slowly start to add some modern touches to the old house too.

Roan's place was a little chilly—especially compared to what Walker was used to—but the blanket and Roan's proximity kept him warm. He felt every whuff of Roan's breath against his stomach and smiled at the little snuffling sounds Roan made in his sleep.

He'd started out nodding at the TV, unable to keep his eyes open. Then his head had drooped on Walker's shoulder, until he'd eventually slipped down. Walker had stretched out a little to accommodate him and now Roan's thick black hair, stark against his white shirt, looked like an invitation he couldn't resist. Carefully he moved the strands from Roan's forehead, brow furrowing at the deep, bruise-like half-moons under Roan's eyes. The need to protect him, to take care of him, surged through Walker until it became almost a palpable thing. He had to breathe through it, or he'd hug Roan tight and never let go. His face twisted at the thought of Roan all alone here, day in and day out, in this empty house.

"Come with me," he whispered. "There's plenty of room for you on my farm."

Roan didn't hear him; he slept on peacefully and so solidly Walker wondered how long it'd been since he'd found some real rest. When Roan didn't wake, Walker kept carding his fingers through his hair and settled a little deeper into the couch. He wished the circumstances of his visit were different, but he couldn't deny the soft, warm feeling burrowing in his chest as he allowed himself to just be with Roan.

When the movie ended, Walker turned the TV off, and oddly enough it was the lack of noise that woke up Roan.

"Mom?" He put his hand on Walker's stomach and sat.

"No, little lion," Walker said, his heart hurting. "I'm sorry."

"Oh." Roan hung his head for a second, then noticed their position. "Oh! I fell asleep on you."

"It's okay. Looked like you needed it. And I enjoyed having you close." Maybe that was too forward, but Walker didn't feel like pretending.

Roan blinked, mouth parting in surprise, then reached for Walker's hand and held it between both of his. He had his legs tucked underneath him, and he pretty much disappeared in the oversized hoodie. He looked so huggable Walker hardly knew what to do with himself. "I'm glad you're here," he said softly. "How did you even find out?"

"Andy told me. Molly had called to find out if they could do a little follow up on—"

Roan shook his head hard. "No, they got all the pieces of me they're going to get for now."

"I understand that. Did you not talk to Molly?"

"No. She must have gotten hold of Lindsay when she called. She was here a lot during and right after. I'm a little surprised she's not here right now, actually." He laughed.

"I think she knows I'm here with you. But, thank God for her," Walker said softly. "I'm so sorry I wasn't here for you, Roan."

"Did you want to be?"

Walker twisted his hand and dovetailed their fingers together. "I'm here now, aren't I?"

Roan nodded, mouth curling in a sad smile as he gently stroked his thumb against the palm of Walker's hand. It tickled in a shivery way. "Yes, you are. I can't really believe it. I'm sorry I didn't try to reach out to you. It was all just...too much."

Walker tugged on Roan's hand and hauled him closer, giving him that hug he'd been aching for. "You can't believe I'm here? Why wouldn't I be here?"

"I thought for sure you'd pick Mike."

"Mike?" Walker gave him a startled look. "No. No way. There isn't anyone I want but you." Roan stared at him with such a vulnerable, soft expression, his eyes tightening at the corners, Walker couldn't stand it. "Roan..." he whispered, but he didn't get any further because Roan closed the distance between them and kissed him.

THE KISS STARTED whisper-soft, like the touch of butterfly wings. Roan eased back a little, and Walker opened his eyes, not quite knowing when they'd drifted shut. Walker searched Roan's face, looking for clues. "Are you sure this is okay?" he whispered.

"Yes," Roan said. He kissed Walker again, a little harder this time, their lips sticking together until Roan wet them. The touch of Roan's tongue was electricity in his veins and Walker shivered as it charged through him. He moaned when Roan leaned back again, followed for a second, then thought better of it. Roan needed to be in charge for this.

"My mom would have loved you, you know?"

Walker's eyebrows flew up as he let out a startled laugh. "What?"

Roan's cheeks pinked. "I just wish she could've met you. If only once—" He turned away, face twisting, trying to hide his pain.

"You don't have to hide from me," Walker whispered, pulling him close again. He ran his hands over Roan's back, then slipped them beneath the thick hoodie. He'd been thin before, but now his shoulder blades stuck out like sharp wings. "You never have to hide anything from me."

Roan tugged himself free, then climbed into Walker's lap and kissed him wildly. It stunned Walker for a second, but then he gripped Roan's shoulders and kissed back, sweet and hard and agonizingly perfect. He couldn't remember ever kissing someone like this, fitting together like lock and key.

"Can we have sex?" Roan gasped, sitting up again. "I know it's weird. I know my mom's only just—but I want to."

"It's not weird." Walker tried to quell the mind-blowing shot of arousal that was already hardening his dick. "You want to feel close to someone. It's normal."

"Not someone. You."

Walker smiled, thumbed Roan's lip, then kissed him again. "Okay," he said. "I'd like that a lot. Here? Or—"

"Upstairs. My bed. I have—I have condoms and stuff."

Oh, God.

"Right." Walker closed his eyes for a second, trying to regain his equilibrium. He shuddered as his brain tried to overload his senses with possibilities, then looked at Roan again, who was grinning slightly.

"Come on, cowboy," Roan said with a quiet chuckle, but when he climbed to his feet, Walker saw he was trembling a little too.

They climbed the narrow stairs, familiar now after Walker had all but carried Roan up earlier before he'd passed out on his bed. He'd slipped him out of his jacket and shoes before repressing the urge to spoon up behind him.

Now, though, Walker had no plans to leave Roan's bed before morning. Roan stepped over the threshold and turned around, but Walker just kept on going until their mouths met. He loved that they were nearly the same height, that they were equal in this, even if Walker was a lot broader.

He fingered the string of Roan's hoodie. "Okay?" he whispered.

"Yeah," Roan said, already breathless.

"Can we have some light? Or do you want it dark?"

Roan hesitated for a second, then stepped away and closed his curtains. Beside the bed stood a small lamp that cast a soft orange glow across the room when he flicked it on.

"Better," Walker said, then reeled Roan in again and put his hands on the bottom of his hoodie. He began to tug, and Roan lifted his arms. Underneath he wore a threadbare T-shirt, the neck so stretched it slid off his shoulder.

"This is the real me," Roan said tugging at the grey shirt. Walker couldn't even tell anymore if that had been its intended color. "All the brands and designer jeans, that's not me. That was my ex in college and his mom."

"I like you in your tight jeans," Walker said, hauling him closer by his ass. "But I like you all soft and comfortable too. I don't care about your clothes, Roan. I care about what they keep warm." Walker winced. "And I don't mean just your body."

Roan laughed, and the tension in his sharp shoulders eased a little. "I know what you meant."

"You've lost weight you couldn't really afford to lose, baby."

"I know." Roan ducked his head, so Walker palmed his cheek and kissed him.

He began to unbutton his own shirt, holding his upper body away from Roan's a little so he could reach. When Roan took over, he let his hands fall and let Roan undress him. Shirt first, then undershirt.

Then Roan undid Walker's pants and let them drop. He knelt to take off Walker's socks, hands lingering. "You have nice feet," he said. "I noticed them before."

"Yeah?"

Roan looked up, but his gaze snagged on the bulge in Walker's boxer briefs. He reached for the waistband, quickly glancing up to gauge Walker's reaction, then tugged them down. Walker's cock swelled to fullness as Roan stared at it, and Walker had to suppress the urge to wrap a hand around and squeeze away some of the sweet demand. He did see what Roan planned to do before he even moved.

"Not yet." He caught Roan's chin before his mouth could descend on Walker's cock. The position made it easy for his thumb to slip inside, and Roan's reaction was instant. His eyes fluttered shut, lashes quivering against his cheekbones, and he moaned around Walker's thumb, immediately beginning to suck.

"Oh, it's like that, is it?" Walker whispered.

He pulled his thumb slowly out of Roan's mouth, dick jumping at the mournful sound he made, then pushed it back in, one millimeter at a time. He kept it up until Roan's breath puffed harshly from his nose, then pulled away. Roan's eyes flew open, and they were a beautiful abyss of lust and need that took Walker's breath away. "Stand up."

Roan grabbed the hand Walker held out and rose to his feet. Walker drew him close and kissed his exposed shoulder, slowly working his way up to Roan's neck. He was naked, and Roan was not, but somehow it felt empowering. He stroked his hands down Roan's chest, deliberately, teasingly close, but avoiding his nipples and the little barbells penetrating them. Then he tugged at the worn T-shirt and removed it.

"Ah, baby." He stroked the flat of his palms over the stark rise and fall of Roan's ribs, the ridges of his hips.

"I know. It's not...pretty."

Walker's gaze snapped up. "You're beautiful to me, Roan. Never not." He gently kissed his mouth, his temple, his shoulder. "Let me make love to you, and then I want to feed you."

Roan's laugh burst out of him like it came as a surprise. "Okay," he whispered, and reached for his sweatpants. They rustled down his legs and fell to the floor. He was wearing nothing underneath.

"Damn," Walker whispered. "I've been wanting to see that again. I see my memory didn't fail me."

"Yeah?" Roan asked. He brought his hand to his cock and gave it a long, luscious stroke. The foreskin drew down, revealing a pearl of precum. When his fist rose back up, the rosy head disappeared again and Walker's dick gave a jealous lurch.

He growled softly. "That's it, little lion. Show me."

CHAPTER 20

ROAN KNEW EXACTLY what that would do to Walker. He kicked the sweatpants aside and spread his legs a little farther apart. His dark, trimmed bush nestled at the base of his cock, and Walker dragged his fingers through it, gently scratching with blunt nails. Roan bit back a moan, not quite ready to relinquish all restraint yet.

"What exactly have you been imagining about me?"

Walker's mouth curled into a slow, wicked smile. "You naked," he said. "Just like this." He finally thumbed one of Roan's piercings. Then he brought his hand up and brushed his fingers lightly over Roan's cheekbones. "I'd love to blindfold you. So you don't know what I'm about to do to you, but you're all spread out for me to see. To watch you give in to the pleasure. The way you did before."

Fuck. Roan's eyes fluttered shut. To drift in darkness at Walker's mercy. It should've been a scary thought, but he wanted to let go. To be free of the pain and sorrow he'd been carrying around since his mom first called him with the news of her illness over a year ago. And he'd be safe with Walker. With a jolt, he remembered the shame he'd suffered through the day after their encounter on the horse.

"I don't know…"

"What don't you know?" Walker kissed him gently, closed-mouthed. "It's just a fantasy, Roan. We don't do anything you don't want."

"It's not that." He looked down, put his hands on Walker's chest and reveled in the smooth softness of his skin. Apart from a few hairs around his nipples and a trail leading like an invitation to his cock, he was bare, and the fragile whiteness of where the sun rarely shone was still startling. "I always feel weird, after," he admitted.

"Did you feel weird after last time?"

Roan bit his lips. Nodded. "I did, the next day." He was surprised when Walker hugged him. He couldn't remember the last time anyone had hugged him, stark naked. Usually being naked meant one thing, and when it was over, clothes came on again as soon as possible. Walker's large hands rubbed his back until he felt warm and pliant.

"This time is different," Walker said. "No matter what we do—and it doesn't have to be any more than this—I'll be here in the morning. You won't be alone. And it's just us. No cameras, no show." His hand slid up Roan's back and cupped his neck. "You and me."

He was right. Roan snuggled closer, and Walker's arms around him tightened. He pressed his nose behind Roan's ear and breathed soft and even.

"Okay." Since Walker's neck was right there, Roan opened his mouth and suckled lightly.

"Okay? To which part?" Walker sounded hoarse, and Roan allowed himself a small smile before moving down a little, sucking harder on the thick muscle of Walker's shoulder.

"The not knowing what you're about to do. The blindfold. Yes."

"Lord." Walker shivered against him, then grabbed a handful of Roan's hair and tugged. Not hard, just a suggestion, but Roan went easily, eagerly, and let Walker plunder his mouth. The room tilted, and he felt disoriented for a second, and then he was lying down, flat on his back, Walker cradling him tight. "What can we use? Scarf? Tie?"

"I have one of those masks. I had crappy curtains in college, so I got this to keep the light from getting through."

Walker looked at him. His tawny eyes were almost all pupil. "You really want this? You're not just doing it for me?"

Roan grabbed Walker's arms so hard his fingers left indentations. "I want it, cowboy. Make me forget, for as long as you can."

"I can do that."

Roan rummaged in his bedside table for the mask. He found the lube and condoms too, and hesitated before taking them out and putting them within reach.

"Just in case," he said, when he saw Walker look at him intently.

"We won't need that for a while," Walker said. "If at all. I plan to take my time with you." He picked up the mask. "Your hands are free, so take it off whenever you want."

"Okay." Roan closed his eyes, then quickly opened them again, sat up, and grabbed hold of Walker's head, fingers entwining at the back. He took in his handsome face, the laugh lines around his eyes, the swell of his full, sexy mouth. They kissed, hard, fast, needy, and then Roan lay back and closed his eyes again. The silky fabric of the black mask was like a sensuous caress as Walker slipped it into place, and he couldn't help a small sound as the world behind his eyelids went black.

"All right?"

"Yes," Roan said. He lay in anticipation for a moment, not knowing what would come next, and he realized he was tense.

Walker seemed to realize it too, because he kissed Roan lightly on the mouth, just a reassuring touch, then began to stroke his calloused palms over Roan's body. Down the outside of his arms and up again. Down the inside of his arms—which tickled in the best way—and up again. Over his chest, but not his nipples, circling his bellybutton, then slipping down to one thigh, then the other. His ankles. His feet. The touches weren't erotic, but they warmed his skin, made it tingle and come awake. He'd lived in his own head for so long he'd forgotten what it was like to just feel. And Walker was making him feel, all right. He had no choice, since his eyes were out of the equation. Listening and feeling was all he could do.

"Turn over," Walker said, his hands still on Roan's feet.

He complied, a little unsteady until he found the safety of the bed beneath him again. He pressed his hardening cock against the sheets.

Walker's fingers dug into the soles of his feet briefly, then he felt his way up Roan's calves, his thighs, to the swell of his ass. Walker's thumb traced where his thighs and backside met, then he palmed his cheeks, squeezing a little, and stars began to dance behind Roan's eyelids. Walker didn't linger though. He moved over the small of Roan's back, up his sides, over his shoulder blades, until every inch of Roan's skin had been drawn out of its long slumber.

"So hot," Walker murmured. "Hot damn, little lion."

Roan burrowed his face in the pillow so he wouldn't make an embarrassing noise. He felt Walker's breath on his shoulder before the actual touch of his mouth, and Roan gasped. The kiss on his sensitized skin was like a touch to his cock, and he squirmed as his groin went from vague arousal to aching hardness.

IT WAS WEIRD. Roan had had massages before, and he'd been with other people aside from his ex. Sometimes just kissing in clubs, sometimes hand jobs, sometimes the full shebang. But he'd never felt this affected by a simple touch before. He must've made another noise because Walker stopped trailing kisses down the juts of his spine and straightened.

"Baby?" he asked. "You still good?"

Roan nodded, swallowed hard, then said hoarsely, "Yeah, good."

"You sure?"

"Absolutely." He squeezed his eyes closed tighter until a rainbow of colors sparked behind his eyelids. Now that he couldn't see, couldn't focus on some small detail to derail himself from feeling, everything came at him tenfold. Walker's mouth started where it left off, and every time he flicked his tongue at Roan's skin, Roan jumped infinitesimally. It wasn't long before he had to open his mouth to drag enough oxygen into his lungs.

Walker reached the swell of Roan's ass, and the bed dipped a little as he sat up. He stroked the flesh, kneaded it, spread Roan's cheeks and pushed them together until Roan's face was as hot as the fire in his groin.

"Walker," he protested weakly.

"I know, baby. Turn over again."

Oh, God. He'd been hard before, but now he was ready to erect a barn with his cock. He turned over anyway because being hesitant about it would only make it worse. His eyes might've been out of order, but Roan knew his body. He knew his nipples would be dark with blood and erect, the piercings protruding on either end, lifted away from his skin. His chest would be red with sex-flush, and his dick would point up his belly, leaning slightly to the left. His balls would be drawn up tight and small, hugging the base of his cock like overlarge chestnuts. He wanted to tug at his balls, wrap a hand around his cock, and as he imagined doing exactly that, blind to Walker's gaze but feeling it anyway, his cock jumped and a surge of liquid dripped onto his belly.

"Shit, Roan," Walker croaked. "I want to fucking devour you."

"Then do it," Roan managed, desperate now.

"Not yet. Would you let me watch again? Just a little bit, like last time."

"Ah." Roan writhed against the bed. He should've known Walker would pluck that fantasy right out of his mind. He tossed his head to the side as he squirmed against the needy pulses in his veins. He wanted—he wanted—

Walker's thumb slipped into his open mouth and instantly Roan went completely still as he closed his lips and tongued him. Walker made a hoarse noise, then there was a rhythmic slapping sound, and fuck, not being able to see Walker jerk himself but knowing he was made it even hotter. Roan reached for his own cock and fisted it, dragging at the foreskin in the way he liked best.

"Fuck, yes," Walker murmured. He pressed Roan's left nipple, and

Roan jolted like he'd been electrocuted. "Too much?" Walker asked, slipping his thumb out of Roan's mouth.

"A little," Roan gasped. "For now. Give me a minute."

"I'll give you anything you want." Walker slipped two fingers into Roan's mouth now, and for a second Roan thought he should feel embarrassed, wanting that so much, but in that moment he couldn't.

Walker didn't touch Roan's chest again, instead rubbing down his belly, fondling the hairs of his treasure trail and gently cupping Roan's balls. Walker rolled them between his fingers, lifted them and soothed them, until his fingers inevitably slipped lower. He froze, and Roan held his breath.

"Show me," Walker demanded, and damn, he sounded completely wrecked.

Roan began to tremble when he bent his knees and let them fall open. The fingers left his mouth, and he bit down on a sound of loss.

"Holy shit, Roan," Walker whispered. The touch to the little piercing through the back of his balls was wet, so Roan knew they were the fingers that had just been in his mouth. "Do you have any more?"

"That's it," Roan said.

His breath hitched when Walker pulled on the guiche piercing a little, then rubbed over it.

"Why did you get them done? Do you like the pain?"

"Not really. And it was over so fast it barely registered. I can't explain it. I like how they feel now, obviously, but in that moment, there's something..." Roan bit his tongue and shook his head.

"You liked lying there with your legs open?" Walker whispered. "While a stranger looked at you and did this to you?"

"Yes," Roan said. He could feel the heat crawl up his chest, over his throat, to his face. "Yes, I liked that. *Ah!*" Roan jack-knifed up and clutched Walker's head as he sank down on Roan's cock, taking him so deep Roan could feel Walker's throat flutter round him. "I'm gonna come, I'm gonna come," he gritted out, trying to hold it back.

Walker wrapped his thumb and forefinger around Roan's base and squeezed, hard. Then he moved up and down, twisting his head on every upturn so Roan could feel his tongue drag over the entire length. The suction created a vacuum around his cockhead that made him lose his breath, even with the makeshift ring around his cock. Then Walker slipped his tongue under Roan's foreskin and he went boneless all over, sinking down into the mattress again as his body succumbed to quaking sensitivity.

Walker sat up. The spit cooled on Roan's cock. "I'm going to let you go of you now," he said. "Or do you need me to hang on a little longer?"

Roan gulped for air and concentrated on holding his orgasm at bay. "I'm good," he whispered.

Walker let go, rubbed behind his balls again, flicking the little ring with his fingernail. Roan's cock jumped and his asshole clenched. Since his knees were still spread wide, he wondered if Walker saw, but he had no way of knowing. "I'm going to play with your nipples now," Walker whispered right into his ear, sending goosebumps down his spine. "You can jerk yourself off whenever you want, but I'd really like you to come with at least some part of me inside you. You can choose." He paused, and Roan held his breath, waiting. "My fingers, my tongue, or my cock. It's up to you."

Roan opened his mouth, which had gone dry, but didn't know what to say.

"You can tell me later," Walker whispered. His voice was incredibly intimate, a caress he could feel all the way to his groin now that his mind's eye was enveloped in silky darkness. "Tell me when you're ready for me, and I'll give you whatever you want."

"Okay. Just…" Roan squeezed his eyes shut as he felt his cheeks go red.

"What is it, Roan? You can ask me anything."

"I'd like to suck you. For a little while. I want you in my mouth."

CHAPTER 21

FOR ALL HIS outward calm, Walker's heart was jackhammering in his chest. He could feel his own pulse pound his neck, and watching Roan, lying there with his mouth slightly parted, already wet and puffy from sucking on Walker's fingers, didn't help. His chest was gorgeously flushed, and his erect nipples looked good enough to bite. He was wanton and aroused.

All for me.

Walker couldn't say anything, his voice was stuck somewhere between his lungs. Instead, he reached for the extra pillows and gently nudged Roan's head. He sat up, let Walker arrange the pillows, and at the smallest touch sank down again. He licked his lips, mouth slick and pink, and Walker's stomach contracted with desire. He shuffled forward on his knees, then planted one hand against the wall over Roan's bed. Holding on to his dick, he smeared it over Roan's lips. He could feel the faint gasp, then the heat of his hot, slick mouth as Roan opened wider. Walker wanted inside. Some primal instinct wanted him to shove forward and delve deep, feel Roan's throat contract around him, wanted to experience it all. Teeth, tongue, palate.

Roan's breath hitched as he waited with his mouth open. He writhed on the sheets, then tugged on his balls as his cheeks went pink.

Walker leaned forward again, slicking Roan's mouth with more precum. This time, he dipped inside a little, just enough for Roan's mouth to close around him. It took all of his willpower to slowly pull back again, but it was worth it, just to see Roan's lips cling to him, trying to hold him as he withdrew. Walker's dick popped out, and Roan fell back, his frustration clear as day.

"Don't close your mouth," Walker whispered.

"*Hnn.*" Roan hid his face in the crook of his elbow for a second. Walker let him, caressed the soft flesh of his underarm, goosebumps rising in his fingers' wake. His patience was rewarded when Roan slowly dropped his arm and opened his mouth. Wide. And there went his willpower. He fed Roan his dick, inch by excruciatingly slow inch.

Roan didn't suck. He just mouthed, pushing Walker's cock into his cheek, then digging the tip of his tongue into Walker's slit.

"Jesus Christ," Walker sighed, slowly starting to withdraw again. Roan made an inarticulate noise, straining his neck to keep Walker in his mouth, sucking hard to prevent him from popping out. Walker had to plant both hands against the wall above them to keep himself upright, and he thrust into Roan's mouth lightly.

The need to deep throat him had left from the moment he realized how blissed out Roan was, just from holding Walker's tip in his mouth, playing with it. He could easily have grabbed hold of Walker—for his own security as well as adding sensation—but that wasn't what he wanted. Walker moved in his mouth a little, because he literally couldn't keep still, and Roan held him in that sweetest caress, sometimes moving his tongue, sometimes sucking so lightly it drove Walker to the very boundaries of his sanity.

"You're going to do this all night if I let you, aren't you?"

Roan let Walker's dick fall from his mouth. "Sorry," he breathed, twisting his face away.

"Ah, there's nothing to be sorry for. I love it. Here." He cupped Roan's cheek, coaxing him back. Then Walker pressed the heel of his hand to his dick so his balls lifted away from his body. "Open those sweet hot lips, baby." Roan did, and Walker maneuvered until he could sink his sack into Roan's waiting mouth. It wasn't an easy position to hold, but he didn't plan on doing it for long.

Roan moaned when he realized what he had in his mouth, and he gently pushed his tongue out, easing Walker's balls apart. He played with the fragile, wrinkled skin, nibbling lightly, then mouthing one ball, then the other. He stretched wide and held them tenderly in the scalding heat of his mouth. His sigh was such a noise of contentment Walker wanted to laugh but didn't. Obviously this was touchy for Roan, despite how much he loved it. And Walker didn't want him to think he was laughing at him.

He softly pulled away, waiting for Roan to break the suction, then he moved to lie on top of him and kissed him. Roan moaned and sucked on his tongue, wrapping his arms tight around Walker. It was the best feeling, being skin-to-skin completely at last. Roan's cock dug into the V of Walker's hip, and he shifted a little, rubbing against him. His entire body tingled, and they kissed and kissed and kissed.

When they finally broke apart, Roan reached for his own nipples and pinched them. "Fuck," he whispered. "I feel so on edge."

"Let me do that," Walker said. He batted Roan's hands away, rolled one nipple between his fingers, and took the other one in his mouth. Roan cried out and arched beneath him, thighs trembling as they wrapped around Walker's waist. Walker kept twisting and biting, testing Roan's limits, until he began to quake so hard they were almost convulsions.

"Too much?" Walker whispered.

"Yes. No. I don't know. God. Don't stop."

Walker laughed softly, and switched, pulling at the wet nipple as he took the other one in his mouth. They were swollen and red, tasted of steel, salty skin, and something earthy he couldn't entirely identify. His dick was throbbing, adding to the sticky, sweaty slick on Roan's stomach, but he ignored it. He couldn't get enough of driving Roan out of his mind. He didn't even care if he came or not, he just wanted to see Roan fall apart. When Roan jerked so hard he nearly knocked Walker off him, he sat up and let go of his nipples.

For a moment he didn't move. Roan's chest rose and fell with harsh breaths. His dick jerked and throbbed as his stomach muscles jumped.

He was tense, waiting, not knowing what was coming next. Walker carefully moved, and Roan held his breath, clearly expecting another assault on his nipples. Instead, Walker gave him the sweetest kiss. He dragged his mouth over Roan's, sighed when he felt it to the marrow in his bones, dipped his tongue inside and tasted leisurely, pulled back a little, then kissed him again. And on. And on.

"Oh, Walker," Roan whispered, holding him tight. For a moment they just breathed together until the need for more began to build again. Roan's cock jumped against Walker's abs, and he gave him one last, slightly dirtier kiss, to let him know the game was changing again.

He lifted himself up, dragged his hands down Roan's pale skin, tugging a little at the hair, and then sucked Roan down. He wished he could take him down to the root, but Roan was a lot bigger than anyone might give him credit for at a glance, and Walker was woefully out of practice. He made up for what he couldn't reach with his hand, and Roan didn't seem to feel the need to complain.

"OH, GOD." ROAN'S legs spasmed when Walker pushed them wider. He tongued Roan's balls, teasing them apart, then sucked first one, then the other. Precum steadily dribbled into Roan's navel now, and Walker paused to lap at the little puddle. Roan let out a startled laugh that turned into a moan when Walker lifted his balls and nibbled on the piercing. His legs jerked again, as did his hands, like he wanted to lift his knees and hold them open but hesitated.

"Do it," Walker whispered. Then he sat back and waited. Watched.

Roan battled with himself. His jaw was clenched tight, and air blew from his nose in loud, almost angry gusts. The line of his throat was exquisite as he fought his embarrassment, head thrown back in the pillow. Unable to help himself, Walker soothed Roan's stomach, gentling him silently.

When the fight left Roan, it was sudden. He breathed out through his mouth, his body relaxed, then he slowly slipped his hands underneath his knees and pulled them up.

"Have you decided?" Walker asked quietly.

"I want your tongue." Roan's voice was so gravelly Walker almost didn't recognize it.

"Is that all?"

"I'll let you know if I change my mind."

He spread his legs wider. The piercing glinted in the orange light. Walker nosed Roan's balls, breathing deeply, then flicked his tongue against the little silver ring.

"Oh, God." One of Roan's legs slipped from his grasp and thumped to the bed. He had to try twice before he could get a grip on it again.

"Okay, little lion?"

"Yeah, I—yeah."

Walker heard the little hesitation. He sat back. "What is it. You need the mask off?"

"Not yet. I just haven't…been with anyone since I got that piercing over a year ago."

A rush of heat shot up Walker's dick and dribbled out. He breathed evenly for a second, closing his eyes so he didn't have to look at Roan's balls, his smooth taint, that sweet little asshole waiting just beneath.

"Walker?" Roan asked, voice small.

"I'm trying not to come," he admitted, opening his eyes. Roan let his head fall back, laughing softly. "Oh, you think that's funny?" He bent and sucked Roan down without warning.

"Ah! God!" Roan thrashed against the pillow, then stilled again when Walker just as abruptly let go of him again. "Please," he whispered, even as it sent a rush of red heat up his throat. "Please."

"I've got you, baby. You don't need to beg." Walker licked Roan's taint, tickled the metal piercing in Roan's tight little balls. Roan's hole contracted and relaxed. Walker grabbed his hips, hauled him up and tongued him open.

The noise Roan made was the dirtiest thing Walker had ever heard. He licked and prodded, nibbled and kissed, until Roan was a writhing, swearing mess. He'd started to shake again, and Walker was glad they weren't back on Cormac, because this time he didn't think he'd have managed to keep Roan from kicking him. Giving him a moment to settle, Walker gently sucked his balls again, always returning to the ring clinging to his sack. He took it in his mouth and softly sucked, listening to Roan's keening noises.

Roan had his head thrown back again, his sharp Adam's apple danced convulsively as he tried to moisten his no doubt dry mouth, and his chest heaved as he gulped for breath. When he calmed a little, Walker lifted his hips up again and brought that gorgeous hole to his mouth again.

"Fuck. Fuck! Walker, I can't——" His legs jerked, hard, and hit Walker in the back. "Shit, shit, I'm so sorry."

Walker eased him down and stroked his stomach, his thighs, gave his cock a leisurely tug. The foreskin had withdrawn completely now, hugging the base of his cock-head, and Walker played with it until he could slip it back up. He shoved his thumb underneath it and drew lazy circles.

"Tell me what you want, Roan," he murmured.

"Fuck me. Please."

"You sure?"

"Yes."

"I want to see you for that."

Roan went still. "Okay," he whispered. "But not yet."

Walker kissed the inside of Roan's knee, then gently eased his thighs down, stretching them out so Roan could relax. He grabbed a condom, made quick work of snapping it in place, and reached for the lube. When he saw an unopened bottle of water and some wet wipes, he grabbed both. Wiping his mouth first—he wanted to kiss Roan again, and while he didn't think Roan'd mind after the rimming, it was only polite—he then opened the bottle.

"Want some water, little lion?"

"Yes, please."

It didn't even occur to Roan to sit up and reach for the bottle. He let Walker lift his head and opened his mouth, so trustingly something warm and wonderful bloomed in Walker's chest. He gave Roan a few sips, then drank some himself, swirling it around his mouth before he swallowed.

"I'm going to work you open with my fingers first."

"You don't need to. I can take it."

"It's been a year. I don't want you to take it, Roan." He leaned close and whispered in his ear, "I want you to love it so much you'll ask me for more. Again, and again, and again."

Roan made a hoarse sound, and turned his face toward Walker. Their mouths slid together like they'd been kissing for years. Without breaking the connection, Walker lubed up two fingers and searched for Roan's hole. He rooted around gently, testing. When one finger traced the rim, Roan instantly bore down, trying to draw Walker in. He withdrew a little, intent on taking his time, then pressed again, mimicking the movement with his tongue.

Going by the noise Roan was making, he yearned as much for Walker's tongue in his mouth as a finger in his ass. Walker gave in, licking into Roan's mouth, then entering his finger, slowly but inexorably surely. When Roan's hole fluttered around him, hot and tight and soft, Walker held still until he relaxed, then worked on opening him up a little more.

Walker stopped kissing when he drew out and returned with two fingers so he could see if Roan was all right. He was trying hard to relax, fists opening and closing against the sheets, lips parted. He still knew what to do, but that didn't mean he didn't anticipate pain, and Walker wanted him to feel as little discomfort as possible. His breath hitched when Walker pushed in to the first knuckle, then he grimaced a little, so Walker touched his nipples, gently at first, then tugged at the piercings a little harder. Roan's entire body shuddered, then capitulated to the intrusion. Walker's fingers sank into his body, drawn in, then held there by Roan.

Chapter 22

I T WAS SO much. Roan was glad he couldn't see anything when Walker's fingers pushed into him. He was so gentle about it, it would almost have been easier to just take the pain and get it over with. But this care, this love, was not something Roan was used to. And he didn't know how to deal with it. His heart stumbled along in a rhythm he couldn't imagine keeping up for long, and when Walker caressed his hair, he inexplicably felt like crying.

The next kiss came as much as a surprise as all the other ones, and each time Roan became needier, a little more unraveled. "Please," he whispered into Walker's mouth.

"Yes, baby. Soon." Walker kissed him again, then was gone. Roan jerked when he prodded deeper, feeling around, then hooked his fingers to the front wall of Roan's rectum and drew down. When he hit Roan's prostate, a shout burst from his mouth, his thighs began their familiar tremble, and Roan wanted to hide his face beneath a pillow.

"God, there too, huh?" Walker asked, sounding reverent. He spread his fingers, this time skirting around Roan's prostate—and Roan was grateful for it—but still stretching. Then he pumped Roan's cock, hard and fast, a few times, and Roan made embarrassing, high keening noises, his orgasm building like a frightening crescendo. He didn't want to come yet. He flailed until the back of his hand hit something, then grabbed hold of Walker's arm.

"I'm ready. I can't hold on much longer. You said…you said I could ask for anything. And you'd give it."

"I did," Walker whispered.

Roan heard the snap of the bottle, the slick, rude sound of Walker lubricating his cock. The bed dipped. Walker's warm hands spread Roan's thighs wider and arranged them over his own. He felt so open and exposed, the moment tore him in two. On the one hand he imagined seeing what Walker saw, his puffy hole, maybe gaping a little, the glint of the piercing. On the other hand, he wanted to get fucked more than he ever had in his whole life.

The need won out. He lifted his hips. His ass contracted in anticipation. Walker swore under his breath, leaned over Roan, kissed him one more time, then set his cock to Roan's entrance. He bore down, ready, needy, and Walker began to push into him. There wasn't a sound apart from the wet noise of sex. They both held their breaths even though Roan fought to relax. Millimeter by agonizing millimeter, Walker pushed his way inside. Roan felt full to the brim before they'd even made it an inch, and he knew it would just keep on coming.

"Okay?" Walker asked. He sounded strained and suddenly all Roan wanted was one thing.

"I need to see you," he whispered. Walker stilled. After a very quiet moment, he softly kissed Roan's mouth, then slid his fingers against the silky mask.

"Keep your eyes closed for a second, so you adjust," he whispered, and then the mask was off. Orange light danced behind his eyelids. Walker tweaked his right nipple. Roan gasped, and when Walker slid all the way inside, the noise he made one of utter relief and satisfaction. He gently pulled out a little, and pushed back in, easing the way. He rearranged Roan's legs so he could lie down more comfortably, and rocked his hips. It was barely a push, but the movement grazed Roan's prostate and his eyes flew open.

It was as if the world had always been black and white and he could see in color for the first time. Walker's face was right there, in sharp relief against the hazy hues of the dusky room. Walker gazed down at him with such affection, Roan wondered if he'd caught him in an expression he wasn't meant to see. But Walker didn't change. Didn't hide. He smiled softly but deeply. Heartfelt. His eyes lifted at the corner.

"Hi," he whispered.

Roan opened his mouth but he choked up. A single tear rolled down his temple. Walker caught it, tasted it, then passed the salt to Roan's tongue. "I'm okay," Roan managed.

"I know," Walker whispered. "It's just so much, isn't it?"

Roan wanted to close his eyes, but didn't. He nodded, wrapped his arms around Walker and held him tight. He rocked his hips while Walker held still, and while he didn't move much, the pressure against his insides was exquisite. He shuddered all over, clenching down hard.

"Ah, Roan, you're killing me here." Walker began to thrust, almost as if he had no choice. His dick slid almost all the way out, stretching Roan's rim, then entered him again in one hard push. Roan jolted, mouth open in shock, and he stared right into Walker's eyes as he did it, like promised, again and again and again.

He'd never been fucked like this before. Their bodies created a co-coon of safety, a harbor from all the pain, but at the same time they created a salacious space, a pocket of sex and lust and primal, earthy feelings that was only theirs and no one else's.

When they reached the point of no return, Roan's body quaked and shook so hard they couldn't keep kissing. Needing something he couldn't entirely put into words he thrashed his head about as Walker worked over him, hitting the sensitive nub inside him relentlessly. He'd been tweaking Roan's nipples at the same time as he held himself up with one arm, but when Roan didn't stop seeking, he dropped down on his elbows and fed Roan two fingers.

They both moaned simultaneously, eyes locking with a desperation that could've been frightening but all Roan wanted was to reach that high, to get there through Walker's doing, to give himself over completely in the purest of ways. Like he knew, Walker worked harder, first with deep, full length strokes, then short, fast jabs. Roan sucked on his fingers, tongued the deliciously salty skin. Walker made a broken noise, then fucked him with all he had, hammering Roan's prostate until the shaking seized. Roan tensed up, rising higher and higher and higher, breath stuttering until that fell away too. For a second the abyss was terrifying, but he wasn't alone. Walker whispered his name, and at the very last moment his eyes slammed shut and the torrent took him, down, down, down, until his balls were empty and his belly sticky, his hole still pulsing around Walker's rigid cock.

He made a pathetic mewling noise when Walker pulled his fingers out. And then he very carefully eased his cock out too. He wanted to say something about that, but then Walker was there, stripping the condom off and feeding his cock into Roan's achingly empty mouth.

His mind was buzzing with blissful relief, his body felt heavy as if the earth's gravity had shifted, and he let Walker push in and out of his mouth.

Roan suckled and drew on him, flicked his tongue against the underside, until Walker swore and shook, thighs hard and twitching with the effort of holding himself up. When Roan thought Walker would pull out, he grabbed hold of his hips and devoured him whole. Walker cried out and the thick pulse of his cum filled Roan's mouth. He swallowed it down.

ROAN ROSE FROM the deepest sleep in a year like a diver rising to the surface of the ocean. He became aware of a soft, rustling sound first. It was soothing and rhythmic. Then light began, soft like dawn's rising, but it was too early for morning. His sleep might've been deep, but it hadn't been a whole night's worth. He wasn't alone. That was the next thing he knew, and right along with that realization came the sensation belonging to the rhythm.

Walker was stroking his chest, leisurely up and down. Roan stretched, limbs a-quiver. With the greatest effort, he unglued his eyelids.

"He lives," Walker murmured, amusement tingeing the tone of his voice. Roan shifted his head, the pillow rustling underneath him, and blinked to wake up his brain a little more. Walker was watching him, probably had been watching him for quite a while because there was no sign of sleep on his handsome, weathered face. Roan reached out and touched the lines beside his mouth, then slid his hand around the back of Walker's head and drew him down for a kiss.

"Can't believe I fell asleep," he croaked.

Walker laughed, a little dazed when Roan let him go. "After you came like that? I'd've been surprised if you didn't." Roan felt his face heat, and Walker stroked his cheek with the tips of his fingers. "No, baby," he whispered. "Don't be embarrassed now. That was the sexiest thing I've ever seen."

Roan frowned in confusion. "What?"

"I never laid a hand on your dick. I've never seen anything like that before." He bit his lip and shifted, and Roan wondered whether, if he reached underneath the sheets Walker had arranged over them while Roan slept, he'd find him hard again. The thought made him tingle, but it also made him wonder where they went from here. "How are you feeling?" Walker asked.

"Fine," Roan said. He stretched his body. It ached, but in the best way. "Better than fine." He smiled a little bashfully.

"No regrets?"

Roan opened his mouth to answer, then took his time to think about it. Last time he'd given himself up like that to Walker, he'd been a mess the day after, but now, with Walker here...

"I feel self-conscious," he said. "I think I always will. I guess that's part of the...appeal. To let go like that even when I don't quite want to. But I'm not ashamed."

Walker tugged him close and held him. He smelled so good. Of sex and exertion and the deep, rich fragrance that was all Walker. "Good."

"How about you?" Roan asked. "How do you feel?"

Walker smiled, the left side of his mouth lifting a little higher than the right. "I don't want to scare you," he softly said.

"What? You won't. What is it?" Roan began to lift himself off Walker, but was drawn back into the tight embrace.

Walker's hot breath tickled his ear. "I feel like I want to wrap you up and take you home and never let you go."

Outside, a car came hurtling down the street, music blaring. Roan stilled. "What does that mean?" he asked softly.

Walker stroked his knuckles down Roan's face, scruffy now with new stubble. "It doesn't mean anything other than I don't want this to end. And it can mean anything from me traveling up here every once in a while and you coming down to see me sometimes, to you leaving this place behind and joining me on the farm."

"You hardly know me."

Walker leaned up on his elbow and gave Roan all of his intense, tawny-eyed attention. "I'm willing to take the chance with you, little lion. Hell, there isn't much I wouldn't do for you."

"That's insane," Roan said, laughing a little giddily.

Walker's smile was a little self-deprecating. "I'm aware. But I'm too far into this to pretend otherwise."

"I don't know anything about farming," Roan whispered.

"I can teach you anything you want to know about farming, if that's what you want. If not, there are plenty of others things to do. Either around the ranch or outside of it. Hell, my step-mom's been going on about starting one of those organic produce delivery side businesses."

"I don't know." Roan bit his lip and averted his eyes. He felt Walker stiffen a little.

"What don't you know?"

"Well…" He couldn't hold back the smirk anymore. "Do leeches eat lettuce?"

Walker stared at him, blinked, then threw his head back and laughed. Roan wanted to gnaw on his Adam's apple.

"No," Walker said. "Leeches live in water." His eyes began to twinkle. "There are other critters though."

"No, don't tell me."

"We have velvet ants, which are actually wasps."

Roan clamped his hands over his ears. "I said don't tell me!" He screeched when Walker tickled his sides and tried to bat him away.

"We have brown recluse spiders."

"I'm not listening!"

Walker got him good between his ribs. "Wolf spiders."

"No!"

Walker sat back a little. "Okay, I'll stop."

Roan sighed and relaxed back in the bed. Walker crawled up the bed until they were lying flush together. His lips grazed Roan's jaw. "Rattlesnakes," he whispered, skimming his hand along Roan's arm. Roan bucked and laughed so hard Walker bounced off him. He reached for Roan and pulled him close again, nuzzling his neck. "Okay, I'll really stop. Although I should warn you about my parents."

"Yeah? Why's that?" It seemed wrong to be thinking about Walker's parents when they were both half hard again, squirming together so their cocks lined up.

"They'll harass you about our sex life at every turn. It's a thing they do. And if you can't run fast enough, they'll share intimate details about theirs."

"Okay, I was getting turned on again, but that's not an issue anymore."

"Hmm. You sure?" Walker nipped his shoulder, twisted the piercing in his right nipple, and then grasped their cocks together.

Roan stopped thinking about everything, parents, snakes, bugs, everything but the man in his arms.

EPILOGUE

"**B**EEN AWHILE SINCE I saw you in skinny jeans."

Roan turned away from the bedroom window of the master bedroom at the farm, where he'd been standing to watch the white tents go up and the mess of wires, lights, cameras, and crew setting up for filming.

Walker looked amazing in his black dress shirt, tight Wranglers, and white cowboy hat. His tanned skin shone with more than the sun's kiss, though. Clearly Kylie, or whoever was doing makeup for the shoot, had already gotten ahold of him. They'd actually added highlight to Walker's cheekbones. Hilarious.

But kind of hot.

Walker stepped into the room and pulled Roan into his arms, cupping his ass and squeezing. "I missed 'em."

"I figured flip-flops and shorts wouldn't be quite fancy enough for our wedding." Roan still had his fancy clothes from before, but he rarely wore them now. He didn't miss them. Not really. His new life with Walker was so real—dirty (in both the delicious way and the actual dirt way), physical, and full of day-to-day joys—that he felt fully at home in his body for the first time ever. He didn't have to dress to impress, though on date nights he still did, because he wanted to. All he needed to do to impress Walker was show up. Every day. And be there.

Walker lifted a brow. "I'd marry you naked."

Roan smirked. "I bet you'd like that."

Walker pulled him in tighter, nuzzling his neck and then kissing his ear. "I should."

"Andy would love it, too. Get those ratings sky high."

Walker huffed a laugh, his head tipping back to expose his long neck, and Roan didn't resist the urge to press a kiss to his Adam's apple. "Screw Andy."

He still couldn't believe they'd agreed to this, but they had. The extra money would be nice for their honeymoon and, besides, it felt right somehow. Full circle. Seeing Andy, Molly, and John again was going to be strange, but they'd done a good job with the first season of Queer Seeks Spouse.

Everything had been edited to pieces, of course, and what made it to the TV screen didn't reflect the reality of their relationship in any way—especially now that they really knew each other—but it didn't portray them in a bad light either. Agreeing to let Andy and company come in for a follow-up special, letting them film the ceremony, so long as they footed the bill for the decorations and cake, plus paid them a handsome sum, hadn't been that hard of a choice to make.

Speaking of handsome.

"You're looking pretty good yourself, cowboy."

Walker's cheeks flushed with pleasure. "Tessa will be upset that you saw me before the wedding."

"Does that make you the bride?" Roan asked, laughing and poking Walker in the chest.

Walker chuckled and kissed Roan's cheek. "C'mon. We should go down. Get you to makeup."

"How long until the guests arrive?"

"Soon enough."

They'd invited important friends and family to the ceremony. Though there would be many more people in attendance for Walker than for Roan. Lindsay had said she couldn't make it, though she'd sent a beautiful card and some photos of him as a child that she'd found in her things. One of which was a very special picture of Roan and his mother. He'd been about eight in the shot, and he'd been curled up at her side on Lindsay's sofa, laughing, both of them. It was priceless to him.

Walker had it framed and placed on the mantel with his own family photos. It still choked Roan up—in a good way—to see it there every morning. Of all the changes made to the old farmhouse in the last year, that was the only one that really mattered to Roan. He smiled toward the photo as they passed through the living room together on their way out.

Stepping out to the front porch, they were greeted by a profusion of reddish-pink azaleas in full bloom. Out in the field where they were setting up and decorating the large white tent under which they'd be married, a white fringe tree provided a cloud-like background for the stunning purple irises he knew Tessa had planted twenty years ago. Another cloud of pink, a mimosa tree, bloomed to his right, and Roan took a long slow breath.

It was beautiful. If only his mother were here to see it…

"You okay?" Walker asked.

"I'm good. Just missing my mom."

Walker nodded and slung his arm around Roan's shoulder.

Roan smiled, his throat tight, and he squeezed Walker's hand. "But let's not be maudlin on our day." Then he spotted someone standing in the shade of one of the oaks, talking with a producer, and he frowned. "Did you have to invite him?"

Walker squinted into the midmorning light, trying to see with the sun in his eyes. "Mike?"

"The one and only."

"You still jealous, little lion?"

"No." Roan wrinkled his nose. "He just bugs me."

Walker laughed and hauled Roan against his body to whisper in his ear, "Because you're jealous. No need to be. I'm marrying you, ain't I?"

"Ain't you?" Roan chuckled. "You must really want me to believe you because you're slipping into deep Louisiana-speak on me now."

"I couldn't not invite him. I've known him forever. Plus, we invited everyone else who was on the show with us."

"Yeah, but did he have to accept?"

"What about him?" Walker said, nodding toward Ben, who had arrived hours earlier than necessary for the wedding. Apparently, Andy had requested to film interviews with him and Mike as the other two frontrunners who had "lost" to Roan. "Did you have to invite him?"

Roan snorted. "I didn't. Andy did."

"Ditto for Mike."

"I know." Roan's eye caught Ben's then, and he smiled, hoping to impart that he considered them to be friends. But Ben ducked his head and moved out of Roan's line of vision into the shade of another oak tree. "He didn't love me," Roan said quietly. "He just thought he did."

"Same with Mike."

Roan shook his head, but he didn't argue. The difference between Ben and Mike was night and day. Ben had let proximity and forced intimacy take on more meaning than they really had. Mike had years with Walker. But whatever. They were getting married today and the last thing he wanted was to talk in-depth about the other men in their lives.

"There you are," Kylie said, hustling up the porch steps and grabbing his arm. "Come with me." She directed her sharp gaze on Walker. "And you! Stay in the air conditioning. I don't want to have to re-do your face later."

Roan waved as Kylie dragged him away to the makeup trailer where he was pushed into a chair, much like the one he sat in at the dentist, and endured half an hour of her attentions. Then it was Tessa's turn, and he stayed behind to chat with her while Kylie glammed her up for the ceremony.

"Walker's going to love your hair," he said, sipping water from a Styrofoam cup that Kylie had pushed into his hand at some point, ordering him to stay hydrated. "He loves the gray."

Tessa pursed her lips, checking herself out in the big mirror. Her gray hair was curled to frame her face, and the makeup was tasteful. "Wish I liked it half as much as he does, but there's no fighting age, baby. Death comes for us all."

"Wow, way to get morbid on my wedding day," Roan said, chuckling.

"Oh, no, now, I didn't mean it like that." Tessa's eyes grew round with worry. "And I didn't mean to remind you of your dear departed mama. I know she'd have loved to be here today."

Roan nodded and took another sip of his water but said nothing more. If he thought too much about his mom, he'd cry. Instead, he teased Tessa some more. "Joe's going to have to keep his hands off you until after the ceremony, or Kylie's going to whip him with her hairbrush."

"Oh, he'd like that," Tessa said with a twinkle.

Roan laughed, his heart swelling in his chest. It made Walker crazy when Tessa and Joe talked about their sex life, but it made him hopeful. Would he and Walker still be so adventurous and eager at their age? He hoped so.

Joe was doing better since they'd moved into the refurbished barn, too. He had been taking his diabetes diagnosis more seriously, saying, "I want a few more years to play with my woman in that fancy new Jacuzzi." Walker had groaned, and Roan had laughed himself almost to death.

When Tessa was completely made up, she rose from the seat with a slow dignity and took hold of Roan's hands. While Kylie cleaned up and readied her area for her next victim, Tessa smiled up at Roan. "You take care of my boy, won't you?"

"Of course, Tess. You know I will."

"And love him for the rest of your days?"

"That's what I'm about to promise to do."

"He might not be my flesh and blood, but he's my heart."

"Mine, too."

"I know." Tessa smiled and touched the tip of his nose with her finger. "I knew the first moment I saw you. That day down by the stables? You weren't supposed to be there, but you were. And somehow I knew."

Roan hugged her, careful not to muss anything. She was older than his mom had been, but she was comfortable, warm, and well-used to hugging. He let her hold him for a few moments and then he whispered, "Thanks, Tessa. For everything."

She knew what he meant by that—the many layers of his gratitude—and she kissed his cheek. "Ditto, Roan."

The rest of the day was a whirlwind. There were final details to nail down with the producers, guests to greet, phone calls to take and texts to reply to, and before he knew it, it was showtime.

Roan's clothes stuck to him in the Louisiana humidity as he stood at the end of a long, red piece of carpet, looking out at rows of white folding chairs and surrounded by sprays of flowers. Their guests all gazed back at him with open, loving expressions. He could feel sweat sliding down his back and the side of his face. He didn't care. Sweat was part of his life now. Like cattle, and horses, and gators. Like chickens, and organic produce, and hummingbirds.

Like Walker, who had arrived dramatically on Cormac's back.

Roan's lips twitched, with laughter or restrained tears, he didn't know for sure. Walker looked damn fine up on that horse. His heart skittered and slipped, his joy rose like a bird in flight, and he lifted his hand to wave. "Howdy, cowboy," he whispered.

Walker slid down to the ground, his boots hitting the earth with a thump. He grinned, tipped his hat back, exposing his face, and then whistled. Dana trotted up from the right with a basket in her mouth. Walker bent to take it from her, and patted her head in reward for her obedience. Then he lifted from the basket a single red rose and a horseshoe.

The guests, a combination of fellow farmers, Walker's cousins, and folks from the show, broke into laughter. Walker grinned cockily, and then, while the string quartet Andy had hired played the Wedding March, he stalked down the aisle toward Roan.

Roan watched, lip between teeth, his heart squeezing and thumping, as the man he loved came at him with such determination and confidence. He lifted his chin, put out his hand, and waited.

When Walker reached the end of the aisle, he grabbed Roan's fingers and then encircled Roan around the waist to plant a kiss on him. Roan's knees went weak, and when Walker pulled back, he dropped down on one knee.

"Roan, will you accept this horseshoe as a token of the luck and love I've found in you? And will you be my husband?"

Roan chuckled, taking the horseshoe and the rose from him. "Was this Andy's idea?"

Walker winked.

"Yes," Roan said. "I'll marry you. Even though you've proposed a dozen times before."

Walker had started proposing to him off and on only a week after he'd moved from Ohio and into the farmhouse. The first time had been out in the field after Roan had watched him deliver a calf. The second time on the back of Cormac when they'd relived their first encounter just for fun. The third time had taken place under the covers, in the throes of passion. But the real proposal had been a month and a half ago, while standing under the stars, watching a lunar eclipse and talking quietly of the future. Walker had gone down on one knee, much as he was now, and asked, sincerely, and with such desperation that Roan had finally given the answer he'd withheld every other time. *Yes.*

"Yes, I'll be your husband," Roan said again.

Walker rose, took his hand and kissed the knuckles, before turning to the minister who'd baptized him as a baby. "We're ready, whenever you are."

The vows were traditional, short and sweet, and the ceremony was over before Roan knew it. They kissed, fast and hard, and then turned to their guests, who applauded and stood for them as they walked back down the aisle to a joyful piece of music Tessa had chosen.

Cormac waited for them, more or less patiently, only stomping once before Walker settled him with a hand.

"Up you go," he said, hoisting Roan with his cupped hands.

Guests spilled from the tent to watch them leave. The sun set in a haze of gold and red, pink and orange, a spill of beautiful color and light. Walker headed directly into it, and Roan settled back against his big body, letting Walker take the reins. He closed his eyes, curious to see what Walker had in store for their wedding night. He only knew it wasn't back at the farmhouse, and that it didn't involve leeches, gators, or a tent.

He trusted Walker. Tonight was going to be beautiful. He couldn't wait.

"You comfortable, little lion?" Walker's voice settled him even more.

"I'm good." He squeezed Walker's thighs firmly. "Ride me off into the sunset, cowboy."

With a laugh, Walker proceeded to do just that.

THE END

Letter from Leta

Dear Reader,

Thank you so much for reading *Cowboy Seeks Husband*! We hope you enjoyed reading it as much as we enjoyed crafting it.

Be sure to follow me on BookBub or Goodreads to be notified of new releases. And look for me on Facebook for snippets of the day-to-day writing life, or join my Facebook Group for announcements and special giveaways. To see some sources of my inspiration, you can follow my Pinterest boards or Instagram.

If you enjoyed the book, please take a moment to leave a review! Reviews not only help readers determine if a book is for them, but also help a book show up in site searches.

Also, for the audiobook connoisseurs out there, many of my other books are available in audio, narrated by John Solo or Michael Ferraiuolo. I hope to eventually add my entire backlist to my audiobook offerings over the next few years.

Thank you for being a reader!
Leta

Standalone

VESPERTINE

by Leta Blake & Indra Vaughn

Can a priest and a rock star obey love's call?

Seventeen years ago, Jasper Hendricks and Nicholas Blumfeld's childhood friendship turned into a secret, blissful love affair. They spent several idyllic months together until Jasper's calling to the Catholic priesthood became impossible to ignore. Left floundering, Nicky followed his own trajectory into rock stardom, but he never stopped looking back.

Today, Jasper pushes boundaries as an out, gay priest, working hard to help vulnerable LGBTQ youth. He's determined to bring change to the church and the world. Respected, admired, and settled in his skin, Jasper has long ignored his loneliness.

As Nico Blue, guitarist and songwriter for the band Vespertine, Nicky owns the hearts of millions. He and his bandmates have toured the world, lighting their fans on fire with their music. Numbed by drugs and fueled by simmering anger, Nicky feels completely alone. When Vespertine is forced to get sober, Nicky returns home to where it all started.

Jasper and Nicky's careers have ruled their lives since they parted as teens. When they come face to face again, they must choose between the past's lingering ghosts or the promise of a new future.

Standalone

STAY LUCKY

by Leta Blake

A second chance to build the family of their dreams.

Dr. Grant Anderson never expected a second chance with Leo Garner. Leo's current significant other is a movie star, and who can compete with that? But when Leo's kidney problems resurface and his relationship falls apart over the care of his adopted daughter, he returns home to North Carolina to start over from scratch. Does he want a do-over with Grant too?

The heat between Leo and Grant is explosive and undeniable, and their affection reignites as well. Can their fresh start survive Leo's health scares, his daughter's anxieties, a return of the jerk ex, and both their insecurities? And can they make a new family for themselves?

This book is a surprisingly deep, sweet, sexy romance with a happy ending you'll love! Written originally under the pen name Halsey Harlow, but soon to be re-released as Leta Blake.

Standalone

THE HOUSE ON HANCOCK HILL

by Indra Vaughn

Pastry chef and bakery owner Jason Wood bakes a mean chocolate soufflé, yet his love life keeps falling flat. He'd blame his past if he wasn't trying so hard to avoid it.

When his family's farmhouse burns to the ground, he's summoned to identify a body found in the ashes. Jason returns to Hancock, Michigan, and reunites with a childhood friend, small town vet Henry McCavanaugh.

After fifteen years apart, their rekindled friendship soon develops into much more. But Jason's baggage threatens their blossoming romance, and he leaves town unannounced to escape his feelings—and Henry's feelings for him. He's learned the hard way if something seems too good to be true, it's best to run for the hills.

Jason stress-bakes more confections than he knows what to do with before wondering if he's running in the wrong direction.

Originally published by Dreamspinner Press. Now published by Indra Ink.

WAKE UP MARRIED, EPISODES 1 – 3
by Leta Blake & Alice Griffiths

Join the fun in this soapy serial as Will & Patrick's fake marriage turns into true love! Written by best-selling author Leta Blake and newcomer Alice Griffiths!

Episode One: Will & Patrick Wake Up Married
After a drunken night of hot sex in Vegas, strangers Will Patterson and Dr. Patrick McCloud wake up married. A quickie divorce is the most obvious way out—unless you're the heir of a staunchly Catholic mafia boss with a draconian position on the sanctity of marriage. Throw their simmering attraction into the mix and all bets are off!

Episode Two: Will & Patrick Meet the Family
Meeting the family is challenging for every new couple. But for Will and Patrick, the awkward family moments only grow more hilarious—and painful—when they must hide the truth of their predicament from the people they care about most. Throw in the sexual tension flaring between them and you've got a recipe for madcap laughs and surprisingly heartwarming feels.

Episode Three: Will & Patrick Do the Holidays
A couple's first holiday season is always a special time. Thanksgiving, Christmas, and New Year's Eve are magical when you're in love. Too bad Will and Patrick's marriage is a sham and they're only faking their affection for each other. Or are they? Sparks fly in this episode of the *Wake Up Married* serial. Will the sexual tension between Will and Patrick finally explode in a needy night of passion? Or will they continue to deny their feelings?

Gay Romance Newsletter

Leta's newsletter will keep you up to date on her latest releases and news from the world of M/M romance. Join the mailing list today and you're automatically entered into future giveaways.

letablake.com

Leta Blake on Patreon

Become part of Leta Blake's Patreon community in order to access exclusive content, deleted scenes, extras, bonus stories, rewards, prizes, interviews, and more.

www.patreon.com/letablake

Other Books by Leta Blake

Any Given Lifetime
The River Leith
Smoky Mountain Dreams
The Difference Between
Heat for Sale
Stay Lucky
Stay Sexy
Omega Mine: Search for a Soulmate
Bring on Forever
Angel Undone

The Home for the Holidays Series
Mr. Frosty Pants
Mr. Naughty List

The Training Season Series
Training Season
Training Complex

Heat of Love Series
Slow Heat
Alpha Heat
Slow Birth
Bitter Heat

'90s Coming of Age Series
Pictures of You
You Are Not Me

Co-Authored with Indra Vaughn
Vespertine
Cowboy Seeks Husband

Co-Authored with Alice Griffiths
The Wake Up Married serial
Will & Patrick's Endless Honeymoon

Gay Fairy Tales
Co-Authored with Keira Andrews
Flight
Levity
Rise

Audiobooks
Leta Blake at Audible
Indra Vaughn at Audible

Free Read
Stalking Dreams

Discover more about the author online:
Leta Blake
letablake.com

Other Books by Indra Vaughn

The House on Hancock Hill
Patchwork Paradise

Christmas Books
Dust of Snow
The Winter Spirit

Shadow Mountain Series
Fated
Fragmented

Co-Authored with Leta Blake
Vespertine
Cowboy Seeks Husband

About the Author

Author of the bestselling book Smoky Mountain Dreams and the fan favorite Training Season, Leta Blake's educational and professional background is in psychology and finance, respectively. However, her passion has always been for writing. She enjoys crafting romance stories and exploring the psyches of made up people. At home in the Southern U.S., Leta works hard at achieving balance between her day job, her writing, and her family.